Also by Jack Heinz

Novels

Rebellion, Love, Betrayal. 2019
Six Spies in Saranac. 2020
Engagement in Saranac. 2022

Nonfiction (published as John P. Heinz)

(with A. Gordon) *Public Access to Information.* 1979
(with E. Laumann) *Chicago Lawyers.* 1982
(with E. Laumann, R. Nelson, and R. Salisbury) *The Hollow Core.* 1993
(with R. Nelson, R. Sandefur, and E. Laumann) *Urban Lawyers.* 2005
(with A. Heinz) *Women, Work, and Worship in Lincoln's Country.* 2016

SUSPICION HARDENS

SUSPICION HARDENS

TWO STORIES

JACK HEINZ

DEEDS PUBLISHING | ATHENS, GA

Published by Deeds Publishing in Atlanta, GA
www.deedspublishing.com

Printed in The United States of America

Cover painting by William Conger, "Ragtime," gouache, 2009

Interior and cover design by Mark Babcock

ISBN 978-1-961505-25-4

Books are available in quantity for promotional or premium use. For
information, email info@deedspublishing.com.

First Edition, 2024

10 9 8 7 6 5 4 3 2 1

Again, for Anne, who makes it all possible.

MISSING IN ST. LOUIS

"The deficiency of strength may be greatly supplied with art, but the want of art will have but heavy and unwieldy succour from strength."

Pierce Egan, *Boxiana*, 1821

"Artists are always facing the menacing choice: make a mark that looks like art or make a mark that doesn't look like art."

William Conger, 2021

1

"Mayor Tucker is here."

"You mean former Mayor Tucker."

"Right. He was mayor for so long that I can't remember anyone else. He was mayor when I was in high school."

"No, he wasn't. When did you graduate?"

"1954."

"You're right. He was mayor then."

"That's a lovely scarf."

"Thank you."

"Who designed it?"

"Jacques Fath. Harry bought it for me when we were in Paris last year."

"Good taste ....Let's talk about something pleasant, like the destruction of the Mill Creek Valley."

"Have you seen the architectural artifacts coming out of those nineteenth century townhouses? Beautiful stuff. An interior decorator's dream."

"What sort of stuff?"

"Acres of walnut and mahogany paneling, some of it handcarved, marble mantle pieces and fireplace fronts by the dozens, elaborate newel posts, cast brass door knobs by the hundreds, some with designs that include birds or flowers. The neighborhood deteriorated badly, very badly, but the things inside those houses were still amazing. St. Louis had money once."

"Where's all the stuff going? The antique shops couldn't handle it. Not even the Landesman Galleries, not enough space."

"There's a man named Filenze who's buying it up in bulk. He owns a couple of big warehouses stuffed with the salvage. You can find remarkable treasure there if you can make your way through the place without tripping over things and hurting yourself."

"Why did they tear down all those old houses?"

"Urban renewal. The neighborhood was renewed right out of existence."

"Don't let Mayor Tucker hear you say that."

"To hell with him! He made the developers happy. Americans want everything to be new. Those houses were old. They had to go. Tucker is old too—it was time for him to be renewed out of existence. He's looking frayed around the edges. Time to be replaced, like last year's draperies."

"Watch out for those martinis. They inflate your hyperbole."

"Good! If it isn't inflated, it isn't hyperbole. It won't get off the ground."

"Is Man Ray coming? We have guests."

"Jay will go to the airport to meet him, but TWA said the plane is going to be at least two hours late, maybe even later, so Jay hasn't gone yet. I think Ray is coming, but I don't know when."

"He'll be tired. The Festival of the Arts at the White

House was just yesterday, and now he's had an extra long time in the airport and on the plane. He may want to go the hotel and rest."

"How old is he?"

"I don't know, but old."

"Yeah, he must be ancient. He was a big deal in the 'twenties."

"I'm told he's still in good shape. Still interesting to talk to. That's what he's here for, to talk. He's going to do a fundraiser at the Museum, an invitation-only thing for big ticket donors. And a couple of dealers are fighting, falling all over themselves, to get him to make an appearance at their galleries."

"Which dealers?"

"One of them, for sure, is Alden Adams."

"Oh, for God's sake. He's a stupid jerk."

"No argument."

"Well that should give Man Ray a good view of St. Louis."

"So what? Were you hoping to sell him some property? He might as well see the truth. Paris has stupid jerks too. He won't be surprised."

2

After fifteen minutes of silence and several inarticulate expressions of annoyance, a young woman sitting in the TWA departure lounge passed the time by talking to the old man seated next to her.

"I'm Betty. What's your name?"

"Well, that's kind of complicated. My parents named me Emmanuel, but that's too long, too many syllables, so everyone calls me 'Man.' You could call me that if you want to."

"Man. That's cool. But isn't it, I don't know, too universal maybe, too much like a claim that you're everybody?"

"No, that's 'Everyman.'" He loosened his shirt collar and pushed his tie down. "Some people wanted to call me 'Manny,' but I didn't like that. Too childish. Too much like a grown man being called 'Jacky.' Maybe okay for a comedian, but not for someone with dignity...I've been 'Man' for a long time now and it saves time when I sign my name."

"Yeah, I see." She closed her magazine, signaling her intention to keep talking. "So, you're going to St. Louis, or at least that's where our plane's going if it ever gets here...Is St. Louis your home?"

"No, I'm just going there for a short visit. A business trip."

"So is D.C. your home? Or near here?"

"No, I was just visiting here too. How about you?"

"I work on Capitol Hill, for a congressman."

"That sounds like interesting work."

"Sometimes it is. Mostly it's just answering letters from people in the district."

"Where's the district?"

"The East St. Louis area. The congressman is Mel Price, Democrat of Illinois. He's on Armed Services, an important man."

"Do you live near the Capitol?"

"No, I live at the Arlington Towers, near the Iwo Jima memorial." Betty looked at her watch. "The plane sure is late."

"There are so many memorials in D.C. that you can tell people where you live that way. Rather like Paris, where people say 'I live near the Arc de Triomphe, or Les Invalides.'"

"Have you lived in Paris?"

"Yup. Off and on."

"Where are you from, Man?"

"Mostly Brooklyn. My early life."

"You don't sound much like Brooklyn."

"I can when I want to." He did.

"Oh, I see." She laughed a bit.

"Have you heard anything lately about the plane? About when it's expected."

"No, but I'll go ask. Save my seat."

"Thanks. I will."

Betty went to the desk next to the gate, then returned

and sat down. "Well, the woman at the desk was vague. She said there wasn't any definite information now but that they'll be making an announcement sometime soon. She didn't sound very hopeful."

"I thought they always sounded hopeful. I thought they were trained to sound that way." Man Ray settled in his chair.

"Dunno. Didn't sound hopeful to me…Tell me about Paris."

"What would you like to know?"

"Is it fun there? Did you enjoy it?"

"Yeah. I still do. I'm living there now. I've lived in Paris off and on over the years. I've made a lot of friends there. Friends who've been very helpful to me in my work."

"What sort of work do you do?"

"Well, I'm an artist, but mostly people call me a photographer."

"Oh, cool! What sort of photography do you do? Weddings, portraits, sports, news, dogs?"

Man laughed. "I've done portraits. I don't do sports or news, might have done a dog or two, I suppose. I would do a wedding if someone wanted me to and if I thought it'd be interesting."

"What sort of wedding would be interesting? I mean, what would you look for? What would interest you?"

"Good question. I'm not sure. It'd have to strike me. The people would need to be interesting. I'd need to see their feelings, their emotions. Maybe something would happen at the wedding. Or maybe you and I, Betty, could make something happen."

"You really are an artist."

"I hope so."

Then there was an announcement over the loudspeaker. It was brief and carefully worded, but the essence was that there had been an accident and the plane would not be coming. Because TWA did not have a replacement on the ground at National, the passengers would be transported by bus to Friendship International Airport, near Baltimore, and the flight to Saint Louis would depart from there.

Man asked Betty, "What does TWA stand for?"

She said, "The Wrong Airline." An old joke.

Betty ran to a pay phone and called her office, which had access to the wire services, AP, UP, and INS. Her friend got on the machine and found that the incoming plane had crashed on the side of a mountain in Virginia, near the border with West Virginia. All passengers and crew were killed. Betty passed the news to Man and in hushed tones the word began to spread around the airport.

Friends and family who had come to greet passengers on the incoming flight were in tears. So were some of the outgoing passengers. "There but for the grace of God" was repeated many times. Some of the St. Louis passengers decided not to fly and left the airport.

The bus trip to Baltimore was somber and mostly silent. People were both grateful that they'd survived and ashamed of being grateful. It would have been hard to miss the message that fortune is distributed without regard to merit.

On the plane, Betty was seated in coach and Man was in first class. At the baggage claim in St. Louis, however,

Betty squeezed Man's arm and said, "I hope the rest of your trip is better."

He grimaced and said, "Thanks. You too."

A TWA steward came up to him and said, "Mr. Ray, there was a reporter from the *Post Dispatch* here hoping to see you, but because your plane was very late he had to go back downtown. He wanted me to tell you that he was here."

Man said, "I'm glad he left. I can do without the press just now."

Betty said, "Wow, those must be some baby pictures."

Man shrugged. "I've found, Betty, that it's remarkable what people are interested in...I enjoyed meeting you despite the awful circumstances. Try to keep the politicians honest."

3

St. Louis in summer ranks with the most uncomfortable cities in the States, right up there with New Orleans, Houston, and Washington, D.C. The river valley is a trough holding a pool of humidity. There is no breeze except for the exhaust from window air conditioners that deposit their heat and moisture on the streets. Collars wilt, creases disappear, shirts stick to skin. In other places, people have the good sense to remove some of their clothing. Not in St. Louis. A national magazine said that it is the only city in the United States where a man can walk down the street wearing a top hat and not be laughed at. That may not have been entirely true, but it captured something of the mores, or perhaps of the pretension.

The streets are empty in midafternoon. Taxis rest then because the drivers know that customers will not be out. Fortunately, Man Ray was able to take an electric streetcar. Tracks ran down the center of the street and the car stopped often.

It delivered him to Euclid and McPherson, half a block from the Alden Adams Gallery and directly in front of a chocolates shop. Through the window, he could see that the shop would have been at home in Vienna, Prague, or Budapest. He went in. Large mahogany and glass cases were filled with an array of candies. There were also a few pieces of Biedermeier furniture that had no obvious function, things that perhaps had come from the owner's home. Man Ray bought an opera cream, which was offered in either milk chocolate or dark. He chose dark. Because the chocolate would melt quickly in the St. Louis weather, he ate it before he left the shop. An elderly matron looked at him disapprovingly, but her companion in a gray pinstriped suit smiled, perhaps enviously.

Ray was scheduled to arrive at the gallery at 4:00. It was now 4:15. He thought that he could be tardy but not obnoxiously late. He walked briskly. The gallery was on the ground floor of a characterless modern building with plate glass windows. Passersby had a view of the art. He liked the openness of it, but he hoped that the gallery's artists used stable pigments—watercolors wouldn't last in those windows. As in all American galleries, the walls were white. There wasn't much woodwork, and what was there was also white. The space was open—no small rooms. He thought that it could have been a showroom for washing machines or automobile tires. The furniture store next door appeared to have the same landlord and the same decorator.

Ray was greeted by a gallery assistant who told him that Alden Adams had not yet arrived but was expected soon. The young man apologized. Some of the gallery's more prosperous clients had been invited to meet Man Ray, and a few of them now approached him and asked the usual questions. He gave courteous replies to most of them. He made good use, however, of silences. Once or twice he said, "That's a very intelligent question," and then gave no further answer. This was received with puzzlement but not hostility.

Man Ray was not physically imposing. He was short, not much more than five feet tall. Nor was he handsome or robust. He had dark hair flecked with gray, and his eyes were large and dark. On this hot day in St. Louis, he wore a well-tailored linen shirt, lime green, tropical weight wool trousers, gray, and no jacket. His glasses were designed to be unremarkable, ordinary, with a dark tortoise shell frame and no tint in the lenses. He did not look like a celebrity, but perhaps he might have been an ex-celebrity—maybe a featherweight boxer long retired. His movements were not quick, no doubt slowed by time. He could be gruff or affable as he chose.

A middle-aged woman dressed in powder blue and wearing pearls asked, "What brings you to St. Louis?"

He said, "The weather."

She laughed, which mollified him a bit, so he said, "I was in the States for the White House Festival of the Arts a couple of days ago, and I decided to accept an invitation to a reception at your museum."

"The City's museum in Forest Park?

"That's the one."

"How was the White House? Was it interesting?"

"Oh yes, I enjoyed it."

She said, "I read in the newspapers that there was some controversy about opposition to the Vietnam War."

"A writer from the *New York Review of Books* was there trying to get people to sign a petition opposing the war, but most people refused to sign. It wasn't the right time or place for that, and most people told him so. Very few artists signed. Robert Lowell, the poet, had been invited to read, but he boycotted the festival. John Hersey attended, but instead of reading from one of his novels he read an excerpt from 'Hiroshima'. It was mostly the writers who were trying to politicize it."

"What did you especially enjoy?"

"In the evening the Ellington band was set up on a low stage on the south lawn. You could walk right up to the stage. I watched Cootie Williams do 'Concerto for Cootie' from about ten feet in front of him. Johnny Hodges took a beautiful solo, as always. Duke's comments between the numbers were his routine set pieces—he was loving us madly and all that. But the band was great. And Cary Grant gave a talk commenting on the crop dusting scene from 'North by Northwest.' Lee J. Cobb and Mildred Dunnock did a scene from 'Death of a Salesman'—in the East Room, just people standing all around them, not on a stage."

"Was any of your work there?"

"Yes, there was one of my Rayographs, printed in the late 1920s. It's now in the MoMA collection."

Martin Schweig, a photographer and gallery owner, joined the conversation. He asked Ray whether any other photographers had been invited to the White House.

Ray said, "Steichen was there, the old buzzard, and he's at least ten years older than I am, probably more."

"Isn't he a nice guy?"

"No, he isn't. He had his beautiful young wife with him, showing her off. He looked like her grandfather."

"You're just jealous."

"Of course, why not?"

"Was your wife with you?"

"No, Juliet is home in Paris, enjoying civilization."

"What don't you like about Steichen?"

"He's very full of himself. Opinionated. He's stuck in a point of view that's at least a half century out of date."

"He was avant-garde for a little while."

"Very briefly." Ray sat down in a chair. "Stieglitz was more important. Stieglitz didn't get along with Steichen either. When Steichen was young, Stieglitz befriended him, almost adopted him, promoted his career, and then Steichen turned on him."

The gallery assistant passed by at that point and Man Ray signaled to him and said, "Has Mr. Adams been heard from?"

"No, I'm afraid not. I'm sorry." The young man looked distressed.

Ray, annoyed, said, "I'm sorry too. The man who contacted me about arranging this visit was named Ben Davos. Is he here?"

"Yes, he is. He's in the office making telephone calls, trying to locate Mr. Adams."

"I see ....Do you suppose I might speak to Mr. Davos?"

"Yes, of course. I'll tell him. I'm not sure how long he may be tied up on the telephone."

"Well, please tell him that, if he is not untied soon, I may have to leave. And what is Mr. Davos's job here at the gallery?"

The assistant said, "He's Mr. Adams's partner."

"His partner in the gallery?"

"Yes, and also in life. Mr. Davos primarily runs the gallery, while Mr. Adams attends to clients and makes contacts in the artworld."

"Ah, an inside man and an outside man."

"Exactly."

Man Ray's hands moved nervously, as if he wanted them to be occupied. He said, "But on this particular day, Mr. Adams appears to be too far outside."

"I'll tell Mr. Davos that you would like to see him."

"Thank you. I would, indeed." Ray considered saying that he was tired, but decided not to.

The gallery assistant hurried to the office and promptly returned with Davos, who was apologetic but obviously distraught.

Davos said, "It's a great pleasure to meet you Mr. Ray, and I'm terribly sorry that Alden isn't here to greet you." He was out of breath and speaking hurriedly, the words tumbling. "I can't imagine where he might be. This isn't like him. And your visit, Mr. Ray, is of course a very special event for us. Several of the gallery's most important clients are here."

Ray said, "Please don't be upset on my account, Ben. But it's clear that you're worried about him. What inquiries have you made?"

"I've called all his clubs and usual restaurants and so on. They tell me they haven't seen him since yesterday, or sometimes the day before."

"Have you contacted the police?"

"Yes, but they say they can't do anything, can't even file

a missing person report until he's been gone for at least forty-eight hours. Unless there's some evidence of 'foul play'—then they'd investigate."

"How long has he been gone?"

"Well, I don't know. He didn't stay at home last night."

"You share a residence?"

"Yes, we do. Our housekeeper looked in his room, at my request, and she tells me that one of his suitcases and some of his clothes are missing."

"Have you checked with the railroads and airlines?"

"Yes. They tell me there's no ticket in his name, going anywhere."

Man Ray looked thoughtful. "I don't mean to alarm you, but do you have today's newspaper? There's a story about the TWA plane crash late yesterday. I was interested in it because I was waiting in D.C. for that same plane to bring me to St. Louis. It didn't get to D.C., so I read the story closely. It was a late edition of the morning paper, the *Globe Democrat*. There's a list of people who were on the plane. I noticed that one of the names was a famous one, John Alden, as in the Pilgrim story."

The gallery assistant said, "The one where Priscilla says, 'Speak for yourself, John?' Alden likes that story."

Davos was pale. He said, "Alden sometimes uses that name—usually when he's doing something naughty." His voice was choked.

Ray looked at the floor, "Something like what, for example?"

"Like sex with someone other than me, for example."

A copy of the newspaper was located and they confirmed that the John Alden name was on the list. Davos excused himself, returned to his office, and shut the door.

Ray said, "I wonder whether this bit of information might be sufficient to make the police interested. I think it's worth a try."

The gallery assistant agreed, "I'll call them." And he did. He was told that an officer would be sent to investigate.

The officer did not arrive promptly. Man Ray inscribed a few copies of his autobiography, *Self Portrait*, and then left.

4

Ray had arranged to meet Mary Ocean, a well-known St. Louis artist, for a drink at a nearby bar, Duff's. He didn't know her, but he'd seen her work and he liked it. The paintings were colorful and sophisticated. He detected a Fauvist influence, especially in the handling of the paint.

He arrived at the restaurant first, took a seat at the bar, and ordered a *pastis*. The bartender looked vacant, so Ray said, "Pernod or Ricard, with some water. I'll mix it."

Mary Ocean was a handsome woman in her mid-thirties, a bit taller than Ray and more robust. She wore a loose-fitting cotton dress with a red and blue print, and a long, heavy necklace with carved sea shells and silver beads, probably Mexican or Navaho. Also amber.

She was a regular at Duff's and was greeted by the manager. Ray recognized her from photos in *Art News*. He stood. "I'm Man Ray."

She said, "I know. I studied you in school." Then, with a big smile, "Besides, there aren't any other old men here." Her laugh was ready and raucous. She made it plain that she was not awed to be in the presence of the master.

He laughed and said, "Let's sit at a table. It'll be more comfortable and give us room to talk."

The place wasn't crowded, so they had a choice of tables.

They settled at one in the middle of the room with a view of the bar. After a waitress had brought a drink for Mary, Man said, "What are you working on these days?"

"Right now I'm painting chairs ....I don't mean I put paint on chairs; I mean I make pictures of chairs."

"Oh, that's much better."

"I hope so. It seems to me that chairs have personalities."

"Yes, of course they do. Van Gogh did chairs, solid ones."

"I know. I don't usually answer that question about my work by talking about the subject matter. But I have a show of chair paintings up now, so I suppose I was thinking about that and was giving the show a plug."

"How do you usually answer?"

"Usually I say something kind of snarky because we know that most people don't really care about the work and wouldn't get it if I tried to explain. Currently the snarky answer is 'very good, expensive art.' Then I give them my card that has one of my paintings of a furious chicken. But you're Man Ray. You're different. I guess I thought chairs might be safer."

"That was probably the right move." Then he said, "Do you have a pen or pencil with you, one that you could use to draw?"

"Of course, always."

"I'll get paper." He walked over to the bartender, inquired, and was directed to the owner's office. Once equipped with two sheets of writing paper, he returned to the table.

He said, "Now we're properly equipped."

"Do I have an assignment?"

"No. The spirit will move you."

As they continued their conversation, both began to draw. Since they were seated across from each other, neither could see much of what the other was doing, and what they could see was upside down.

Mary said, "Does an older artist have different problems than a younger one? I think I'm not looking forward to it."

"I don't know that being an old artist is so bad. It's just being an old person that's bad."

"How so?"

"As you get older, Mary, your world becomes smaller. Your range of interests narrows. Years ago Gertrude Stein told me that, and now I find it's true. You become less adventuresome, not necessarily less curious, but your curiosity becomes more specialized. I'm still interested in my art, but not in much beyond it." He found his chair uncomfortable. It was an old wooden chair with no padding. Then he said, "No, that's not true. I'm still interested, but I don't have enough energy to deal with it."

Mary persisted. "Do you and I need to be interested in things beyond art?"

"Oh, I think so. There's so much amazing stuff in the world. Beautiful things. Horrible things. It's all stimulation. We need it. There are books to read, wonderful stuff — one can never get through the wonders, of course. The books pile up, but we have to try ....Do you read German?"

"No."

"Too bad. There are eloquent letters written by Rainer Maria Rilke to his wife—published in a book as *Briefe uber Cezanne*. They are about much more than Cezanne."

"Maybe I should learn German."

"The letters will be translated someday."

Mary could see that Man was drawing a female nude, quite small. It occupied only the top quarter of the page. Mary used her hat to conceal what she was drawing.

She said, "Speaking of other interests, I understand that you and Duchamp play chess."

"We do, indeed. Marcel is very enthusiastic about chess and he's recruited several artists, including me, to design chess sets. The sets are sold to raise money for the promotion of the game."

"If you live long enough, I suppose you get some idea of how well your work is going to hold up after you're gone."

Man said, "Perhaps, but I think it might be better for most of us if we were spared that. The simple fact is that most people, regardless of their line of work, are forgotten within a few years after their deaths. The odds favor oblivion." He seemed comfortable saying it.

"I suppose . . . "

He interrupted. "When you say 'how the work will hold up,' I assume you don't mean whether it will physically survive, will avoid deterioration, but how it will be regarded in the popular taste."

Mary raised her eyes from the drawing. "Yes, I meant the market."

Man looked at his drawing and frowned. He said, "Ah, the dear old market. I think you can count on it to be changeable over time. Even Titian has had his ups and downs. But he doesn't care now. Why should you care after you're gone?"

Mary said, "Pride, I suppose, pure ego maybe. Don't we all want to produce things that remain in demand? Isn't that a measure of quality?"

"No, it's not. Quality turns on values more lasting than popular taste."

"Like what?"

Man changed the angle of his sheet of paper. He said, "It's hard to put labels on them, and people will differ about whether a work has those attributes, whichever of them you choose, but things like truth, honesty, insight, originality. The fickleness of the market reflects these values only imperfectly, if at all. Alma-Tadema, Burne-Jones, and Rossetti were once all the rage. No more. Will they rise again? Who knows? Who cares? You care only if you were so foolish as to buy art as an investment."

"People have made money on Jackson Pollock."

"No doubt. No doubt. But it was a very risky venture. Do you want to try to make money by buying a piece of truth? Good luck! Who holds the key to that? Can you lock up truth?"

Mary decided to change the subject. She said, "You're drawing a nude."

"Indeed, a classic subject."

"Is it Kiki?"

Man smiled at the knowing reference. "It's Venus, relaxing. And what are you creating?"

She said, "We'll see what it turns out to be." She added

a line or two to her drawing. "What was on your list of things of value? Honesty, integrity, originality? Pretty hard to grab hold of any of those."

"Granted. But do you know any artists who sell out? I sure do—and they know they're doing it."

She could see that he had started a second drawing. She said, "What counts as selling out?"

"Dishonest work."

"What's a dishonest work of art?"

"One that panders. One that scores easy points with popular gestures or cliches. One where you didn't really try for excellence but just cranked it out." He paused. "I think honesty is a matter of what's in the artist's heart, or what isn't there."

She said, "Speaking of honesty, how do you feel about forgeries? Can they ever be good art? There are a lot of people out there making van Goghs and Monets. Some of them are damn good. Some persuasive Vermeers were produced. I'm sure there are people producing Man Rays."

"Ah, that's difficult. Forgeries are problematic. In my view some of them are works of art and others aren't. The difference lies in originality and honesty. If all the artist does is copy an existing painting, then it's no better or worse than any other reproduction. It's simply a picture of a picture. But if an artist works in the manner of van Gogh and produces a new picture, then it might be a work of art. We all borrow devices and mannerisms from other artists. Originality, of course, is a matter of degree, and so are truth and insight and honesty."

"That makes them very hard to evaluate."

"Yeah, but I think artists know when they're cheating. I've destroyed my work when I thought it wasn't original enough—among other reasons for destroying work. I'll bet you've done that." He paused. "It's an interesting question whether honesty or truth can be compartmentalized. If the work that looks like a van Gogh is misrepresented, sold as a van Gogh when it's not, then that's dishonest, a fraud. But the fraud is in the presentation of the work, not in the painting. Now, if the artist who did the painting had intent to deceive, then we could say that it's a dishonest painting. But is the painting art if the artist's intent was pure, but not art if it was painted with bad intent? Does the artist's intent to deceive somehow infect the painting, so that it becomes bad, corrupt? Maybe a piece of art isn't responsible for what somebody does with it."

She said, "The thing below Venus is a bit peculiar. It looks like a clock."

"It is—it's an alarm clock. Venus has an appointment, and she doesn't want to be late. Probably a lover is coming to call."

Mary said, "No doubt."

"I'm sure you've played exquisite corpse. It was very popular in Paris in the twenties. Andre Breton, Yves Tanguy, and Henry Miller used to play it. So did I. I think you really need at least three people to do it properly. We took one sheet of paper and folded it in thirds. The three of us each drew a piece of a figure—one drew the head, one the torso, and one the legs and feet. The paper was folded so we couldn't see what the others were doing, and it was marked in advance so that each artist began and ended at the right place, so that the drawings fit together. We got some interesting results."

"We did that in art school, but we used separate sheets of paper and worked on them at our separate desks." Then she said, "I've read that you've made copies of your own work."

"Yes, I have. Lots of them. Reproductions made by my own hand or under my supervision. One of my first pieces of sculpture, the object called Le Cadeau, 'the gift,' was stolen on the first day it was placed on exhibit. It was a flatiron with a row of tacks glued onto the smooth surface. Made in 1921. That was three years before Andre Breton wrote 'Manifeste du Surrealisme.' Did it matter that the piece was stolen? Not really. I've made many, many copies of it. And Le Cadeau was also photographed. All of the objects I've made over the years were photographed before the objects themselves were destroyed or stolen or lost or sold. Does it matter? Of course not—the idea was the art, not the object. Entrepreneurs want me to license five thousand copies of Le Cadeau, which they will make and sell for three hundred dollars each. But they would be sold as reproductions. They'd be honest."

Man leaned back. Then he said, "Let me see your drawing."

She turned her sheet of paper around, slowly. She had made a detailed, highly realistic rendering of one of the patrons of Duff's, a rear view of an overweight man seated on a barstool. He was in Mary's direct line of sight.

Man Ray laughed and said, "Bravo!"

She said, "You've had a long career. Going back to 1921."

"Even before that. I had shows in New York before I moved to Paris. I'm an old man. Why are you interested in this? You're young."

"I hope to be old someday. I'm curious to know what it's like to age as an artist."

"It mostly isn't so bad. But one of the things that happens in your old age is that your friends die. And that doesn't just happen to them, it happens to you. When a friend dies you lose something real, something tangible. You can feel yourself losing your grasp on it. The closer the friend, the bigger the loss of course. This is cumulative. The losses mount up. I started counting, making a list—Eluard, Matisse, Leger, Derain, Picabia, Brancusi. All gone now. My dear friend Duchamp is still here, but possibly not for long…Something that was important in your life will be missing, gone. There's a hole. It's as if someone took away one of your paintings or the favorite chair where you sit to read. Even worse than that. Then you end up in a small room in a nursing home." He was silent. So was Mary.

Then Man said, "All of this blather has made me thirsty. I need another drink. And then you can tell me what you know about Alden Adams."

Mary said, "He's a sonofabitch. A rapacious bastard."

"Ah, it sounds like I'd better get drinks for both of us." But the waitress had disappeared, so he went to the bar.

When he returned to the table, he said, "Tell me about it."

"I had my most successful show ever at his gallery. My 'angry chickens' show—the work for which I'm now best known. He raised my prices, and it was a brilliant move.

Everything sold. We made a lot of money. But I haven't seen a nickel of that money and it's been ten months."

"Has he been paid by the collectors?"

"Yes, he has. I know some of them, and they tell me they paid him before they picked up their paintings."

"If you don't mind my asking, how much are you owed?"

"In round numbers, more than fifty thousand dollars."

"Serious money."

"It sure is for me. I could use it. And now there's talk that he's disappeared."

Man said, "What I know is that he hasn't been seen for a few days, and one of the passengers on the TWA flight that crashed was listed as John Alden. Ben Davos told me that Adams sometimes used that name. The police are investigating."

"So what do I do?"

"Davos is a partner in the gallery. Why not get the money from him?"

Mary said, "I tried that. Ben doesn't have the money. Ben's a good guy. I believe him. He says Alden is the money guy, Alden provides the capital and handles all of the financial transactions."

"But the gallery owes you the money and Davos is a partner."

"Yeah. My lawyer tells me that I could sue the gallery and probably get a judgment against them, but that's not worth anything unless the gallery has the money to pay the judgment."

"You might be able to bankrupt them and put them out of business."

"How would that help me?"

Man closed his eyes, "Where did your fifty thousand go?"

Mary said, "That's what I'd like to know."

5

First an ordinary policeman came, a patrolman. He talked to Mr. Davos, wrote down the basic facts, and reported to his supervisor. Then, a few hours later, at about 8:45 p.m., a detective went to the Davos and Adams residence.

Detective Garavelli was a large man. His size was what impressed one first; other qualities came later. He was six feet four inches tall and weighed nearly three hundred pounds. Despite that, he walked gracefully on the balls of his feet in cordovan shoes, wing-tips, polished to a sheen. A tropical wool suit, well-cut, was the work of J. W. Losse, custom tailor, established 1894. Garavelli wore a silk tie, red and blue, a regimental stripe. His iron-gray hair was luxuriant but under control. He was fresh-shaven, but you could see that he needed to shave often. His manner was gentle. Davos took all of this in, as was intended. If the dtective's manner of dress lured a suspect into offering a bribe, the suspect would find that he had made a serious error.

At first both men stood in the entry hall of the apartment. Then the detective said that he had several questions and he suggested that they move into the living room. They did, but both still stood. Garavelli took a small notebook from a side pocket of his suit jacket and rummaged in an inside pocket. He brought out a retractable ballpoint pen, immediately clicked the pen, and then looked at the point. He clicked it again and the point retracted. Apparently satisfied with the pen, he said, "When did you first become aware that Mr. Adams was missing?"

"I first became concerned about him when he didn't come to Man Ray's visit at our gallery, a big event."

Detective Garavelli clicked the pen and wrote "Man Ray?". Then said, "That's when you first became concerned about it. When were you first aware that he was gone, not around?"

"I'm not sure."

"Did he sleep here, in your residence, every night this week?"

"Not for the last two nights."

"And before that?"

"I'm not sure."

"Does he ordinarily sleep here?"

"Ordinarily, yes."

"But not always?"

"No, not always."

"Do you know where else he sleeps?"

"I could speculate."

"Let's save that." Garavelli paused. "Does Mr. Adams have any special friends?"

Davos raised his eyebrows and then appeared to study his knees. "*Special* friends?"

"Yes."

"You mean lovers."

"I suppose lovers would count as special. Unless they were just routine."

"That's insulting."

The ballpoint clicked closed. "No, it isn't. Don't misunderstand me. I don't care about morality. I'm only interested in facts. I've found it to be a fact that some people take lovers routinely. In a missing person case, I'm not much interested in the routine ones. But the special lovers are important because they might be more likely to know where he is or perhaps more likely to become emotional."

"I don't know of any lovers, Mr. Garavelli."

"Okay." The detective seated himself without being invited to do so. "Well, of course, Mr. Davos, I suppose you would be the most special friend of all." Garavelli changed his position in the chair in order to make himself more comfortable. "I'll need to know where you've been for the last three days, all day long."

"All day?"

"Yes, all day."

"I was at the gallery every day from nine until six, except tonight when I stayed later because of the Man Ray event and because of Alden being missing, and the policeman came."

"Dinner at a restaurant?"

"No, dinner at home, after work."

"Lunch?"

"At my desk, at the gallery."

"Your employees at the gallery and your housekeeper will confirm this?"

"There's only one employee at the gallery. I'm sure he'll confirm it. Also the housekeeper."

"Who is Man Ray?"

"A famous artist. American born, now living in France."

"What's his real name?"

"It's Man Ray, I think. He's been known by that name since at least the 1920s."

"How old is he?"

"Mid-seventies, I think."

"Is he a long-time friend of Alden Adams?"

"No, I don't think Alden has ever met him."

"Then why was Man Ray at the gallery today?"

"Because he's a famous artist."

"Did he come from France just to go to your gallery?"

"No, of course not. He's in the U.S. because he was at the art festival at the White House a few days ago."

"So it's just a coincidence that he showed up at your gallery on the day that Alden Adams went missing? Just a coincidence?" Detective Garavelli clicked the ballpoint pen three times — open, then closed, and open again. He wrote nothing. "Did Alden Adams arrange Man Ray's visit?"

"No, I did."

"When did you arrange this?"

"I wrote to Mr. Ray while he was still in France and then I talked to him on the telephone, once when he was in Washington."

"When did he arrive in St. Louis?"

"Very late on Wednesday night, I believe. He was on the TWA flight from DC, the one where the plane crashed on its way to DC."

Next to the name Man Ray, the detective wrote, "Wed. nite, TWA." Then he said, "He was supposed to be on the plane that crashed?"

"Yes, but on the DC to St. Louis leg, not on the flight to DC when it crashed."

"H'mm. Close call."

"Yes." Davos lit a cigarette and offered one to Garavelli. The offer was declined. Then Davos said, "Mr. Ray pointed out to me this afternoon that one of the passengers in the crash was listed as John Alden, and I know that's a name Alden sometimes used."

Garavelli said, "We'll have to look into that, won't we?"

"Yes."

"So if the TWA plane hadn't crashed, and it had arrived in DC, then Man Ray would have boarded the plane that a passenger ticketed as 'John Alden' just got off of?"

"Yes, that's right."

The detective clicked the pen twice. He wrote 'John Alden,' clicked the pen again, and put it and the notebook back in his pocket. "Another coincidence. I'm interested in coincidences. Some people don't believe in them. Where can I find out more about Man Ray?"

"Almost any library. Or at the St. Louis Art Museum. He's in lots of books."

"He's a big deal then."

"Yes, a big deal."

"You'll have to forgive my ignorance. I'm an overgrown Italian boy from the Hill. Like Yogi Berra and Joe Garagiola." He looked at Davos. "Famous baseball players."

"Yes, I know."

He took out the ballpoint and clicked it. "Italians like art, but my taste runs more to Tintoretto, Guardi, and Tiepolo. Do you know their work?"

"Not really well. "

"They're worth a look." He took the notebook out again and handed it and the pen to Davos. "You said you could speculate about where Alden Adams slept when he wasn't sleeping here. Write the names. I'll need to talk to them. Include all the special friends."

Davos wrote the names and the detective looked at the list. He didn't comment. There were six names. Garavelli clicked the ballpoint four times.

Then he said, "I'll need to have you check your bank accounts—the gallery's account and whatever other accounts you and Mr. Adams both have access to. See if there have been any unusual withdrawals. Do you have a safe deposit box?"

"No, but Alden does."

Detective Garavelli looked at the ballpoint as if it might hold a secret. It was open. He made a note, and then clicked it closed. "I'll be in touch."

6

Jay and Fran Landesman moved to London in the early 1960s, but they returned to St. Louis from time to time and stayed at the Loomis House, a small hotel owned by a friend of Jay's. On Sundays, the hotel's restaurant was closed and Jay had the use of the kitchen, which gave him opportunities for bad judgment. At a cocktail party on Friday evening, in an excess of enthusiasm, Jay invited Man Ray to come for Sunday lunch and, to Jay's surprise, Ray accepted.

Jay's projects were pursued with energy and imagination. His plan for the lunch was characteristically ambitious, with elements of heresy. In a city located on the banks of the Mississippi, Jay decided to make *bouilliabaisse,* perhaps assisted by Man Ray. Assembling it would provide entertainment.

Jay devoted all of Saturday to locating a variety of fish. The essential one, *rascasse,* a type of rockfish found only in the Mediterranean, was not available, but he was able to get monkfish, mackerel, striped bass, snapper, flounder, and conger eel. No shellfish. Jay doubted that Ray observed dietary laws, but the omission of shellfish would be authentic. A true *bouillabaisse* does not include shellfish.

Ray was punctual. He arrived at the hotel at noon. Fran

greeted him and led him to the kitchen, where Jay was at work.

During the greetings, Ray said, "You are a native St. Louisan, Jay?"

"Born and bred. I lived in New York for a time, but I came back. My father immigrated from Germany in 1904 to paint murals for the German pavilion at the World's Fair."

"Ah, an artist."

"Not a very original one, I'm afraid. He painted cherubs and seraphim, all very Germanic."

Jay started slicing potatoes. Man Ray said, "There are a lot of Germans in St. Louis."

"Yeah, but my father was Jewish. Also my mother."

Man said, "My father was a tailor, working in the garment trade in Brooklyn."

"You and I are cut from the same cloth. Two Jewish boys who grew up in modest circumstances."

Man said, "In my case, very modest circumstances."

"And now one is living in Paris and the other in London."

"Both living comfortably."

Jay said, "One of them more comfortably than the other."

Man surveyed the kitchen, "What's that dish you're preparing? I see fish."

"It will be a *bouillabaisse*."

"It can't be done away from the Mediterranean."

"So they say. But it will be a work of art. And all art involves magic. I'm sure you agree."

Man laughed nervously, wondering what he had got himself into. "Where are the *rascasse*?"

"They are in Marseilles, where they belong. But this will be a Dada version of *bouillabaisse*."

"Dada, like many good things, can be carried too far, as I should know better than most. But, I suppose that since something is art if I say it is, then perhaps this dish will be *bouillabaisse* if you say it is. In any event, I'm sure it will be good to eat."

"Would you like to help?" Jay handed him an apron.

"I'm not sure this is my *metier*, but I will be happy to be your assistant."

"*Sous-chef*."

"Okay. I assume we can talk while we work."

"I sure hope so."

May Ray tied the apron around his waist and said, "I'm told you are a successful theatrical producer and an author and an editor. A multi-talented man."

"Yeah, well most of those things are in the past tense. They're history."

"You've got time yet. Tell me about your work."

Jay said, "I've already sliced some onion. Hand me that frying pan and the bottle of olive oil. I'll saute the onion and then when it's soft we can add some tomatoes and garlic." He turned on the gas burner. "But I think you meant other kinds of work. Early in my career I created a small magazine called *Neurotica*. I started it here in St. Louis and then I moved it to New York. We published Alan Ginsberg, John Clellon Holmes, and some of the other beat-generation authors. After I got married and sold *Neurotica*, I came back to St. Louis and my brother and I started a nightclub called the Crystal Palace, decorated with a collection of crystal chandeliers. At first we had just singers and a piano, but then we moved on to improvisational theater — the Compass Players from Chicago, including Mike Nichols and Elaine May. And my wife, Fran, was writing songs in collaboration with the club's pianist. She wrote the lyrics and he put them to music. 'Spring Can Really Hang You Up the Most' is the best known. Then we did a musical about the old *Neurotica* gang in New York. I wrote the book, Fran wrote the lyrics, and Tommy Wolf, the pianist, wrote the music. It was a big hit here in St. Louis and we took it to Broadway, where it received mixed reviews and didn't last long. The New York producer changed the cast, fiddled with the script, changed the ending, and generally screwed things up. Then I was back in St. Louis once again. I tried to produce musical reviews and generated bursts of enthusiasm, but I was tired and burned out. So was Fran. We moved to London. My life story."

Man said, "An ambitious life. Critics can be unkind. You don't want to pay much attention to them."

"I didn't want to pay attention to them, but they stopped people from buying tickets." Jay turned off the gas burner. "We're going to make the broth now. Since we don't have the small rockfish, I've ground up some red snapper. We'll boil that with the onion, tomatoes, and garlic for about fifteen minutes and then add the diced fennel, parsley, salt, and pepper."

"Where's your wife?"

"Resting. She doesn't like cooking. She's a poet."

"You're a brave man. I was married to a poet"

"I hope you're enjoying the cooking."

"I am." As he washed the spatula Jay had used to stir the onions and tomatoes, Man said, "At first, American critics attacked me because my paintings had 'European influences.' They meant Cubism and abstraction. A terrible affliction. That's why I went to Paris."

"You've been very successful by any standard."

"I've lived a long time now, three-quarters of a century. It's been a full life. Not always pleasant, of course, but I've had some success. Unlike most artists, I never had a regular, continuing dealer. I've had shows all over the place."

Jay said, "Check the onions in the frying pan. Are they sweating?" Then, "Without a regular dealer, who promoted your work?"

"I don't know. Was it ever promoted? Certainly my friend Duchamp recommended me to important people."

"How did you find an audience? What brought the customers in the door?"

Man laughed. "Tell me more about the Crystal Palace. I get it that it was chic, but surely there were other chic saloons in St. Louis. What was special? Everything needs a motivating idea. What was the concept that motivated the place?"

"Well, the Palace was beyond chic. We didn't spell it out exactly, not even to ourselves, but I think we were selling sophistication, or maybe the illusion of sophistication. We threw around a lot of ideas and pursued some. We never really settled on one thing. That may have been a problem—we made it up as we went along."

"Continuous creativity is a good thing."

"Even if you don't know where you're going?"

Man said, "Sure. Do we ever know where we're going?"

"I know where we're going with the broth. First, we're going to put it through a sieve, push it firmly to get all the liquid, and then we'll strain it. Then we cook the potatoes in the broth." Jay assembled the implements and the sliced potatoes. "Actually, there were two versions of the Crystal Palace."

"Like many works of art."

"Right. The first one, the better one, the purer one, was on Olive east of Grand. That's Midtown. It was a small place. It had been a bar called Dante's Inferno."

"A poetic name."

"We got rid of it. We gutted the place, took it down to the bare brick walls and painted them black. The ceiling too. Everything black. The chandeliers stood out. Without them you couldn't see your hand in front of your face. As soon as you came in, there was the bar, a beautiful piece of polished mahogany. You couldn't miss it. A big, gregarious, talkative bartender greeted everyone. He thought he was a scholar, started a lot of lively conversations, and we did a big bar business. Farther back we had small, round soda fountain tables and a very small stage. It was set up for couples, not big parties. My family owned an antiques gallery, so we had access to decorative pieces, old mirrors, a few paintings that you couldn't see. They were just a shadowy presence. My brother Fred, an artist, designed the Palace. Fran helped. It looked great—not like any other place in town."

"People liked it."

"You bet. it was a big success. The entertainment was good, smart. But then, after a few years, we thought we could make even more money with a bigger place. We needed more space. So we moved several blocks farther west on Olive to the neighborhood where the antiques stores were located. We acquired two and later three of those old stores and tore down a lot of walls. We built a new, much larger saloon, much more open, a cabaret theater. It had more light, more color. It was splashier, lots of red and gold. Stained glass. Someone, I think maybe it was Lenny Bruce, said it looked like a church that had been turned into a whorehouse."

"Did the customers like it?"

"For a time, they did. The customers kept coming. And then they didn't."

"What happened?"

" A lot of other nightspots tried to copy our success. They moved into the same neighborhood. At first, most of them were nice, tasteful. They drew people to the street. We put in gas streetlights and called the area Gaslight Square. The Square was like a roman candle. It flew up high, created a beautiful blaze of glory, and then it died. It didn't last long."

Man said, "When do the fish go into the broth?"

Jay frowned. "They don't go in. The fish are cooked separately and the *bouillabaisse* will be served in two large dishes, the fish on a platter and the broth in a tureen. A slice of toasted French bread with a dab of *rouille* will be in the bottom of each soup plate."

"You are a real Frenchman."

"A Midwestern Jewish Frenchman."

"Every bit as authentic as a Brooklyn Jewish Frenchman."

Jay added the potatoes.

Man pursued Jay's story. "Why did Gaslight Square die?"

"The nightclubs attracted crowds of customers, people looking for a good time. And then the customers looking for a good time attracted prostitutes. The Square became tawdry. People with taste stayed away. The audience for sophisticated humor and music disappeared."

"Where did it go?"

"Beats me. There was nothing good on the TV, so maybe they just put LPs on the turntable."

"Couldn't you or the police stop the prostitutes from coming in?"

"No. The police couldn't, or wouldn't, assign enough officers. They were more concerned with violence. Or maybe the whores were paying the cops. I don't know. We hired private security guards, but it wasn't good for business if they roughed-up the paying customers. The whores were there because the same people who were buying drinks at the bars were paying for their services. Drugs were also available—the customers were also paying for those. Drugs go where the money is, and the Square was coining money, for a brief time."

"Sounds lively."

"It was. But then the fun stopped. By the early 'sixties, we were losing money and running out of money to lose, so we closed the Palace."

"You're lucky. The decision was made for you. You didn't have to struggle with it."

"It was painful. Still is." Jay looked on the shelves. "Where's the saffron? Man, see if you can find it in the cabinet behind you, so we'll have it when we need it."

Man said, "Any artist gets satisfaction when his work begins to sell, but there's a danger in it. Ambition for popular success can be a terrible thing. It's the old Icarus story—there's danger in flying too high, flying too close to the sun."

Jay said, "Do you think the potatoes are done now?

Man toyed with the spatula, then picked up a fork and speared a potato slice. "I'll try one."

"We don't want them to fall apart. They'll continue to cook a bit in the warm liquid."

"Still crunchy. Maybe a little more time."

Jay said, "Right ... I had ambition and some success, but I couldn't sustain it. My new ideas didn't work. It's a problem of balance. If you don't have an audience, you aren't reaching anyone, and what's the worth of that? But if your focus is on getting attention, it'll ruin your work. There's probably a difference between a showman and an artist." He stirred the pot. "The goddamn fickle audience. As they say, can't live with 'em, can't live without 'em."

Man said, "Every artist needs the audience, and every artist complains about it at one time or another. Nobody creates art for no audience."

"We got a lot of applause, and I liked the applause. I also liked the money."

"Of course. But an audience is good for more than paying the bills. It provides validation, support, esteem. Some of that may be essential. Confidence is a big problem for artists."

"Did you find the saffron?"

"Yes. Here it is."

Jay said, "Are artists just insecure people, by personality?"

"I think it's inherent in the nature of the work. If you're in the business of selling shoes and your shoes don't sell, you know you're doing it wrong. You change the shoes and find something that will sell, or you quit. With art it's more complicated. It's pretty clear that selling, making money, isn't the purpose of art. Somebody who wanted to make money would be crazy to choose art as the way to do it." Man speared another potato slice. "Part of the ideology of art is that quality can be separated from or distinguished from what the market wants. Something can be good art but not 'commercial,' or it can be popular but dreck. Even the artist who has independent means needs an audience."

Jay said, "It's time to start cooking the fish now. The firmer fleshed fish go in first. In a genuine *bouillabaisse* like this one, the fish are kept whole until they're taken to the table. They aren't cut up until they've been presented, unless they're too big to fit on the platter. So we don't want them falling apart." He moved the pot onto the flame. "First we put a bit of olive oil into the water, bring it to a good boil in order to emulsify the oil and bind it with the water, and then we reduce the heat so that the fish doesn't overcook."

Man said, "The recipe is in the name of the dish. In the old Provencal language, *boui* means boil and *abaisso* means to turn down the fire. The French care about both food and language."

"Good to have a man who knows what he's talking about ....So, then, how do you know whether your art is any good? It must take a pretty powerful ego to continue insisting that the stuff is good if it doesn't sell. How do you know it's good?"

Man said, "That's an older man's question, Jay. Young artists tend not to worry much about the audience. They don't really know whether it's going to sell or not, and they're in an early stage of the romance. They're in love with the work. They just crank it out with enthusiasm. But the aging artist is more reflective." He picked up the spatula again, to no apparent purpose. "It becomes difficult to sustain your confidence as you age—especially if the audience goes away. If the audience was never there, that's a different problem. Then you should seriously consider whether you're in the right line of work. But if the audience was once there and then went away, something changed—maybe you changed, maybe your art changed, or maybe the audience did. It's hard to know whether you're wrong or the audience is. Or maybe you and the audience are just out of sync." He paused. "The audience will usually prefer the familiar. They like hearing the old songs, the old routines—until they get tired of them. Like entertainers, artists are often tempted to play to the audience, to entertain, but artists like to think of themselves as a priesthood, serving an especially demanding, jealous, quixotic god. Of course, even priests sometimes give the audience what it wants—the Latin mass, the incense and gongs, the shofar.

But priests are supposed to feel slightly shabby when they do that in order to please the crowd."

Jay was more practical. "But how does the artist arrange to live?"

"Intelligent appreciation is harder to come by than money. The audience doesn't need to be large, if they're the right people. But there's a difference between appreciation and adulation. We need appreciation, but if you need adulation, that's a character defect. Fame can be, and usually is, a pain in the ass. What good is it?

Jay said, "Maybe I was trying to sell shoes when I should have been trying to create art."

"Art as entertainment is a special case. I think it depends on the purpose of the entertainment. Our friends tell me that the Crystal Palace presented some Samuel Beckett. There's a difference between Beckett and Bob Hope. I don't mean to say that Bob Hope isn't an artist—I'm sure that there's art in his performance and, maybe, through the right eyes, there's even a kind of beauty. But if the only purpose of a particular piece of art is to entertain, then it's more like shoes. The work either entertains or it doesn't, much as a shoe is comfortable or it isn't. Of course some buyers may like the shoe while others don't, but the reception by the market is dispositive. The question is, how many shoes do you need to sell? How many people were amused?"

Jay said, "Okay, the potatoes are done now. How long have the firmer fish been in the pot?" He looked at his watch. "We need another minute or two, I think. They need to cook for about twenty minutes, but the flounder only wants about five minutes. So we'll hold that until we're ready to eat. Now you could put a small amount of *rouille* on the toast slices and then put one in the bottom of each soup plate. But not too much *rouille*. It's spicy."

"What's in the *rouille?*"

"It's basically an *aioli* with the addition of hot pepper and a bit of saffron. So I started with a garlic mayonnaise—mashed garlic, olive oil, egg yolk, and a small bit of lemon juice—and now I'm adding the cayenne and saffron." Jay made sure that all the fish were covered by liquid. Then he said, "I don't think fine art used to work the same way as popular entertainment. But maybe they're the same thing now. My father could draw and paint recognizable figures. But that isn't necessary anymore—Jackson Pollock, Mark Rothko. Is success in art as changeable, as subject to changing popular tastes, as entertainment is? You've had a long career and continuing success."

Man said, "I'm sure Pollock and Rothko took instruction in drawing. I know Pollock studied with Thomas Hart Benton—a Missouri man, I believe. Pollack wasn't especially talented in drawing, but he was trained in the technique. I studied drawing. My early art was traditional. And my career has had some ups and downs. I'm not as fashionable as I used to be. But I've been fortunate. One of the things fame will do for you, I suppose, is smooth out some of the rough spots." Man poured Mountain Valley Water into a glass and drank. "I think art is more stable, on the whole, than show business. Thank God! In entertainment, you have a Number One hit, and you are at the top of the charts. Great! But if the success doesn't repeat —and repeat pretty damn soon—you're done. And numeric measurement of success is especially nasty. Numbers are tyrants. They're inherently incompatible with art. There's no ambiguity in numbers, no subtlety, no flexibility. You can measure to tenths of a point, or hundredths of a point, but the number is always definite. Do you rank 433rd or 434th? One outranks the other. Art isn't like that."

Jay said, "The *bouillabaisse* is almost done. I'll go wake Fran. I have a couple of bottles of Muscadet on ice. Would you open them? I think Muscadet is very good with seafood."

When Jay returned, he said, "After lunch, we could go see Gaslight Square, the remnants of it. A few of the clubs are still there, struggling to survive."

"No, I think not. A burned-out roman candle is rather sad."

7

Since he was a co-owner of the gallery's bank account, Ben Davos was reasonably certain that the account had not been closed. The bank would have required his consent before closing it. He found, however, that on Tuesday, the day of the White House Festival of the Arts and of the TWA plane crash, $35,000 had been withdrawn. The balance remaining was only $500. Davos reported this to Detective Garavelli.

He also reported that the bank was not immediately able to identify the person who had made the withdrawal. Since only Davos and Alden Adams had signatory authority, however, Davos said that the money must have been withdrawn by Adams. But because Davos was still "a person of interest," Garavelli would need to confirm it.

Garavelli went to the bank. He talked to one of the vice-presidents (there were several). The man was in his late fifties, paunchy, and had thinning hair and round glasses with pale tortoise-shell frames. Garavelli pegged him as a Protestant. He certainly was not an Italian with a sensible diet. The man's office was six feet wide and eight feet deep and his small desk was uncluttered. What work did he do? At Garavelli's request, the vice-president checked the posted records and determined that the withdrawal had been made in person, not by writing a check. Garavelli then asked whether the records indicated which teller handled the transaction. A call was made and the teller was identified.

She was a woman of dyed hair and indeterminate age, wearing a white blouse with a peter pan collar. It was clear from her businesslike manner and from the vice-president's deference to her that she had worked at the bank for many years. She was addressed as "Miss Kitzmiller." Detective Garavelli took out his small notebook and the ballpoint pen. He intended to ask her to describe the person who withdrew the money, if she was able to. Because Alden Adams was in his mid-forties and had dark hair and eyes, while Ben Davos was ten years younger, blond and blue-eyed, Garavelli thought that one was unlikely to be taken for the other. He need not have worried.

Miss Kitzmiller said, "The withdrawal was made by Mr. Adams. I recognized him. The gallery has been a client of the bank for quite some time." She removed a pencil from the bun in her hair. "On a withdrawal of that size, it is my practice to make a note. If you wish, I could produce the note, but the withdrawal was perfectly proper."

Garavelli asked, "Weren't you concerned that he was cleaning out the account?"

"No, I wasn't."

"Did you ask him about it?"

"Certainly not. It is not my business to inquire into the financial transactions of our depositers. I assumed that he was going to make an investment or buy an expensive piece of art."

"But this was an unusually large withdrawal."

"No, not especially. People buy houses and make down payments. People give us their money to hold, and when they ask for it back, we give it to them. I made a note."

Garavelli said, "Thank you, Miss Kitzmiller, you've been very clear."

And that was that.

As he left the bank, Garavelli said, to no one in particular, "He's done a runner." A woman on the sidewalk stared at him. The detective was startled to realize that he had spoken aloud. He mumbled, "Pardon," and walked on.

When he arrived at his office, he found a message that Davos had phoned. Garavelli immediately returned the call. Davos said that a different bank, a smaller, more convenient, neighborhood bank, held their personal checking account. He had been about to contact that bank, but the bank called telling him that the account was now overdrawn and no further checks would be honored.

Garavelli asked, "How much money did you have in the personal account?"

"When I checked the balance recently we had $18,000, plus a bit. And now we're $2,000 overdrawn."

"Can Adams write checks on the account?"

"Yes, it's a joint account."

"Did the bank tell you where the money went?"

"No, they just said that in the last few days they'd received checks that had overdrawn the account."

"How many checks?"

"They didn't say."

"Who were the payees on the checks?"

"I don't know."

"I want you to tell the bank that they have your permission to give me the full details on it—so I don't have to get a court order. I'm going to have to find out when and where those checks were written and for what purpose."

Davos agreed to give the bank the necessary authorization.

Then Garavelli said, "You told me that Adams has a safe deposit box."

"The gallery doesn't have one, but Alden has one that his parents used."

"Where is it?"

"It's at the Security National Bank, downtown."

"Do you have access to it?"

"No."

"Does anyone else?"

"I don't know."

"I'll find out."

The personal checking account was at Brewers National, located just a block from the Davos and Adams apartment. The detective took an unmarked police car and parked near the bank. Then he realized that it was early afternoon and he had not had lunch, so he restarted the car and drove three blocks to Kopperman's Delicatessan. Garavelli thought Kopperman's wasn't as good as Volpi, but it would have to do. He needed to maintain his strength and the bank would still be there. A potato pancake or two would suffice, maybe with a side dish.

Once fed, he drove to the bank. He found that Davos had already called and the bank was expecting him. They had assembled the information. According to the bank's records, at the beginning of the week there had been a balance of $18,050. Then seven recent checks arrived, all written by Alden Adams, and the account was now overdrawn by $2,100. Since the bank knew both of the accountholders, who lived nearby, it had honored the overdrawn checks but had called Davos. Two of the checks were written for cash, one at the Missouri Athletic Club, where Adams was a member, and one at the Ritz Bar, a place Adams visited often. Another check was made payable to a travel agency, and a large one was written to Jaccard's, an upscale jewelry store. Garavelli was especially interested in the last two. He asked the bank officers and employees whether Alden Adams had been there within the past week. He had not, so far as anyone could recall.

It was only 3:30. There was still time to check the safe deposit box at the Security National Bank. A quick trip downtown got him to the bank just before 4:00, the bank's closing hour. Two keys were required to open the box, one held by the bank and one in the possession of the boxholder. Since Ben Davos didn't have the key, opening the box would require drilling out and removing the boxholder's lock. The bank manager refused to do this without either the consent of the person who had rented the box or a court order. People who wanted to access a box also had to sign a register, and Garavelli asked to see that record or to be told who had been in the box last, but the bank would not provide that information without a court order. So Garavelli requested a meeting with the president of the bank. A rather officious middle manager told him, with what Garavelli took to be some pleasure, that "Mr. Denby has gone for the day." It was exactly 4:05 pm. This annoyed the detective. He did not want the bother of going to a judge, so he decided to extend the president's work day.

Fred Denby lived at the Park Plaza, a residential hotel overlooking Forest Park and the private streets of Portland Place and Westmoreland Place, the most elegant neighborhood in St. Louis. Garavelli didn't know anyone who lived there. The Park Plaza was an art deco tower, with a lobby that included a newsstand, a barbershop, a shirt shop that also sold ties and cufflinks, a florist, and a small jewelry store. Everything one needed. Garavelli showed his badge to the hotel's assistant manager and was told that Mr. Denby's suite was on the twelfth floor. The elevator operator had an understated uniform, no braid, tasteful. There were only two apartments on the twelfth floor, one on the south side overlooking the park and one on the north overlooking the residential neighborhoods. Denby had the park view.

The bank president himself opened the door. Fred Denby was a tall, courtly gentleman, erect, as tall as Garavelli but much more slender, with handsome white hair, well-combed, and he was still wearing his business clothes, banker's gray. He might have been seventy years old or perhaps ten years younger.

He immediately said, "How may I help you, officer?" Denby knew who had rung the doorbell. The hotel's assistant manager had called him.

Garavelli said, "Detective Garavelli, sir."

"Yes. Please come in." Denby led the way from the entry hall into a spectacular living room, two stories tall, with windows a yard wide and twenty feet tall looking down on the trees in the park. The room was flooded with afternoon light. Garavelli was impressed, as he was meant to be.

Denby said, "Please sit down, Detective. May I get you coffee, tea, or a drink?"

Garavelli chose an overstuffed armchair that was big enough for his bulk, then replied, "No, thank you. This won't take long, I hope." Garavelli explained that Alden Adams was missing and feared dead, that both the gallery's bank account and the Adams and Davos personal checking account had been emptied, and that he needed to determine whether the money had been transferred to the safe deposit box at Security National Bank.

Denby asked, "Does Davos have the key to the box?"

"No, he doesn't."

"Is Davos on the list of those who are permitted access to the box?"

Garavelli took out his notebook and the ballpoint pen. He clicked the pen twice and said, "Your bank tells me that he isn't."

Denby asked, "Do you have proof that Alden Adams is dead?"

"No, we don't. We don't know what's become of him. We're investigating."

"If you had proof that Adams is dead, then we would need authorization from the executor of his estate in order to open the box. A representative of the tax authorities might need to be present. Without a ruling that he's dead, or missing and presumed dead, and also without the court's appointment of an executor, we can't open it without a court order."

Garavelli clicked the pen again and wrote "Denby uncooperative." He clicked the pen three more times, leaned forward in the chair, and said, "But this may be a case of homicide or kidnapping. Adams may have been forced to clean out his bank accounts. If I have to get a court order, that will delay our investigation and a man's life may be at stake."

Denby was calm. "I'm sorry, but I suppose you will be able to call that urgency to the attention of the court."

Garavelli clicked the pen again. "But there are suspicious circumstances here and the box may contain evidence that would shed light on the matter. The material might even suggest where we should look for Adams, or who might have a motive to harm him."

Denby's manner was polite. "If there were a court order, our bank would of course be very happy to cooperate. Without that order, however, I'm afraid I'm unable to help you." Denby didn't move or change his expression.

Garavelli clicked the pen twice and wrote "Why?" Then he said, "Has Alden Adams had a long relationship with your bank?"

Denby hesitated. "No, but the Alden family—the family of Mr. Adams's mother—is well-known to us. I was acquainted with his parents." Denby remained seated.

Garavelli wrote, "Old friends." He said, "If anyone shows up with the key to that box, alert me and stall them. You may consider that a police order." Garavelli put away the notebook and ballpoint, put his hands on both arms of the chair, and pushed himself up into a standing position. He said, "Well, I hope we find him."

As Garavelli walked to the door, Denby rose and said, "So do I, officer. Excuse me, that should be 'Detective.'"

Garavelli turned and said, "It doesn't matter what I'm called." And he left.

*

Garavelli still needed to talk to the travel agency and Jaccard's Jewelry, but it was now after 6:00 and the businesses would be closed, so he went back to his office and wrote a memo that a lawyer could use in applying for the court order. There was a motions judge who might be able to act on it in the morning. But since Adams had been gone only a short time and there was no evidence of violence, the matter could be a bit sticky. The judge might be reluctant to act.

The travel agency, Worldwide Travel, which was located downtown on Washington closer to the river, was his first stop the next morning. Garavelli showed a copy of the canceled check to the manager of the agency, who consulted records and found that Alden Adams purchased a ticket on Pan Am for a flight from New York to Paris and a Eurail pass good for ninety days. Garavelli asked whether they had also sold him a ticket to New York.

"No. Apparently he planned to make his own arrangements to get to New York—on another airline, or by rail, or bus, or driving."

"Right. When was the flight to Paris?"

Records were consulted again. "It was scheduled for last

Friday. The ticket was purchased on Wednesday, two days before that."

"Was the ticket used?"

"I don't know. The airline could tell you that."

Garavelli looked at his notebook. "So he was planning to fly from New York to Paris on Friday, the day before the big event at his gallery, but he didn't tell anyone about that."

The woman who ran the agency said, "We don't know anything about the gallery."

"I'm sorry. I was just talking to myself. It's a bad habit. Especially bad for a policeman."

She said, "I find it charming."

He raised his eyebrows. And then said, "Could the ticket have been exchanged for another time, or another destination, or another airline?"

"Yes, it could, subject to the discretion of the airlines. Some of them have agreements with each other on exchanges, but there are rules or limits about the available options."

"So there are a lot of possibilities."

"Yes, there are."

"So the ticket is almost like cash?"

"Well, almost, not quite. And you have to be able to show that you're the person named on the ticket."

"It sounds like we'll need to explore the possibilities."

"I'm afraid so."

There was no point in checking with the airlines, not yet. Even if Adams had been willing to lose money on the deal, the Pan Am ticket to Paris couldn't be exchanged for a ticket from St. Louis to Washington for a passenger named John Alden. The man, at least, would have needed to use the name on the Pan Am ticket. Airlines didn't let passengers freely transfer tickets from one person to another. But he could have had a false ID in the John Alden name and he could have bought a separate ticket for the domestic flight from any airline he chose.

Garavelli's next stop was the jewelry store. He knew that Mermod Jaccard King was an old St. Louis firm, but most people now just called it Jaccard's. It had been around a long time. So had the man Garavelli spoke to there. He must have been eighty. The suit he was wearing had many miles on it, but Garavelli recognized the fine tailoring. The man was a jeweler. His name was Alvin Herzberger.

When the preliminaries were out of the way, Herzberger said, "Oh yes, I remember the transaction well. I handled it myself. Mr. Adams was very particular. He wanted a special piece, and he looked at a number of our better rings with gemstones."

Garavelli said, "The check was in the amount of $14,830, a large purchase."

"Oh yes. It is a fine piece."

"You let him pay by check."

"Yes, that's not unusual. Purchases of that size are seldom done with cash." Herzberger paused. "Unless we know the customer well, however, the piece doesn't leave the store until the check has cleared. It is always handled discreetly and comfortably. In any event, there was no problem with it."

"What was the stone he bought?"

"It was a very fine emerald set in a ring in gold, a simple setting."

"Was it a man's ring or a woman's ring?"

"Oh, a woman's ring. Some might call it a cocktail ring. I assumed he was buying it for his wife or a very special friend."

Garavelli said, "I doubt it." He paused and thought about it. "If someone who had that ring needed money and wanted to sell it, where could he or she go to do that?"

Herzberger didn't hesitate. "Oh, any large city, if you know the right people."

"In the world? That is, any large city in the world?"

"I should think so, yes."

"That doesn't narrow it down much, does it?"

"I'm afraid not." Herzberger adopted a professorial manner. "The great centers of the trade in stones are Antwerp, New York, and Israel, but any large city would have buyers."

*

The next day, one of the better lawyers working for the City was able to persuade a judge to sign the order permitting the Security National Bank to drill out the lock on the safe deposit box. The judge was the lawyer's uncle.

With the court order in hand, Garavelli returned to the Security National Bank. He had informed Fred Denby that he was on the way. Denby looked at the order briefly and said, "Everything seems to be in order. We will drill the box." He then told his secretary to pass the word and see that the work was done.

As Garavelli had expected, the box was empty. Only a paper clip was left in it. Denby came to the vault room and saw the result. He said, "Unfortunately, Detective, the box doesn't appear to be helpful."

Garavelli said, "Oh, I think it tells me something. But we aren't done. I need to know who had access to the box recently."

Denby said, "I think we can get that for you."

An assistant produced the register and Garavelli examined it. The only person who had visited the box since the death of Adams's mother the year before was Alden Adams, who last signed the register on the previous Wednesday, the same day he bought the ticket to Paris and the Eurail pass.

Garavelli pulled out his notebook and pen, made a note, and said, "Thank you, Mr. Denby, I think I have what I need ....I assume you'll be able to put a new lock into the box."

"It can be repaired."

"You might need a new customer."

Garavelli went back out into the heat and humidity.

8

The art and architecture schools at Washington University were located on what was known as "the white campus." The buildings were clad in limestone. The main campus, a hundred yards away and up a small hill, had red granite buildings. On both campuses the architecture was conservative, fusty. The dean of the art school had invited Man Ray to teach a master class for graduate students, but some of the undergraduates majoring in art came back to the campus when Ray's visit was advertised.

The class was held in an ordinary classroom, with seats arranged in straight rows. There was no stage or dais; Ray was at the level of the students. This was a disadvantage, especially because he was a small man, but he stood in the front of the room, behind a lectern, and could be heard. He began with material from the "Paris" chapter of his autobiography, describing the years immediately following his arrival in France in 1921, his collaboration with the Dada group, and his relationship with Kiki de Montparnasse, the model in many of his most famous photographs. The story was interesting enough, but his delivery was lackluster. He mostly read, and the students were disappointed and bored. When the question and answer session started, however, student interest picked up.

The first inquisitor was a young man in the fourth row who seemed to have come straight from a studio. There was paint on his jeans and a little on his face, but he had put on a clean shirt. The student introduced himself as "Miles."

"I'm trying to get established with a gallery. Do you have any advice for me?"

Ray said, "Sure. Learn to be articulate."

"What do you mean?"

Man Ray answered quickly, "Artists like to say, 'the art speaks for itself.' But, of course, it doesn't. It just sits there like a mute beast and people stare at it."

Miles said, "Not every piece of art is an object."

"No, of course not. But even if the art is incorporeal, even if it's light, or a mist, a vapor, even if it's transient, you're trying to create something. Some effect. What is it? Be articulate about it. What are you trying to do? You aren't trying to create nothingness. There's enough of that in the world already. The idea may be that the world is irrational, but the artist then needs to be able to express that idea—in a somewhat more nuanced form, I would hope. Learn to be articulate."

But Miles had taken art theory classes. "What we are taught today, and what students have been taught for a long time now, is that a piece of art doesn't need to mean something. It's enough that it is something, something that exists in the world and can evaluated for its own worth."

Man Ray moved out from behind the lectern and shifted his weight to his forward foot. "Maybe I'm too old, or have been in Europe too long, but I know that line. That's an old dodge. I'm not talking about meaning. I'm talking about intention. What are you trying to do? What's the idea? Explain it. I'm tired of lazy artists who won't do the hard work of articulating what we're up to, what we're trying to accomplish. We claim that words are impoverished, but they will do some work. Use them. Are the objectives purely formal? Is it an experiment in form or color? Or an exploration of flat space versus three-dimensional space, or of movement versus stasis, for example? Or are the intentions more substantive, referring to literature, history, religion, or some such? If you're reaching for truth, do you have any ideas about what the truth is that you're reaching for?"

Miles persisted. "But some art is hard to explain. What's motivating it may be complex, multilayered. There may be ambiguity. I may not even understand fully all of the things that motivate my painting."

"Yes, okay. Some things are hard to explain. But let's start simple. There are questions we should be able to answer, the sort of questions people often ask. For example, why is this painting small while that one is large? Pretty profound question when you think about it. Or, why is this painting predominately red? Now, if the answer to the first of those questions is that you had a stretched canvas that size and didn't have any other use for it, and the answer to the second is that you had a lot of leftover red paint, then we'd probably all be better off if you just admitted that. Shrouding the answers in mystery doesn't really make it better. Often, at least, we have more subtle, more important answers to those simple, fundamental questions."

A young woman in the first row had her hand up. There

was something about her that reminded Man of Kiki. Perhaps it was because he had been talking about the 1920s. He pointed at her and nodded.

She said, "What's the good of being articulate? Will it make people like art more?"

Students farther back in the room didn't hear her, so Man repeated her question. Then he answered. "Not necessarily, but it may help people understand. Understanding, enlightenment, is a good thing. Why do you suppose so few people are interested in art? Maybe we would have a larger audience if we bothered to explain. But, of course, there'd be a risk in that. It would expose us. If we remove the mask, tear away the curtain, we'll be open to criticism. We might then be seen as superficial. So much the better. Maybe the criticism would make us think about why we're doing what we're doing. That wouldn't be a bad thing."

The young woman said, "Most artists are not very good at talking."

Man replied, "People in general, artists or not, aren't very good at talking. That's why I say *learn* to be articulate. I think it's a skill, like drawing. You may or may not have much natural talent for it, but you can get better at it with hard work and practice."

A student wearing a suit and tie asked the last question. He looked like he was on his way to an interview for a job on Wall Street, and his question suggested that salesmen should do the selling of art. "Why can't we just let the museums and curators and gallery owners do the explaining?"

Man Ray said, "That's what we've done, mostly, and it hasn't worked very well. I think the reason it hasn't worked is that we, the artists, make the creative decisions. The people in those other jobs don't really know why we made those decisions, or often they don't. They can make guesses, but unless we've told them, they don't know. So why shouldn't we explain? An automobile maker expects to have to tell you what's good about his cars. A real estate broker will tell you what's good about a property — or maybe, if the broker is honest, what's bad about it. We have something to sell, or we hope we do. Why should we be special? What's different about us? The answer to that, I think, is that we're a priesthood. And priests aren't supposed to be salesmen. Priests are in fact advocates, but they are supposed to be advocates for the Faith, not the collection plate. And we should be advocates for art. Our parishioners are voting with their feet. Our congregations are small. I think we need to be articulate."

As Man Ray spoke, he became more energetic and positive, and by the end the students were with him. They applauded enthusiastically.

9

Garavelli made a list:

AA is gone
large money is gone
did AA take it?
he wrote the checks, withdrew gallery account, signed for safe deposit,
bought expensive ring, bought travel
could Davos or someone else force or con him to do all those things?
highly unlikely
the money is probably with AA. where?

———

what does Man Ray have to do with this?
he arrives here just as AA disappears
he has connection to AA's gallery
he is in airport waiting for the TWA that crashes
was the Alden on that plane AA?
was MR waiting for AA?
was MR there to get the money?
is this art trouble or homosex trouble? both? neither?

— — — —

talk to MR
talk to Davos again re AA and friends

It was only ten AM. He should arrange to see Man Ray. Modern art, like modern music, was not to Garavelli's taste, and he didn't mind telling you that he didn't get it.

The Mayfair Hotel, where Ray was staying, was where celebrities found refuge — Douglas Fairbanks and Cary Grant had stayed there. Before going to the hotel, however, Garavelli did a little reading about Man Ray in the *Post Dispatch* files. The reporters at the *Post* found it useful to share small pieces of information in the hope that detectives might reciprocate. A friend at the *Post* compiled a summary of the paper's Man Ray stories, including those on his current visit. Garavelli reviewed the material.

Then he went to the Mayfair's front desk, called Ray's room, and suggested that they talk in the deserted dining room, where they would have privacy. The two of them at the same table made an odd picture, something like a version of Laurel and Hardy, but without the humor. And Ray wasn't tall enough to be Stan Laurel.

Man Ray said, "I'll order tea."

Garavelli said, "I'd rather have coffee."

"I'm sure they'll be happy to bring coffee. Shall we order pastry?"

"Not for me. Gina, my wife, has made ravioli and I'll be expected to eat heartily."

"Isn't ravioli a little heavy for this hot summer weather?"

"Gina's ravioli is so light it almost elevates up off the plate."

"I think you may have said that before."

"I don't doubt that I have. It's still true."

Then Garavelli said, "Thank you for meeting with me, Mr. Ray."

"Call me Man."

"Sure. And you can call me Al."

"Short for Albert?"

"No. I'm an Alphonso."

"I was Emmanuel."

"Where did you grow up, Man?" Garavelli already knew the answer.

"Brooklyn."

"Are you Jewish?"

"Yes. By birth."

"I'm Italian."

"I thought you might be."

Garavelli laughed. "Yeah, it doesn't fool people when I wear green on St. Patrick's Day … So we're not so different. I don't really know Brooklyn but I'll bet it's something like the Hill. That's the old Italian neighborhood in St. Louis."

"Yeah, pretty similar, but the accent is a little different."

"Okay, but then you become an artist and I become a cop. Do you keep in touch with your family?"

"Yes, I do."

The tea and coffee arrived, a pot of each.

Garavelli said, "Was your father an artist?"

"No, a tailor. But he made things with his hands."

"Mine owns a restaurant. So neither one of us followed in the family tradition."

"I always wanted to be an artist."

"And I wanted to be a cop. But you've really moved up in the world, Man. I respect what you've done with your life. I had advantages—Garavelli's Restaurant is a successful business—and what have I done with the advantages I had?"

"You've made detective, an important, responsible job."

"I suppose so." He paused. "I don't know much about art, Man."

"It's all about life, Al. And you know about that. Whether you're solving crimes or making art, what's important is understanding life." He held up a hand, palm forward, a stop sign. "That's just a sample of art world blather. I don't know what I'm talking about."

Garavelli spoke softly, "No, you're right. I think solving crimes may be a bit like painting a picture. What I'm always trying to do is develop the picture, see it, get a view of what happened."

"Yeah. Your use of the word 'develop' is interesting. In my work, I've done a lot of photography. One of the best parts of it—sometimes even exciting—is in the darkroom when the print is in a tray of developer, and you're working under the safelight, a very dim red light, and you see the image begin to emerge on the paper, and it's very indistinct at first and only gradually becomes more clear. You're working in the dark, or in very dim light."

Garavelli refilled his cup with coffee. "That sounds exactly like what I do. But you can alter the image, can't you? You can manipulate it."

"Yes, I can. But I'll bet you can do that too."

"I try not to, but I'm sure it happens." Garavelli thought the coffee was not as warm as it should have been. "How do you know where the picture is going? Is it all clear to you in your head when you start to work on it? Or do you follow leads?"

Man said, "I have an idea when I start. But the idea can change as I do the work. Not every idea works out or is successful. I don't, when I start, necessarily know where it'll end up."

"Just like me again. When I start an investigation, I direct it. I'm in control of it. I determine where it goes. But then, at some point, the facts take over and I just follow the facts."

"But your technique, your craft, still shapes it."

"No doubt." Garavelli lit a cigarette and offered one to Ray, who declined. "Do you prefer your pictures to be direct in their meaning, or do you like them to be subtle, or perhaps ambiguous?"

"Well, the images in my pictures and sculptures are usually pretty direct, but the meaning of them may be unclear or ambiguous."

Garavelli said, "Okay, I get it." He pushed the coffee to the side and leaned forward. "I want the questions I ask to be clear, but sometimes the reasons behind them may not be obvious. So, with that in mind, here's a direct question. Are you a homosexual, Man?"

"Is that relevant?"

"I don't know. You tell me. So, are you?"

"No, I'm not. It should be pretty easy for you to confirm that."

"For some reason, Man, I believe you."

"Why is that relevant?"

"It may not be. Sometimes I ask questions that turn out to be irrelevant. You told me that you often make pictures that turn out to be something different than you expected. The process leads you in another direction."

Man Ray shifted uncomfortably in his chair. He started to pour more tea, but only poured a quarter of a cup. He said, "The work that either one of us does can be ruined if we go off on a tangent. But this is all very abstract."

Garavelli said, "Let's make it more concrete. Davos tells me you're the person who pointed out that a man named Alden was on the TWA plane."

"Yes, I did."

"How did you know that?"

"I was interested in the passenger list because I would've been on that plane if it hadn't crashed on its way to DC, so I paid attention to the stories in the newspapers. The *Globe Democrat* published the names of the people killed. I noticed John Alden because it's a familiar name."

"The Pilgrims."

"Yes."

Garavelli reached for the ballpoint pen but thought better of it. He didn't think it would work. He said, "I don't want to be difficult, I'm just trying to develop the picture, to see where it goes, to see where it leads."

"I think there's more to you than meets the eye, Al."

"I certainly hope so, Man, because what you can see doesn't amount to much."

"Uh huh. I'll bet there will be more questions."

"There's money missing. Do you have any idea where it might have gone? Could you help me find it?"

"No. I don't know anything about that."

Garavelli pressed him. "Someone who was trying to find the money might think that you were in the departure lounge at National Airport waiting for Alden Adams to arrive, and that maybe he had a bundle of money he was bringing to you."

"That picture isn't going anywhere, Al. You need to just scrape it off and start over."

"No? Maybe when I look into it I'll find that Adams owed you a substantial sum, or maybe you were about to sell him a valuable work of art. You showed up at the gallery on Saturday."

Man Ray finished his tea and looked toward the door to the lobby. He said, "When you're developing a photograph, if you turn on the white light in the darkroom while the print is in the developer, you can get an effect called 'solarization.' Portions of the image reverse so that light areas become dark and dark areas become light. It can produce some interesting pictures. Sometimes pleasing. But it's very hard to handle solarization and often destructive. If you try to push it too far, the whole picture will become black. Then you can't see anything."

"Thanks for the lesson, Man."

"My pleasure, Al."

They stood and shook hands. Man Ray said, "Enjoy the ravioli, Al."

Man Ray didn't know whether they would need to meet again, and neither did Garavelli.

*

The corporate headquarters of TWA was in New York City, but there was a local business office at Lambert Field, the St. Louis airport. Garavelli decided to start with the local office to see whether he could get what he needed. Face-to-face contact was always best. He called ahead to locate the right person and was transferred to Mrs. Dempster, who handled governmental relations.

The airport building was an impressive piece of modern architecture, less than ten years old, with soaring concrete barrel vaults intersecting at right angles. The concourses were large and cavernous, but the TWA offices were down a long corridor, away from the passengers. Mrs. Dempster turned out to be an energetic young woman, somewhat bubbly, who was eager to be helpful. Garavelli explained that a man was missing.

Then he said, "This is a fishing expedition, but Alden Adams dropped out of sight at about the time that your plane crashed in Virginia, and we noted that one of the passengers was listed as 'John Alden.' It was the Alden name that interested us. It's a pretty thin lead, but I thought we should check it out."

"Okay, let's do that. What would you like to know? We've been receiving lots of inquiries from the families of people on that plane, of course, and so have the New York and Washington offices. We've been cooperating with them. I have a whole file on it."

"Have you had anything from John Alden's family?"

"Let's see." She went to a filing cabinet. "The files are alphabetical. Alden should be near the beginning." She looked, and then looked again. "No. I don't find any communication about Mr. Alden."

"Have you tried to contact the passengers' families?"

"Well, most of them have contacted us. We haven't had to look for them. But I suppose if someone was on that plane and we hadn't heard from anyone, we'd try to locate family. I'll check upstairs—that's New York—and see. Of course, often people are traveling on business and then we have the name of the business. But not always."

Garavelli took out his notebook and pen. "You don't routinely get information from passengers on husbands or wives, or next of kin?"

"No, we don't. I think that might alarm some passengers."

"Yes, I suppose it might."

"But we do often have a home address. Or a business address. But not always."

"Not always."

Her hand brushed a few stray strands of hair away from her eyes. "No, I'm afraid not. If customers pay in cash, we just sell them a ticket and don't require them to tell us where they live. Or whether they are married. And so on."

"And so on."

"Yes."

"Will the people upstairs be able to tell you whether Alden's family or business has been contacted?"

"Oh, I'm sure they will. I'll pursue it."

"Good. Thanks." Garavelli made a note. "Can you tell me when and where the Alden ticket was purchased?"

"I don't have that information here, but I could try to get it for you."

"Thank you. I'll need it." He looked at his notebook.

"Can you tell me whether the ticket was used? That is, whether Alden checked in and boarded the plane?"

"Yes, I should have that." She looked. "Yes, Mr. Alden is on the list of boarded passengers, I'm sorry to say. What a tragedy!"

"Yes." Garavelli made another note. " Is there any definite information yet on the cause of the crash?"

"No, not yet. All we know now is that there was bad weather in Washington. But of course the authorities are investigating. The plane had been properly serviced and inspected. It was certified as safe. I know that."

Garavelli said, "Well, I'll be in touch with the Feds to see what the findings are." He paused and looked out the window. "Was the plane boarded through one of those flexible tunnels that attach to the plane or did the passengers walk from the terminal across the tarmac and climb stairs into the plane, in the older system?"

"I don't know. I don't think anyone has asked that question. I haven't heard it discussed."

"Could you find out?"

"I'll try."

"I'd greatly appreciate it. It's very important for me to be certain that Mr. Alden was on that plane."

"Okay." She made notes. "Let's see. Next of kin. Home address, if possible. Where the ticket was purchased and when. And how the plane was boarded. Is that what you need?"

"And you were going to find out whether anyone upstairs has tried to locate his family."

"Yes, that's what I meant by 'kin.'"

"I think that's everything then, for now."

"If you think of anything more, just let me know."

"I'll do that. Thank you." As he left, Garavelli said, "It's summer, but you're wearing a light sweater."

"They turn the air conditioning in this building up so high that it's freezing, and it blows right on my desk. I get chilly. You men are fine because you get to wear suit jackets, but we're supposed to have bare arms and freeze."

Garavelli said, "That's the first time I've heard a suitcoat in a St. Louis summer called a blessing ....I'll be expecting to hear from you."

"Yes, indeed."

*

Shortly before noon the next day, Garavelli got a call from Mrs. Dempster. She told him in a very organized manner that:

1) TWA did not have on file any address for John Alden, and they didn't know whether he was married.

2) They had not yet made an effort to locate Alden's next of kin or business associates. She didn't know whether they had any way to do that.

3) The ticket was purchased at the TWA check-in counter at the airport on the day of the flight. Alden paid cash, and therefore no ID or address was required.

4) The flight was boarded at "ground level," which meant that passengers walked from the gate to the plane.

Garavelli called her back. "Thanks very much for the information. It's helpful. There's one more thing. Can you be sure that Alden actually got on the plane?"

"Well, we can't question the stewardesses. They were all killed. Everyone on board was killed. But he had a seat assignment and his ticket was collected. He would then have been given a boarding pass, and the boarding passes were counted. The number of boarding passes collected matched the number of passengers on the list, and John Alden was on the passenger list. That's standard procedure."

"Where are the boarding passes collected, on the plane or at the departure gate?"

"They're collected at the door of the gate, just as the passengers go out to the plane. If they were collected on the plane, then they'd have to be counted there and there'd need to be communication between the stewardess on the plane and the person working the desk at the gate. So it's easier to just have them collected at the gate. We also don't want to have people going out onto the runway if they're not supposed to be there."

"Does the boarding pass have the passenger's name on it?"

"Yes, it does. And we have the one for Mr. Alden."

"It sounds pretty certain. But I just wonder, would it be possible for someone to wander away during the boarding process — that is, to just walk away between the gate and the plane, after handing in his boarding pass?"

"It seems unlikely, but I don't really know much about that. I could ask."

"Could you do that, please? And did he have baggage?"

"I'll check that also,"

She did, and called back. "There's no record that he had checked baggage. And I'm told that the passengers aren't really being watched very closely when they're walking to the plane. Everyone is usually eager to get to their seats and they line up and move promptly, in an orderly fashion. There's a stewardess standing at the door of the plane who might notice if someone stepped out of line and moved away, but of course we can't ask the stewardess. I'm also told that very occasionally, not very often, a passenger forgets something and leaves it at the departure gate — a briefcase or a hat or an umbrella — and goes back to get it. We don't keep any record of that. It's just handled informally by the gate personnel."

"So I gather it might be possible, speaking hypothetically, for someone to disappear."

"Yes, I suppose so, but why would anyone want to do that?"

"Good question. I suppose the answer is, for any one of the reasons that people usually want to disappear — money troubles, marital troubles, trouble with the law, you name it."

"You see the dark side of things, Detective."

"Not as much as priests do, Mrs. Dempster. There are worse jobs. My uncle was a mortician in the Army Medical Corps during the Battle of the Bulge."

Then the chief of detectives walked through Garavelli's door with another assignment, an urgent one — homicide, a 39-year old mother of two, shot, burglary gone wrong? The Alden Adams case would be on the back burner. That man was long gone. Wherever he was, dead or alive, he would keep. One of the frustrations of police work is that not every case is neatly resolved. Some of them remain open.

10

Before returning to Paris, Man Ray arranged to meet Mary Ocean for a drink at the Gaslight, one of the few remaining clubs near Boyle and Olive. It was late afternoon and the club was dark. The lights weren't on, but the Gaslight was open for business. In a St. Louis summer, lights are not left on when they don't need to be. Every lighted bulb is a small furnace, and that is unwelcome.

Tables near the front get outside light from the only window, so Man and Mary settled at a small table near the entrance. The place was curiously formal, a refuge, a gin and tonic or martinis place, not a beer joint. In the evening, the owner, Paul Mutrux, often played flamenco guitar. He was good. But in the afternoon the music came from tape — the Modern Jazz Quartet's famous version of "Softly, As in a Morning Sunrise" and Miles Davis doing "Someday My Prince Will Come." On Monday nights, chess was played there.

Man said, "St. Louis has excellent taste in music."

Mary smiled. "Some parts of St. Louis, some of the time."

"That's the most one could possibly ask." Then he said, "Is it always hot in this town?"

Mary leaned back. "No. In January and February we have cold damp weather instead of hot damp weather."

"Oh dear, I'll miss it."

Then she asked, "Why are you still here? I thought you were going back to Paris."

"I'm stalling. I gave a talk yesterday at Washington U, corrupting yet another generation."

"Did they applaud?"

"Oh yes. They have proper manners. Midwesterners. But the truth is I'm avoiding going back to a painting that's waiting for me in Paris."

"Ah, I know the feeling. The terror of blank canvas."

"I wish it were blank. Actually, it's on a board, not canvas, which is a damn good thing because I've scraped it off so many times that a canvas would be frayed by now. There've been about six versions of it so far."

"What's the problem?"

"If I knew the answer to that, I'd be back in Paris now, painting. I don't want to talk about it."

Mary said, "I'm told it frustrates you that you're better known as a photographer than as a painter."

"That's another subject I don't want to talk about."

"Some people have suggested that you're schizophrenic—that the painter in you is jealous of the attention and the money that the photographer gets."

"And that's exactly why I don't want to talk about it."

"Okay. Let's return to the threatening painting in Paris. What's the idea behind it?"

He lit a cigarette. "Being and nothingness."

"Oh, the usual. It's hard to do that one new."

"Yeah. There are two things that are hard to do—one is to paint something that hasn't been done before, and the other is to improve on something that has."

Mary stirred her G&T with her finger. Then licked the finger. "Who was it always saying, 'Make it new?' Was that Mies van der Rohe? No, he was 'Less is more'. Three little words, that's the key."

"I always wondered what the key was."

Mary said, "Formulas don't work, do they?"

"Those words aren't formulas, they're cheers—they should be shouted by girls with short skirts and pom-poms."

"So, the problem with the painting. What do you do when you're stuck?"

"I go to St. Louis."

"That doesn't work either, does it?"

"No." He studied the burning end of the cigarette as if he might do its portrait. "The irony is that just yesterday I was telling the art students at Washington U to be articulate. I told them they should learn how to explain their work. So why am I so tongue-tied? Is it because I'm seventy-five years old and burned out?"

"I don't think so. It's just goddamn difficult to do."

Man said, "So let's talk about the Alden Adams case. I heard that Detective Garavelli has given up."

Mary was better informed. "I don't think it's so much that he's given up—I heard that he got assigned to another case. But I still hope to get the money Adams owes me."

"How are you going to do that?"

"I'm gonna cause trouble."

"Good! That's the thing to do." He raised his chin. "Since I'm not usefully employed, could I help you?"

"Are you a good detective?"

"No, but I'm well-connected. I could mobilize some influential people. I could call the mayor. I've met him."

Mary knew how St. Louis worked. "Better than the mayor, I'll give you a name. Call Bob Knox. He was Mayor Tucker's number one deputy. You'll like him. He's an interesting man and he did all of Tucker's difficult tasks."

"Bob Knox. Tell me a bit about him."

"Middle-aged. Generous in size. Looks like he enjoys his food, and he does. From Baltimore, originally. When Bob was young, H. L. Mencken would come over to the Knox family home in the evening to play in a chamber music quartet. Bob went to the University of Virginia and then Harvard for graduate work, and you can still hear the eastern shore in his accent. A cultivated man."

"Should I call him?"

Mary said, "Let me set it up. I'll grease the skids."

"Okay, I'll wait to be called." Man looked at a young couple walking past on the sidewalk. "Tell me about Alden Adams."

"Well, he's homosexual."

"I got that part. What else?"

"His mother's people, the Aldens, are old St. Louis. They had money he inherited."

"Are there still Aldens around?"

"Not that I know of. He had a sister, but she died. Unmarried. Also homosexual, I think."

"What about his father?"

"From somewhere else. Maybe a small town in down-state Illinois. He wasn't a big name."

Man finished his gin and tonic and signaled to the bartender. Then he said to Mary, "Did Alden inherit big bucks?"

"I think so."

"How'd he go about getting rid of it?"

"I don't know. He's a jackass, but as you and I both know that's not a barrier to making money or even keeping it."

"Gambler? Drugs? Expensive hobbies?"

Mary looked thoughtful. "I never heard about any gambling. Drugs, not especially, so far as I know. Maybe LSD for the artistic experience. On your last one, hobbies, he buys and sells art. But that's supposed to be a business."

"Does he know anything about art?"

"Not much. He has a degree in art history, but he's by nature and inclination a con man."

The gin and tonic arrived and Man lit another cigarette. It was from his last pack of Gitanes.

Mary said, "I'm surprised you're not smoking Gauloises, the artist's favorite."

"Too smelly for a classy joint like this." He straightened his tie. "Okay, so you don't like Adams. Was that also true before he stole your money?"

"Yeah. I liked it that he raised my prices and sold my paintings, which was good, but he's still a jackass."

"You and I should track him down. Maybe that'd be as good as finishing a painting." Again he seemed to study the burning end of the cigarette. "I've had other paintings I couldn't finish. This isn't the first time. But it's always disappointing. The lack of resolution is frustrating. It's like a story when you don't know how it comes out."

Mary said, "Maybe it's the same as any problem you can't solve. I have a faucet I don't know how to fix. It's frustrating."

"Yeah. But you're not in the business of fixing faucets. I've been an artist all my life. I should be good at it by now."

"The faucet drips. I hear it. It's annoying."

Man said, "Sounds exactly like my painting. But maybe that's the solution. Maybe what the painting needs is a dripping faucet. I'll work on that."

11

The Chief of Police called Garavelli. "Al, I've had a visit, an in-person visit from the Mayor's office, expressing interest in the Alden Adams case. I understand that's been one of yours."

"Yes, it has. But I was taken off it for a homicide."

"Well, you don't need to give me the details now. That might be necessary in the future, but not now. All I want to do is let you know that Adams is a heater case. Keep the mayor's office informed about where it stands. Knox may be best. You know who he is. He was a Tucker man, but he's still in the mayor's office helping with the transition to Cervantes. Be polite. Knox is an easterner and a Harvard boy, but don't let that bother you."

"Chief, polite is my middle name."

"Right. Keep me informed. But not too well informed."

"Okay. I'm flat out on this homicide now, but I can give the mayor what we have so far on Alden Adams. It's pretty clear that Adams has taken a stroll with some money, but there may be more to it than that."

"I'm sure you'll handle it."

"Thanks, Chief."

*

Two days later, Detective Garavelli was back at work on Alden Adams. The homicide had been solved quickly. As usual, the husband did it. There was a movie that Garavelli didn't like called "Divorce Italian Style," but the family in this homicide was north St. Louis Irish. Some marriages just didn't work.

Two things needed Garavelli"s attention. He needed to interview the people Adams spent time with, people who might know where he had gone. The second thing was the plane crash. Had all of the victims of the crash been identified, how certain were the IDs, and had the search of the site turned up money or property that might have been carried by Alden Adams?

To get names of friends, Garavelli went to the gallery intending to talk to Ben Davos, Adams's partner, and to the young man who was employed as the gallery assistant. Davos had given Garavelli a few names of Adams's friends, while saying that he didn't know where Adams slept when he wasn't at home, but Garavelli hoped to persuade him to be more forthcoming. Questioning the gallery assistant would probably be easier. Garavelli assumed that the young man was gay. He recognized it was merely an assumption, and an uninformed one at best. He didn't know anything about the assistant's personal relationship with either Adams or Davos. The younger man might not like either one of them. Employees often didn't like the boss. Garavelli also didn't know how often the assistant saw Adams. Perhaps he saw him only at the gallery, and Adams didn't spend much time there. Davos appeared to be the man who ran the place. Garavelli decided to talk to him first.

The office at the rear of the gallery was designed to be shared by Davos and Adams, with the understanding that it would be used primarily by Davos. That was not an issue now. Garavelli knocked and entered. He took out his notebook and ballpoint. "Mr. Davos, I'm sure you'd have told us if you'd heard from Alden Adams, but I'll ask. Have you?"

"No, I haven't."

"How about friends or acquaintances? Have you heard anything from them about where Mr. Adams has gone?"

"No, nothing."

Garavelli made a note and clicked the pen twice. Then he said, "Does Mr. Adams have any vacation places he especially likes, any parts of the world he finds especially attractive?"

"No."

"No he doesn't have any, or no you don't know?"

"I don't know of any place he especially likes."

"The south of France? Saint Tropez? Cannes?"

"No, I don't think so."

"Someplace else, maybe…Does he like islands, or beaches?"

"I don't know."

"Fly fishing or bass fishing?"

"Sorry."

Garavelli clicked the pen three times. He looked at it. The point was retracted. Two years ago, when he started the pen-clicking, he'd intended it as a subtle irritant. He thought it raised the level of tension and increased the pressure. Some interviews needed it more than others. But now the pen clicking had become a habit. He probably did it more than he should. He said, "What sort of music does Mr. Adams like? Classical, jazz, opera, rock, show tunes?"

"I'm not sure."

Garavelli closed the notebook and put the pen back in his pocket. He looked at Davos for several seconds. "You live with the man, but you seem to know remarkably little about him. Alden Adams appears to be mysterious. I'm having a hard time getting a description of him. Is he mysterious? Does he have secret life?"

"I wouldn't say that. I don't think so."

Garavelli leaned back in his chair and spoke quietly, but there was no missing his intensity. "Do you want us to find Alden Adams, or would you be happier if he just stayed away?"

"Detective, I'm happy to cooperate, but I can't give you information I don't have."

Garavelli stood. It was a small office with no windows but lots of pictures. There wasn't much room to walk around. "Okay, fine. You gave me some names when we last talked. I'll check those out. Have you thought of anyone else I should talk to?"

"No, those are the only ones I know."

"If you think of more, let me know. What has Mr. Adams's state of mind been in the last month or two? Was he worried about anything?"

"Well, of course he was worried about money. We owe some of the artists for paintings we sold, and some of them were pressing us for payment."

"Were any of those artists angry?"

"Well, sure, some of them were unhappy."

"Did he or you receive any threats?"

"I didn't. Alden didn't tell me about any threats."

"Which artists are unhappy? Names."

"Mary Ocean, Willard Lowdermilk, Elwood Thibault, known as Woody, but I think Woody moved to San Francisco a couple of months ago. Maybe others. They talked to Alden, not me. They know he's the money guy."

Garavelli took out his notebook and pen and wrote. Then he said, "How much were they owed?"

"Thousands. Many thousands."

"Were any of the artists angry enough to do violence?"

"That would be very hard to imagine."

"But not impossible?"

"You have more experience with that than I do. Who knows what's possible?"

"Where's your assistant? Is he here today?"

"No, I had to let him go."

"That's too bad. Why?"

"I couldn't pay him. Alden took all the money. I may have to close the gallery if customers don't come rushing in soon."

"That's a good reason to find Alden Adams and see if there's any money left." Garavelli walked out the door of the office and into the gallery space. "I'll need the name of the assistant."

"Harold Strand."

"Where could I find him?"

"He's been living in University City, on Westmoreland, sharing a third-floor walkup with an accountant who keeps books for the Bishop. But Harold may have gone to look for a job elsewhere."

"I'll find him." Garavelli turned back toward the desk. "By the way, the mayor's office expressed interest in Alden Adams. We got a call. Did you generate that?"

"No, I didn't contact any politicians."

"Okay. Policemen, generally, think politicians are only a nuisance. I share that view."

*

Davos had given Garavelli seven names of people who knew Alden Adams. The detective spoke to six of them. Three were other art dealers, none of whom seemed to know anything personal about him. They'd done business with Adams, but they hadn't really come to know him, or so they said. One of those not a dealer was Mary Ocean, who gave Garavelli an earful but nothing that would help locate Adams. The remaining two he could find were also artists who had exhibited at the gallery at one time or another. Willard Lowdermilk was an older man who had taught at St. Louis University and was now retired. His story was similar to Ocean's, but less extreme. Adams owed him money for paintings sold, but only a few thousand. Lowdermilk didn't like Adams, but he didn't hate him. He said he would do business with him again if Adams paid him what he was owed. Garavelli got the sense that Lowdermilk thought Adams was not beyond redemption.

Garavelli tried to call Elwood Thibault, "Woody," but was unable to locate him in San Francisco, so he turned that problem over to the California police. They could ask questions.

The last name on the Davos list was Zane Goodspeed, another artist, a young man with orange hair and several tattoos. He was apparently less successful than Ocean and Lowdermilk—Adams didn't owe Goodspeed money because his paintings hadn't sold. Garavelli and Goodspeed didn't share a natural affinity, but the young artist provided the most productive tip. He gave Garavelli the name of a man who was not a regular in the St. Louis art crowd.

"There's this young guy who was often hanging with Alden. Ray Robinson."

Garavelli said, "Like the boxer?"

"Yeah, but younger. Instead of 'Sugar Ray,' he's called 'St. Louis Sugar'."

"Does he box?"

"Nah. But he tap dances."

"Is he a homosexual?"

"I sure hope so."

"A Negro?"

"Yeah, but light-skinned."

"You know where he lives?"

"Somewhere near the Wabash station on Delmar. Maybe on Clemens. I saw him with Alden at the White Castle by the station. The station's men's room is a cruising spot. You probably know that. Your men go by there regularly."

Garavelli didn't comment, but he wrote it down. Zane Goodspeed seemed to take pleasure in that. Garavelli wasn't sure why.

*

Later that day Garavelli drove west to the University City neighborhood where Harold Strand was living. He'd called ahead and Strand met him at the door. Garavelli was only a little winded by the walk up to the third floor.

When he got his breath, Garavelli said, "I was sorry to hear that you've lost your job. Bad news."

"Yeah, it is."

They went into the living room. It wasn't a large apartment. Garavelli sat in a Barcalounger, a reclining chair, the largest chair in the room. "Before we talk about Alden Adams, tell me about Ben Davos."

"Ben's a good guy. He's a good boss, easy to work for, straightforward."

"How's his relationship been with Adams in recent months, so far as you could observe?"

"Okay, I think. I haven't seen any big arguments."

"They've been living together for some time now. Does Davos have any other lovers?"

Strand answered quickly. "No. I don't think so."

"Have you been intimately involved with either Davos or Adams?"

"No, I haven't. Not all homosexuals are promiscuous."

"Just trying to get simple facts, Mr. Strand. It's in the nature of my job. You and I will both do better if we just think about it that way."

"I'll try."

"Does Alden Adams have lovers other than Davos?"

Strand hesitated. "I don't know anything definitely."

"How about what you know indefinitely?"

"I've seen Alden with other men, younger men."

"Seen him where?"

"In a bar."

"A gathering place for homosexuals?"

"Yeah."

Garavelli said, "Did Alden being with younger men bother Davos?"

"I wouldn't know. I doubt it."

"Why do you doubt it?"

"Ben's a pretty level-headed guy. He takes the world as it comes."

Garavelli pulled the Barcalounger full upright. "You like Davos better than you like Adams. Right?"

"I suppose so."

"That's okay. You're entitled to have a preference.... You said that Davos takes the world as it comes—does he ever worry about anything?"

"He worries about money. Some of the gallery's artists haven't been paid their share from sales."

"I've talked to some of those artists. They're pretty unhappy. But there was money in the gallery's bank account, or there was until recently. Why didn't Davos just write checks to the artists?"

"Alden handled the money. It was his responsibility to pay the artists."

"And Alden would have been angry if Ben wrote checks to the artists? Is that it? Ben had a check book. He could've written checks, but he didn't."

Strand said, "Yes, Alden would've been angry if Ben did that. And I don't think there was enough in the account to pay Mary Ocean. She was owed a lot."

"Aha. I see." Garavelli leaned back. "So Davos worried about money, but he didn't argue with Adams about it."

"Not that I knew of."

"Mary Ocean's work sold for big money. Where did that money go?"

"I don't know."

Garavelli looked at his notebook. "There's one of the artists I haven't been able to track down. His name is Elwood Thibault. I'm told he may have moved to California."

"Yeah, I heard that Woody went to San Francisco, probably for the hippie scene. Why do you want to talk to him?"

"I want to find out what he knows about Alden Adams."

Strand shook his head. "I don't think he'd know anything. Woody is a sad case. He's fallen apart. He's a druggy and I doubt you'd get anything coherent from him. And he wouldn't be capable of engineering a ham sandwich."

"Who said anything about engineering?"

"Well, it's pretty obvious that you're trying to determine how Alden managed to disappear so neatly."

"Sometimes detectives are obvious" Garavelli straightened the chair. His weight kept pushing it back. "You said you'd seen Alden with younger men. One of the people I talked to gave me a name, Ray Robinson, known as 'St. Louis Sugar.' Does that ring a bell?"

"Yeah, he's about my age. Semi-famous."

"What do you know about him? I heard he lives near the Wabash train station."

"I don't know where he lives, but I believe he's in the Army, or Army Reserve. I've seen him in uniform. There's a Reserve unit stationed at the airport."

"Is Sugar a pilot?"

"Nah, helicopter maintenance."

"Sounds like you know him."

Strand said, "We've talked."

"Is Robinson an artist?"

"No."

"Why would Alden Adams know him?"

"Come, now, detective."

"Meaning?"

Strand didn't reply. Garavelli relented.

"Okay. That's all I need to know." Garavelli stood. "You've been helpful. Thank you. I hope you find a new job. Will you stay in this area?"

"Don't know. Will you find Alden Adams?"

"Don't know."

*

To locate St. Louis Sugar, Garavelli recruited colleagues in the Vice Squad who kept tabs on the public part of homosexual sex, the bars where homosexuals gathered, and the trade in sex-for-sale. Neighbors didn't like it when things got too open and raunchy. Garavelli's friends in Vice told him that they knew Sugar and that he was relatively well-behaved. In the neighborhood, he was visible on the bar scene, and Vice had been aware of him for some time, but he was careful to stay out of trouble — he didn't want to lose his Army gig.

Garavelli looked for Sugar, but no one was at home at the apartment on Clemens. He'd try again later. In the neighborhood, he found people who might have been Sugar's friends. Most of the men wouldn't talk to him. They were evasive. The men didn't know Garavelli, but his colleagues in Vice had regular contacts in the community and some of those contacts were helpful informants. Garavelli didn't know what quid pro quo was exchanged and he didn't want to know. The information on the street was that Sugar hadn't been seen recently. He had dropped out of sight at about the same time that Alden Adams went missing.

Garavelli's next stop was the Reserve unit at the airport. He found that the Army also wondered where Ray Robinson was. Robinson had missed duty and exercises and was listed as AWOL. When (or if) he turned up, he'd be in trouble. But, so far as Garavelli could determine, the Army hadn't really looked for him. It had more important things to do, like training for Vietnam.

While he was at the airport, Garavelli went to the other side of the field and paid another call on Mrs. Dempster in TWA governmental relations.

He said, "I need to talk to your gate personnel who handled the flight that crashed, and probably also talk to the people who worked the check-in for that flight at the counter on the concourse. I'm trying to track another passenger."

Mrs. Dempster said, "I'll arrange it, but they won't all be here today." She paused. "First, I'll need to find out who worked that flight and then contact them. The most efficient way to do it, both for you and for us, would be to get them all here on one day, and then you could talk to all of them with one trip."

"That sounds right to me. I'd appreciate it if you could arrange it. And is there any more word on the cause of the crash?"

"The National Transportation Safety Board is still investigating. I'm sure they'll give you what they know so far."

Garavelli thanked her and left.

*

When he returned to his office, he found that he had received a call from Bob Knox, from the mayor's office. He returned the call.

Knox said, "The first thing I want to make clear is that I don't intend to interfere with your investigation and I don't want to get any information that's confidential or that you're not comfortable giving me. The mayor's been asked to express interest in Alden Adams, so that's what I'm doing. If there are important developments that you can tell us about, I'd like to know about them. Do you have any leads?"

"Not really. We think it's possible that Alden Adams was a passenger on the TWA plane that crashed recently, using the name John Alden, but we haven't been able to confirm that. His bank accounts and safe deposit box were cleaned out and he bought an expensive emerald ring shortly before he disappeared. It looks like he's gone, and he's probably taken the money with him."

Knox asked, "Did he have a traveling companion? The emerald ring is interesting."

"Women are not his thing."

"I see."

"We're not aware of any traveling companion, but there's another missing person, a young Negro man, who dropped out of sight at about the same time that Alden Adams did. The young man was acquainted with Adams, at least. It's striking that they both disappear at the same time, so I'm looking into it."

"What's the young man's name?"

"Ray Robinson, same as the boxer, so the kid is called 'St. Louis Sugar'."

"Is it confidential that Robinson is missing?"

"No, that's known on the street."

"Thanks for the information. If you find Adams or get a good lead on where he is, please let me know."

"I'll do that, sir."

"I'm called Bob."

"Got it."

*

Garavelli's meeting with the TWA ground personnel was scheduled for the next day. He didn't sleep well that night. He was trying to figure out how much time and effort he should devote to looking for Ray Robinson. That wasn't his assignment. But the disappearance of Robinson would probably shed light on what happened to Adams.

Five employees were present at the meeting, three who had worked at the ticket counter and two who had been at the gate. All of them were women. Garavelli explained the problem:

"We have two missing persons, both of them men, who disappeared at about the time of the flight that crashed in Virginia. I'm told that all of you worked that flight, some of you on ticketing and some at the gate. I want to find out whether any of you can recall a particular passenger. I'm in touch with the NTSB, but they've not yet succeeded in identifying the remains of all the people on board. The destruction was pretty complete. Most of the passengers had family who have come forward, but they haven't yet heard from the family of a passenger named John Alden. Do any of you have a recollection of a passenger by that name?"

They all shook their heads, no. One said, "We see a lot of passengers."

Garavelli said, "Of course, but I thought I would ask."

One of the women said, "If John Alden flew, he'd have had to check in and have a boarding pass."

Garavelli said, "Yes. He had a boarding pass, and it was collected, but we don't know who used that pass." He cleared his throat. "Let me approach the problem in a different way. Do you recall a passenger on that flight who was a young man, about in his early twenties, maybe twenty-five at most, not tall, slim, a Negro? I have a picture of him that I got from the Army. He's in uniform in the picture, but he may not have been wearing a uniform when he flew. You can pass the picture around."

One of the TWA employees said, "Would he have been flying on a military ticket or on a reduced rate ticket?"

Garavelli opened his hands, palms up. "Unfortunately, we don't know the answer to that, but probably not."

Another woman spoke, "Is he John Alden?"

"We don't know that either." He paused. "The two missing men are named Alden Adams and Ray Robinson. There was no ticket issued in either of those names, but one or both of them may have traveled under a false name. And no family has turned up inquiring about the passenger who was ticketed as John Alden. So it's possible that either Adams or Robinson might have been on the flight using that name. That's what I'm trying to determine."

Then a desk clerk said, "There were some Negroes on that flight. There was a whole family, but I think the children were younger. And we do often get soldiers as passengers here, many of them from the Army Reserve unit on the other side of the airport, just beyond the runways."

Garavelli remained silent. One of the women was looking at the photograph intently. Finally, she said, "I think I recognize him. He was afraid to fly. I was working the gate and he said he'd never flown before. His fear was bothering some of the other passengers. He looks different in the picture, calmer, but I think it's the same person."

Garavelli said, "If I could get another photograph of him, I hope you'd be willing to take a look at it."

"Sure, I'd do that."

"Was the passenger who was afraid to fly a Negro?"

She replied, "I'm not sure—I don't recall. But this man in the picture is light-skinned. You can't always tell—or at least I can't. I might not have noticed, especially if he was wearing a hat."

The building was well air-conditioned, but Garavelli was warm. The room was small, and he thought perhaps the number of people in it had overwhelmed the ventilation. Or maybe women with bare arms had turned the thermostat up. In any event, he asked the TWA employees whether it would offend them if he removed his suit jacket. He thought it was unprofessional to do that, but he was uncomfortable.

Mrs. Dempster responded for the group. "Not at all, Detective. We understand. Please be comfortable."

He said, "Thank you," and took the coat off. His shirt was damp with perspiration. It was a two-shirt day, maybe even a three-shirt day. The laundries would make a fortune.

He had more questions for the woman who thought she recognized the man in the picture. He asked her, "How tall was he?"

"I can't remember really, so he probably wasn't especially tall or especially short."

"How heavy?"

"Slim, not heavy."

"Thank you."

Another woman said, "You don't suspect that he was carrying an explosive device, do you, and that's why he was nervous?"

"No, we don't suspect that at all. I'm just investigating what became of two missing persons, trying to find them. The NTSB is still investigating the cause of the crash but they don't think an explosion was the cause." He paused and retrieved the photo. Then he said, "Thanks very much for your help. You all did your jobs properly, and you've given me useful information. I'll get back in touch when I get hold of another picture of the young man."

His friends in Vice were able to get a photograph of

Ray Robinson from one of their contacts. The woman who thought she recognized him looked at the new photo, but was still uncertain. She thought he was the frightened passenger, but she wasn't sure.

Garavelli reported all of this to the Chief of Police. The chief said, "So what do you do now?"

"I try to find out whether there was a young Negro male, not too big, among the bodies recovered from the crash site."

"Yes, you're right, that's the next piece."

*

On his way home, Garavelli stopped by the corner of De-Baliviere and DeGiverville. He liked the two old St. Louis names, but that wasn't why he went there. The address was the location of Garavelli's, the family's restaurant, and he wanted to visit his father. The older Garavelli had a reserved table at the far end of the large room, near the kitchen, the restrooms, and the back door. Regular customers stopped by his table to pay their respects, and, once per hour, on the hour, Giovanni Garavelli (known as John or, to a select few, as Jack) made a circuit of the dining room, welcoming one and all.

The father was a smaller, older version of the son. He was shorter, slimmer, and had white hair, but the face was the same.

Al said, "How's it goin,' Pops?"

"The waters are smooth, thank you. Smooth as glass."

"Anything interesting happening?"

"Mayor Tucker was in today, but then Mayor Cervantes came, so Tucker left. I think only a few of our customers noticed it or realized what was happening."

"There's no love between those two…There's a man named Knox who was Tucker's *consigliere*, but now he's working for Cervantes. I think Knox is supposed to smooth the transition from one mayor to the other, provide some continuity. I've talked to him."

His father said, "He also dines here."

"What do you know about him? What can you tell me?"

"I can tell you that he has a good appetite and he likes calamari. Does that help?"

"You are a goldmine of useful information, Pops…I see you are keeping a close watch on the back door, as usual, watching out for deadbeats."

"I have to. A few of the customers are not Italian."

"The Italians are the ones you need to watch, Pops."

"What a terrible thing to say!"

They both laughed.

12

While Garavelli was visiting his father, Bob Knox called Man Ray at the Mayfair Hotel: "Mr. Ray, this is Bob Knox in the mayor's office. I understand that you've contacted our office to express concern about the disappearance of Alden Adams. I've been in contact with the police department and I have some information on the investigation."

"Thank you for calling."

"I think you suggested that the passenger listed as John Alden might have been Alden Adams. The police are interested in that idea and they've pursued it."

"Yes, I met with Detective Garavelli and we discussed that."

"Garavelli's a good man, I think."

"I got that impression. Smart."

"Right. Diligent, too. He's found that a young Negro called 'Saint Louis Sugar,' who was in contact with Alden Adams, disappeared at about the same time as Adams."

"Is the young man an artist?"

"No, I don't think so. Garavelli could tell you."

"What's the young man's name?"

"Ray Robinson. He's called St. Louis Sugar because of Sugar Ray." Knox's voice was quiet. "May I ask, apart from the fact that Alden Adams owns a gallery, what's your interest in the matter?"

"Well, first of all, simply curiosity I suppose. I was scheduled to fly to St. Louis on the plane that crashed before it got to Washington, and then I made an appearance here at the Alden Adams gallery and Adams didn't show up and it turned out that he was missing." Ray decided to give Knox more information. "Do you know Mary Ocean?"

"I know the name. She's one of the prominent artists in St. Louis."

"Well, she tells me that Adams left town owing her a considerable sum of money. She'd like to find him. I'd like to help her, if I can."

Knox said, "Are the police aware that Adams owed her money?"

"I'm sure they are, but I'll talk to Garavelli."

*

The NTSB was not helpful. Garavelli tried to get information by telephone and Telex, but that didn't work. They gave him pieces that had been reported in press releases, but not much more than that. He wasn't satisfied. So he mobilized. He contacted Senator Stuart Symington, with whom he was acquainted because Symington sometimes ate at Garavelli's. The senator's office contacted the NTSB and arranged a meeting, but Garavelli would have to come to Washington. The officials who knew about the TWA crash were busy investigating and didn't have time to go to St. Louis, and there was no money in the budget of the St. Louis Police Department for this sort of travel. Garavelli's Restaurant was profitable, however, and his father was generous.

Garavelli's desk was next to that of a detective named Tim Metzler. Al told Metzler, "I'm going to take Gina to Washington, DC, for the cherry blossoms."

"This is the wrong time of year for the cherry blossoms."

"I was misinformed."

Metzler said, "It must be nice to be the crown prince of the spaghetti aristocracy, the Baron of Bolognese."

"Goddamn German. Don't expect a postcard."

Since the crash site was only a short drive from DC, a visit there would also be possible.

The NTSB man, who was several rungs down the ladder of the office's hierarchy, was civil and proper, but no better than that. He began by saying, "Detective Garavelli, Senator Symington has requested that we give you our cooperation, and I intend to do that to the extent I'm able, but we're very busy and I can only give you limited time. You are a public servant and I am a public servant, and I'm sure you will understand that we have to do our work with too few staff and too little budget. Senator Symington understands that. Now, what do you want to know?"

Garavelli had told them in advance that he was primarily interested in determining whether Ray Robinson, a young man of African descent, had been found among the victims, but NTSB gave him a canned briefing, with slides. Garavelli was impatient.

In response to his questions, he was told that the cause of the crash was probably a combination of errors by both the pilot and the control tower at the airport. Radio traffic during the approach suggested this — the flight recorder preserved evidence of confusion in the cockpit. The investigation was continuing. TWA and the traffic controllers were now each blaming the other, but the NTSB would try to reach a conclusion and issue a report. There had been strong cross-winds on the runways at National, so the flight was diverted to Dulles Airport, but the pilots were not familiar with the approach route to Dulles and had difficulty following the map. Visibility was very bad.

The flight recorder showed that the pilot thought he had been cleared to descend to 1,800 feet. Perhaps he had and perhaps he had not, but in any event the wind currents produced downdrafts. The plane would have needed to be considerably higher than 1,800 feet to clear Mount Weather safely. It is 1,754 feet high. The plane crashed at an elevation of 1,670 feet. Essentially, the plane flew into the side of the mountain.

It first sheared off trees, which it hit at a speed of 228 miles per hour, cutting a swath sixty to seventy yards wide and a quarter mile long. Then the plane hit rock. There was an explosion, but the explosion followed the crash, it did not precede it. There were no big pieces of the plane at the site. Investigators said that it "disintegrated" upon impact. An employee of TWA, Richard Easton, said, "If you didn't know it was an airplane, you'd never guess it. There's no tail or wing that you could make out." The men sent to the site were called a "rescue" squad, but no one was rescued.

After the briefing, Garavelli asked whether one of the passengers was a young Negro, in his early twenties, slim, not tall. He was told that some bodies had been identified as Negroes, but none was a male in his twenties. He was also told that, in many cases, the race of the victim could not be identified. He was handed a statement by Loudoun County Medical Examiner George Hocker: "For about half of the bodies, you can recognize that it is a human. But with the rest of them, you're just dealing with pieces." Another report said that, of the ninety-two passengers and crew, only nine could be "identified by sight." In addition to the dismemberment caused by the impact, the remains were made unrecognizable by the fire that followed. The first person on the scene, a farmer who lived nearby, thought that a gasoline tanker truck had exploded. The fire burned for several hours.

One of the NTSB men told Garavelli, "Some of the passengers' families just got a package containing a more-or-less miscellaneous collection of body parts, and most families accepted the packages without question. They were better off if they didn't inquire too closely about what was in there. It was sometimes the only possible way to handle it. Were any of those parts from a twenty-some year old Negro man? I couldn't tell you and I don't suppose anyone else could."

Putting aside the search for Ray Robinson, Garavelli then asked whether anyone had found a large amount of cash or an emerald ring at the site.

He was told, "If anyone found those things, they didn't turn them in."

Garavelli said, "Would it have been possible for them to walk away?"

"There were a lot of workers on the site—people from a number of different agencies, federal, state and local. Firemen, police, medical technicians, crash site investigators, clergymen, reporters, TWA people. There was a lot going on. Who knows?"

"Wasn't there any security on the site?"

"There was an attempt at security. Initially, military police tried to establish a secure perimeter with a five-mile radius. Have you read about the federal facility built inside Mount Weather? It was supposed to be secret, but reporters attracted by the crash put it into the newspapers and onto TV. With all of the workmen at the site, the Feds were unable to maintain the security."

Garavelli said that he had seen the stories. Then he said, "What is it, exactly?"

"It's the evacuation bunker or refuge for top officials of the government in case of nuclear attack. The facility is sometimes called a bunker, but that term hardly captures the size and sophistication of the place. It has private bedrooms, all inside the mountain, for the President, Vice-President, and all cabinet-level officers, plus beds for 2,000 other officials and staff. There's a lot of stuff inside that mountain, built at enormous expense, and the plane crashed only a mile and a half from the fortified entrance to it. So then it's all over the newspapers."

"A very costly plane crash."

"Yeah. In lots of ways."

"I'd like to look at the site. Could I do that?"

"No, I don't think so. It's still a restricted area because of the security for the evacuation facility."

"But the secret is out of the bag."

"Yeah, but people are not permitted to just prowl around there."

"I'm a law enforcement officer."

"City of St. Louis. Maybe you could ask for special permission."

"Who would I need to talk to about that?"

"CIA."

Garavelli was referred to Charles Maranville, the CIA's director of domestic operations, and given directions to the headquarters at Langley, just off the George Washington Parkway, west of the Chain Bridge. He was told, "Look for the sign that says, 'Bureau of Public Roads."

The building was a gray limestone monolith. Garavelli had to pass through several security checkpoints and then he was given an escort to Maranville's office.

Charles Maranville, known as "Rabbit," had been a corporate lawyer in Chicago, and later an officer in Naval Intelligence during World War II, assigned to OSS. He was spotted there by General "Wild Bill" Donovan, the most decorated American officer of World war I, who recruited Maranville for the CIA when it was organized after WWII. He was not an impressive man to look at, modest, rather colorless on the surface, but he was interesting. In his spare time, he played jazz piano and palled around with Eddie Condon, Pee Wee Russell, and Benny Goodman. He'd been in the spy business a long time, and in the jazz world even longer.

Maranville had a corner office. An American flag on a pole stood at the corner between the windows. The furniture was government-issue, high quality, not Cabinet officer grade but not far below it. There was an inscribed photo of the sitting president, Lyndon Johnson, on the wall behind the desk, and photos of other men Garavelli did not recognize. All in government frames. No family photos. He was a career man—except that there were the stories about jazz piano.

Garavelli said, "Thank you for seeing me, Director. A question first, if I may. Rabbit Maranville played baseball for the Cardinals and the Boston Braves. Was he your father or a relative?"

Maranville's smile was faint. He'd heard similar versions of that question too many times. "No, but he's the source of my nickname. The boys I went to school with thought that any Maranville should be called Rabbit."

"He was before my time, but I'm told he had good moves."

"What may I do for you, Detective?"

"I'm investigating a case involving two missing St. Louis men, one an art gallery owner from a prominent family and the other a young Negro man from the wrong side of town. They were acquainted. We think that one or both of them may have been on the TWA plane that crashed on Mount Weather."

"Since you aren't sure whether either of them was on that plane, I assume neither was a ticketed passenger and neither was among the identified bodies."

"Correct on both counts, sir."

Maranville looked at the flag, or perhaps he was looking out the window, it was hard to tell. He said, "What makes you think they might have been on board?"

"There was a ticketed passenger named 'John Alden.' The missing gallery owner is named Alden Adams. No body identifiable as John Alden has been found and no-body has come forward seeking to claim such a body. We think John Alden may have been Alden Adams, or perhaps even the other man who went missing at the same time."

"Is that all you have?"

"Bank accounts and a safe deposit box were cleaned out, and Alden Adams bought an expensive emerald ring on the day before the flight."

"And there are people who want their money."

"Yes."

"It's not my business, Detective. I'm concerned with national security."

"I'd like to get permission to search the site of the crash."

"I can't help you. It's a secure site. Since the news media have now publicized the government relocation facility, I assume you know about it."

"Yes, I do."

"Well, it's still a secure site. No one is permitted to be within two miles of the entrance."

"Why not?"

"That's need to know, Detective, need to know. In any event, your chance of finding anything useful there is essentially zero. A metal detector would find a lot of metal. Fragments from the plane are strewn and buried all over the site. Literally dozens of forensic investigators have combed it thoroughly. You can be confident that there's nothing of interest left to be found."

"I'd like to try."

Then both were silent. Garavelli took out his pen and clicked it three times. He did not take out the notebook.

Maranville had an unlit pipe. He held the bowl of the pipe in his right hand, pointed the stem toward the window, and moved the stem in small circles and arabesques. To Garavelli, Maranville appeared to be exercising his hand. The two men stared at each other. Garavelli had been in such meetings before, so he knew that this one had ended. He clicked his pen again and put it back in his pocket. Then he smiled. And Maranville smiled.

Maranville stood. "Sorry. Can't do it."

As Garavelli went out the door, Maranville called to him.

"How's Sportsman's Park, Detective?"

"Now on its way out, Director. It'll soon be replaced."

"I saw one game of the 1944 World Series there, the Cardinals versus the Browns. Sportsman's Park was the home field for both teams."

"It was wartime. The best players were in other uniforms."

Maranville said, "The Cards won the Series, four games to two."

"Also won the Series last year. Thanks again for your time."

13

When Man Ray met with Mary Ocean at her studio on North Compton near Grand, the cab driver asked, "Are you sure this is the right address?" There was no one on the street, no foot traffic, and the building, formerly a warehouse for industrial refrigeration equipment, was three stories tall, all concrete. The facade had no identifying mark except the number. The door was painted the same gray as the walls. Windows at ground level and some of those on the second floor had been filled in with concrete blocks, also painted gray. There was no mailbox, only a narrow slot in the door.

Ray explained to the cab driver, "It's an artists' studio. Artists generally prefer understatement in the design of the space, so as not to compete with the appeal of their art."

The cab driver said, "Okay."

Ray pushed an unobtrusive doorbell beside the door. There was then a long wait. He had a 2:00 p.m. appointment and it was now 2:05, but Ocean's studio was on the second floor and she was descending on a freight elevator enclosed by a folding wooden fence. It was slow, but it worked.

Mary opened the door to the street, Ray entered the building, and the two of them walked through a garage to the elevator on the back wall. Mary unfolded the wooden gate, and they both stepped in. She refastened the gate, the elevator rose to the second floor, and she opened the gate into her studio. On the wall next to the elevator, a four-foot long sheet of shelf lining paper was hung with architect's push pins. The sheet had pen and ink drawings of birds, with written notes on the anatomy. There was a heron standing, five birds flying with wings spread, a vulture, and a skeleton of a bird that may or may not have been a heron, with the bones labeled. There was also a detailed study of the feathers of a wing, extended. Man Ray was fascinated by it.

Mary said, "Birds, birds, birds…Do you ever start with no plan whatsoever? Just begin somewhere, in the middle or at some edge, and make something—a figure, or a bird, or an abstract shape, a color—and then see where that leads?"

"I did that forty-five years ago when I was stuck, and young, and I didn't have anything to lose."

"Now you have things that you don't want to lose, but there isn't much risk that it wouldn't work."

Man said, "The trouble is, people are paying attention now. I have a body of work that's weighing me down, preventing me from becoming airborne."

"What do you mean?"

"I have a reputation now. It creates expectations."

Mary picked up a brush, dipped it in a strong blue, and made a bold stripe diagonally across a blank canvas. "To hell with expectations! What do you think this might become?"

Man Ray looked at the stripe, but couldn't think of anything to say about it. Instead, he said, "In the old days, I'd paint a shape, a quite finished shape, perhaps a piece of machinery, maybe a gear, and then I'd add other shapes, one at a time. Sometimes the shapes weren't coherent, not immediately, but they usually added up to something. It was fun because I didn't have any models of past work to guide me. It gained something from spontaneity, I think."

Mary expanded the blue line. It was becoming more curvaceous. "Did you change things as you went along?"

"Always, but sometimes I tried not to. That required discipline. And imagination. To do it I had to invent my way from one edge to the other, through the picture. It was difficult. I don't work that way now, maybe because I'm too old and tired, or maybe too risk averse. Now I always have an idea before I start to paint. I'm trying to do a specific thing. The painting may turn out to be different from what I'd intended, I might change my mind, but I have an idea in mind."

"You're more disciplined now."

"That's true. That may or may not be a good thing, of course."

Mary Ocean added a dark red form to the blue stripe on her canvas. She said, "Ed Paschke came down from Chicago to do a class for my students. He started a painting and it turned into a baseball glove, a catcher's mitt as I recall it, and then, in the palm of the glove, in the mitt, he started to paint pubic hairs."

"In the great Surrealist tradition."

"Yes, indeed. He sure knew where the painting was going, what it should look like, but he couldn't tell you why."

Man said, "When I urge young artists to be articulate, I do it because giving students advice they will be unable to follow builds character." He picked up a brush and approached Mary's canvas. Then he smiled and put the brush down. "That's enough of that. Let me tell you about developments on Alden Adams. I talked to Detective Garavelli. He's checked out my suggestion that Adams might have flown under the name John Alden on the TWA flight that crashed in Virginia. The police have been unable to establish that. If he was on that flight, he's certainly dead. But none of the remains at the crash site could be identified as a piece of Alden Adams. A lot of the pieces were unidentifiable, however. Some might have been him. Garavelli went to Washington and talked to government officials. Does the name Ray Robinson mean anything to you? A young Negro man?"

"The boxer, but he isn't young."

"No, not the boxer. This one is young and is called 'St. Louis Sugar.'"

Mary said, "Doesn't sound familiar."

"Well, Garavelli found that the young man disappeared at the same time as Adams and the two of them were acquainted. It may be relevant, or maybe not. More uncertainty, indeterminacy. Duchamp would love it."

"But it doesn't get my money back. What does Garavelli do now?"

"He does what an artist does when he's stuck, I suppose—he tries to build a picture piece-by-piece."

*

Garavelli didn't have a regular partner in his work. He preferred to investigate on his own and he had enough seniority and standing in the department to be permitted that freedom. There were younger men available to carry out routine tasks if he needed help, but he hated to delegate. If someone else did the interviews, he never felt certain that the right questions had been asked in the right way. If they weren't, he might not get all of the relevant information.

His wife, Gina, was usually willing to listen to him, but she got tired of hearing about police business—it wasn't her special interest—so Garavelli also tried out his thoughts on Tim Metzler, the detective who had the desk next to his. Metzler was an old South St. Louis German, even more senior in the department, and Garavelli liked him. He was a family man with five children and four grandchildren. He wasn't as big as Garavelli, but his consumption of Budweiser had produced an ample waist. He wore suspenders. On special occasions, he also wore a belt, just to be sure. He would not have been taken for a physical fitness advocate, but he had a vise-like handshake. He always seemed to be freshly shaved. Garavelli said that Metzler was "never more than fifteen minutes beyond Barbasol."

The two of them had talked about Alden Adams and, after the trip to Washington, Garavelli wanted to talk again. He said, "Tim, why did Adams leave town? What was the reason?"

Metzler leaned back in his chair and loosened the suspenders. "Why are you sure that he left? Maybe somebody disposed of him here."

"Adams went around gathering up money and he bought a plane ticket. That sure looks like someone who was leaving."

"But the plane ticket hasn't been used. Right?" He paused but Garavelli didn't answer. Then Metzler continued. "Maybe he wanted us to think he was leaving, to throw us off the track. And money's always useful, anywhere. Or maybe he was trying to raise enough money to pay someone off. And maybe that someone got tired of waiting. Or, all that money he accumulated, that's a good enough reason to kill him, don't you think?"

Garavelli resisted the urge to click his pen. "Certainly people have done it for less. But, if he wasn't planning to run away, why was he closing his bank accounts and emptying the safe deposit box?"

"He owed money to a bunch of artists; maybe he wanted to hide the money from the people he owed. Or maybe he was planning to pay the artists."

"Then why didn't he just do that?"

"Maybe there wasn't enough to go around. Maybe somebody wanted more."

Garavelli didn't see Adams as a victim. "I don't think Adams was killed. Not here anyway. There's no evidence to suggest that he was. No blood. No witnesses. Unless he was on that plane, I'm betting he's still alive."

Metzler sat up straighter. "Do you think he just ran out on his debts? The art gallery was a successful business, right? A going concern. He could have kept that going and made money."

"Maybe not. He'd stiffed a lot of artists, and some of

those artists are important ones. They didn't like giving him paintings and not getting money for them. Adams was going to have a hard time finding artists who were willing to give him works to sell."

"So his motive for leaving, you think, was probably just to start over somewhere else. And fleece artists again." Metzler pulled on the suspenders. "What's happened to the airplane ticket he bought?"

"As far as I can determine, it's still out there somewhere. That's consistent with the idea that he wanted to disappear."

"Yeah. The ticket would've been a way to trace him if he'd used it."

Garavelli said, "And he had enough money to be able to move without using it. But did Adams intend to return to St. Louis, sometime in the future, or did he plan to disappear permanently?"

Metzler rubbed the top of his head. Not much hair was left there. "The answer to that is probably related to the reason why he left. If he'd borrowed money from the wrong people and couldn't pay it back, or if he knew something, some information that could damage those people, he'd want to stay gone, at least for a very long time."

"Yes."

Metzler had another thought. "Or, if Adams had committed a crime, a serious one, and he thought we might be onto him, that might be another reason to disappear permanently. Do we have any unsolved cases where he might be a candidate?"

"I can't think of any, but I'll consider that."

Metzler looked at the ceiling, "On the other hand, if this was a homosexual love affair gone bad, with hurt feelings, or jealousy, Adams could just be taking a little vacation. Then he might plan to return when things cool down."

"Ben Davos claims that he doesn't know of anything like that."

"Maybe it's true. But maybe he wouldn't know"

"Yeah. I thought I was getting a nice, simple, straight-forward missing person case, and I'd just look around a bit and either I'd find him or I wouldn't. But now I've got, added on, grand theft, maybe loan sharking with muscle, a second missing person, a plane crash with unidentified bodies, a homosexual network with a possible vendetta ,and heat from the mayor's office (on a low simmer). And they ask me why I don't dispose of these cases in a hurry." Garavelli pushed his chair back. "This has been helpful, Tim. Thanks. Let me buy you a Coke from the machine."

Metzler said, "Make that a diet Pepsi. I'm in training."

Garavelli laughed and said, "Sure."

14

At five pm in the Mayfair's lounge, there seemed to be a convention of cocktail pianists. The resulting cacophony forced Jay Landesman and Man Ray to take a cab to Duff's. They settled at a small oak table against an old brick wall.

Man said, "When do you leave?"

Jay said, "Tomorrow," and ordered a martini.

Man ordered a *pastis*. This time Duff's knew what it was.

Then Jay said, "I'll be glad to get back to London and the 'Beyond the Fringe' crowd. St. Louis is a bit retro. You must be eager for Paris."

"I am, and Juliet is easily as attractive as the Beyond the Fringe crowd."

"What's kept you here?"

"Partly I've been avoiding a painting in Paris that I don't know how to solve, and partly I've been curious about the disappearance of Alden Adams."

"The gallery owner?"

"Yeah."

"Why do you care? Does he owe you money?"

"No, not me. But he owes several artists."

Jay's martini and Man's *pastis* arrived and were greeted with enthusiasm. Then Jay said, "Gallery owners always owe artists. In the business world, they're known as slow-pay experts, not to say deadbeats."

Man said, "But Alden Adams carried that to an extreme. Do you know Mary Ocean?"

"Yes. She's a character. I don't know her well, but I've met her at art wingdings. She's a St. Louis celebrity."

"Well, I've had some conversations with her, and I like her. She's authentic. She tells me that Adams owes her a bundle. I offered to try to help her get it."

"How do you think you could do that?"

"Well, I thought maybe I could put some pressure on Adams, using my position and my visibility in the art world to get him to pay his debts."

Jay said, "You mean you'd put him out of business if he didn't pay up?"

"A bit more subtle than that, but that's the general idea. Obviously, I can't do it unless he turns up or the police find him."

"No, you couldn't."

Man Ray didn't like his chair. He moved to another one. "I'm not in any hurry. I'm an old man. I can do as I please and take my time. Maybe Adams is dead, but they searched for him among the bodies in the plane crash and didn't find him. I'm told that a lot of the bodies were impossible to identify. So the police don't know where he is, and I'll be going home soon."

Jay said, "If you don't go soon, Juliet will think you found a new girl here."

"I'm too old for that sort of foolishness."

"I'm surprised to hear that."

"I feel my age."

"In what way?"

Ray finished his *pastis* quickly and signaled for another. "Unless you're seriously depressive or seriously ill, aging happens in subtle ways, but there's an underlying awareness that your life is ending. You don't feel it as a crisis; it's just an undercurrent, a slow erosion. It's a process of subtraction—first something is taken away, hearing maybe, and you adjust to that, and then another thing is taken, and then another. Not all at once. You get hearing aids, which help a bit, but not much. Your eyesight gets worse, so you get stronger glasses. And then you have cataract surgery. Maybe you see better, for a time, and then you have macular degeneration. Then balance, dexterity, concentration, energy, digestion, and dignity go, one at a time. You adjust. You do without. You might be surprised at how much adjusting you can do." He smiled. "Your life becomes quieter. One of the worst subtractions is your friends. They die. But, again, you adjust. And at what point do you no longer have enough left to make life worth continuing? Well, it turns out that one is willing to do without quite a lot. You tolerate it, but you know you can't go on much longer, and that fact curbs your enthusiasm for new projects and you tend to review what you've already done, what you've accomplished."

"Is your work now repeating old triumphs?"

"I worry that it is. I try not to repeat, mostly."

Jay said, "You mentioned new projects. I've got a great one—I think this will be the big one. It's a musical version of the Dracula story. I'm calling it 'Dearest Dracula'. Fran will do the lyrics. We're still shopping for the composer and there's a lot of interest. I'm hoping you'll design the sets! Think of it—Transylvania! It's a natural for Surrealist sets—castles, mountains, caskets, blood. I'm talking to Busby Berkeley about him doing the choreography. A chorus of dancing vampires. Biting everyone in sight. So let's talk about the set designs."

"It's an interesting project, Jay." A middle-aged woman on the other side of the room was wearing a flamboyant hat trimmed with numerous flowers—faux roses, daisies, tulips, poppies. Man Ray studied the hat.

Jay said, "A natural. Can't miss. Let's work together."

Ray looked at the door. "I've never done theater work or set design, and I'm too old to start now. It's a different art."

"This would be just what you need to give your life and your art a jolt. A jump start! It would get you out of those end- of-life doldrums you were talking about. And there'd be real money in it. Your name would help a lot in building the package, and your percentage of the profits would reflect that." Jay finished his martini. "Read the script. It's full of laughs—chills and laughs."

Man Ray lit a Camel. "It's not my kind of thing. Too camp for me. You should get Andy Warhol."

"Warhol has his own movie and theater projects. He won't do sets for a production that he doesn't totally control."

Ray looked at the ceiling. The setting sun coming through Duff's front windows produced changing patterns on the pressed tin panels. "Mary Ocean has imagination. And a wild streak. She'd design interesting sets."

"Her name wouldn't attract the New York investors. She's bigtime in St. Louis, but St. Louis isn't New York. To get the show to Broadway, I'll need names New York recognizes, names they can market. Like Man Ray."

"Why don't you try talking to Mary? See what she comes up with. I'll bet she'd have ideas."

*

Since Landesman was leaving for London the next day, he needed to move quickly. He called Mary Ocean and went to see her at her home, a substantial Arts and Crafts house in the Parkview neighborhood near the Washington University campus. By New York or Paris standards, houses like that were surprisingly affordable in St. Louis. Mary's four children were home from school and were having a good time. They contributed a celebratory atmosphere.

The house was decorated with Mary's paintings and work by several of her friends. Mary's pieces were the most exuberant. The recent ones were studies of chairs, paintings that hadn't been used in a recent show. A sunporch with a tile floor was dominated by succulents, so thick that you couldn't walk through it. Fortunately, the succulents didn't often need watering. Jay and Mary sat in the kitchen.

Landesman made essentially the pitch he had used with Man Ray. The result was similar.

She replied, "First of all, what you need to know—and not only know but appreciate—is that I'm not in the slightest interested in understatement."

"Surely you don't want the sets to be garish."

"Not garish, no. But, if I decided to do the sets, I'd want them to be breathtaking. When the curtain at the theater went up—or opened, or whatever the hell it does—I would want the audience to gasp. And not gasp in horror. I would want them to gasp in awe at the beauty."

"That would be just fine."

"It would be a symphonic Dracula, Beethoven's Dracula. It would make Wagner look puny."

"You're even more full of bullshit than I am."

"That's very difficult to accomplish, but I'm trying."

"How can we make a deal about this?"

Mary said, "Well, to start, you can give me a large sum of money."

"But I don't have any money coming in yet."

"Nor do I. Nor do I. You'll need front money."

"I'll have investors but, before I can get those, I need to have people like Mary Ocean committed to the project."

"Alden Adams left me without what I need to live on."

"I heard he owed you money. What happened?"

"He disappeared. Just vanished."

Jay said, "But he's getting lots of attention. You don't suppose that's what he intended to do, attract attention?"

"No, no. He's an entrepreneur, but he's not nuts. And not that free I think."

"I had Vincent Price lined up for the lead. He's originally from St. Louis, you know. But then the producer backed out. I lost my funding and the deal fell through. Some people have no imagination."

"Flaubert said that you don't make art out of good intentions. You actually have to do it, Jay."

"I know. I'm willing, and I've proved that I can do it. 'The Nervous Set' was great. But then the Broadway producer screwed it up…The money people take control and they have no taste, no sense."

Mary said, "Why did you leave St. Louis, Jay?"

"I left because I'd run out my string. I couldn't come up with new stuff, couldn't keep it going. I have lots of ideas, but the problem is to separate the good ones from the bad. You should help me."

Mary put on an apron. "Has anyone ever told you how insufferable you are?"

"It happens seldom, really. Most people appear to find me charming."

Jay Landesman returned to London without having recruited a set designer.

15

Harold Strand was packing his bags. He wasn't sure where he was going, but there was nothing keeping him near the Mississippi. He'd lost his job, and the St. Louis art community wasn't all that exciting. Then the telephone rang. He considered letting it ring, but decided to answer and was glad that he did. To his surprise, Man Ray was inviting him to come to the Mayfair for a drink.

Strand was a bit overwhelmed by the call. Ray was a genuine art world star, on the international level. The invitation was certainly welcome, but why would Man Ray want to talk to him? What was up? Strand took a shower, shaved, and put on a suit and tie. The suit was his summer one, blue and white seersucker, a staple of summer in St. Louis. The tie was yellow. Celebratory, yes, but tasteful. Maybe Ray needed a studio assistant.

The university streetcar line provided inexpensive and reasonably efficient transportation from University City to the hotel. Strand arrived there at midafternoon and the lounge wasn't crowded. Ray was waiting for him.

With few preliminaries, Ray said, "I'm trying to locate Alden Adams. The police seem to think I know something about his disappearance because I was at National Airport waiting for that TWA plane to arrive, and then I went to his gallery, so the police speculate that Adams may have been bringing money to me. He wasn't, but now I'm involved whether I like it or not. As they see it, as soon as I show up in town, he disappears—both things happen at the same time. They wonder whether the two have anything to do with one another."

"I don't know why they would." Strand nursed his gin and tonic. "Why are you bothering with this? You're an international celebrity." Strand was curious about Ray's involvement. It didn't make sense to him.

"People have been hurt, Mr. Strand, and I have the time. Why shouldn't I try to help?…"I've played the art game a long time. I'm intrigued by this, and I can afford to do what I want at this point in my life. It seems important. The disappearance of Alden Adams has consequences for several people, including you and the artists the gallery owes money, especially Mary Ocean." Ray lit a cigarette. "So what happened to Alden Adams?"

"Maybe he just left. As you say, he owed money. Maybe he got on the plane and the plane crashed, and his body was burned."

Ray said, "Yes, maybe, but there's no real evidence that Adams was on that plane. And, yes, he owed money, but not such a large amount that his situation was desperate. There was money in the gallery's bank account and there was probably some in his safe deposit box, and he was able to buy an expensive emerald ring. With reasonable prudence and intelligent work, he could have paid his debts. Why disappear?"

Ray offered Strand a cigarette, which was declined.

Then Strand said, "He's a homosexual. You know that. Maybe he has a lover somewhere. Men who are homosexual sometimes live complicated lives."

"Not really all that complicated."

"Do you know that from personal experience, Mr. Ray?"

"Please call me Man, and I don't think my sexual activities need concern us. You can be sure, however, that I'm sympathetic. You won't shock me."

Strand smiled. "You are a man of the world."

"I hope so." Ray was drinking tea. He poured more hot water from the pot into his cup. "Detective Garavelli tells me that some of the members of the homosexual community here haven't been willing to talk to him, or haven't been very forthcoming about Alden Adams. Could you help with that?"

"Well, relations between the St. Louis police and the community aren't good. They hassle us. So when the police want cooperation, they don't get it...Maybe I should have given the detective more of it, but I don't trust cops. They give us a hard time."

"I think Garavelli's okay. He's not in Vice, and he doesn't give a damn about that stuff."

"Some Italians are serious Catholics, and some of them are crusaders."

"Yes, some are. Not Garavelli."

"Well, I told him that he should take a look at the relationship between Alden and Ray Robinson, known at St. Louis Sugar."

"Yes, and I know Garavelli has done that—or has tried to, at least. What can you tell me about Robinson? I know he's not an artist, and he's much younger than Adams, and then there are the race and social class differences. On the face of it, apart from the fact that they are both homosexual, they don't have much in common. Why was Adams attracted to him?"

Strand paused. "Alden said that Sugar did the best blowjob north of New Orleans."

"Was that enough?"

"Don't underrate it."

"Granted. On another subject, what can you tell me about Robinson's circumstances? Family? What are his living arrangements?"

"Don't know about family. He lives with two men. One of them is called 'Bathhouse Noble'. He works at the Finnish Baths. I don't know the other man's name."

"How old are they?"

"Bathhouse is maybe thirty. I'm not sure that I've ever seen the other guy."

"And they live on Clemens?"

"I think so, yes."

Harold Strand finished his gin and tonic, Man Ray finished his tea, the two men stood and shook hands, and Ray thanked Strand for his help.

Ray said, "I'm off to 6043 Clemens. That's the address Garavelli gave me. It's nice to be in a town where they know Mark Twain's real name."

It was raining when they came out of the hotel, but the rain had done nothing to cool the day. Properly, he supposed, it was more of a mist than a rain. But there were droplets in the mist and it should have been cooler. It wasn't. Ray wondered whether the steam on the sidewalks came from water that turned to vapor when it hit the hot pavement, or whether the steam in the air was heating the cement. Either way, he knew it would destroy his oxford wingtips.

The doorman flagged a taxi. Ray offered to share it and give Strand a ride home, but the younger man said he had things to do downtown. That wasn't true. He declined because he was uncomfortable with Man Ray. Perhaps it was a simple matter of too much horsepower. But Strand was disappointed.

The taxi had no trouble finding the building on Clemens, a six-flat, brick. The block was handsome but worn. There were mature trees and some substantial houses, but little had been spent on maintenance recently. The properties were beginning to fade. The building was a few steps up from the sidewalk, but the apartment was on the first floor. Ray was grateful for that.

Bathhouse Noble was a large man with a big stomach and a stubble of beard. He was the opposite of the popular stereotype of the slender, lithe, well-groomed homosexual. Ray could not imagine why anyone, male or female, would find the man attractive. His voice was more rumble than words, and their conversation was brief.

Noble confirmed that Ray Robinson lived there, or had lived there until he dropped out of sight. When questioned, Noble also said that Robinson's mother was still living and that her son was in touch with her. Mrs. Robinson lived on Hamilton, near Page, several blocks north of Clemens, Noble was sure of that, but he was unable or unwilling to

be more precise about the address. Noble also asked Man
Ray to tell Sugar that he should return to the apartment,
and that he would not have to pay rent.

*

Ray asked for Garavelli's help. He was told that police,
perhaps Garavelli himself, had interviewed Mrs. Robinson but had not received useful information. Garavelli was,
however, able to give Ray her address and telephone number. When Ray called her and explained that he was hoping to find her son, to his surprise she invited him to tea.

Ray noted that the hallways of the building where she
lived were spotless—in need of paint, but spotless. He rang
the bell and Mrs. Robinson eased herself out of a rocking
chair that faced an electric fan. She opened the door cautiously. The dapper, elderly white man introduced himself
as he took off his beret, which was soggy with rain. A china
teapot and two cups were laid on the table in the living
room, and the kettle was on the stove. She took the pot to
the kitchen and filled it, and then asked whether he took
his tea with sugar, milk, or both. Lemon wasn't offered. He
took milk. He thought that iced tea would be more welcome, given the weather, but of course he didn't say that.

She poured and said, "They tell me you are a famous
man, Mr. Ray, a famous artist."

"Well, I'm an artist, but I don't think I'm famous. Very
few people recognize my name or know who I am."

"The postmaster tells me that you were at the White
House."

"That part is true. I was there last week, along with a lot of other people."

"Why are you interested in my son, Raymond, a famous man like you taking an interest in a poor Negro boy?"

"Please call me 'Man'".

She said, "Thank you, but I'm not sure I'd be comfortable with that." She paused. "My name is Estella, but my friends call me 'Stella.' Some even call me 'Stell'."

"Yes, well the reason I'm interested in your son is that he was acquainted with an art dealer named Alden Adams. Mr. Adams has disappeared, and I'm told that your son also hasn't been seen recently. I thought it was possible that the two of them travelled somewhere together."

"Do you have a romantic interest in Raymond, Mr. Ray, a love interest?"

"No, Mrs. Robinson, I don't. I'm not attracted to men. I'm married to a very lovely woman and we're happy."

"Good for you." She leaned back in her chair. "That's a fine Christian way to live."

Man Ray did not feel it necessary to tell her that he was not a Christian. That fact wasn't relevant.

He said, "Did your son, Raymond, mention Alden Adams?"

"Oh yes, and I've met Mr. Adams. He was helpful to Raymond. Mr. Adams is a kind gentleman."

"How was he helpful? In what way?"

"Raymond felt that he needed to get away."

"Get away from what?"

"He doesn't like to be cooped up, don't you know. He likes to have his freedom, to be out and about, as he often tells me. It may go back to when he was quarantined."

"I beg your pardon?"

"It was measles, they said. There was a red sign nailed to our door. Well, tacks, really, I suppose. One of the Sheriff's men put it up. Hammered on our door. The sign said that nobody could come in or go out." Her voice failed, and she took a small drink of water from a glass on a table beside her chair. "They told me that my husband couldn't come to visit. I didn't tell them that my husband didn't want to visit anyhow. They didn't need to worry about that. But we couldn't go out."

"It must have been difficult, annoying."

"Oh, it was at least difficult. That's a kind word for it. It was worse than that. It was like being held prisoner. Or, at least, I think it was. I've never been held prisoner, except then." She took another sip of water. "When you've been locked up, and then you get to go outside, the sky looks beautiful. Even if there's smoke, the sky looks beautiful." She paused. "I was held by police once."

"What happened?"

"I was in a dime store, looking at the toys, when I was about eleven or twelve years old. I was looking at a doll, a very pretty doll, and the owner said I was shoplifting. I wasn't shoplifting, I was just looking at it, but the man called the police. I hadn't left the store." Mrs. Robinson shook her head slowly from side to side. "A big policeman came, and the store man lied. He said I'd taken things before. He knew he was lying, and I think the policeman knew it too. Then the man told the policeman that he didn't want 'pickininnies' in his store. That's what he called me. A pickininny."

"What did the police officer do?"

"He grabbed hold of my arm and took me to the police station. Then he called my mother, and they kept me there until she came and got me."

"How long were you there?"

"Forever."

Man Ray stared into his teacup. "Was the doll a Negro or white?"

"Oh, white. All the dolls were white. That was the only kind of dolls there were."

Man Ray didn't know how to respond, so he returned to the problems of her son. "Ray wasn't quarantined just recently, just before he left town, was he?"

"Oh my, no. That was years ago, when he was a child."

"So, then, how did Alden Adams help him?"

Mrs. Robinson had reading glasses attached to a black ribbon and hung around her neck. She put the glasses on her nose, adjusted their position, and picked up from the table a folded piece of blue paper. She unfolded it and appeared to read it. Man Ray could not see what was written on the paper.

She said, "My son had trouble with some white men. They called themselves preachers, but they certainly were not good Christians. They threatened him."

"Why? What did they threaten him about?"

"In March, he went down to Selma, Alabama. He went on a bus and was gone for a week. He walked with Dr. King and the Reverend James Bevel, and they walked from Selma to Montgomery. I don't know whether Ray walked all the way to Montgomery, but he was on the Pettus Bridge, you know. They were marching for voting rights."

Mrs. Robinson took off her reading spectacles and stared at Man Ray. He felt that she was examining him, perhaps assessing his trustworthiness. Then she said, "When Ray got back to St. Louis, only a few days after he got back, he was visited by four white men. They called themselves 'Christian Patriots for Purity'. This blue paper says that they stood for…" She put the glasses back on. "Purity of the soul, Purity of the blood, Purity of the Word.' Hogwash! They're thugs. Nothing but thugs." Mrs. Robinson carefully folded the blue paper and put it back on the table. "They gave Raymond a beating."

"That's terrible. Did you call the police?"

"No. One of the men told Raymond that he was a policeman and that if we called the police there would be another beating."

"How bad was the beating?"

"Not too bad. Raymond could walk. They said the next one would be worse."

Man Ray pulled a pack of cigarettes out of his pocket, but then remembered where he was and put them back. "So how was Alden Adams able to help?"

"He talked to Billy Miller. He calls himself Reverend, but I don't believe it."

"What did Miller say they wanted Raymond to do?"

"They wanted him to stay out of politics."

"Has Raymond been in politics?"

"Well, he went to Selma, and he went there because he heard Stokely Carmichael speak at a meeting at the AME church, just down the street. Reverend Bevel was at the meeting and he was signing people up to go to Selma."

"Were you at the meeting?"

"Oh my, no. That was for young people. I live a quiet life. But the white men didn't want colored people to vote. I think that's what they meant by 'politics.' And they asked for money."

Man Ray said, "Money. What was the money for?"

"Money for a gift. Billy Miller said it would be a contribution to the good work of their church." She took a sip of water. "They just wanted money." She took another sip. "If they didn't get the money, they said the police would crack down on Raymond and his friends."

"Crack down on what?"

"Sex. They said it was illegal and Raymond would go to jail. They also threatened to beat him again."

"What makes them think Raymond has money?"

"I don't know what makes them think it. He doesn't."

"How much money did Miller want?"

"I don't know exactly, but a thousand or more. Way more money than Raymond and I have."

Man said, "Since Alden Adams was involved, Miller probably figured that even if Raymond didn't have money, Adams did. So he could get money out of Adams."

"Probably so."

"Adams helped Raymond by paying money, is that it?"

"Yes. He didn't give money to Raymond but he told Raymond that he'd given it to Miller."

"How much?"

"I don't know, but a lot."

"If Miller had been paid off, why did Raymond leave town?"

She said, "He was afraid. They frightened him. And they hurt him. He thought they would do it again."

Man Ray's eyes surveyed the room. There was a picture of Christ on the cross. "Ray might well have been right. It sounds like Miller and his friends have a racket. It's called extortion." He raised his index finger and pointed at the door. "So Raymond just decided to leave? Is that it?"

"I guess so, I'm not sure."

"Did he say goodbye?"

"Well, he kissed me and hugged me. He does that sometimes."

Man Ray paused. "Did he say where he was going?"

"No."

"Did Alden Adams go with him?"

"I don't know. I hope so."

"Where do you think they might have gone?"

"I don't know, but I'm very grateful to Mr. Adams. I hope they are both well."

16

Man Ray called Detective Garavelli. "I've talked to Ray Robinson's mother and I've got some information I think is important."

There was a pause. Then Garavelli said, "Okay, is this a short report or a long one?"

Man Ray took pride in being brief, but he said, "Well, I suppose it might be long."

"In that case, you'd better come to my house for dinner. This would be the perfect night. Gina has made lasagna, and there will be more than enough for the three of us." He gave Ray an address on the Hill and they agreed that Ray would arrive at six PM.

It was a brick bungalow on a street of brick bungalows, but a little larger than the others. It had three bedrooms and a small front yard. The houses on the block were not all built at the same time—some of them fronted right on the sidewalk, but the Garavelli house was set back several feet.

Gina Garavelli, an attractive woman in her early fifties, had black hair streaked with gray. She was small and slim, unlike her husband, and was wearing a linen sundress, navy blue. The Garavellis's daughter and son, Katie and Peter, were not there. Katie was married and living in Kirkwood, and Peter was away at college. Gina and Al Garavelli talked as they set the table and waited for Man Ray to arrive.

Gina said, "Why is Man Ray coming to dinner?"

"He's interested in the disappearance of an art dealer, Alden Adams, and he's talked to people connected to the case. Now he wants to tell me what he's found out."

"What's an internationally famous artist doing investigating a missing person case in St. Louis?"

"In part, I think it's something we see pretty often. He's playing detective. The TV is full of detectives, and it looks romantic, better than selling insurance, so they try their hand at it. And this case involves the art world. It's on his turf. He was in close proximity when it happened…But I think there's more to it than that."

"What?"

"I'm not sure. Probably something to do with his personal life."

Then the doorbell rang.

After the customary introductions, Man Ray began the small talk. "Is Gina a shortened version of Regina?"

She replied. "Ordinarily it would be, and that would have been fine with me. I wouldn't have minded being a queen. But in my case Gina is a distortion. My birth name is Angelina. That led to being called 'Angel'. In about the third grade, after being called 'the little angel' a couple of times, I put a stop to that. I became Gina."

Man Ray said, "A good solution. Practical."

Gina still wondered why he had been invited to dinner. She said, "Al tells me that you came especially because we are having lasagna tonight."

"Well, I'm enthusiastic about lasagna, but I am even more enthusiastic about meeting you."

"Al also told me that you were a charmer."

Man asked, "What sort of lasagna do you prefer, northern, southern, or in-between?"

"Well, tonight we will be having an eggplant version. The eggplants at the Soulard Market look very good this summer. This lasagna is basically Sicilian, but I also make a pesto one from Genoa and a fish one from the Piedmont."

"I've never had a fish lasagna."

"It was popular once, many years ago. You don't see it now."

"What's in the eggplant version?"

"The usual - — tomatoes, capers, balsamella, oregano, salt, and pepper. And the pasta, of course. Homemade."

"I'm impressed that you make lasagna even in a St. Louis summer."

Gina said, "Lasagna is one of life's constants. It's a nice, light, summer lasagna. No meat. And we have air conditioning."

Man said, "I feel the air conditioning, and I look forward to the lasagna."

Gina made it clear that police business was not to be discussed at dinner. Man Ray had to hold his news until the two men retired to the living room with coffee. Then he gave Garavelli a summary of what he'd been told by Mrs. Robinson, including the information about the trip to Selma, the Patriots for Purity, the Reverend Billy Miller, the beating, and the role of Alden Adams.

As soon as Ray had finished, Garavelli said, "How

did Miller and the Patriots find out that Robinson had marched at Selma?"

Man replied, "As I was leaving, Mrs. Robinson said that her son was proud of being on the Pettus Bridge with Dr. King and he told people about it. Maybe some of them were the wrong people. A few of them, certainly, were in the Army Reserve. She said he thought maybe Army men got him into trouble."

Garavelli said, "That could do it."

Ray finished his coffee. There had been a Barbera D'Alba with the lasagna. Six years old. Very good. Now Garavelli offered Man Ray cognac or scotch. He chose the scotch. As they continued to talk, the conversation became more speculative and personal.

Man Ray said, "The information from Mrs. Robinson suggests that Alden Adams is not quite the thief we thought he was."

"No, not quite. Maybe he's a more complicated thief."

"A Robin Hood type, redistributing wealth."

Garavelli pushed back. "Yeah, except the people he's taking it from are artists, not exactly the rich, and the person he's redistributing it to is his boyfriend, a sexual partner. A somewhat warped form of altruism, maybe even self-indulgence."

"But let's not be too hard on him. If what Mrs. Robinson told me is true, Adams was helping a young man who was a victim of violence, racist violence, and the police were not any help."

"The police didn't know anything about it. The Robinsons haven't made a complaint and, when we asked Mrs.

Robinson for information about her son, she didn't tell us a damn thing. She waits until she's having tea with a famous artist from Paris France before she chooses to tell her story."

"According to Mrs. Robinson, one of the men who did the beating and the extortion claimed to be a police officer."

Garavelli hung his head and looked at the floor. "Any name?"

"No, no names."

"I'll look into it. This is very serious."

Man said, "Okay, so what do you intend to do?"

"What can we do? It's all hearsay. By her account, Mrs. Robinson doesn't have any facts from her own personal knowledge. All she knows is what she's been told by her son or by Alden Adams. She hasn't talked to Miller. She doesn't even know the names of the other three men, including the one who claims to be a police officer. She hasn't actually observed anything. And we still don't even have a complaint."

"She observed that her son had been beaten."

"What did she see? Maybe she saw that he had some cuts and bruises, so maybe he got into a fight. Maybe it was a lovers' quarrel. So there's maybe again. Unlike you, we actually have to prove things. You can bet that Miller and his friends aren't going to tell the same story that Mrs. Robinson told you…And why did Alden Adams spend money and effort on protecting Ray Robinson? If Miller's men are as violent as they're supposed to be, Adams took a big risk by meeting with them, by putting himself in their line of sight. Why would he do that?"

"Affection, maybe?"

"Real affection or just sex?"

Man Ray finished his scotch and Garavelli poured another for both of them. Ray looked into his glass. "Ben Davos showed me a drawing that Adams had done, a figure study. It was a young Negro male, nude."

"Was it Ray Robinson?"

"Davos thought it was, but he had never seen Robinson. He assumed it was Robinson because of the way Adams regarded the drawing. But, with the shading and all, it's difficult to tell even the race of the subject. You can't be sure. Robinson is, or was, light-skinned. The man in the drawing is well-muscled, lithe. He looks like an athlete on a Greek vase."

"What's the pose?"

"He's standing, one arm up in the air."

"Genitals visible?"

"Yes."

Garavelli said, "So, what does all this tell us?"

"My picture of Alden Adams has been solarized."

Garavelli smiled. "Yeah, but I've read up on it. Tell me if I've got this wrong, but in a solarized photo some of the light areas become dark and some of the dark areas become light, but that doesn't happen evenly all over. If it did, you'd just get a negative image. But it's more complicated than that. There are areas that are in-between, that have partly shifted or changed, especially at the edges of people or objects, at the boundaries. Have I got that right? There are still some murky parts. We should try to clean it up. The emerald ring, for example, was probably not bought for the Reverend Billy Miller."

Ray smiled. "I'm impressed by your scholarship. But maybe we have too much contrast. Photos sometimes need a long gray scale."

"I could do without the long grays. I'd like some clarity."

"Yes, but we have to recognize ambiguity when we see it."

"You've become quite a detective." Garavelli looked closely at Ray. "Why are you doing this?"

Ray paused and sipped his scotch. "There's an injustice somewhere here. There's an injustice, isn't there? Somewhere, here." He looked at his hands, as if he might be able to draw a picture.

"Yes, of course there is, but it isn't your fight. It's my duty. I'm required to deal with it. You're not."

Man Ray looked out the window. He thought he could see the incomplete Arch. The Gateway. He said, "My father was a tailor in Brooklyn. Not a J. W. Losse Custom Tailor. My father did piecework for sweatshops. I'm comfortable now, but I remember. I suppose I have sympathy for the downtrodden, the vulnerable, the wronged."

"You've come to the right place. We've got plenty of those people. You can find your life's work here."

"I'm seventy-five years old, my life's work is almost done. Juliet's in Paris. I'm going back there." He finished the scotch. "I'm following one of the rules or lessons I taught myself many years ago. When a painting isn't going well, you should do something else. The painting can wait."

"But the something else might not go well either."

"That's the reason to make it something different, not just another painting. 'Make it new,' Ezra Pound's words to live by." Man hadn't supplied to Mary Ocean the source of the quote, but he knew where it came from. He looked out the window again. The gateway was gone. "Pound is troubled. He was a fascist. Fan of Mussolini. Also nuts. Also brilliant. The U.S. government locked him up in a mental hospital for several years after the war. He's now living in Italy."

Ray shifted in his chair. "If I screw up an investigation, they won't blame me. They'll say, 'That investigation wasn't Man Ray's responsibility, that was Garavelli's job.'"

Garavelli said, "I think there's something more you're not telling me."

"Ah, the detective's radar is at work."

"You have to grant me some professional skill…There are a lot of differences between my work and yours."

"Yeah, you use up more shoe leather in yours. But we're probably about equally likely to dodge a bullet. In fact, I'll bet that more artists die of gunshot wounds. I don't think many detectives are actually shot."

"Just like most artists don't cut off their ears."

"Right! But both jobs are creative work. The people who choose to do it have to like problem-solving."

Garavelli said, "They also have to live with uncertainty, doubt."

"Yes, and failure."

"That too."

Ray looked at his hands. "Do detectives like to solve puzzles?"

"Different kinds of puzzles for different tastes. I don't like crosswords."

"Me too."

"But I like chess."

"So do I."

Garavelli turned away from Ray. "Is there trouble in Paris?"

"Why do you ask?"

"You don't seem eager to get back there—and, as compelling as summer in St. Louis may be, I'm told that Paris has it's attractions."

"I'm as transparent as that, am I?"

"If I were investigating, I'd bet that the problem involves a woman, either here or there. Since I haven't observed one here, she'd more likely be there."

Man Ray spoke softly. "A deduction in the classic form. Worthy of Holmes."

"If I'm on the right track then, and since I know you are married, there are at least three possibilities. The problem might be inside the marriage, outside of it, or a combination of the two. If there's a woman other than your wife, that might well create a problem inside the marriage."

"You've done this before."

"Elementary. I'm told you have a somewhat an adventuresome romantic history."

"I think adventuresome is the wrong word."

"What's the right one?"

"I'd accept 'epic.'"

"How many times have you been married?"

"Only twice. About average for the twentieth century. Probably below average for people in the arts."

"But there were lovers."

"Serious ones, yes. Long-term relationships."

"Tell me about this epic. I'll refill your glass."

Had it not been for the drink, Man Ray might not have complied. As it was, he thought he had nothing to lose. "First I was married to a Belgian poet, Adon Lacroix. We met in New York City when I was twenty-three and we married the next year. We were happy for a time, about five years, and then we separated—but we remained married for almost twenty more years. A legal formality."

"What happened?"

"There were no major issues in the marriage. It wasn't that one of us wanted children and the other didn't, or that one of us was only able to make love while dressed in a clown suit. Nothing like that. It was just that we annoyed one another."

"And then?"

"In 1921, I moved to Paris. A short time later I fell in love with a model who used the name Kiki de Montparnasse. She was rather famous in Paris. I took many photographs of her. It's some of my best-known work."

"But you didn't marry her."

"I was still married to Adon…You need to get your notebook. You could click your pen."

Garavelli smiled again. "How long were you with Kiki?"

"Until the end of the 1920s."

"What happened then?"

"I met Lee Miller. Beautiful. When she walked into a room, heads would turn to look at her, both men and women. She was a model, had worked for *Vogue*, but she became a great photographer. I taught her. She was 17 years younger than I. She liked older men. I think she liked their power."

"What happened?"

"We had three years. Then she left me."

"And then?"

"Then there was a dancer from Guadeloupe. She also modeled."

"Name?"

"Adrienne Fidelin, but I prefer not to talk about her."

"I'll respect that. When were you with her?"

"The second half of the 1930s."

"And what happened next?"

"World War Two."

"I know that, but what happened to your relationship?"

"The war happened to it. In 1940 the Germans occupied France. I got the hell out of there. Adrienne stayed with her family."

"You came back to the United States."

"Yes, to Los Angeles, and I met Juliet Browner there. She's now Juliet Man Ray. She was also a dancer and an artists' model. A lovely person. Beautiful, kind. We've been married since 1946."

"And you're still together?"

"We are, yes, but now I'm in St. Louis."

"So, what's the problem?"

"I'm not sure. Perhaps marital fatigue. I've been with Juliet for almost twenty years — far longer than with any of the others."

"Is there someone else?"

"Not for me, there isn't."

"Has Juliet found someone else?"

"Oh lord, I hope not. That would be very bad."

"It does happen, you know."

Man said, "I know that better than most." He rubbed his head. "When you review your lovers, you know you're getting close to the end."

"How's your career going?"

Man savored the scotch. "The trouble is, you remember when it was better. You remember when *you* were better. The world looked, then, like a bundle of opportunities. *Vogue* wanted to publish your photographs. Conde Nast wanted to have you do design work. Your notebook was full of new ideas for paintings, page after page of them. You remember when there were discoveries every day, or almost every day."

"And now there are not so many?"

"No. Not so many."

"And yet, you're still working. You still enjoy it?"

"Yes, I do. And, from time to time, some of the work I'm doing now seems to me very good. But there isn't the same applause. I'm old news."

"Do you have regrets?"

"Of course. I made some bad decisions. I was young and in a hurry. One of the good things about old age is that life slows down. You don't have as much to prove, or you don't care as much about whether you prove it.... None of it matters as much now. Mercifully, by the time you get old there are very few people left who remember the stupid things you did. Of course there are a few malcontents, people of ill will, people who bear grudges. Screw them. None of it really matters anymore. Not even the failures."

Garavelli said, "I think you should go back to Paris. You spent a lot of time looking around, but it sounds like you've found the right woman now. You say you're a problem-solver, so solve this problem. Make it new with Juliet."

"But if I go back to Paris, who will help you find Alden Adams and Ray Robinson?"

"We'll muddle through. My radar, as you call it, tells me that Ray Robinson is dead. I don't have proof of that, but I'll bet it's true. He may have been on the plane that crashed, or maybe he was disposed of by someone who thought he could get them into trouble. If he was alive, his mother would've heard from him. You tell me they were close. When he had trouble with the Patriots, he turned to her. She even met with Alden Adams."

Ray said, "And what about Adams?"

"He's scampered. Maybe he didn't take all the money with him, but I think he took enough of it. We don't know how much there was in the safe deposit box."

"Why would he run away and leave his business?"

"Plenty of reasons. The debtors were closing in, his lover was in serious trouble that had the potential for violence and police involvement, and he probably had to choose between Robinson and Davos. That would have been inconvenient, probably unpleasant—especially if he chose Robinson. It was time to go. He wanted a new start."

"Where would he go?"

Garavelli said, "A big city, a place with an art world."

"Europe?"

"The most likely choice of country is always one where you already speak the language."

"Will you look for him?"

"How can I do that? Of course we'll put out the standard missing-person notice that goes to other police departments. It'll be filed."

"And Mrs. Robinson?"

"I'll pay a courtesy call and see if she wants to do anything. We've already checked with all the coroners for many miles around to see whether they have any unidentified young black males. They don't. The Army also put out an AWOL notice with no results."

"What about the Patriots for Purity?"

"I'll make inquiries. But, without a complaint being filed, I won't be able to get a warrant."

"Maybe Mrs. Robinson will file a complaint."

"Maybe. But she might have good reason to be scared. I suppose she hopes her son is still alive." Their glasses were empty. "I'll call a taxi for you."

17

Garavelli and Metzler were at their desks.

Garavelli said, "Tim, got a minute? I'd like to talk about the Alden Adams case."

"Never too busy to talk to you, my friend. What's up?"

"I've been looking at the Reverend Billy Miller and his Patriots for Purity."

"What have you got?"

"Not much. But, because Mrs. Robinson told us that Adams had given them money, I've been trying to see if Miller has been more flush lately. I haven't found anything useful."

"Why are you investigating him? Do you think he got rid of Adams?"

"No, I don't think that. Why would they do it? Unless maybe they thought he could hurt them some way. Maybe then. But if what Mrs. Robinson tells us is right, Miller might know where Adams is or where he's gone. Anyway, if Miller is running a scam, putting an end to it would be worth doing, worth the effort, especially if a policeman is involved."

Metzler leaned back in his chair and loosened his suspenders. He said, "What have you done so far?"

"So far, not much. There isn't enough evidence to get

a warrant, so I've been using public records and reliable informants."

"And you've been trying to find the money, the money that Adams owed the artists and the money he gave to Miller, which is probably the same money."

Garavelli swiveled his chair to the right, and then to the left. "Right. But, according to Mrs. Robinson, Miller was working with several other men, so maybe the money was divided-up, shared among the Patriots."

"Which makes it harder to trace because the pieces will be smaller, less conspicuous."

"Yeah, and besides, we don't know the identities of the other men, so we don't know where to look."

Metzler said, "And it's pretty hard to trace cash. If the payments were made in cash, and they almost certainly were, they weren't made with traceable bills."

"No. So I doubt that'll get us anywhere."

"Have you questioned Miller?"

"Not yet, but I've been asking around. I'm being careful because he might be able to connect the investigation to the Robinsons, mother and son, and I don't want her to get hurt."

Metzler took a cloth from a desk drawer and, without getting up, buffed the polish on his shoes. Metzler's armchair was made of oak, with a leather seat. The leather was polished to a sheen by many years of sitting, and the seat held the contours of Metzler's substantial body even when he wasn't in it. Metzler's chair, like Garavelli's, swiveled. Unlike Garavelli's, however, the swivel was noisy. Any time Metzler moved, the chair creaked. Then he said, "Is there anything further about the location of young Robinson or Adams?"

"Not a trace. Nothing—either alive or dead."

"Is the famous artist still in town?"

"Man Ray? Yes, he's still here, but he's leaving soon to go back to Paris, to his wife, to his work. Which will be the right thing for him to do."

"Then who's going to solve your cases for you?"

Garavelli laughed. "Man Ray is alright. He's a good guy. If I had his address, I'd send him a Christmas card."

"It's the wrong time of year."

"It's always Christmas in Paris. Or at least I think it would be if I ever managed to get there."

"The Army didn't send you?"

"I didn't get any closer than Fort Bragg…. Man Ray isn't your stereotype starving artist. First of all, he's not starving, far from it. And he hasn't had a tragic life. He doesn't suffer, he's not an alcoholic or drug addict, and none of his wives or lovers have died. Apart from the fact that he paints pictures, he's pretty much he's just your ordinary Jewish guy from Brooklyn who lives in Paris."

Metzler rubbed his bald head. "So what do you plan to do now?"

"Talk to you."

"Swell." He paused. "Is the money the only way to trace them? Wasn't there an emerald ring?"

"Yes, there was."

"Where is it?"

Garavelli said, "I think the emerald's probably where Alden Adams is." Garavelli looked up and raised his chin. "I assume Adams took it with him."

"That's if he's alive. But what if he's not?"

"Then whoever killed him probably has the ring — unless it was too hot to hold, or unless they needed cash. Then they'd fence it."

Metzler said, "We haven't been able to find Adams, and we've looked. So if the ring is here, that probably means it was stolen from him. I don't think he would have bought the ring and then sold it a few days later."

"Right. But he might have given it to his boyfriend, Ray Robinson." Garavelli swiveled his chair side to side again, twice. "I think Adams probably has the ring, so the odds are that we won't find it. But, if we do, it would tell us something." He stopped the swivel. "Maybe Reverend Billy Miller has the ring."

"It's a possibility, I suppose." But Metzler had doubts. "Looking for it might be a waste of time. Why would Miller prefer an emerald ring rather than cash?"

Garavelli leaned toward Metzler. "He probably wouldn't prefer it, but Adams might have needed the cash for traveling money."

Metzler said, "Or maybe Miller has a taste for gems, or maybe he has a fancy woman who does."

"In my poking around so far, Tim, I haven't heard about any fancy woman, but Adams could have told Miller that the ring is convertible to cash, which it probably is. I'll look into it, starting with pawnshops. And our burglary guys could do a survey of fences. Maybe the ring has been on the market."

"An interesting question, at least."

"Yes, it is. Thanks, Tim, once again."

"I hope it's worth it."

Later that same day, Garavelli went down the hall to the office that handled burglaries and thefts of property. He knew several of the detectives who worked there, all of whom had frequent contact with dealers in stolen goods. The fences would have preferred not to have the contact, of course—they made efforts to conceal their transactions—but inevitably the police learned about some of them. Fencing is a tricky business. If it's too visible, burglars won't use the services. The fence would then no longer be one. But for fences to get a good price for things they have for sale, there has to be competition among potential purchasers. Fences need to advertise in one way or another and police are not deaf. A fence, therefore, is required to make strategic choices. On the one hand, he cannot be overly forthcoming with the police; on the other, antagonizing the police will invite more scrutiny. On balance, the result is that detectives often know who to talk to about stolen property.

Pawnbrokers, like fences, must be able to look at a piece of merchandise and know what it's worth. The skills and knowledge needed for the two trades are therefore similar, and the occupations, indeed, overlap. Detectives have informants in pawnshops, as they do among fences, and the clever and nimble informants are, of course, rewarded.

Garavelli explained to the burglary detectives that he was looking for an emerald ring, and he told them why. They told him it would be helpful to have a photograph of the ring. It was easier to question a fence or a pawnbroker when the identification of the property at issue was precise, and precision provided less latitude for evasive responses.

Garavelli contacted Jaccard's, the jewelry store that sold the ring, but no photograph was available. He was told that the design was a fairly common one — the value of the piece was in the size and quality of the stone. The man who had sold the ring, however, said that he could make a drawing or sketch of it, and he was confident he would recognize the piece.

Over the next week, some of the dull, methodical interrogation got done, but the conversations burglary detectives had with fences were not productive. No source had seen or heard of any large emerald on the low-visibility market within the last year.

Garavelli then met with one of the burglary detectives he knew best, Rocco Barberra, and asked the obvious question — whether the fences were telling the truth. Barberra said, "Al, you've questioned a lot of people in your time. Do you always know when they're telling the truth and when they're not?"

"Not always."

"There you are."

Garavelli said, "Thanks. I know you tried."

*

He dealt with the pawnbrokers himself. Most of them were afraid of cops and that helped a bit.

The first seven pawnshops he visited were what he called "dry wells." There were a few small green stones that by some stretch of the imagination might have been emeralds, but no sizeable candidate. Then he went to Lou's

Loans, located in Herculaneum, in the far south suburbs. The owner, Louis Winthrop, had been in the business a long time. He was pleasant and cooperative.

Mr. Winthrop said, "I have a ring that fits the description."

Winthrop went into a back room and returned with a beautiful ring that had a clear green stone in a simple yellow gold setting. He said, "It's a very fine piece. I thought I was lucky to get it."

Garavelli said, "When you have a ring of this quality, you probably make a mental note of who brought it in."

"I do better than that. I write it down. I don't trust my memory."

Garavelli said, "Smart man."

Winthrop handed Garavelli a sheet from a loose-leaf binder.

Garavelli put on his reading glasses. The sheet included a date, a brief description of the ring, the name of the customer, and the amount that the shop had loaned, accepting the ring as security, $10,000.

Garavelli said, "That's a large amount to loan."

Winthrop replied, "I have no doubt that it's a genuine emerald, and one of fine quality. It's the real thing."

Garavelli said, "There's a name of the customer here, 'Wilmer Rasor.' Did you know him?"

"No, I didn't know him, but when I make a loan of that size I always ask for good ID. It all looked right. I don't want to be accepting stolen goods. Not good business."

Garavelli said, "That's the way it's always seemed to me. But if the thing is stolen, the person surely wouldn't give you their real name. What do you know about Mr. Rasor?"

"Sergeant Rasor, I believe. I checked him out a bit. He's an officer in the St. Louis Police Department, or at least that's what he purports to be. He had police ID."

Garavelli said, "Shit." He looked at the floor for a few seconds. Then he said, "Sorry, that was a major disappointment."

Winthrop said, "I've heard worse. Do you know him?"

"No, I don't. But I sure hope it's not true. Would you recognize the man if you saw him again?"

"I'm sure I would."

Garavelli took out his notebook and pen, clicked the pen three times, looked at the ring and the sheet of paper closely, and wrote several notes. He said, "I'll give you a receipt for the ring, Mr. Winthrop, but I'm going to have to take it to the jewelry store for identification. It's possible that the ring is stolen property. In fact, this may even turn into a murder investigation, so we are dealing with a serious matter."

Winthrop replied, "I understand, Detective. It's a hazard of being in this line of work."

"You have a substantial amount of money invested in this ring. I hope I can handle it so that you either get the loan repaid or you get the ring back, but that's not entirely within my control."

"I appreciate that. Thank you. I know a little about the law on contraband."

Garavelli said, "It may be necessary for me to ask you to identify Sergeant Wilmer Rasor, or the man claiming to be Sergeant Rasor. Would you be willing to do that?"

"I'm happy to cooperate. I find that's good business. I

know you'll protect me if you possibly can. But there are some hazards."

"Yes, there are."

Winthrop said, "That's the world." He put the ring into a small box lined with velvet and handed it to Garavelli.

*

Garavelli made an appointment to meet with Mr. Herzberger at Jaccard's. Having been reminded about the ring by Garavelli's earlier visits, and having drawn a sketch of the ring at Garavelli's request, Herzberger was eager to see the piece once again. It had become an item of considerable interest at the store. Herzberger greeted Garavelli warmly, took the ring from the box, and placed it on a black cloth under a strong light. The old jeweler affixed a loupe to his spectacles and examined the ring for several seconds. Then he said, "This is it. I'm quite sure this is the same ring."

Garavelli said, "Is there an identifying mark or number on it?"

"There's a maker's mark stamped on the inside of the band, but there's no ID number. It would be unusual to have one."

"Can you exclude the possibility that it's a very similar ring, but not the same one?"

"I can't exclude that possibility entirely. I'm sure it's the same ring, but I can't absolutely prove that. The maker's mark could be duplicated, if someone really wanted to do it, but there wouldn't be a lot of reason for that. The value of this ring is in the stone, not the gold. There's also a standard mark of the purity of the gold, but that's common."

"But you recognize the ring and you feel sure about the identification?"

"Yes, that's right."

"I think that's good enough, for present purposes. I don't think we're going to have to use the ring as evidence in court. At least I hope we don't need to."

Herzberger said, "Are you able to tell me about Mr. Adams, the gentleman who purchased the ring?"

"Well, I can tell you that he's missing. That's no secret. We don't know where he is."

"I'm sorry to hear that."

"Yes … Thank you for your help, Mr. Herzberger." Garavelli put the ring back in its box and put it in his pocket.

Then he scheduled an appointment with the chief of police. He reported that the ring was found in a pawnshop and that the person who pawned it identified himself as Wilmer Rasor, a sergeant in the department.

The chief got up and pulled a file. He said, "I know about Rasor." He sat again. "He's in sex crimes, and there's a lot of overlap there with drugs, as you know." The chief frowned. "It's goddamn difficult to manage. In truth—don't quote me—it's a zoo. There's too much goddamn money to be made. Rasor is a bad actor—he's got a stack of civilian complaints, and there'd be more of them if people weren't afraid of him." The chief stood, walked over to the window, and looked out at the park. There were children playing. Garavelli stayed seated. The chief said, "I'd love to get rid of the sonofabitch, but I'd need something more than I've got now."

Garavelli said, "He may be able to give us Billy Miller."

"I'll tell you, Al, I might rather take down Rasor than Miller. Rasor's sure a bigger pain in the ass for me, and he may well do more harm to the city."

"That call is for you to make, Chief. I think I could squeeze Rasor, maybe see what I can get."

"Okay, Al, buy us some time. See what you get, but watch yourself! Rasor has friends in the department. People of like mind."

"What mind is that?"

"Same old crap—latest model of the Klan."

"You don't mean that literally, do you?"

"Why not?"

"I didn't think the Klan was still around. This is the 1960s."

"Don't fool yourself. They're still here, and some of them traded in their robes for police uniforms." The chief went back to his desk. "And they don't much like Italian Catholics either, Al. Watch yourself."

"Okay. First I need to see how Rasor got hold of the ring. I think I know, but I'll see what his story is."

"And then what?"

"I think he'll lead me to Miller, so then I'll have a conversation with the Reverend."

"You've been in this business, Al. You don't need me to tell you this, but I'm an old meddler, so I'll say it anyway. Don't make your move until you've got something solid. Charges that won't stick are not in our best interest."

"Got it. For a fat man, I tread lightly."

The chief laughed, for the first time that day.

18

The call arrived at 9:30, just as Man Ray was finishing the light continental breakfast delivered by room service. The caller was Bob Knox, the man in the mayor's office.

Knox said, "Garavelli tells me that you've been investigating."

"If investigating is the right word. I've talked to some people."

"He says you've discovered more about the missing men than the police were able to get, and that some of what you've found is of concern to the mayor's office."

"I hope I haven't been causing trouble."

"No, not at all. Garavelli says what you learned is helpful. I'd like to talk to you about it."

"I'm flying to Paris today."

"Ah. Do you have time to talk? When's your flight?"

"It's an overnight flight, about an eight P.M. departure."

"Are you free for lunch? I'd be happy to meet you wherever you like."

"Sure, I could do that. I know where Duff's is, and I know how to get there. Would that work?"

"Duff's it is. What time?"

"Would noon suit you?"

"It would. I'll see you there."

Ray had a leisurely morning. He finished reading the paper, drew pictures in his notebook, packed, put on a clean shirt, and took a taxi to Duff's.

Knox got to the restaurant first. He knew what Man Ray looked like, and the place wasn't crowded. Ray recognized the deep voice that greeted him. In addition to the Tidewater, there was a bit of Harvard Yard in the voice. Knox had done graduate work there.

Knox's head was large and perfectly round. Its size suggested that much went on inside it, which was certainly true. Before going to work for Mayor Tucker, he had taught political philosophy at Washington University. His clothes were professorial—khakis, a light tweed jacket, comfortable shoes. Given the weather, he wore no tie, but he was freshly shaved and combed. He was mild-mannered, but he'd been a military policeman in World War II. During the Normandy invasion, he landed on D-Day plus two. He'd seen combat.

During lunch, Man Ray told Knox about Mrs. Robinson's account of her son's troubles with the Reverend Billy Miller, and Knox told the artist about the realities of St. Louis politics.

Ray asked, "Do the Christian Patriots for Purity have real political power?"

Knox said, "Not in the conventional sense, they don't. They have no real organization. They're mostly running a con game. But they have the ability to make noise and, for some purposes, that's all you need. The right kind of noise can stir up things and cause trouble. There's a lot of working-class whites in St. Louis. Many of them, and many of the middle-class too, don't want to live with dark-skinned people. That's a simple fact. The mayor's office and the political pros are pretty good at keeping a lid on it, but sometimes the pot boils over. We try not to have people shoot each other."

"Can't the police control it?"

Knox held both hands out in front of him, flat, palms up. Then both hands curled shut. It looked like he was trying to grasp something, or hold something up.

He answered. "Police are drawn from the community. They go home at night, back to their families, their churches, the American Legion club. They *are* the community." He paused. "I'd love to clip the wings of Billy Miller and his Patriots, but to do that we'll need something really solid. Garavelli will pursue it, following-up on the leads you gave him. I talked to him this morning."

At some point during lunch, the conversation turned to the Vietnam War. Ray said, "I'm not a man of politics. I know little about it and I try to stay away from it." That was that.

So Knox changed tack. "How long have you been an artist?"

"Always, as long as I can remember."

"Have you ever had any other occupation?"

"I did design work to support myself when I was young. But I was also making art, at night. I suppose it was the creative drive or urge, the need to create. But I had to eat. I sell my work."

"Let's take the need to eat out of it. If you inherited money, would you still make art?"

"I didn't inherit money."

"I know, but let's suppose that you had. Would you still do art?"

"Sure. I can't imagine not doing it." Ray used his hands in a gesture that was somehow French. "There are some wonderful ancient paintings in a cave in Lascaux, France. Very powerful paintings. Did the people who made them expect them to be seen by humans? There weren't many humans around. What did the people who made those paintings think they were doing? Did they have some sort of concept of art? They were probably trying to communicate, but what were they communicating? We could ask the same question about modern art. Duchamp submitted a urinal to an art exhibition. He said it was sculpture. It was rejected. The urinal was manufactured as plumbing. Did it become art when Duchamp said it was?"

"Ah, the famous urinal. Not everyone's idea of art."

"Yeah, and that was certainly a part of what Duchamp intended." Ray paused. "But Stieglitz took a photograph of the urinal and the photo was very beautiful. So Duchamp was playing with the idea that we can find beauty in unexpected places. Maybe beauty did have something to do with it. Duchamp is a complicated guy."

They had finished eating and were about to pay the check. Then Ray took Knox by surprise. "Would you like to go for a long walk?"

Knox said, "I'm not ordinarily a long walk sort of guy, but how often do I get to take a walk with Man Ray?"

Ray smiled. "I like to get some exercise before an overnight flight. It relaxes me. It helps me sleep on the plane. I won't eat again now before the flight. The damned airline is always waking you up and trying to feed you when you just want to sleep. And a walk would also let me see a bit more of St. Louis. You can explain it to me."

"I'm not a native."

"No, but you've worked in the mayor's office. I'm sure you learned a lot. And before that you were at Washington University. Max Beckmann was there. Also H. W. Janson."

"I didn't know them. Before my time."

"Yes, of course. Beckmann was a great artist."

"The St. Louis Art Museum has some of his work. It has a fine German Expressionist collection."

"I know. I've seen it."

When they left Duff's, the two men turned left and walked south on Euclid. The street was broad and lined on both sides with mature sycamores that provided welcome shade. As on the other days, it was humid. They had a good view of trees and passing cars, but from Euclid they could see only the sides of houses. All of the houses faced east-west streets that intersected with Euclid. After a block or two, they turned left again at a street called Lenox Place. The houses there were all large and had well-tended lawns. It would have been very difficult to know when the houses were built without examining the state of their masonry. They tended strongly toward red brick trimmed with limestone at the corners and around the windows and doors. But they varied a bit—there might be a small limestone front porch, or perhaps a sunroom or a screened porch appended to one side. All very civilized.

Ray said, "These houses exist apart from time."

"That's a nice way to put it. If the essence of good taste is to avoid giving offense, these houses are doing a very good job of keeping their mouths shut."

"Yes. They make no statement at all, apart from the obvious one about the bank balances of their owners." Ray paused. "They transcend mere style. Indeed, they transcend time. Wealth, these houses say, is eternal. The businesses of the present owners may go bad, but someone else will have money and the houses will endure."

Knox pointed. "One of those over there is the Pulitzer's in-town mansion. They also have a summer place out in the County. This one is affectionately known as 'the Winter Palace.' The neighborhood is called 'the Central West End,' not a pretentious name."

"Good."

Then Man Ray said, "You worked for Mayor Tucker, but he didn't get reelected a few months ago. Now you're working on the transition to the new mayor. Is that right?"

"Yes. Tucker served three terms, twelve years, four years each term. He wanted a fourth term, and that had never been done. He was challenged in the Democratic primary and he lost."

"Why was he defeated?"

"When you're in an important political office, you have to make choices. Those choices have costs. Some people win and other people lose. The losers remember the choices you made, but the winners think they earned it or did it all themselves. Over time, the resentments, the disappointments, accumulate."

They both stopped walking.

Knox said, "As Jay Landesman puts it, Mayor Tucker had run out his string. Times change. Politics changes. I cut my eye-teeth in Baltimore watching the politics of Theodore Roosevelt McKeldin, a Republican mayor of Baltimore and governor of Maryland. McKeldin carried rosary beads in a pocket on one side of his jacket and a yarmulke on the other, ready for any occasion. That doesn't work so well anymore. As I said, the resentments and disappointments accumulate. Eventually, the burden becomes too heavy. You can no longer carry it."

They resumed walking.

Ray said, "Some of the U. S. senators seem to have been around for a very long time."

Knox distinguished the cases. "Granted, but the few politicians who stay in office that long are usually the ones who are off in Washington. Most voters aren't really paying attention to what's going on there, and congressmen aren't seen in the district very often. But if you have to make choices close to home, people will be watching. Then it's harder to avoid annoying them."

They reached an area where there were apartment buildings, some of them large and some of them six-flats with "railroad-style" apartments that had rooms on only one side of a long hall, the kitchen at the rear. Two apartments per floor. There were also small shops on those blocks.

Then they saw a large cathedral. Knox said, "The seat of the archdiocese. Some of the less pious residents refer to this neighborhood as Vatican City. A lot of these apartments are filled with people who work for the Bishop, some of them are priests or nuns and some not."

Ray said, "It's a large establishment."

"It is. This is St. Louis—Irish, German, Italian, Polish, old French. St. Louis University, a Jesuit institution, is just a few blocks over."

They walked past a pizza place, not takeout but a place where diners sat at tables with red and white checked tablecloths and drank chianti from raffia-covered bottles. The sidewalk outside smelled of garlic, olive oil, and dough baked in a wood-fired oven. Had they not just eaten, it would have been appetizing.

Knox said, "Smoke. That's how Tucker got his start in politics."

"What?"

"Before he became mayor, he was the smoke commissioner."

"Was that a big deal?"

"In St. Louis, at the time, it certainly was. In the 1920s and 1930s, St. Louis had a major smoke problem. It was sometimes dark in the middle of the day from the pall of smoke. There were trees that wouldn't grow in St. Louis because they didn't get enough light. For those varieties of trees, you see very few now that are more than twenty years old. Evergreens wouldn't survive here, mostly. The industries in St. Louis used soft coal from southern Illinois, and it had a very high ash and sulphur content. There were actually droplets of sulphuric acid in the air. Nose and throat specialists did a brisk business. Also lungs. So the man on the street was concerned about smoke because the man on the street was sick. Tucker is a mechanical engineer and he was then the chairman of the mechanical engineering department at Washington University. The mayor at the time recruited Tucker to solve the smoke problem, and Tucker became a smoke expert. He organized business executives and bankers who were concerned about the fate of business in St. Louis. Smoke was killing business. Eventually, Tucker got legislation adopted that prohibited the hand-firing of soft, high-sulphur coal. The legislation, in effect, required the use of 'Arkansas anthracite,' hard coal, that was shipped in from farther away. Because transportation costs were higher, that increased the price of coal, but Tucker got railroads to cooperate and lower their freight rates for trainload lots. Businessmen also supplied mechanical stokers to fire the furnaces because the stokers were more efficient than hand-firing. Furnaces with stokers burned more cleanly. Tucker argued that the greater efficiency would compensate for the increased cost of fuel. In any event, it worked, the air became cleaner, and Tucker became a popular hero, for a time. He's by nature a reformer. But reform is sometimes popular and sometimes not."

They were getting tired. They stopped again. Fortunately, there was a neighborhood saloon across the street that had air-conditioning, cold beer, and tables with chairs. In mid-afternoon, it wasn't crowded.

When they were refreshed, Ray said, "You mentioned Jay Landesman. I know that the Crystal Palace failed. What happened?"

"The original Crystal Palace was restrained and tasteful—black, elegant in a quiet way. The newer one, the one at Gaslight Square, was much bigger, glitzy, all red and gold and stained glass. Very now. It was a mistake motivated by greed. The original made money, but not enough to satisfy the Landesmans. They thought they could make more. They were wrong." He paused. "I assume you've seen the Gateway Arch?"

"Yes, it's very impressive. The work looks nearly complete."

"It's almost done. It'll open soon. What do you think of it?"

"It will be very beautiful, simple but breathtaking. I think it will be a modern Eiffel Tower."

Knox smiled. "That's the ambition. I hope it gives the city a boost."

Ray returned to the Tucker theme. "I believe Mayor Tucker also did a major slum-clearance project."

"The Mill Creek Valley, in the center of the city. It's been cleared, mostly, but not much has been built there yet. Some of the residents, almost all of them Negroes, moved into Pruitt Igoe, which is not a great success, maybe a disaster, but the houses in the Mill Creek Valley didn't have reliable running water or toilets or electricity. The wiring in some of those buildings was a fire waiting to happen. At the same time that the Mill Creek neighborhood was being demolished, white people were moving to the suburbs, leaving houses and apartments in other neighborhoods unoccupied, especially on the north side of town. So property values declined, which made houses available that were more affordable, but the people who lived in the Valley still couldn't afford them. The tax base of the city took a big hit. It's a similar story in other cities. The automobile built the suburbs, and the suburbs demanded the expressways, and the central cities suffered, and so on and on. Not so much in Paris, I think."

"No, not so much. It's happening, but more slowly."

Knox said, "The art world has changed since you became an artist."

"Yes, it sure has."

"Has the art become better or has it deteriorated? Do you feel good about the directions it took or where it's going?"

"I don't think it works that way. Of course many people seem to think that it does. You hear them: 'modern artists don't know how to draw,' or 'modern art is a fraud, or ugly'. Artists like Duchamp and Picasso and Braque showed us new pathways, new opportunities. But change is directionless, it's merely something new. It's usually refreshing."

"But not the change in the Crystal Palace."

Man Ray poured the last of a Budweiser into his glass. "A failure of taste is the sort of thing that happens all the time, and it would happen even if art remained static."

Knox said, "Yes, failure is inevitable. People want to do something new, and so they think about how things could be done differently. But, because people are fallible, some of those changes don't work. There's usually a reason why things are done as they have been done."

Ray brought the conversation back to St. Louis. "The change in the Mill Creek Valley may turn out to be a great success, or perhaps not. Most things evolve, and it's hard to see at the beginning where they're going." He drank some beer. "Art, of course, changes in bits and pieces, and in different ways in different places." He waved a hand, perhaps drawing in the air. "Picasso and Monet overlapped considerably, you know. Picasso was forty-five years old when Monet died." He paused. "I wonder whether they ever met. Picasso had certainly looked at Cezanne. You can see it in the work." He drank from his glass and finished the beer. "Art is a funny business. Sometimes, as you age, it becomes hard to remember why you're doing it, but the truth is I love to paint. I wouldn't tell you this if you were an artist, Bob, because then you'd laugh, cynically, but it makes me happy to paint—just the process of putting paint on canvas. Except sometimes."

"What about photography?"

"Ah yes, photography. There was a time when I was enthusiastic about photography, but I've done what I wanted to do with it. I think I did some good work. The work for *Vogue* may have been a mistake. People paid attention to that and ignored my painting." Man Ray tried to pour more beer from his bottle, but there wasn't more. "It annoys me a bit that I've received more recognition as a photographer than as a painter. That's something of a disappointment."

Knox said, "But you're famous as both."

"Maybe. The White House showed only an old photograph." Ray looked at his empty beer glass. He took out a folded sheet of paper and a fountain pen, bent over the table, and began to draw. He said, "Thinking about the past is a mistake. Indeed, worse than that, it's a morass of regret, a sinkhole. We were talking about Jay Landesman and the failure of the Crystal Palace. Jay's an instructive case. He was a writer and an editor; then he tried to become a showman, a theatrical producer. He's talented, but his problem is that he has too many talents. If you want to be famous, Bob, do only one thing, do it well, and do it over and over. Don't branch out, don't explore new directions, and, above all, don't have another skill. It confuses people if they see you doing more than one kind of work—they don't know what label to put on you. They need to be able to look at your work and immediately say, 'Ah, that's a Man Ray!' It's a curse to be multitalented. When I was young, I was progressing well on a career as a painter. I began getting solo shows in galleries, but then I became interested in photography. I took pictures of models—I liked the models—and I found that I could make money doing fashion photos. Before I knew what was happening, people started calling me a photographer. Therefore, I was no longer a painter. I didn't realize it at the time, but that was a disaster. They think that you can't possibly be serious about painting or you wouldn't be doing photography. They appear to believe that God distributes talent only one to a customer and it isn't fair to get into the line a second time." Ray thought the conceit about getting into line a second time was probably something he had heard or read, but he said it anyway. It was something he thought about often.

He paused. "It accomplishes nothing to regret the past. I went through life deliberately. You can resist some of the effects of aging, of course, or at least you can try to do that. I exercise, moderately, but I can't see that it makes much difference. I still get older and weaker, and slower. Not more stupid, I think. Not yet. I'm just more deliberate, more cautious perhaps. Am I less brave? I hope not—that would be terrible. But I'm less agile."

He picked up his empty glass and stared at it, then said, "For many of us there comes a time when all you have left is your work. You may be fortunate and have a wife, perhaps even one who loves you, or says she does, despite everything. But you still do the work. You may be able to walk, at an age when most of your friends and contemporaries are dead or hopelessly demented. You walk and you work. You do it because you can—for no other reason, really—because you can. There's no longer demand for your work. It isn't needed, it isn't wanted, but it's what you can do. So you do it. Maybe you even work every day, or try to."

Knox said, "You came to the States to receive recognition at the White House. You have honor."

"For work I did thirty years ago, or forty."

"Your art still has value, the new work."

"Perhaps it will. Perhaps it'll be recognized someday. Who knows? Culture changes." He lit a Gitanes. "My signature has value. I can sign copies of my old work, and I do. Perhaps I should be thankful that I can still sign my name. But I continue because I can. It's who I am. And all I am. That's all there is. The work."

"Are you usually able to sleep on planes?"

"If I get tired enough, I'll sleep. The problem is that I have ideas. And then I want to draw. But at least I'm still having ideas. They don't all need to be pursued, of course. In fact, it would be better if some weren't."

"You sound unhappy."

"Yeah. I'm just a pitiful old man. More fortunate than most. Never mind my blather." He finished the sketch, wrote "For Bob," signed it, and gave it to Knox. It was a drawing of Duchamp's urinal.

He said, "I need to be getting back to the hotel. I want to take a shower before I leave, and I need to check out, pay my bill, and get to the airport."

They went out onto Lindell Boulevard and hailed a taxi. As he was getting in, Ray said, "There's a perceptible sadness in this town. I think it's a result of the loss of past glories."

19

Sergeant Rasor worked out of the eighth precinct, which was on the North Side, not far from Mrs. Robinson's apartment. Garavelli decided to visit him there, but didn't call ahead. He'd talk to Rasor before he talked to Miller. If the two of them hadn't coordinated their stories, something closer to the truth might emerge. Sometimes it did; not always.

The disadvantage of this strategy was that Garavelli had to make three trips to the precinct before he found Rasor there. Policemen are often out investigating, or having coffee. Another problem was that each time Garavelli showed up he needed to have a plausible reason for being there other than looking for Rasor.

Eventually, it worked. Rasor was at the station and came down quickly when he was told that "Lieutenant Garavelli" wanted to see him. Garavelli said, "We need to talk. I think you'll be more comfortable if we do this in a private room."

Rasor said, "The only private room here is an interrogation room, and that would look bad."

"Can't be helped. We need privacy."

"Why am I being questioned?"

"That will become clear."

Rasor realized that he had no alternative. As soon as they were in the room and the door was closed, Rasor said, "What's this all about?"

"It's about an emerald ring."

"An emerald ring?"

"That's right. The ring you pawned at Lou's Loans in Herculeneum."

Rasor did not respond.

Garavelli said, "Do I need to get the pawnbroker to ID you as the guy who pawned it?"

"No, that's okay, I remember now."

"Yeah, you got $10,000 for the ring. I thought that was probably the sort of thing you'd remember."

"Yeah, sure."

"It's a nice ring, Sergeant, I've seen it. Was it an old family treasure—maybe one you or your wife inherited?"

"No, I bought it."

"For $10,000! That's a big expenditure for a police sergeant."

"I didn't pay that much for it."

"Who'd you buy it from, Sergeant?"

"A guy…A man."

"What man?"

"Just a man I know."

"That's not good enough, Sergeant. That's not gonna fly. I can prove that the ring was purchased from Jaccard's jewelry store, downtown, not long ago and for more than $10,000."

"Well, maybe the guy I bought it from got it from Jaccard's."

"Do you have a receipt for the money you paid for it? Or a bill of sale for the ring?" Garavelli loosened his tie. "When you pay money for an expensive ring like this one, Sergeant, you need to get a receipt. Otherwise cops might think the ring was stolen."

"You don't have any proof of that. If you could prove it, you wouldn't be questioning me."

"As a favor to you, Sergeant, just as a matter of professional courtesy, I'm giving you an opportunity to explain. But I'll tell you what I do know. I'll tell you that the ring was bought from Jaccard's by Alden Adams, the owner of an art gallery, and that Mr. Adams is now missing. And here's something else that the police might believe—when we find that a man has a valuable ring without any receipt or bill of sale to explain how he got it, and the rightful owner of the ring is missing and cannot be found, the police might even think that the guy who has the ring was involved in making the owner go missing, making him disappear. Does the phrase 'missing, presumed dead' mean anything to you?"

About halfway through Garavelli's speech, sweat began to appear on Rasor's forehead. He said, "You've got theories or speculation, but I still haven't heard any proof."

Garavelli remained seated and said, very slowly and calmly, "You're going to have to do better on how you got hold of the ring, Sergeant. Otherwise, you're going to face charges. Don't doubt it. We can tie you to the ring. You've got to explain it. And then there's the little matter of Alden Adams. Where is he? Is he alive? Is this a murder investigation? We can start with Internal Affairs. You'll be off the force, out of a job, maybe looking at a felony charge. You'd better give us something we can use."

Rasor pushed back from the table and stood up quickly, which knocked over his chair. It was steel and made an impressive amount of noise when it hit the cement floor in the small interrogation room.

Rasor's face was red. He looked shaken. "Sorry about the noise." He picked up the chair and put it back beside the table. He said, "I'm a fellow officer. The union isn't going to like what you're doing to me. I'm entitled to some consideration."

Garavelli was impassive. "I'm a member of that same union." He took out his notebook and pen and made a note. It said, "Union." Rasor was standing by the wall. Garavelli looked at him and said, "Where'd you get the ring?"

Rasor paused, and then gave up. "From Reverend Miller."

"Just to be clear about it, that means Reverend Billy Miller, of St. Louis?"

"Right."

"And did Billy Miller give you the ring as a gift, a present?"

"No. He asked me to pawn it for him."

"Why? Why didn't he pawn it himself?"

"I don't know. Maybe he didn't want people to know he needed money."

Garavelli said, "Or maybe the ring was hot and Miller thought he would let you take the heat."

Rasor did not respond.

Then Garavelli said, "Where did Miller get the ring?"

"He told me that it had been contributed to the church."

"If the ring was contributed to the church, then Miller wouldn't be pawning it to get money for himself, would he? That doesn't sound right."

"I don't know why he wanted to pawn it."

"So where did the $10,000 go that you got for the ring?"

"I gave it to Miller."

"And Miller put it in the collection plate?"

"I suppose so."

"So it was the church's money?"

"I guess so."

Garavelli made more notes.

"Why were you doing this errand for Miller, Sergeant?"

"I'm a member of his congregation."

"A congregation isn't the same thing as a gang, Sergeant. I'm not sure that the difference is defined in the law, but it should be." Rasor glared at Garavelli and Garavelli showed no emotion. He said, "Was Alden Adams also a member of the congregation?"

"No."

"But you said Miller told you that the ring was contributed to the church, and I've already told you I have proof that Alden Adams purchased the ring. Did Adams contribute the ring to the church?"

"I don't know. Maybe he did. You should ask him."

"You know I can't do that, because Adams has disappeared, and maybe you also know he can't answer questions because he's dead. If Adams's body turns up, Sergeant, you're going to be on the hook for obstruction of justice, at least, maybe accessory to murder." Garavelli closed his notebook and put his pen away. "Miller's church, if that's what it is, seems like an odd charity for Adams to choose to support. Maybe somebody leaned on him, hard. That wouldn't be good for you, but it would be better than having Adams turn up dead. Where is he?"

"I don't know."

Garavelli pushed back from the table. His chair screeched on the floor. He stood and walked to the door. "Have a nice day."

*

The day was hot and Garavelli was uncomfortable. He would have loosened his tie, but it was already loose. He thought maybe he should tighten it. He wanted to look crisp and well put-together for his meeting with Billy Miller. That wouldn't make any difference in the outcome, but it was the right thing to do. The professional thing. He had a picture of what happened between Miller and Adams, but the man wasn't going to admit it. Garavelli thought he'd just put some pressure on and see what he could get. It was the best he could do.

Miller's office had once been a mom and pop grocery store. At another time it was a barber shop. More recently it had been a dentist's office—Garavelli thought that Miller was in the same line of work. The sign on the door now said only "Rev. Billy Miller, Christian Patriots for Purity." There was no use of the word "church." The office inside, however, was decorated with a cross and a print of a portrait of Christ. The Jesus in the picture was the standard, familiar one—white, with flowing light brown hair. Garavelli always wondered how that Christ happened to be born in the Middle East.

The office was furnished with both a desk and a lectern. Garavelli was glad to find Miller seated at the desk and not standing at the lectern. He was ordinary looking—forty years old, with a pudgy face going to fat, a pasty complexion, thinning hair, and small eyes. You wouldn't want to play poker with him. Garavelli said, "Good afternoon, Reverend. Thank you for seeing me."

"Did I have a choice?"

Garavelli sat in a chair in front of the desk and ignored the question. "If you don't mind my asking, what do you use the lectern for?"

"Why do you ask, sir?"

"Oh, you don't need to call me 'sir'. 'Detective' would work, or 'Lieutenant,' or just 'Mr. Garavelli.' I was just curious about the lectern."

"I use it to practice sermons."

"Ah. I thought maybe you are sometimes visited by Patriots who need an extra dose of moral renewal." He paused. "I'm sure you know by now that Wilmer Rasor has told me you asked him to pawn an emerald ring for you."

"Yes, that's right."

"Why didn't you pawn it yourself?"

"It was a task I thought someone else could handle, and Rasor was willing to do it, so I let him take care of it. Besides, I didn't want the bother of driving all the way out to Herculaneum."

"That raises another question. Why did you do the transaction there instead of using a pawnshop in the city?"

"That was Rasor's decision. Maybe he thought he could get a higher valuation there."

"Oh, I thought perhaps you didn't want the ring to be seen, recognized, and that would be less likely to happen in Herculaneum."

"You are a suspicious man, Detective."

"Yes, I suppose that's true. I guess I am. It's a useful attribute sometimes." Garavelli walked over to the lectern, stood behind it, and grasped the top with both hands. He looked at Miller. "Where did you get the ring, Reverend?"

"You know the answer. You told Wilmer Rasor that Alden Adams bought the ring at Jaccard's, so I think you know that I got it from Adams."

"Did you buy it from him?"

"No, he gave it to me."

"A gift? Why did he do that? Were you a close friend of Mr. Adams?"

"No. It was a contribution to support the good work of my ministry."

"Your ministry being the Patriots for Purity?"

"The *Christian* Patriots for Purity, that's right."

"Why would he want to support that particular cause?"

"I suppose he feels that we do good work."

"I think we should probably say he 'felt' instead of 'feels,' don't you? ...Is he still alive?"

"I don't know."

"Why did he give you an emerald ring instead of making the contribution in cash?"

"He said he couldn't write a large check because he didn't have enough money in his account."

"But why an emerald ring? Did you especially want the ring?"

"No, but I don't look gift horses in the mouth, Detective."

Garavelli left the lectern and went back to his chair. "And what are the good works done by your organization?"

"We promote prayer and the recitation of the pledge of allegiance to the flag in the schools, we monitor the content of textbooks and all books in our schools and libraries to prevent the spread of immoral, sacrilegious, or subversive materials, and we oppose premarital sex and all deviant sex practices."

"That's quite an ambitious program. I imagine it keeps you busy."

"Yes, it does."

Garavelli said, "How about race-mixing? Do you do any work on that?"

"I don't see what this has to do with the emerald ring or with anything else that's your business, Detective."

"I'm just trying to understand Adams's motivation for giving you the ring. From what I know about him, he doesn't seem to be a likely candidate for membership in the Patriots for Purity."

"I believe in redemption."

Garavelli stood, walked over to the picture of Christ, and looked at it. It hadn't improved. "As you've noticed, and have pointed out, I'm a suspicious man, Reverend. In fact, given what I know to be true, I suspect that Alden Adams wasn't a supporter of the goals of your Patriots at all. Indeed, I think you were giving him a hard time. You've told me that the Patriots oppose deviant sex practices—and I believe that brought you into conflict with Adams. I know Adams was a homosexual, Reverend, so I don't think he was your kind of guy. It may even be that you pawned the ring because you didn't want people to know that a fairy had given you an emerald ring—a ring for ladies. Not the kind of thing a real man would wear, or even carry on his key chain. So I can understand that you would want to hide the ring, Reverend."

Miller said, "The sexual conduct of Adams and his friends was illegal as well as sinful. He should have been arrested and prosecuted, but the St. Louis police department wasn't doing anything about it."

Garavelli turned toward Miller. "Your friend Sergeant Rasor is a St. Louis police officer—for now, at least, but I don't know how much longer he will be—so why didn't he prosecute and arrest Adams if you thought that was what should have been done?"

"I don't assign Rasor his duties. That's not my job."

"No, but you assigned him to pawn an emerald ring that was obtained under suspicious circumstances."

"Adams gave me the ring. I didn't steal it."

"No, you probably didn't. But to a suspicious guy like me it looks like you squeezed it out of him by extortion. You threatened him that bad things would happen if he didn't pay you off."

Miller smiled. "Exposing him as a homosexual would've been no threat to him at all. Everybody already knew that's what he was, or is, living openly with that partner of his at the art gallery. It's a scandal, an outrage, offending decent Christian people. So how would it have been possible to threaten him by exposing that? He didn't even try to make it a secret."

"No, I suppose Adams wouldn't have minded much if you talked about Davos, the man at the gallery, but what about Ray Robinson, the young Negro man known as St. Louis Sugar? I think Adams would've been more worried about that. Robinson was in the Army Reserve, and he would've been dishonorably discharged if it became known that he was a homosexual."

"If soldiers are not permitted to be doing homosexual acts, then that law should be enforced. That's why we need vigilant citizens like the Christian Patriots for Purity to see that the law is serious, has meaning. Again, Detective, that would just be a matter of enforcing the law."

Garavelli said, "And the race-mixing in the Adams and Robinson relationship made it even worse, didn't it?"

"That's your conclusion, not mine."

"But it's true, isn't it?"

"It was a sin and it was offensive. It violated God's law and man's law. God doesn't intend any two men to have sex, and God intended the Negro and the white races to be separate and to live apart. So, yes, race-mixing is a problem. That's our belief—what of it? This is a free country, still, I hope."

Garavelli went back to the lectern. He said, "Every time you say 'Negro,' you pause before you say it as if the word isn't familiar to you. I'll bet that's not the word you usually use, is it?"

"Is that against the rules?"

"Just an observation."

"Are you a *Negro*-lover, officer?"

"Not especially. Like all people, some of them are good and some aren't, but they are human beings and deserve to be treated that way."

"Are you here to do police business or to practice your sermon at the lectern?"

Garavelli raised his eyebrows. "Fair enough." He took out his notebook, put it flat on the lectern, opened it, and read a few pages. He took his time. He did not click his pen Then he said, "Why were you paying attention to a young Negro like Raymond Robinson? He wasn't a big shot. Why was he worth your bother?"

Miller put the tips of his fingers together to form a church steeple. "Robinson was involved in political activity with Stokely Carmichael, Martin King, and all of that rabble, and Alden Adams was using his money to support their politics. It's subversive. It's ruining this country. Like Lyndon Johnson, and Hubert Humphrey, and Stuart Symington, and all the Communists they've put in the government."

"Do you think Senator Symington is a Communist? He was the president of the Edison Electric Company."

"That's the worst kind of Communist, the most stealthy, the kind that can do the most harm."

"And you call me a suspicious man, Reverend! I'm not in your league when it comes to suspicion." Garavelli went back to the chair and sat, but he held the open notebook in his hand. "And, of course, now that Adams has disappeared I need to investigate what happened to him. I have to find out what's become of him, whether he's alive or dead."

Miller replied, "Yes, that's your job, I suppose."

Garavelli changed the subject once again. "I'm told that you've been on the radio program of the Reverend Billy James Hargis."

"Yes. I have been a couple of times. Reverend Hargis and I studied together at Ozark Bible College and then later at Pike's Peak Bible Seminary. He's a fine man."

"I heard that the Disciples of Christ revoked his ordination."

"That was the work of Communists. Reverend Hargis has his own church now."

"And the FBI tells me that Hargis takes in more than a million dollars a year in contributions through his radio program."

"Praise the Lord! The money is well-spent."

"So the $10,000 that you got from the pawnshop for the ring went to pay for expenses of the ministry and not for your personal expenses. Right?"

"There's no difference between my personal expenses and the expenses of the ministry. I am the minister. Putting food on my table keeps me alive to do the good work. I live for the ministry."

"I don't enforce the tax laws, but there's good money in your good works, isn't there?"

"The faithful are generous. That's been true for a long time. Tell me about the Vatican, Lieutenant Garavelli. Have you ever seen it?"

"No, I haven't, but I know that it's a disgrace. I know it consumes money that could be used to feed the hungry."

"Many people believe that spiritual sustenance is important, Detective. The ceiling of the Sistine Chapel has been a source of inspiration and comfort to millions of troubled people over the ages. You should look at it some time. Maybe it would give you a broader view of the world."

"This isn't getting us anywhere." Garavelli put the notebook back in his pocket.

"No, it isn't."

"But this conversation has given me a better understanding of the nature of your work. I'll let the folks at the Internal Revenue Service pursue it further."

"I'll be happy to talk with them. I'm always looking for converts."

"Look, Miller, let's lay it on the line. You probably would've gotten away with your extortion if Alden Adams hadn't disappeared. But, once we started investigating Adams as a missing person and investigating assets that disappeared along with him, then we were going to find out about the emerald ring. If Adams hadn't gone missing, you'd have been Scot free, whistling Dixie. But now the cops know about the emerald, and they wonder how it ended up in the pocket of Billy Miller. A jury is going to find that highly incriminating. If you got rid of Adams, that was a very big mistake. And, if he went missing on his own, that's just your bad luck. Either way, it's pretty clear that you strong-armed the emerald ring. And, if Adams turns up dead, or Robinson turns up dead, you're going down hard. You'd better start praying that they're healthy. It's a test of your clout with the Almighty."

The speech was all bluster. Garavelli knew that he didn't have the evidence to prove extortion, much less the more serious charges. Nonetheless, he hoped it would give Miller a bad day or two. And there was some truth in it.

*

Garavelli returned the ring to Louis Winthrop at Lou's Loans. There was no proof that it was obtained illegally. Not yet. It was obtained in suspicious circumstances, but suspicions aren't proof. Miller knew that. Then Garavelli went back to the office and talked to Tim Metzler.

As he entered the office, Metzler was typing on an old upright Royal. Garavelli said, "You're busy."

"Only one finger on each hand is busy." For a two-fingered typist, Metzler was fast. He stopped typing and looked at Garavelli. "Reports, reports, reports."

"Never a dull moment," Garavelli said.

Metzler leaned back. His chair squeaked. "How's Gina?"

"She's fine, thank you. Why do you ask?"

"Did you really feed Gina's fine lasagna to that Frenchman? Somebody told me that you did."

Garavelli stood by his desk, and then he paced. "Frenchman? Oh, you mean Man Ray. He's no Frenchman. He's from Brooklyn. He's an okay guy. You'd like him."

Metzler loosened his suspenders. "Frenchmen are not my favorite people."

"If you Germans wouldn't invade them so often, you'd get along with them better."

"My people have been in this country longer than the Garavellis."

"Yeah, about fifteen minutes longer."

They both laughed.

Then Garavelli said, do you have a minute?"

"Sure. The reports'll wait."

"Don't let the chief hear you say that." Garavelli paused and removed his jacket, draped it over the back of his chair, and then sat. "In the Alden Adams case you suggested trying to find out what became of the emerald ring. So I did that."

"Yes, and you found it."

"Yeah, in a pawnshop. And now it's back at the pawnshop. Miller almost certainly extorted the emerald from Adams—we can't prove that—but here's what bothers me. Why pay off Miller with the ring instead of cash? Adams paid more to buy the ring than Miller was able to get by pawning it, and Miller, I assume, would have preferred to have cash. So why does that make sense? Does it add up?"

"We talked about this before. Maybe what happened wasn't the original plan. Maybe circumstances forced Adams to do it."

Garavelli swiveled his chair and looked out the window. "My first thought, when I saw the check from Adams to Jaccard's and then when Jaccard's told me it was for the emerald, my first thought was that the stone was an asset that was easy to carry. So, if Adams was planning to leave town, he would just put it in his pocket."

Metzler said, "But he didn't do that."

"No, he didn't, and I was surprised when we found it at the pawnshop. I thought the ring had probably gone to Ibiza or Madagascar or somewhere with Adams, or maybe it went down with the TWA airplane. But it didn't. Why not? You said that maybe he was forced to change his plans. Forced by what?"

Metzler turned toward the Royal and typed a note about a different case. "Probably forced by timing. People were closing in on him. He owed a lot of money to artists and they were after him, and Miller's mob, or church, was beating up Robinson and threatening Adams. Adams needed to get on the road. We don't always get to do what we planned."

"I've noticed that. But Adams had cash. Why not just give Miller the cash? I'm sure the preacher would have preferred it."

"Sure, but so would Adams. The ring could be converted into money, with some trouble and at a discount, but that would take time. Cash is a lot more liquid than a stone. As I said before, Adams needed to get on the road."

Garavelli swiveled back to face Metzler. "Do you want a Coke?"

"Diet Pepsi."

"Right." Garavelli stood and walked toward the vending machine. "I asked Miller why, if Adams wanted to support the church, he didn't just give him cash."

"What did Miller say?"

"He said Adams told him that he couldn't write a large check because there wasn't enough money in the bank. It was true that there wasn't money in the account—because Adams had taken it out. But Miller didn't know that. So Miller took what he could get. He used the old line about looking in the horse's mouth."

Metzler said, "They all like to pretend to be country boys. I suppose Adams was probably bargaining with Miller, bargaining to save his skin, and the emerald gave Adams a way out."

"That sounds right to me." Garavelli delivered the Pepsi and got a Coke for himself. "But I guess we won't know for sure until we find Adams."

"When are you going to do that?" Metzler turned back to his typewriter. The chair squeaked again.

Garavelli leaned back, "Not today…. But I don't think he's dead."

20

Four years passed. St. Louis continued to be hot and wilting in the summer, gray and dreary in winter, but glorious in spring when dogwoods are in bloom, and crisp and bracing in the late fall. The symphony, the art museum, the botanical garden, the zoo, the Cardinals, and the beer were still enjoyed, not necessarily in that order of preference. Popular taste was slightly retrograde, traditional—Carnaby Street never caught on. The Gateway Arch was completed, and Joel Meyerowitz came to town to take pictures of it.

Man Ray returned to Paris and resumed his career. Jay Landesman was in London, still trying to mount a production of "Dearest Dracula." Al Garavelli made captain, and was put in command of the homicide squad. At a reception in honor of the new chief of police, Garavelli saw that the mayor's wife was wearing a necklace with a pendant that held a sizeable green stone of beautiful color and clarity. He considered asking her if she bought the piece at Lou's Loans in Herculaneum, but he decided not to. He thought that might be graceless. Mary Ocean painted almost every day and had solo shows, but none at which her work sold as well as at the last Alden Adams show, from which she still had received no money. Mrs. Robinson died without having heard from her son. The Reverend Billy Miller continued to prosper. Gina Garavelli made lasagna year-round and Al ate it enthusiastically. Alden Adams did not return to the city. There were some records of recent activity by people using that name, but investigation found that none of them were the former art dealer.

21

Jay Landesman walked through Covent Garden on his way
to the restaurant. He liked the old market, and one of the
townhouses on the north side of the square had a colorful history that interested him. It had housed the National
Sporting Club, where professional boxing matches were
held for the amusement of toffs. In 1913 Bombardier Billy
Wells, the English heavyweight champion, fought Georges
Carpentier there for the European title. The Bombardier
was knocked out in the first round. And the building, or
perhaps another townhouse nearby, had earlier been the
home of Sir Charles Sidley, where he played a small but
memorable role in English legal history. Sir Charles, during
an evening of celebration in 1663,, went out on a balcony
naked and either "made water" on the people assembled
below or "cast down bottles" in which he had urinated, or
possibly did both. In any event, a court found his behavior
offensive. The decision in Sidley's case became important
in establishing the principle that the Crown was the custodian of public morals, a principle that Landesman, as an
impresario, had wrestled with on occasion.

From the market, he walked along Maiden Lane, which
took him past Rule's. It would have been a convenient

place to meet with Lancaster, but Landesman knew that he would be paying the tab and he wouldn't look forward to that. Rule's, a well-preserved relic from Edwardian London that made the most of its yellow walls, dark wood, and period decor, did not do as well, in Jay's opinion, with its lobster, pheasant, and grouse. "It's coasting," he thought. At Charing Cross, Landesman strolled at a leisurely pace and considered pausing to examine the marvels offered at one of the many bookstores, but he was due at Le Moulin d'Or on a side street south of Soho Square, just out of the high rent district.

Diners went through a small vestibule before entering a large room, the only dining room . Plate glass windows, useful when the building was a shop, faced the sidewalk. They were now draped with white curtains to give diners privacy. The decor was simple, welcoming, homelike. Small lamps covered by pink silk shades, one on each table, suffused the room with rose-colored light.

Jay Landesman arrived at half past six. The man he was meeting, Osbert Lancaster, was already seated at a good table. Lancaster was an extraordinary character, rather famous for the single column cartoons he published in *The Daily Express*, but in addition to drawing cartoons he wrote architectural history and social satire, which were combined in a series of essays on real estate development published as *Progress at Pelvis Bay*, and he designed sets for Sadler's Wells, Covent Garden, Glyndebourne, and the Old Vic. Landesman was hoping to persuade him to do the sets for "Dearest Dracula."

Lancaster fit the restaurant. He was dressed in Edwardian style — a houndstooth check suit with waistcoat and a colorful silk handkerchief flowing out of the breast pocket. It was a country suit, not at home in London, but it was handsome. Lancaster had been a fixture of the social set when he was at Oxford, and he knew what he was doing. He was in his early sixties, but looked older. In a strong, deep voice, he greeted Jay enthusiastically.

After a brief consultation, both men ordered white-bait, a specialty of the house, with a simple green salad and a bottle of Smith Haut-Lafite, white. Whitebait are baby fish, usually either herring or sprat, served and eaten whole with the heads, fins, and tails. They arrive in a mound, deep-fried, accompanied by half a lemon on each plate. The fish at Le Moulin d'Or were fresh and excellent.

Until seven p.m., all guests of the restaurant were greeted by Mrs. Emerson, a woman of uncertain age, perhaps ageless, who welcomed them with the grace and formality of the second daughter of a baronet, which she may have been. She was dressed in silk organza, a print with large flowers. Her red lipstick was carefully but generously applied. Diners who arrived before seven, as both Lancaster and Landesman did, were able to observe the changing of the guard when Mrs. Emerson relinquished her post to a gentleman known as "the Major." He wore a dark business suit, not evening dress, and was perhaps seventy, portly. If he had a surname, it was never used, and the source of his rank was not specified, but no one doubted that it was well-deserved.

When the Major arrived, he kissed Mrs. Emerson's hand, she curtseyed, and she then departed. One of the diners, a man dining alone at the next table, chuckled at the ceremony. The man sat ramrod straight and had iron gray hair, dark eyebrows, and impressive military bearing. The Major inclined his head toward him. Indicating the diner, Lancaster mumbled to Landesman, "Retired officer. Grenadier Guards." Jay wasn't sure it was true, but there was no extra charge for this entertainment.

Jay used essentially his standard Dearest Dracula sales talk, even though it had not persuaded either Man Ray or Mary Ocean. He didn't have anything else to offer. As in his presentations to Ray and Ocean, Jay emphasized the potential that set design offered for original artistic expression. But Lancaster had done set designs before, several times, and did not require persuasion on that point.

Lancaster said, "Picasso did set designs, you know. Also costumes."

"No, I didn't know that. Was that recently?"

"Oh no, it was fifty years ago, at least."

"Did you ever talk to him about it?"

Lancaster warmed to the topic. "No, but I was a student of Vladimir Polunin, who worked with Picasso on the sets. Vladimir had stories about the experience."

"What was the show?"

"It was 'The Three Cornered Hat,' a Spanish-themed ballet presented by the Ballets Russes and directed by Diaghilev. Music by Manuel de Falla. Picasso being Spanish fit the theme."

Jay said, "Have you ever met Picasso?"

"Yes. I met him in the south of France, and we had a brief conversation. We spoke French. He didn't like my accent, and I didn't like his." Lancaster didn't laugh.

But Jay did. "Picasso was always doing something new."

"Yes, he's a risk-taker. Still is."

"So, why not do the sets for Dearest Dracula? It would be something new, something different."

"I've done many stage sets. That wouldn't be new."

"But Dracula would be a new subject. Not your usual thing. It would be a romp, it would suit your sense of humor."

"Yes, it'd be different. It would be that. But I fear I'd be out of my element."

"What do you have to lose?"

"A great deal. I value my reputation. I don't want to become a laughing-stock in my old age."

"Picasso hasn't worried about losing his reputation when he changes styles and media, and then changes them again, and again."

Lancaster agreed, "True. Picasso is extraordinary, in many ways. He has great talent and artistic intelligence, of course, but also great courage. Or perhaps it isn't courage, perhaps it's just extraordinary self-confidence. He truly believes he can do all these different things and do each of them well. One could call it arrogance."

Jay said, "But he *has* succeeded at each."

"Perhaps. Some more than others…Once one has acquired his level of fame, one becomes nearly impervious. He can do anything he wants and he will still be Picasso. The fact that it is his work gives it standing. His imprimatur elevates it."

Jay poured more wine. "People have told me that fame isn't worth seeking—that it's a false god or a bitch goddess, or some such bullshit. But you've just explained why fame is valuable, why it's an asset. "

Lancaster said, "I find this a depressing conversation. Let's talk about something uplifting, inspiring, such as our invasion of Anguilla."

Jay gave up. "What about Anguilla? If some ambitious local politician comes along who decides to proclaim himself the chief executive of an independent nation, is the Crown then required to throw in the towel? England wasn't willing to just give the island away."

At that point, Man Ray arrived at the restaurant, accompanied by another man. As they were being seated, Jay and Man recognized one another and exchanged smiles and nods. Landesman and Lancaster were then in the midst of their whitebait, and it would have been disruptive in the dining room for them to stand to greet the newcomers.

Jay said to Osbert, "That's Man Ray. Do you know him?"

"I recognized him. We met once, years ago."

"I didn't know he was in London."

"I saw in our paper that he's here to receive a medal from the Royal Photographic Society."

Jay said, "He's moving slowly, leaning on his cane."

Osbert replied, "He's slow, but look how he moves. You can see that he's lame, but his movements are precise and smooth, well-designed, composed."

Jay said, "We should congratulate him when we are leaving the restaurant."

"Yes, that would be appropriate. But you are wrong on the facts about Anguilla. What took place was an attempt at democracy, which we have now extinguished. Two years ago there was a popular uprising on the island and we sent British troops to put that down, and then we withdrew the troops last year, and now we have sent them in again because a referendum was held in January and ninety-nine percent of the votes supported independence. Our objective was to prevent democratic government. And have you seen what we did today?"

"No, what?"

"We sent troops to Northern Ireland to help the Protestant minority repress the Catholic majority in Derry. For good socialists, the Wilson government doesn't appear to have great fondness for the downtrodden and oppressed."

"I assume, Osbert, that you are a Conservative."

"I've voted Tory, and I've voted Labour, and once, in the absence of mind, I may even have voted Liberal."

They had finished the whitebait, their salads, and the Smith Haut-Lafite, all of which were excellent, and were enjoying an elderly calvados.

Jay said, "I think maintaining order is a duty of government, a matter of principle."

"Ah, yes, the Imperial Principle. Mustn't let the Empire fade...I was at Oxford with some of the ministers of the present government, notably Dick Crossman. 'Broad of Church and broad of mind, broad before and broad behind.'"

This last was delivered in his strong voice accompanied by a roar of laughter. The restaurant was not large enough, nor were there enough conversations taking place, for there to be any possibility that it might have been inaudible. The gentleman with Man Ray was facing Lancaster, and he looked toward the disturbance, then quickly looked away.

Jay took advantage of the break in the conversation to ask, "Osbert, do you know the man who is dining with Man Ray?"

Lancaster, without being obvious about it, looked. Then he said, "I think he's an art dealer."

"Yes. I think so too."

"He's probably a dealer of the promoter type. The talk in the art market is that Ray is interested in licensing reproductions of some of his classic work—to be produced in large editions. That's probably the topic of discussion during their dinner."

That was a well-informed assessment. Ray and the other man at his table were, in fact, planning to license five hundred high-quality copies of Ray's photo known as "Noire et Blanche." It is a picture of the head of Kiki de Montparnasse, recumbent. Standing beside her head, at a ninety degree angle, is an African sculpture, a tall, narrow mask, black.

Osbert said, "I'm sorry that Ray is doing these multiples."

"Why? It will put an excellent photograph, a classic photograph, onto a wall that couldn't have afforded it otherwise."

Osbert summoned the waiter, requested the check, and put on wire-rimmed glasses, perched on the end of his nose. "It's a question of authenticity, I suppose. I'm not objecting to reproducing pictures, God knows. My cartoons are printed in the daily newspaper and distributed in many thousands of copies, but no one is going to clip it out and frame it and hang it on the wall as a work of art."

"The Man Ray photographs will be sold as copies."

"Perhaps, but who knows what will happen when it leaves the artist's hands? And Ray's hands won't even have touched those copies. The pictures will no doubt be marked—on the back, where the mark can't be seen when the thing is framed. And, indeed, apart from the mark, the object will simply be another print of one of Ray's photos, indistinguishable from the original except by the age of the paper. Indeed, it will be in effect a duplicate original. Why should it have less value than the exhibition print? But it will have."

Jay said, "The real problem is misrepresentation—representing the piece as something it isn't."

"Yes. Authenticity. Exactly the problem."

"But authenticity and veracity aren't always what the market wants. In the original script of my show, 'The Nervous Set,' the female lead commits suicide. That version was powerful, and the show was a hit in the original production in St. Louis. But, when the show got to Broadway, the money people intervened. The producer said to me, 'We gotta change the ending. It's a musical, Jay, you can't have a downbeat ending. The audience has to leave the theater smiling.' Broadway made it false."

Osbert said, "So the Broadway version failed because it lacked authenticity."

They finished their calvados and paid the check. As they left the restaurant, they stopped by Man Ray's table.

Ray stood and greeted them. "Jay, wonderful to see you again."

Introductions of the other two men were then ex-changed. Ray's companion at the table introduced himself as "Clive Sedgewell, art dealer." And then said, "And of course I know the work of Mr. Lancaster, I see his tren-chant cartoons in the *Express* almost every day. Cleverly done!"

There were two more chairs at the table. Ray said, "We were about to order an after dinner drink. Please join us."

Jay said, "Thank you, but we've just had calvados."

Osbert Lancaster quickly said, "But perhaps we could have another."

Clive Sedgewell agreed. "There is always that possibil-ity."

When they were all seated at the table, Landesman and Lancaster both ordered another calvados and Ray and Sedgewell ordered cognacs. Jay and Osbert then congrat-ulated Man on the medal awarded by the Royal Photo-graphic Society.

Man said, "Thank you." He ran his forefinger around the rim of his glass. It whined. "It was for old work."

Jay moved on. "This is almost a professional meeting, perhaps tax deductable. All four of us are in the art world, two work in production and two in distribution."

Osbert said, "Which am I, production or distribution?"

Clive said, "Oh, Mr. Lancaster, you are clearly an artist."

Osbert replied, "Thank you, I think."

Man said, "Have you been in St. Louis recently, Jay?"

"No. I'm living here in London, near Camden Passage and the Angel tube stop."

Clive said, "Oh, are you from St. Louis?"

"Yes. Do you know the place?"

"No, I've never been there."

"Ah, I see. I thought perhaps I'd met you there. I owned a nightclub in St. Louis, the Crystal Palace, and I thought I'd seen you there."

"No. I'm sorry I didn't have that opportunity."

Man said, "It would have been interesting, I'm sure. I'm told that the Crystal Palace was an elegant room."

Clive said, "Named for the nineteenth century marvel here in London, I assume."

"Yes. I'm sorry all three of you missed it." Jay then turned to Lancaster and Ray. "I had thought that, since Clive is an American, he might have been there."

Clive replied, "But I'm not American, I'm British."

Jay toyed with his calvados. He said, "Oh, perhaps because I'm an American I thought I recognized a kindred spirit, a fellow countryman."

Clive shrugged. "Sorry. English born and bred." This last was said in exaggeratedly plummy tones.

Osbert intervened. He turned to Sedgewell. "Are you related to the famous Sitwells? Dame Edith and so on?"

"No. I'm Sedgewell, not Sitwell. Different name."

"Sorry. I'm a bit deaf."

Jay said, "Perhaps you may be a distant cousin. Perhaps a very distant cousin."

Sedgewell replied, "I don't think so."

Jay persisted, "Ah. I thought perhaps the name might have evolved. Names do change."

Osbert said, "There's a rather good painting of the family, you know. By Sargent."

Man said, "What family?"

Osbert replied, "Why, the Sitwells." The silk handkerchief was threatening to escape his breast pocket. Osbert stuffed it farther in. "One of the Sitwells is an Osbert, you know. We Osberts must stick together. Probably endured the same teasing at school." He paused. "He isn't well." The other three men looked at him. Osbert smiled, but he wasn't rescued.

Then Osbert said, "I'm afraid, Jay, we may have interrupted the business that Man and Clive were conducting. We should take our leave."

Jay said, "But we haven't finished the drinks they so kindly invited us to share, and I'm enjoying the conversation." He turned to Man. "I've been trying to persuade Osbert to design the sets for a new production of 'Dearest Dracula,' my musical version of the Dracula story."

Man replied, "Yes, I remember that project. I wish you well. Both of you.'"

Clive said, "Sales resistance appears to be in the air tonight. I've been trying to persuade Man to let me do an edition of one of his famous photographs, but I'm not succeeding. He isn't interested in money."

Jay examined his cufflinks, set with tiger eyes. "That's the problem with dealing, or trying to deal, with successful artists who are near the end of their careers. They're uncooperative."

Osbert said, "Insufficiently entrepreneurial."

Man said, "Too independent."

Jay said, "Or, perhaps, too discerning."

Then Man added, "It's true that older artists, or most of

them, are less interested in money. Certainly that's true if you've had some success. You've already bought most of the things you really wanted to buy, and you know you won't have many more years to spend the money. So it doesn't matter as much."

Then Jay changed tack again. He said, "Osbert and I were just discussing authenticity, and the subject brought to mind St. Louis bouillabaisse. Man, do you remember when we made that in St. Louis? It wasn't a real bouillabaisse, was it? It wasn't authentic."

Ray replied, "No, I'm afraid not. But it was tasty."

Jay said, "I suppose it was a sort of copy of a bouillabaisse, but not a very close copy, certainly not one that would have fooled a Frenchman."

"As I recall, Jay, you told me exactly what was in it. I saw the ingredients. It wasn't intended to fool anyone."

"No, that's right. It was all legit fish." Jay paused. "When you were in St. Louis, did you go to the Alden Adams gallery?"

"Yes, I did, but Mr. Adams wasn't there. He had disappeared."

Jay said, "So who invited you to make an appearance at the gallery?"

"I was invited by Ben Davos, Adams's partner, and I then met Davos at the gallery."

"But you didn't meet Adams?"

"No, I didn't."

"A pity." He paused again. "Did you get to see more of the town?"

"I did, yes. On my last day there I had lunch with a man

from the Mayor's office and then we took a walk around the neighborhood known as the Central West End."

Clive said, "In London, the theater district is called the West End. Is the Central West End the St. Louis theater district?"

Jay replied, "No, but some of the people who live there play different roles, from time to time."

"Oh yes?"

"Yes, you never know where they may turn up — in different guises."

Clive said, "How amusing!"

Jay said, "Perhaps."

Man Ray looked at Sedgewell. "At public events, if there's a question I don't like, I say, 'That's an interesting question.' And then I say no more. It works. Many times the best remedy for a problem is simply to ignore it. Not every comment or question deserves an answer, and it's often better to leave those without one."

Osbert said, "We should run along, Jay. Perhaps Man has business with Mr. Sitwell."

Jay said, "Not just yet. We'll be leaving in just a moment."

Osbert said, "Must go. Terribly sorry. An engagement, you know." He stood, said goodbye, and left.

Jay looked directly at Sedgewell. "The new mustache suits you. It's handsome. And your temples are a bit more gray. And the new accent is very cultured, very British, almost persuasive." Jay stood and shoved both hands into the side pockets of his suitcoat. "But I'll bet you're missing the good old days in St. Louis."

"I'm afraid you've mistaken me for someone else, sir."

"Oh come on, Alden, as one old con man to another. Don't try to fool a fooler."

"You've had too much to drink, sir." This was said in clipped British cadences.

"Born in the Central West End, on Portland Place..."

"No, I wasn't."

"...in the shadow of the Park Plaza...."

"No, you're mistaken."

"...only a hundred yards from Forest Park. Now that I've found you, what do you think the odds are that Mary Ocean and the others won't come after you?"

Man Ray looked down at the table and, in a low voice, said to Landesman, "Jay, I don't really know you well. We spent a part of one day together in St. Louis four years ago, cooking fish, but that's all the time I've ever had with you. You appear to believe that this gentleman, Clive Sedgewell, is in fact Alden Adams, the missing St. Louis gallery owner. But Mr. Sedgewell has a good reputation as an established dealer here in London. Perhaps you're right, Jay, or perhaps you're not. I don't see any real proof one way or the other."

Clive said, "I'm sorry that our dinner has been disrupted. Perhaps Mr. Ray and I could conclude our business."

Man Ray looked at his cognac and swirled the glass. He turned toward Landesman. "I suppose it would be a good thing if Sedgewell were Adams — that would provide closure, and maybe the St. Louis artists would get some of the money they are owed. But my hope isn't evidence. Since I never met Alden Adams, I don't have any real basis for having an opinion about this. If you're confident about your identification, Jay, you could contact Al Garavelli in St. Louis. If he's still on the police force, I'm sure he'd pursue it. But the question that bothers me most is, what happened to Ray Robinson? I had tea with his mother at her apartment. She's a nice lady. She told me that Alden Adams was helpful with her son's problems and provided money. But she missed her son and she's going to need him in her last years. She deserves better. Where is he?"

Sedgewell remained silent. So did Landesman.

After an awkward interval, Man Ray said, "I'm going to walk away from this table and I'm not going to do business with either of you." He opened his wallet, removed a stack of banknotes, put them on the table, and left the restaurant.

Sedgewell turned to Landesman. "You, sir, are either a charlatan or a fool. I intend to sue you for malicious interference with contract, and I will prevail. If you are a competitor of mine, you may have had a business reason for doing it. If not, you are just a reckless jackass. Consult your solicitor."

Landesman said, "Screw you, Alden."

Their voices were raised. The Major came over to the table. "Please, gentlemen, think of the other guests."

Jay said, "I'm just leaving." And he did.

Sedgewell remained at the table.

22

Juliet hired a car and driver to meet Man at Orly. He was tired, but he soon returned to work on a painting that was in progress. While he was cleaning his brushes, he told Juliet about the extraordinary dinner in London. Since she was not in St. Louis and had not met the various characters in the drama, the story required a bit of explaining. She seldom listened closely to Man's accounts of negotiations concerning proposed shows or editions of his work, even if those negotiations had taken place in glamorous surroundings or had been accompanied by nice meals. She was not much interested in the business side of art. But this story had some unusual elements. It got her attention. Then the conversation and their lives moved on. Man had ideas for new paintings and sculpture.

Several months later, Man and Juliet treated themselves to a celebratory dinner at Lucas Carton. Man had a new commission, and it was a good one. It was to be a large mural, made as a mosaic of pieces of colored glass, reproducing a painting he had done thirty years earlier. The restaurant was at 9 Place de la Madeleine, between Place Vendome and the Elysee Palace, near the intersection of Rue Saint-Honore and Rue Royale and Man and Juliet started at the Louvre and walked west along Saint-Honore. They could have turned at the corner of Rue Royale but they continued on to Chanel's shop at number 21 and Hermes at 24, taking a short detour to look at the latest designs.

As they entered the restaurant, the maitre d' greeted Man Ray by name and said, in French, "It is good to see you, sir. I trust that you and Madame have been well."

Man was leaning on a stick. "We have, thank you, and we've been walking to enjoy this beautiful day. Juliet is a bit footsore."

The maitre d' smiled and said, "We will remedy that."

He conducted them to a table at a beautifully upholstered banquette along a side wall. A waiter appeared carrying a small footstool covered in silk, and it was placed at Juliet's feet. The long tablecloth permitted her to slip off her shoes. She was enormously grateful.

Halfway through the entrecote and an excellent bottle of Chateau Cantenac-Brown 1947, and after having exhausted the topics of the day, Juliet said, "Whatever happened about the St. Louis art dealer who may or may not have turned up in London?"

"I don't know. I haven't heard."

"Are you going to inquire?"

"No."

"Why not?"

"That's not my art."

"It wouldn't hurt you to worry a bit more about the young man, St. Louis Sugar."

"My friend Garavelli is paid to worry about that, and

he's in a better position to pursue it. He has more information and more resources to work with."

"The St. Louis dealer walked off with a lot of money that belonged to the artists. I know you're concerned about the welfare of artists. I've seen your concern about that here."

"Paris has artists who need money. I can probably do more good here than I could there. I'm not going to live long enough to right all the world's wrongs. And you and I will certainly not accomplish it while eating entrecote at Lucas Carton."

"You have skills. Use them."

"I've had my shot at it."

"You can still paint."

"Maybe. How do I know it's good? What proof is there?"

"Money. Money is the proof. People want to buy your work."

"It's my name. They're paying for what I did thirty years ago. Or more."

"You still have ideas."

"I'm tired. I'm done. I had a good run."

"This is supposed to be a celebratory meal. You don't sound very celebratory."

Man said, "You brought up St. Louis. St. Louis is not a very celebratory story."

"You're back in Paris now. Turn the corner."

"St. Louis or Paris, it doesn't change the facts. I'm still Man Ray."

"That's a good thing to be."

"There are things to celebrate. Some things. Old things."

"You're not that old."

"Hah…I still have ideas. But I'm not sure I have the skill to execute them. Or maybe it's the energy. Or maybe the will. It requires discipline to do it. It's work. It has to be fun. The less it is fun, the more discipline it takes. Art is not a repetitive task. With a repetitive task, you can force yourself to do it, more or less. If you know it needs to be done, you will do it, but art isn't like that. Not real art. You can't just will yourself to do it. You can't will yourself to have imagination, instinct. It has to come from within."

"I've heard you say that any artist needs an audience. That sounds like external motivation, not something coming from within."

"It's complicated. If I think the work is good, I don't care about the audience. I'm satisfied. But if I'm not sure whether it's good or not, then I sure as hell need the audience. So, if your self-confidence weakens and the audience isn't there to support you, you're in trouble. You question why you keep painting."

"You keep painting because that's your identity. That's who you are. You define yourself as a painter. Without painting, you'd see yourself as having nothing. I think there's more to you than that. I think you're a good man, humane, intelligent. But for you, it's all about painting."

The waiter poured the last of the wine from the decanter.

"Demand for work I did thirty years ago doesn't help much—except to put food on the table."

Juliet said, "Maybe we should pay some attention to the food on the table."

"Perhaps .... Shall we have another bottle?"
"Maybe just a half."
The meal was excellent.

AUTHOR'S NOTE

The corporeal Man Ray was, in fact, at the White House Festival of the Arts in 1965. I had a brief, pleasant conversation with him there. Meeting him was one of the highlights of my early life. He was friendly and unpretentious. I have no reason to believe, however, that he ever went to St. Louis. It will be safer to regard the Man Ray in this book as a character in a novel.

I also knew Jay and Fran Landesman, and the person called Bob Knox here, and an artist who sometimes used the name Mary Ocean. None of them are responsible for what has become of them in this story.

The emergency evacuation shelter for high-ranking officers of the federal government was, in fact, housed within Mount Weather in Virginia. Like Man Ray in Chapter Two, I sat in a waiting room at National Airport expecting to board a TWA flight to St. Louis and, like the airplane in this novel, the one I was scheduled to board crashed on Mount Weather on the doorstep of the national mega-bunker. All passengers and crew were killed. It was Thanksgiving weekend of 1974, nine and a half years after the crash in the story. But the scene in the waiting room was essentially the same. The woman I talked to was a newspaper reporter rather than a congressman's assistant, but, like

Betty, she had access to the newswires. I took TWA's bus to Baltimore and flew from there to St. Louis very quietly.

Many of the details in the book are true, or at least partly so. Duff's existed then. Not now. The Moulin d'Or existed then. Not now. Anne and I ate there. J. W. Losse Custom Tailor was then in St. Louis. Gone now. I saw Mike Nichols and Elaine May perform at the first Crystal Palace. Garavelli's restaurant was in fact at the corner of DeBaliviere and DeGiverville for many years, and it was very successful, but Joe Garavelli retired at the age of 57 and the business then passed through a series of owners and several locations. Stan Musial and his business partner owned it for a time. The original building was demolished in 1987. Sic transit.

The whitebait that Jay Landesman and Osbert Lancaster ate at the Moulin d'Or in 1969 was often on London restaurant menus. Ecologists, however, advocated the rather obvious proposition that harvesting baby fish in large quantities, frying them, and serving them in sizeable mounds was not a good way to provide for future fish supplies. Nonetheless, it is still sometimes seen on menus.

In writing the story, I received expert advice and often had the good judgment to follow it. Evan Meagher, a professional baseball player, lawyer, chief financial officer, author, harmonica player, and friend, gave the manuscript a close reading and made extraordinarily valuable suggestions. William Conger, a distinguished Chicago artist, devoted many hours to educating me about the art world and the life of an artist. The book owes much to his expertise. Irvin Slate, a friend for sixty-six years and an avid reader, provided both discerning appraisals of the manuscript and needed encouragement, as he has on many other projects. The Rt. Hon. Lord Justice Longmore, another friend of long standing, advised me on the London chapter. He knew about Sidley's case without having to look it up. Anne Heinz was my constant adviser on innumerable issues, large and small—word choices, chapter deletions, structure, voice. She was a part of it all. This is one of those relatively rare occasions that calls for sentiment, but words are inadequate to express the extent of my thanks.

Jay Landesman wrote two memoirs, *Rebel Without Applause* (1987) and *Jaywalking* (1992), both of them good. The first has more on his St. Louis and New York years; the second covers the years in London. There is also a book about Jay and Fran written by one of their sons; see Cosmo Landesman, *Starstruck: Fame, Failure, My Family, and Me* (2008), which is candid and humorous. Ernest Kirsten's *Catfish and Crystal* (1960) is a detailed and authoritative picture of St. Louis in the middle of the 20th century. On the plane crash, see Adam Shaw, *Sound of Impact: The Legacy of TWA Flight 514* (1977). See also Edward Adams, "Weather Hampers Aircraft Probe," *Free Lance-Star*, Fredericksburg, Virginia, December 2, 1974, p. 1, at 12. I have learned from all of these, but the story told here is nonetheless a work of fiction.

J. H.
April, 2022

THE BENEVOLENCE
OF OLD MEN

"So do not believe for one minute that there is very much difference between one human being and another. We all have a will to survive, but it is stronger in some than it is in others; and the urge for revenge, that too is stronger in some than in others."

Ward Just, *An Unfinished Season*

1

"Joe Cioni's is the place to go / the place to go to spend your dough." As he walked, he sang, not loudly but audibly. "Joe Cioni's is the place to go / singin' boh doh dee oh dee oh dough." A woman nearby who was almost his age smiled. That made him slightly self-conscious, but it didn't stop his singing. The stiff breeze off the water suited the song. The path was not the most direct route to Cioni's grocery, but the detour was a small, private pleasure.

While adding up the groceries, Cioni said, "Were you in business, Mr.Maranville?"

"No, government."

"Oh, with the Park Agency?"

"No, I was in sales tax."

"Oh."

"Yes. I thought of it as law enforcement. You wouldn't believe the amount of cheating. But we were watching. I always say, if you look after the pennies the dollars will take care of themselves."

Joe Cioni said, "That's what my dear mother always told me." He completed the transaction expeditiously, without further questions.

After he left the store, Rabbit Maranville considered whether the news that he had been a tax collector would spread. It was obvious that he was now retired, but he knew there was speculation about the sort of work he had done. The sales tax story would do no harm.

*

Back at home, he took his morning coffee to the screened porch. The wicker armchair wasn't the most comfortable seat in the house, but it would do and in good weather it had a view of the Seward Range in the distance. Seward. An up-state New York man. Seward's Folly had caused Maranville a certain amount of trouble, mostly because the land and waters were too close to Russia and the Russians wanted them back. Not bloody likely. The struggles over missile launching sites, distant early warning installations, and shipping lanes were constant worries, and Rabbit had devoted many hours to them, but they were someone else's problems now.

Caleb Ironwood would be arriving soon. The conversation would be difficult and Rabbit preferred to have the meeting on his home ground. It helped that Caleb's house was at Raquette Lake on a point with water access only. Rabbit's house was easier to get to. A good excuse.

He worried about what there was that he could give Ironwood for lunch. He had some decent cheddar, and he could do a ploughman's lunch, with pickle. Very British. But the bread was only store-bought, stale. If he made grilled cheese sandwiches, the butter and the frying pan would fix that. He knew that Ironwood cared little about eating.

The visit was three hours off and Rabbit had the morning for reading. He told himself to drink water, not just coffee. Water was better for his blood pressure and his stomach and, besides, its lack of flavor was consistent with his lifestyle. Perhaps he'd revisit Trollope or maybe Twain. Anything but a spy novel. Well, not anything. He drew the line at bodice-rippers. And he thought most spy novels were damned nonsense. "Eric Ambler, John Buchan, and Ian Fleming are silly. Drivel." He liked LeCarre's writing, but found the plots preposterous.

Clouds had descended and the weather was now gray and damp. Given the heavy overcast, he could barely see the Seward Range. The rain was reluctant, as if the heavens were determined to make the day wet but had only a limited supply of water and were parceling it out slowly. The fall colors would arrive soon. Not soon enough to suit him.

*

Ironwood was ramrod straight. Rabbit wondered why it was always a ramrod that was straight. Why not straight as a ruler? A ramrod, after all, might be bent — they were often bent in use - but a ruler has to be straight to do its job. How many people now even know what a ramrod is? Not much call for them. No doubt the image is meant to suggest strength. A ramrod is more aggressive than a ruler. Rabbit, however, had a teacher in grade school who did what he could to change that. He disciplined students by slapping their open palms with the flat of a ruler, hard. It didn't help the teacher control the class, but it made Rabbit think that a ruler could be aggressive.

It was just noon, precisely. General Ironwood was never

late. If an artillery barrage arrived late, our troops might already have invaded the area. Ironwood said such things, but he wasn't really entitled to that excuse for his punctuality. He'd served in intelligence. Rabbit had worked with him often.

*

The general stood and looked through the screens at the lake. He said, "There's a loon. It'd better leave soon."

"They're pretty good at timing it. They know when there's enough open water."

"Need a long runway."

"A bird not really designed for flying."

Caleb Ironwood turned and faced Maranville. "Have you heard the news, Rabbit? Bobby Fischer defeated Boris Spassky. The first time an American has won the world chess championship."

"No doubt there'll be dancing in the streets of Greenwich Village."

"But possibly not in Peoria or Dallas."

"No, probably not." Rabbit settled into the wicker chair. "So what else has happened, especially in our nation's capital?"

Ironwood said, "Sarge Shriver is getting good reviews for the job he's done filling the empty place on the McGovern ticket. Shriver made a couple of speeches recently that were well-received by the faithful."

"And not received at all by anyone else."

"Yes, of course. So it goes. McGovern's getting a lot of

criticism for a sloppy, careless job of vetting Tom Eagleton. The fact that Eagleton had been treated with electro-shock wasn't widely known, but some people knew about his history of depression. A reasonably diligent inquiry would've discovered it."

Rabbit said, "Yeah, it sure came out quickly as soon as he was on the ticket. And that's fair enough, but I'm told that McGovern offered the nomination to several other people and they all turned it down. Eagleton was a rush job."

"The nomination wasn't a plum. The pros knew from the beginning that Nixon was going to cruise. The Chicago convention in sixty-eight is still splitting the party."

"Yeah. It's amazing what a weak candidate McGovern has become. When he was a bomber pilot he was awarded the Distinguished Flying Cross and the Air Medal with three oak leaf clusters, but the Republicans are calling him a 'peacenik.' Spiro Agnew makes McGovern sound like a conscientious objector."

Ironwood said, "McGovern is a lost cause. Nixon's going to blow him out of the water. Eagleton's withdrawal killed whatever small chance McGovern had. The Democrats have nothing but problems."

Rabbit lit his pipe. "I'm told that McGovern talked to psychiatrists when he found out about the shock treatments, and he was told that Eagleton's depression could be a danger to the nation if he was serving as president. So Eagleton had to go."

"It's hard to imagine why the Republicans thought that the Watergate burglary and the illegal wiretaps and the 'dirty tricks' were necessary. Surely they saw that they were going to win easily."

"They did those things just from force of habit. It's business as usual. For them, politics is a game with no holds barred. They don't distinguish between tricks and crimes."

"It wasn't a game for the Watergate burglars. They, or at least most of them, were anti-Castro Cubans from Miami. Reports are that they spoke Spanish during the burglary. They hated Castro, and they thought Republicans would do more to get rid of him than Democrats would. Kennedy failed them at the Bay of Pigs because he didn't provide air cover. That got a lot of their friends killed. They had reason to want the Democrats to lose."

Rabbit said, "No doubt there was some ideological motivation, but when they were arrested they were carrying a large amount of cash in crisp, new, hundred-dollar bills, consecutively numbered. They were paid for the burglary. They were also well-equipped with tear gas fountain pens, walkie-talkies, and surgical gloves, typical CIA gear. These weren't your average burglars picked up at the corner saloon."

Ironwood said, "True. The local prosecutor in Miami started his own investigation because the burglars were from there. Since the hundred-dollar bills were new, the serial numbers could be traced to the bank they came from. It was all from one Miami bank, and records of accounts at the bank were subpoenaed. One of the burglars had a deposit from a man who was a fundraiser for CREEP." CREEP was a commonly used label for the Committee to Re-elect the President.

"They've only started to trace the money. Walter Lippmann says that the planning of the burglary will go all the way to the President."

"He may well be right."

Rabbit said, "Here we are, two old men demonstrating that we paid attention to the news and we can remember some of the details. Pretty soon we'll start talking about doctor visits."

"Or about the time I met Delores del Rio."

Rabbit laughed. He relit his pipe. "How's Mary getting along?"

"She's dealing with it. Accepting it." Ironwood coughed, paused, and then coughed again. "You know she's expecting another child?"

"No, I didn't know that. I was asking about her handling of John's death. The pregnancy must make that especially difficult."

"She misses John, of course, but she knows he's gone and there's nothing to be done about it." Ironwood put his hands on the arms of the chair, pushed himself up, and slowly stood. "My knees hurt. She's having trouble sleeping."

"Get her a pair of wool socks. They'll keep her feet warm. Warm feet relax the body."

"Thick socks or thin?"

"Thick. And real wool. No imitations."

"Those will solve her problems?"

"No, but it'll give you something to do." Rabbit refilled Ironwood's cup and said, "The child will want to know what happened to its father, want to know how he died. There'll be questions."

Ironwood looked away. "The loss will be abstract, not personal. The child will have no personal knowledge of John."

"But he or she will want to know who killed John."

"Nonsense."

"That sort of inquisitiveness or curiosity is natural, innate."

"Bullshit."

"I'll bet you any sum that the child will search for the killer. Watch out for it."

"You old fool, by the time this child has the ability to search for anyone, you and I will both be well beyond the ability to collect on a bet."

"No doubt. Also well beyond the ability to pay off on one, which makes it a safe bet." Maranville emptied his pipe into an ashtray. "Nonetheless, I think there's something to what I said."

General Ironwood turned toward the Seward Range. "You've become peculiar in your old age."

*

The medical examiner's verdict was that the death was accidental, the result of a fall. John Waverly's body had been found at the bottom of a flight of stairs, but there were only five steps. Apart from some bruises on his chin that could have been the result of being struck with a fist, the only significant injury was a broken neck. His head was attached to his body at a peculiar angle. The pathologist who did the autopsy found that he died quickly.

2

"Do you like your grilled cheese sandwiches lightly toasted, chestnut brown, or burned black?"

"Chestnut brown sounds appealing."

"I've always pegged you as a moderate."

"And yours?"

"The same. You don't think I'm a radical, do you?"

Ironwood joined Rabbit in the kitchen. It was a large room, a bit smaller than the living room but the same size as the bedrooms. There was a cookstove with four burners, fired by bottle-gas, an unpainted wood table and three chairs, all well-worn, and a sink where dishes were washed with water pumped up the hill from the lake. Drinking water came from gallon jugs. There were hummingbird feeders outside both of the windows.

Ironwood said, "Do you have any soup? I like to dunk a grilled cheese in soup."

"False teeth?"

"No, I just like soup."

"The only soup in the house is Taylor's Butterbean. But it's not made for dunking; it's a hearty soup."

Ironwood said, "Never heard of it."

"No, I'm not surprised. It's only available by mail from a small town in central Illinois."

"Why mail?"

"It's a small operation. No distribution. They make the soup in a kettle on a stove, but they can it and the soup is excellent. A meal in itself. It has a lot of black pepper in it."

"Black pepper? Maybe some other day. The grilled cheese will be just fine."

Rabbit said, "You're not very adventuresome today."

"Unlike most days." Ironwood pulled out one of the kitchen chairs and sat at the table. "We worked together on many problems over the years, but I never asked you about how you found your way to the Agency. How did that happen?"

"It was a job."

"Did you go there right out of law school?"

"No, at first I stayed in Chicago and practiced law in the family firm."

Ironwood said, "You come from a family of lawyers?"

"The firm was Maranville and Maranville, and I wasn't either one of those. My grandfather and my father established the firm."

"Were they also Rabbit?"

"No, just me."

"How did you come to be called that?"

"Are you a baseball fan, Caleb? Cast your mind back. When you and I were young, Rabbit Maranville was a famous shortstop, first with the Boston Braves and then later with the Cardinals. A Hall of Fame player. My last name was Maranville, so on the playground I became Rabbit."

"I always thought that Rabbit was a peculiar nickname for a high-ranking official at the CIA. Bunnies are timid, cuddly, peaceable creatures."

"I was peaceable, maybe not cuddly. Many years ago, there was a young man who called me Bunny. Once."

"With what result?"

"We had a disagreement about his parentage, and we both had to stay after school. Since I retired and bought this place, I've wished that I could persuade people to call me Beaver, a proper Adirondack animal, an industrious animal, good at building, good at blocking streams."

Caleb said, "A useful skill. Some streams need to be blocked."

"You and I blocked a few."

Caleb returned to Rabbit's biography, "Were you ever covert?"

"At the law firm?"

"When you first went to the Agency."

"Never. My job was to know people and get information from them."

"What kind of information?"

"All sorts of things. Mostly useless stuff. Mostly about who knew whom."

"How did the Agency find you?"

"I was in Navy intelligence during the war. Wild Bill Donovan was running the OSS and he spotted me. After the war, when he put together CIA, he recruited me."

"Did they hire you to be a lawyer?"

"No, I was hired because I had contacts. My grandfather had been president of the Chicago Bar Association in the 1890s, and my father was a member of every club Chicago had to offer—the Union League, University, Mid Day, Attic, Racquet, Evanston Country, and Glenview Golf. I was a member of the Triangle Club at Princeton. I knew people. And they'd talk to me."

"Those sound like strange credentials."

Rabbit said, "Oh, I don't know, I think it's the sort of thing that gets jobs for many people. My credentials were much like those of the Dulles brothers, except that they came from Watertown, a smaller town than Chicago. But rich."

"You had contacts, but Wild Bill must have thought that you had good sense. Did the job require you to have good sense?"

"Maybe I didn't need that to get in the door. But, in truth, I think some skill was required to stay there or get ahead."

"What skills did you have?"

"Good sense? I was always just a lawyer from Chicago who had the benefits of a prominent family and a good education. That gave me a leg up." Rabbit scraped the bowl of his pipe. "I wasn't interested in the romance of covert work. That's for the boys who enjoy deception."

"And you don't?"

Rabbit pushed his glasses down his nose and looked at Caleb over the top of them. "I have, at times, found it necessary to be less than straightforward. You may have observed that. But, of course, if you mislead people often, you run the risk that you'll wear out your welcome."

"One thinks of some of our friends and colleagues."

"Who shall remain nameless?"

"Oh, I don't see why that should be the case."

Rabbit said, "It's too nice a day to count bodies. There's

a gentle rain. Sunshine would spoil it. How did you find your way to the Pentagon?"

"Like you, I was selected. From a different sort of gene pool, but selected nonetheless. I was born and raised in West Virginia, near Harper's Ferry. In fact, my people were there while it was still part of Virginia. They were farmers and machinists, not lawyers. One of them worked at the Federal Armory at the time of John Brown's raid."

"What role did he have in it?"

"History doesn't record that. He wasn't a writer…. From West Virginia, I went to Yale."

"How did that happen?"

"I was a good student. The local librarian liked me and she was married to a Yale alum. He got me in. I think they had some money."

"It was ever thus."

"And then the Army sent a recruiter to Yale looking specifically for intelligence officer candidates…I was lucky. Things were pretty grim in West Virginia in the mid-1930s."

"What are you doing to occupy your time these days?"

"Oh, I keep busy with household chores, deferred maintenance, improvement projects. Right now I'm organizing an upgrade of the air conditioning in our apartment."

"How do you organize air conditioning?"

"We want to put in central air, get rid of the window units, but it's a co-op building so I need to get permission from the board to put in duct work. I need access to some of the common space."

"Co-ops are a pain."

"The political maneuvering in the building is treacherous. It makes the National Security Council seem like ring around the rosie."

"Your neighbors pay a high price for their antisemitism."

"True, but it's improving."

"The price?"

"The prejudice; it's diminishing."

"Slowly, no doubt."

"Slowly. Mindless nonsense, but pernicious."

"Air conditioning is well and good, but what are you doing to keep the mind alive? Are you listening to music, listening seriously?"

Rabbit knew that Ironwood had an encyclopedic knowledge of classical music.

Caleb said, "I've been listening. Indeed, I heard some musicians recently who were playing your sort of thing."

"My sort of thing?"

Rabbit played piano, mostly jazz. When he was in the Triangle Club shows at Princeton, he met the Dorsey brothers and sat in with them, and back in Chicago he knew the Austin High Gang, especially the McPartlands, Jimmy and Richard. He still played with pickup groups.

Caleb said, "I went to a club in New York, and they had a band made up of old-timers. At the break, I stood at the bar and had a conversation with the drummer, Tommy Benford. He was in Jelly Roll Morton's Red Hot Peppers."

"What did he have to say?"

"He said that Jelly was an amazing character. Unpredictable, but brilliant. Benford's brother, Bill, was also in the Peppers, played bass. And Gerry Mulligan was at the club in the audience. He didn't play, but he was introduced and was applauded."

Rabbit said, "Having Mulligan there was a tribute to the musicians." Rabbit raised his eyebrows. "Was there a saxophone in the band?"

"A younger fellow named Eddie Chamblee."

"Not younger than Mulligan, but a little younger than the Benfords. Chamblee was married to Dinah Washington for a short time — an experience that would test the mettle of any man. Who was the trumpet?"

"I think it was Bobby Stark."

"Couldn't be. Bobby Stark died thirty years ago, maybe more."

"It was Bobby someone, perhaps someone using Bobby Stark's name."

Rabbit laughed. "A false Bobby Stark! What a wonderful world that would be! A world in which Bobby Stark was so well known and so honored that there was something to be gained by being a false Bobby Stark. A day to live for."

"He played well."

"What songs did they do?"

"I can't give you the whole playlist, but I remember that they did 'Someday Sweetheart,' 'A Hundred Years From Today,' and 'C Jam Blues.'"

"The classics. Jelly wrote Someday Sweetheart. It's not surprising they played it."

"All very good."

"I'm very glad." Rabbit thought that they had exhausted the subject. "Have you done any canoeing lately?"

"Just a short trip. I put in at our camp on Raquette Lake last week and went up the Marion River to the carry, left my canoe at the landing, walked up the carry to Utowanna Lake, poked around, and then went back to the canoe and floated home. A quiet day."

In the northeast of the United States, the term "camp" refers to a vacation home or getaway that in other parts of the country would be called a cottage or second home, and a "carry" is a portage.

"See any wildlife?"

"A beaver was working."

"Is that big white pine still leaning out over the river? The last time I saw it, its roots looked like they were just barely holding onto the bank."

"The tree is still there. If it falls, it'll block the carry."

Rabbit took the sandwiches off the stove. "All done." He brought them to the table. "Then what happens? The Marion River is a navigable waterway, navigable by small boats. If they can't get through, will the rangers cut the tree and get it out of the way?"

"I don't know. They don't like to interfere with nature, but they also wouldn't like to close off access to the carry. I don't know what the rules say."

Rabbit said, "My view is that nature is adaptable. Consider evolution. I think we should agree that in this day and age nature has evolved to a point where the gasoline powered chainsaw is now part of the natural order. Your average black bear will not be at all surprised by a chainsaw. A beaver might even welcome the competition." He paused. "Do you miss the Pentagon?"

"Yes and no. I don't miss the pettiness or the long hours, but I miss working on problems that have real substance and the feeling of being in on decisions that really matter."

"You've earned your retirement. Why not just relax, read a book, put your feet up?"

"Reading books is fine, for a day or two. Then I get bored. So I take walks. Then I get bored with taking walks."

"Golf is a traditional solution."

"A walk is not improved by chasing a small white ball. I want to solve real problems. Not the invented problem of how to put the small ball into a distant hole."

Rabbit said, "Did you fancy that in your work you were doing some good in the world?"

"In truth, sometimes I did."

"Yes, we had the occasional success, the occasional disaster averted. It was nice to feel that we might have mattered."

"It was."

"Perhaps we should try to do it again."

"How?"

3

The next day General Ironwood again came to visit. Rabbit was listening to a news program on the radio.

Ironwood said, "The first reports had all of the Palestinians killed and the Israeli hostages rescued, but our people in Munich now tell me that the attempt to ambush the Palestinians at the airport was a complete disaster with grenades and a helicopter that exploded, and almost everyone was killed, both Palestinians and Israelis."

Rabbit poured two cups of coffee. "The sports reporters who were there to work the Olympics got it all wrong. They're not used to covering terrorists and hostage situations."

"Does the Agency have anyone there?"

"I'm sure we do, but I'm not in contact with them."

"The attempt to rescue the hostages was done by Munich police. Under German law, the army can't use force within the borders of the country, and the police didn't have trained snipers, they didn't have sniper rifles with long barrels, didn't have telescopic sights or infrared scopes, and didn't have armored personnel carriers. It was incompetent. They weren't trained for this and they weren't prepared. Of course, I'm hearing American Army men talking."

Rabbit said, "The Germans tried to negotiate with the

terrorists, but the Palestinians wanted concessions from Israel and that was a non-starter. The Israeli government is very firm in its position that they never negotiate with terrorists, that negotiation only encourages more terrorism, more taking of hostages."

"West Germany offered the Palestinians a very large amount of money for the release of the hostages, but the reply was that they weren't interested in money and they also weren't interested in preserving their own lives. So the West Germans killed them. Unfortunately, the hostages died too."

"When you have absolutists on both sides, it seldom ends well. How many dead?"

"When the Munich police started shooting, the first thing the Palestinians did was execute the hostages, rapidly. What I get from U. S. Army sources in Berlin is that five Palestinians were killed at the airport, all eleven of the Israeli hostages died, and one German policeman was killed. Three of the Palestinians were arrested and are being held for trial. I think they were wounded. The count could change."

Rabbit rubbed a hand through his thinning hair, "There's talk, mostly suspicion, that German Nazis helped the Palestinians."

"We both know that there are still Nazis in Germany, but I can't believe that the West German government would want a high-profile disaster like this, just when they are getting international attention for their Olympics. Part of the problem here, I think, is that the Germans were trying to minimize their militarist image, so there really wasn't much security at the Olympic village."

Rabbit refilled their coffee cups. "There's enough blame to go around. Lots of it. A real tragedy. Good intelligence work might have prevented it." The coffee was hot and he winced. "Speaking of intelligence work, we have some skills, some valuable experience, and there's certainly no lack of wrongs to be addressed. You and I should team up to tackle them."

Caleb said, "What could we do?"

"The same sort of work we always did, investigate, find out what the facts are and see where they lead us."

"Then what?"

"Speak up. Make the facts known. There are some wrongs that exist only because they haven't been exposed. Joe McCarthy was brought down by Edward R. Murrow and his colleagues. We don't command an army at this point or any police force, but we know people who do."

Caleb said, " 'Tail-gunner Joe' was brought down with some help from Joseph Welch and McCarthy's own stupidity. What could we work on?"

Rabbit said, "I have an idea. Instead of talking about this further, why don't we put a canoe in the water and see what's going on in the fresh air?"

"Could we see whether the fish might be interested in what we offer them?"

"No doubt a pursuit that would be equally productive."

*

In the Midwest, the Stony Creek Ponds would certainly be called lakes. But they are next to the Saranac chain of lakes, Upper, Lower, and Middle, and to Tupper Lake, all of which are big—not big by Great Lake or Champlain standards, but big. In the Adirondacks, "pond" commonly means a body of water that is smaller than its neighbors. There is inconsistency in this. A few of the waters called ponds are larger than some called lakes. This is probably attributable to the fact that most were named by people standing next to them, not by someone with a wider perspective.

The Ampersand Brook flows into the ponds near Rabbit Maranville's camp, and then the water almost immediately turns and goes out into the Stony Creek, just a few yards away. The ponds are also fed by springs and by the runoff from the mountains. The water level fluctuates. Maranville's dock was mounted on floats, so that it rose and fell, but its range of movement was limited to about two feet. In the spring, when the waterways are at flood stage, towns downstream want water to be held, spillways are closed, and the dock is then under water. But this was the fall. The dock was dry.

Maranville and Ironwood eased the canoe out of the slip, Rabbit in the stern and Caleb in the bow, an arrangement that recognized Rabbit's greater experience in canoeing. The stern has more control over the direction of the boat. They could have used their hands to pull and push the canoe out of the slip, but Rabbit thought that was inelegant. He preferred to use his paddle.

Their first stop was a bog, a flowage off the Ampersand Brook, perhaps only a half-mile from the ponds. The bog has an unobstructed view of Ampersand Mountain, and there are always wading birds. Open water in the middle of the bog is partially covered by lily pads. Tussocks of aquatic grasses support the shores of the open water. At the far end of the bog, a small stream carrying runoff from the mountain enters, and the grasses close in on that stream until it becomes so narrow as to be impassible.

As they floated almost motionless in the middle of the bog, Caleb said, "I value our friendship, Rabbit. The older we get, the more I value it. At our age, we have to treasure our friends. They become fewer. There was a time when you and I both had many. I know you've had the same experience I've had."

"Yes, as you age your world gets smaller in many ways, and that's one of the worst of them. But I don't know how to prevent friends from dying in their eighties. I don't suppose being in the Adirondacks helps to alleviate the isolation of old age, but it makes the isolation more beautiful."

"It's certainly beautiful in this bog."

"It's less beautiful in the black fly and mosquito season. The fall is the best—a day like today. The swamp maples are already losing their leaves, but the tamaracks are turning golden."

"I call them larch."

Rabbit said, "Most people here call them tamaracks. The base of their trunk, where it flares to form the roots, is the traditional wood used to make the stem of an Adirondack guideboat."

"One of the most beautiful watercraft ever created."

"If you know what you're doing, they're a joy to row. They go through the water like sharp shears through silk."

They paddled out of the bog into the brook. Rabbit said, "That floating tree was a near miss."

"Sorry."

"You'll see obstacles ahead about a second before I do. You're twelve feet closer to them, so it's the bow paddler's job to be the lookout. Shouting a warning is fine, but a bow rudder is even better. Don't try to power your way through it. You can seldom avoid a problem in a canoe by speeding around it. Ease your way by it. You may even need to back water."

"What?"

"Backing water means paddling backward, paddling in reverse. Slow down. 'The deficiency of strength may be greatly supplied with art, but the want of art will have but heavy and unwieldy succor from strength.'"

"That's obviously a quote. Who is it?"

"Pierce Egan. He covered Regency period boxing. The quote is from his *Boxiana*, written in either 1820 or 1821. One of those — or close."

"It might have been said by Cezanne or Duke Ellington."

Rabbit said, "Or anybody smart, if they knew how to use a bow rudder."

"Do you often memorize things you read?"

"Very seldom. That just seemed to me to be well-expressed. And the sentiment is right, or at least usually right. Force is sometimes necessary, but in any event the 'heavy and unwieldy succor' is correct."

Ironwood partially turned on his seat. He talked over his left shoulder. "Most professional soldiers don't like going to war. Some do. But they know the reality of it. Some are actually good at it. There was a Confederate general named Bushrod Johnson. He commanded a division at Chickamauga. He was a West Pointer who'd been working as a chemistry professor before the war, but he executed one of the most decisive attacks. He read the battlefield correctly, broke through the Union lines, seized control of a ridge that overlooked the main road, set up artillery on the ridge, and destroyed a large Union force that was trying to escape. He captured a lot of ammunition and many prisoners. He succeeded because he moved quickly and effectively. But what's always interested me is his character. He was born and raised in the North, in Ohio, in a Quaker family that supported abolition. He'd worked in the Underground Railroad. Yet, for reasons unknown to me, when the war came he served the South. After the war, he was chancellor of the University of Nashville, and then he moved to central Illinois and settled on a farm. A complex man. He had a reputation as a scholar. People do things for reasons that are sometimes not apparent."

"Not apparent, no. But the reasons are usually understandable if we have the facts, so that we can see what he was thinking. Now watch out for that rock!"

"Ever alert, ever alert."

They continued upstream on the brook. There were sandbars created by abandoned beaver dams. When the dams stopped the water, the sand it was carrying settled to the bottom and it remained long after the logs and brush used to create the dams had washed away. Rabbit and Caleb had to watch out because sandbars are hard to see and a boat can run aground.

They soon came to a beaver dam that was still active. They heard it before they saw it. Water coming around and through the dam made a deep roar as it was pushed by the weight of the pool upstream. It was impressive to see how much pressure the dam withstood. The beavers knew what they were doing.

So Rabbit and Caleb had a choice. They could get wet, or they could turn around and go back the way they came. The wet option was to land the canoe downstream of the dam, get out, and wade while they lifted and pulled the boat around the obstruction. If they were lucky and didn't step into a hole, they might only get wet up to their knees.

They decided to retrace their strokes. They turned the canoe around and floated downstream on the brook, past the entrance to the bog. At several places, trees that were close to the brook now leaned over the water and had a precarious hold on the land. He wondered whether the trees had been close to the brook when they were seedlings or whether the stream had eroded the land to meet the trees.

Rabbit said, "I have an idea. Why don't we investigate something close to home, something of direct concern to us, John's death."

Caleb said, "Too close to home. Mary and Ellen would be uncomfortable."

"But you'd have the benefits of an insider. You have more information. You'll have insights." Then he stopped paddling. He said, "Switch sides. We've got wind blowing across the bow from your side, so I'll paddle hard on the opposite and try to fight the wind." They corrected the course of the canoe. "That's okay now." Rabbit caught his breath. "Nailing down the cause of John's death would be a gift to his unborn child. As I've said before, the child will want to know why his or her father isn't there."

"How could we investigate? We don't have police powers."

"We could ask questions. As usual."

4

Later, they sat on the screened porch again, still looking at the water and the Seward Range. A loon was swimming across the pond, diving, disappearing for an amazing length of time, and then resurfacing far away.

Caleb said, "How are we going to do the investigation? You didn't have experience in the work on the ground."

"I didn't wear disguises or use invisible ink, but you damn well know that's not the real world of intelligence gathering."

"You handled ops, but you didn't see action."

"It depends on what you mean by action. In my job, the action was intellectual. I didn't do my work by shooting guns or breaking down doors and arresting suspects. What I did was think and speak and read and write. I deployed agents. The action was in meetings, in the conversations and the memos, in the decisions that were made." Rabbit rubbed his chin in a parody of a thoughtful look. "My job didn't build muscles. A woman once told me that I had too much fun from the neck up."

"That was an invitation."

"Maybe. Or perhaps she was simply telling me that she found me dull."

"Did you test the proposition?"

"That's personal." He paused. "But the answer is, I didn't find her attractive. She was boney."

"Boney?"

"Yes, boney. Her skeleton was large and prominent."

"Okay, that's enough."

Rabbit was back in the wicker chair, pointing the stem of his pipe at the Seward Range and using it to describe small circles and figures. It looked like he was writing in the air. He said, "Was Mary in the house when John died?"

"No, she and Max were at our place, visiting Ellen while I was at the Sea Island conference. She found John when she went home. Max, thank God, was still with Ellen."

"Did the police come to the house before the body was removed?"

"Yes. Mary called an ambulance, and the ambulance men called the police. I suppose the death must have looked suspicious."

"I think they have to call the police whenever there's a violent death. Do you know where John had been that night, before he died?"

"No, I don't."

"Did the police record what he was wearing when he died, or take photographs?"

"I don't know. I assume he was wearing pajamas or boxer shorts."

"Was he wearing a bathrobe?"

"I don't know. What does it matter what he was wearing when he died?"

"If he was wearing a bathrobe, it might suggest that he'd received a guest. If he was dressed in a dinner jacket, black tie, it would suggest that he'd been to a party. Perhaps a party with the Georgetown set, brandy and cigars after dinner."

Caleb said, "He wouldn't have been to a party. The medical examiner's report said that there was only a very small amount of alcohol in his blood, maybe a glass of wine with dinner or one drink before dinner."

Rabbit continued. "A party with the Georgetown set. The things that are hatched in those private rooms are pretty arcane. God knows what gets talked about in those rooms, during the brandy and cigars, a breeding ground for treachery. Maybe John became privy to the secrets of the wrong person, maybe he heard something he shouldn't have."

"You're prejudiced against upper class society. You're unfamiliar with their customs and conventions, and you find 'the other' threatening."

"Yes, I'm a Midwestern lawyer, and we don't separate the men from the women after dinner and 'retire' to separate rooms. Yes, I'm a provincial. And I find Georgetown's social customs alien, brittle, superficial, rather offensive. In truth, I find it all stupid."

"Superficial is the right word. The fact that their customs are different from yours doesn't make them evil."

"Perhaps not. But they're still offensive."

Caleb said, "You come from the establishment, a long line of prominent lawyers. Princeton!"

"Yes, professionals, people of substance, serious people. And I'm a Midwesterner—that's important. People with some morals."

"People with different morals, not necessarily the right ones or the wrong ones."

"My sort of people are not slipping stealthily from one bed to another, a pattern of behavior that sometimes leads to murder."

"For a sober Midwestern lawyer, you have a mischievous, fanciful streak."

Rabbit said, "Yes, I don't fit in…Speaking of fitting in, we'll need a covert agent who can collect information without being obvious about it. I said we should ask questions, collect information, but we can't do that ourselves. We need someone who can blend in. If the two of us were to go around asking intrusive questions, we'd accomplish two things—offend people mightily, and close off sources of information. The guilty parties would run for cover, and so would frightened ones. "

Caleb said, "Blend in where? We're going to have to identify the possibilities, tell the agent where to look."

Rabbit went into the living room and walked over to a small desk. He started pulling on the hardware and pushing buttons. First, the top of the desk lifted to reveal an open space below it. Then there was a click. A side panel of the desk swung out and provided access to six small drawers that weren't visible with the panel in place. He said, "This old desk isn't really secure, but that's okay because the stuff in it isn't really secret." He took a children's book from one of the drawers. He said, "This was once a tool. A book code. No more." Then he pulled, from deeper in the drawer, a small spiral notebook. He said, "What agent? Who do we know? And who's available?" Rabbit turned the pages in the notebook. "There are retired agents out there who'd be happy to have some extra money."

"How much can we offer?"

Rabbit said, "How much are you willing to spend?" He went to the kitchen, taking the notebook with him. When he returned, he held two opened bottles of beer and he handed one to Caleb. He said, "What about Butler?"

"Don't know him."

Rabbit said, "He's an odd case. Most covert agents try to be inconspicuous, but they accomplish that in different ways. Some are amiable but not the life of the party, personable but not gregarious, friendly but not a close friend. Butler, however, simply tends to disappear. This result is mostly a product of his natural assets. To begin with, he's small—small hands, small feet, small eyes. But not a midget. He's maybe five feet three inches tall. And he's taciturn, with a sour disposition so far as anyone can tell. He isn't eager to talk and no one is eager to talk to him. I've heard him laugh only once or twice, very briefly and very quietly. He's clearly uncomfortable laughing. But he's bright and hardworking. Single-minded. A close observer. It's amazing what he comes up with. And he can analyze facts"

"Does he have a family?"

"He has a wife and a daughter. I have a hard time trying to imagine the process by which that might have happened. He's bloodless. I once asked a colleague how Butler would handle it if he had to kill someone. The colleague replied, 'It wouldn't bother him. He'd just get the job done.'" Rabbit drank from his bottle of beer.

Caleb said, "Competent agents have people skills. They

know how to maintain relationships, keep sources open, how to watch a trotline. But they aren't trained to figure out how a murder was done or who did it."

"Yes, agents aren't detectives. They don't know how to solve crimes. That isn't what they do." Rabbit pulled out his pipe and considered it. "Mostly what they do is conversions. They're like Pentecostal preachers looking for converts. They're good at identifying people who could be persuaded to give us the goods, people with weak morals or a need for money. They also do mundane tasks. Watching. They empty dead-letter boxes and put notices on bulletin boards and assemble the goods."

Caleb said, "But the work is risky. The job takes courage."

"I distinguish between the harvesters and the gleaners. The harvesters get the big chunks. The more obvious stuff. But the gleaners often get the most valuable material, the things that are really hidden. That's the more dangerous work."

"Which was Butler?"

"He was a gleaner, probably what we need for this job."

Caleb said, "Okay, give it a try."

"I'll call him, if I can find him. And I'll have Butler find out what John was wearing."

*

Rabbit made one of his frequent telephone calls to his wife, Penny, who was still in D.C. Since it was his usual time to call, she answered the phone by saying, "What's new?"

He said, "The Ironwood's daughter, Mary, is pregnant."

"Oh! And so soon after John's death. I wonder whether he knew. How long has it been? I assume John is the father."

"Of course I didn't ask. And I haven't tried to do the math."

"Well, I hope the child will be a comfort, a gift to look forward to."

"Caleb and I have decided to examine John's death. We don't think the broken neck was accidental. I'm planning to hire a man who did some work for the Agency, a man named Butler, to do some investigating."

"Is that a good idea? There was a verdict in the death. Isn't that settled?"

"As I continue to age, it becomes easier to say that nothing matters. It becomes tempting to say it. And, of course, it's true that things won't matter to me, personally, because I won't be around much longer. So, then, an old man ends up withdrawing from the world. Anger is probably healthier. Then, at least, you remain engaged with what's going on. You care about something instead of letting it all pass you by."

Penny said, "There was a movie called something like 'The Last Angry Man'—with Paul Muni. He played a crusty old doctor who was a sort of hero."

"Yeah, that's what I'm shooting for, to become a beloved crank."

"You're well on your way to it."

5

Rabbit found a telephone number.

"Mr. Butler, call me Rabbit. What should I call you?"

Butler made a mumbled reply that escaped Rabbit.

Rabbit said, "I see in the files that your first name is Hamish. Should I use that name?"

"How about you just call me Butler?"

"Okay…I have a job for you if you want one."

"Is it national defense?"

"It's related to national defense, but it's an investigation of a possible crime. If we can get together, I'll tell you more about it."

"What kind of crime?"

"There was a death. The verdict was that it was accidental, but General Ironwood and I don't think so. We want to investigate."

"Are you working for the government—national, state, or local?"

"No, none of those. The person who died was General Ironwood's son-in-law. It's personal. I, we, want to find out what happened."

"We can talk about it. Where are you?"

"I'm in the Adirondacks, upstate New York."

"Do you want to travel or do you want me to?"

"I'm an old man. It would be easier for me if you could come here. Of course, I'd pay all your expenses. And, if you go to work for us, your pay would come from General Ironwood and from me, at your normal rate."

"How do I get there?"

"You could fly to either Syracuse or Albany and then rent a car. It's about a three hour drive north from either one of those airports. Or you could fly to Burlington, Vermont, but there aren't as many flights there."

"When do you want to do it?"

"At your convenience."

Butler said, "Next Thursday."

"That's five days from now. Could you do it sooner?"

"No."

"Thursday it is."

*

They arranged to meet at the Full Moon, a coffee and newspapers place on the main street in Saranac Lake. It had good food, but they chose to meet in mid-afternoon, a time between meals when it would not be crowded.

There were a few customers in the front room, so they walked past the serving counter to the back room, which was mostly empty. The cafe would have been busy in mid-summer at the peak of the tourist season, or in mid-winter when the skiers were in town, but this was between the seasons. There was no one at the tables near them.

Rabbit said, "The victim's name is John Waverly. His

death doesn't make sense. He died in his own house, a place he was familiar with."

A waitress who looked as if she were in high school came to the table. She was probably twenty. Rabbit said, "No school today?"

She just looked at him, briefly. She said, "The coffee is on the counter. Help yourself." Rabbit had been there before. Then she put two menus on the table and said, "If you want food, we have some." She left.

Rabbit took his pipe from his jacket pocket. "Don't know whether I can smoke this here. Maybe not. But I can wave it around, make them nervous." He looked at the menu and started speaking. "It happened in the middle of the night, and there may or may not have been lights on—we don't know for sure about that. The body was found by his wife, Mary, in the morning, and she may have turned on the light or it may have already been on. She isn't sure which. But the victim knew the house, there were only five steps on the stairs, and he hadn't had more than one small drink. Blood tests established that. There's a wall on one side of the stairway that he could have used to help his balance. He wasn't carrying anything, or at least nothing was found near the body. He was at the bottom of the stairs. His only real injury was a broken neck. Damn funny fall."

Butler said, "The medical examiner found accidental death."

"Yes. That's because he was at the bottom of stairs and the police report said that the outside doors were locked and there was no one else in the house and he had a broken neck. So the medical examiner took the path of least resistance, accidental death. I think they wanted to clear the docket."

"Was there any evidence that he'd been hit or pushed before he fell?"

"There was no bruising on the body except internal bleeding from the broken neck and a few small bruises on his chin that could have been a result of the fall or could have been old."

Butler said, "A professional job. A broken neck, you know, doesn't necessarily result in death. In fact it usually doesn't. It has to be done right. You have to know how to twist." He waited for a reaction but didn't get one. "What sort of work did John do?"

"He was a data analyst at the Navy's Bureau of Ships. He was good with numbers."

"Highly classified material."

"Sure. Top clearance."

"Work record?"

"Good, I think. He'd had promotions. You could check."

"Kids?"

"One. A boy. But his wife is pregnant. I'm not sure whether he knew about that. He may have died before it became clear. You could check on that, too."

"How old was he?"

"Forty."

"I'll want to look at the house. The place where he died. And talk to the wife."

"I'm sure I can arrange that."

"Where was his office? I'll need to talk to people there."

"He first worked at the old Main Navy and Munitions Building on Constitution Avenue, the temporary buildings built during World War I, but then his office moved to new space at Crystal City. I'll talk to the Agency about getting you access to people there. We may need to give you some sort of cover job."

"Okay. Don't know much about ships. What did he work on?"

"All I know is that it involved the detection of the movement of submarines. I don't even know if it dealt with finding enemy subs or with making ours harder to find."

The waitress brought cream and sugar to the table. She said, "Cups are at the counter."

When she had left, Rabbit said, "We need to create a more complete picture of John Waverly. I want to know who he was. I believe that when someone's been killed, intentionally, you'll be a lot closer to knowing who killed him if you really understand the victim — his life, what made him tick. I'm sure you know this. This wasn't a random killing by some deranged twerp. This killer made some effort to make the death look like an accident. There was a reason for the killing of John Waverly. If we can find that reason, we can probably find the killer."

Butler said, "If he was having an affair, he might have been killed by the woman's husband."

"Yes, and we should investigate that. That's what I mean when I say that we need to know who he was. General Ironwood can give us the outline of John's bio, but we need to know more than that. Ironwood probably won't know, for example, whether John was having an affair. Ironwood's daughter, John's wife, might know, but the general might not."

"What about a burglary gone bad; John interfered with it?"

"The police report says that nothing was taken from the house."

"Who has the police report?"

"Ironwood."

"What about money?"

"Money is always good to know about. Have you got someone who could give us the FBI file from John's security clearance?"

"No, those files are pretty tightly controlled. The FBI protects their informants."

Rabbit got up from his chair. "Okay, so we'll need to dig. That's your job." Rabbit picked up an abandoned newspaper from a nearby table. "I had a friend at the FBI. He told me that when they were doing my security clearance they went to my hometown and interviewed one of their 'reliable informants'. She was an elderly woman. She told them, 'I don't know the young man, but his grandfather was a lovely person.' He said that quote's in my file. So much for the FBI's reliable informants."

"Why did he tell you that?"

"Because he thought it was funny."

"Right." Butler went to the counter and filled a coffee cup.

Rabbit said, "I could order you some toast, or bacon and eggs."

"Just toast would be good. Lunch was a long time ago."

Rabbit signaled to the waitress. He ordered toast for Butler but nothing for himself.

Butler said, "I want to start with the wife, Mary, and the house. Where does she live?"

"In Arlington, at fifty-two twenty-seven north eleventh road. I'll set it up, or General Ironwood will."

"I don't want Ironwood to be there when I'm interviewing his daughter."

Rabbit said, "She might be more relaxed and speak more freely if her father were present."

"Maybe, or it might be the opposite. I watch reactions. If they're both present I'll have to worry about watching the reactions of both of them. I don't know what the relationship is between the two. If I need to ask her about whether her husband was unfaithful, or whether she was unfaithful, that's a much trickier business if her father is present. She'd probably clam up, be embarrassed, and then he'd want to protect his daughter. I'd get less from both of them."

"What you say makes sense, but it may be difficult for me to move him out of the way. He may want to be there."

"It won't work with him present. I can't do it that way. You need to ask him whether he wants to get the job done, to find out the truth."

"General Ironwood was an intelligence officer, but I'm not sure how much he dealt with investigations. He did military intelligence—troop movements, information about the types of armaments the enemy has available at the time and place, estimates of numbers and kinds of troops—but at least some of the information came from covert agents."

"You might ask him whether he's ever tried interviewing two people at the same time."

" I don't think he'd see it as you interviewing him." Rabbit took out his wallet and signaled to the waitress. "I'll handle it, and I'll get you a copy of the police reports."

"What comes next?"

"It might be good if you could make a courtesy call on General Ironwood while you're here, but he's at his camp on Raquette Lake and it's only accessible by boat. It's a hassle to get there. I don't want to use your time that way."

"I have a ticket for a flight to Washington tonight."

"Okay, I'll explain it to him. You can get started by visiting John's widow at their house in Arlington.

6

It had rained the night before and the road was muddy. When snow melts in the spring, the mud season, many Adirondack roads are closed. Barriers are put up at their entrances so stuck cars don't block ambulances and firetrucks. But this was fall and the roads were open. Nonetheless, there was mud. The state highway to Coreys and the Coreys road were clear, however, and General Ironwood girded himself for another session with Rabbit Maranville.

The rain wasn't visible from inside. Through the windows it looked only gray out, but as soon as Rabbit went beyond the porch roof he felt it on his skin, and he breathed it in. There were small droplets floating in the air. They made wet spots on his cotton windbreaker, but not immediately. It took a few minutes for them to get through the cloth.

Rabbit greeted Ironwood and the two men went inside quickly. Rabbit hung their coats near the stove to dry.

Rabbit said, "What's the latest news from Watergate?"

"They've found a California lawyer named Donald Segretti who traveled to cities where Democratic primaries were held, planting false stories and disrupting the Democrats' campaign events. The FBI discovered that Segretti made telephone calls to Howard Hunt, one of the Watergate burglars. And all of this appears to be tied in with a man named Jeb Stuart Magruder—and also Maurice Stans, the former Commerce Secretary. They're running Nixon's campaign."

"It's getting closer and closer to Nixon."

"Yeah, it is, but he'll still be re-elected handily."

Rabbit pointed Caleb toward a chair in the living room and then put a record on the turntable. He said, "Listen to this pianist. It's Jay McShann, accompanied by just a bass and drums."

The music began.

After an especially lyrical passage, Caleb said, "What's he playing?"

"Probably a Steinway."

"Very funny. Very funny."

"It's just a blues. I think he calls it something like, 'Baby, With Your Black Dress On'. But the song doesn't matter. Listen to the technique. It's so crisp. The notes are like cut glass. The releases are other-worldly."

"It sounds old-fashioned."

"Well, in a sense it is, but it has modern elements and ideas in it. McShann is a transitional figure in jazz. His origins are in Oklahoma blues, but Charlie Parker got his start in Jay McShann's big band. Led the saxophone section. McShann brought Parker to New York, so he's a bridge between traditional blues and bebop. One of the bridges, not the only one. But he's a great musician."

Caleb said, "This music transports us back to a simpler, gentler time."

"Yes, that's right. To a gentler time that, as it turns out, was the run-up to World War Two."

Rabbit turned off the record player. "Speaking of a simpler and gentler time, I had an extraordinary dream last night. Do you remember your dreams?

"Sometimes, not often. Was your dream about the Agency?"

"No. I find that I've stopped dreaming about the Agency." Rabbit started scraping the bowl of his pipe. "Last night's dream had a performance of popular music, archaic popular music, the canon. I was in a long, narrow room; or it might have been a railroad car. If it was a train, I was in the parlor car. A number of young women were seated in comfortable chairs along the longer walls and one of the women started to sing. The song was 'Wrap your troubles in dreams/dream all your troubles away.' It was a performance worth being asleep for, worth the time. I seldom have dreams that I think are worth the time. I wish I could capture it fully, completely. I'd like to see and hear it again."

"Who'd the singer sound like?"

"Well, she had a small but pleasant voice and sang very precisely, she hit the notes cleanly, so I suppose you could say that she sounded like maybe Blossom Dearie. A rarefied taste."

"I don't know her."

"A New York cabaret singer. That's her birth name, by the way. Irish. Her sets are like little concerts. "

Caleb said, "That was a pretty tame dream."

"Yeah, well, I didn't want to excite you, but I thought it was intriguing, perplexing, sort of a mystery. I'm not sure what it meant .... Music. My dreams are mostly about music and about music performance. I often wonder whether

I could've made a living as a jazz pianist. The answer is really pretty clear—I would've starved."

Caleb said, "Do you think dreams have meaning?"

"I think some of them do. Do you ever have nightmares? Have you ever read Freud?"

"No."

Rabbit said, "Neither have I. Does anyone read Freud these days?" He rubbed his forehead with the thumb and three fingers of one hand. "What are your dreams like now?"

"I had a dream recently in which I was at a conference on urban planning."

"I think that qualifies as a nightmare."

"Oh, I don't know. I'm an expert on the location of highways."

"What is there to know about it? You just build the roads where poor people live. The route knocks down the houses of people who don't have clout at city hall. Problem solved."

Caleb said, "You have a weird sense of humor....Why are you telling me about dreams? I've never understood why people think that their friends should be interested in their dreams."

"Not sure why. I thought the dream was important somehow. Sometimes my dreams are so real that, when I wake up, I feel it really happened, that I really experienced it. I worry that I won't be able to remember which things happened and which I only dreamed."

"Why do you care?"

"It's my life! I need to know what happened and what didn't."

Caleb said, "Impossible things happen in dreams—you fly or you return to the past, and you make foolish mistakes, things you would never do when you're awake. It's silliness. Strange stuff. And mistakes that you made in your life. And it's not worth your attention."

"Oh, I think you're too hard on your subconscious. Your brain is working all the time. Perhaps you're more creative, more imaginative, when you're sleeping. Maybe you could put things together in different ways, in new ways."

"Oh, for Christ's sake."

"You have no imagination."

"Or no interest in silly drivel of unspecified content." He stood. "Is Penny still in D.C.?"

Rabbit took out his pipe and said, "Right about now, I'd wager that she's at the Corcoran, or maybe at the Philips, in either case enjoying herself."

"Isn't it hot and humid there?"

"You can be very sure that it is."

Caleb said, "I have a more checkered past than you realize. When I was at Yale, I got into a little trouble."

"Tell me about it."

General Ironwood stretched his shoulders and assumed a speaking posture. "Alums were gathering in an assembly hall for some sort of procession. It wasn't going to be a proper academic procession, but they were planning to walk across the green, in an orderly fashion, to a church to present some sort of award to someone. I led a group of students, a rather small group, in a protest. We ran across the green in the general direction of the church, all of us shouting, 'Rupert Brooke.'"

"Rupert Brooke? Wasn't he a homosexual?"

"Yes, I think he was. A poet. Died young during the Great War, of an infection, on his way to Gallipoli."

"That frolic of yours could've been a bad career move."

"I kept waiting for a review board to ask me about it, but they never did."

"We should thank the Good Lord for blessing us with poor recall."

"I believe there was some drink involved in it. I didn't really know at the time who Rupert Brooke was, but the name just came into my head."

"No one is ever going to believe that."

"No, probably not."

"So there was a flap?"

"There was a spot of bother."

"What was the penalty?"

"I don't even remember. Nothing major."

"So you got away with it. You paid no price."

"Yeah, I suppose you could say that."

7

The Waverly residence was a modest, two-story brick house built soon after the end of World War II. The first floor had a living room, a small dining area, and a kitchen, and there were three small bedrooms and a bath on the second floor. There was no sidewalk on the block, and the front of the house was close to the street. The only trees were in the backyard, but the yard was rather large. It was the smallest house on the block.

Mary, John's widow, met Butler at the front door. A small boy was beside her.

Butler said, "Thank you for agreeing to see me, Mrs. Waverly."

"My father told me that you are helping investigate my husband's accident. I was satisfied with the medical examiner's report, but Dad and Rabbit were not, so I'm happy to cooperate. I'll answer any questions."

"I'd just like to see where it happened. It won't take long."

The boy said, "What does the man want, Mommy?"

Mary said, "This is my son, Max." Then she turned to the boy, bent over, and ruffled his hair. She said to him, "I'm just going to talk to Mr. Butler for a few minutes. Let's go get your Richard Scarry book and you could also play with your trucks." She led the boy into the dining area, found the book on the floor, handed it to him, and took three toy trucks out of a large cardboard box.

Max said, "Can I have a cookie if I don't bother you?"

She said, "Sure." Then she turned to Butler and said, "Bribery."

Butler said, "It's the way of the world."

"Okay, you want to see where John fell.'"

"Yes, please."

She went into the kitchen, and then into a small hallway that provided access to the back door. A vacuum cleaner, a broom, and other tools were stored along the walls of the hall. There were five steps leading down from the kitchen level to a vestibule at the bottom of the stairs.

Butler said, "Where did you find your husband?"

Mary pointed down the stairs, "There."

"At the bottom, all the way down, just inside the back door?'"

"Yes."

"How was he lying? On his back, or on his front, face down?"

"Mostly face down… but twisted."

"With his legs under him?"

"He was sort of in a heap."

"What did you do when you saw him there?"

"I went down the stairs and looked at him."

"Was he on the stairs or on the floor?"

"Mostly on the floor, maybe partly on the bottom stair. The police took photos."

"Did you move him or touch him?"

"I don't think I moved him. I may have touched him. I probably did. I thought he was dead."

"Why did you think that?"

"He didn't move, he didn't respond, his head was at a crazy angle."

"This was in the morning?"

"Yes."

"Was your husband dressed?"

"Yes, but not much."

"What do you mean by 'not much'?"

"He was wearing a t-shirt and boxer shorts."

"As if he had just got out of bed?"

"Yes."

"What he ordinarily wore to sleep in?"

"Yes."

"If someone knocked on the back door or rang the bell, is that what he would have worn to go to the door?"

"I don't know. We don't have people coming to the back door in the middle of the night."

"Right. The police report says that the door was locked. Did you lock it?"

"No, I didn't touch the door."

"Until the police arrived?"

"The police came in the front door."

"And when you arrived home that morning you came in the front door?"

"Yes. We don't have a garage. I parked on the street and came in the front. And then I went upstairs, and when I saw that John wasn't there, I came back down looking for him."

"What did he have on his feet?"

"Nothing."

"Do you think the bare feet might have made him fall?"

"I don't know."

"Were the stairs wet, or slippery for some other reason?"

"I don't know."

Butler said, "The police didn't find anything slippery on the stairs." He looked again at the door. "Surely there must have been someone at the back door. Why else would your husband go down the stairs? Surely he didn't intend to go outside in the middle of the night wearing boxer shorts and with bare feet. There must have been someone at the back door. But the door stayed locked."

"Since he fell, he wasn't able to unlock the door."

"Ah, that's true. But there must have been someone there, someone who would've heard him fall. Someone who hasn't come forward and hasn't been identified. Who could that be?"

"I don't know."

"Where was your son while this was going on?"

"He was still with my mother. We stayed there for two days while Dad was at a conference in Georgia."

"The police said that there was no sign of forced entry into the house, so either your husband was alone in the house, or he let someone in. Do you think someone might have arrived unexpectedly, perhaps a family member?"

"No, I don't think so. I've talked to family members."

"Did anyone else have a key to the house?"

"My parents."

"And also your husband's parents?"

"Maybe, I don't know. But they live in Indianapolis."

"Did your husband have any friends who might have been staying here with him?"

"What are you suggesting?"

Butler replied, "Perhaps a colleague needed a place to stay for the night?"

"My husband was alone in the house. He fell, he died. It's obvious, for God's sake. Leave it alone. John is dead."

Butler looked at his wristwatch, removed a handkerchief from his pocket, looked at it, and then put it back. "You have my sympathy…. It's very sad, especially with your pregnancy. Did he know about that?"

"No. He didn't."

"That's too bad. I assume he would've been very happy if he'd known."

"Yes. He would have."

"Do you know where your husband was during the evening before he died?"

"No, I don't."

"You didn't call him? Or Max didn't?"

"No. We weren't far away."

"Do you know of any person who might have had a strong dislike for your husband or have had a grudge against him?"

"John fell, Goddamnit. There was nobody else in the house."

"Okay. Thanks for your cooperation. I was just trying to get facts, and you were helpful." He started toward the front of the house, then stopped. "Why did he go down those stairs?"

She didn't answer, and he continued walking.

As Butler passed through the living room, he said to Max, "What kinds of trucks do you like best?"

"Emergency vehicles," in a small voice, carefully articulated.

*

Rabbit was reading the newspaper when Butler called. The long black cord on the phone made it possible to take it to the kitchen table and answer it there. Butler said, "There are only two reasons to go down those stairs—one is to meet someone at the back door, and the other is to go outside. There's no basement. He was wearing a t-shirt and boxer shorts. Bare feet."

"He wasn't going outside."

"If he met someone at the door, that someone broke the neck and left him there."

"And then locked the door from the outside."

"Which they could have done, with a key."

Rabbit said, "With a key. Or someone who was already in the house could have broken his neck, thrown him down the stairs, and then gone out the front door. Does the front door automatically lock behind you?"

Butler said, "Yes."

"But if the killer was already in the house, why not put John at the bottom of the stairs to the second floor, a longer flight of stairs, which would be more persuasive?"

Butler said, "Those stairs have a landing in the middle, where they make a ninety degree turn. And, according to the police report, Waverly weighed 210 pounds. Maybe the body was too heavy for the killer to carry. A skillful woman could have broken the neck, maybe."

Rabbit said, "A woman trained in lethal technique? Or a man who couldn't carry him?"

"Maybe. Or maybe they thought the longer stairs weren't necessary. They got the verdict they wanted, after all.... Did someone put in a fix on that?"

"I don't think so. Who would have fixed it?"

"Yeah...But it seems pretty obvious that John Waverly didn't break his neck falling. Are the Arlington police too blind to see that?"

Rabbit said, "Maybe they saw what they wanted to see or expected to see, or what the family wanted them to see."

Butler said, "I talked to the cop who had the case. I asked him what he thought happened. He told me that, as he figured it, Waverly was on his way to bed and decided to check the back door to make sure it was locked. I asked him what about the bruises on Waverly's chin. He said those were superficial, of no significance, could be anything."

"The police must've had other cases that were more interesting or where victims were pressing them."

"And what about General Ironwood? Surely he'd been in that house many times. He knew what those stairs were like and knew that they don't lead anywhere but outside. Why couldn't he figure it out?"

Rabbit said, "Maybe he was caught up in family chaos, in the family's anguish about John's death. The family was probably focused on their loss, on the fact that John was gone, and not on the cause of his death. Maybe Caleb was just accepting the explanation that was most comfortable for them at the time. They wouldn't have welcomed the idea that someone had invaded their house and murdered him." He paused. "Or, what if he didn't fall walking down the stairs, but walking *up* them?"

Butler said, "You think he'd been outside in his boxer shorts and bare feet?"

"Maybe he met someone at the back door and didn't go outside, or went outside only briefly, or he went down the stairs to say goodbye to someone who was leaving."

"Like a lover?"

Rabbit said, "That's one possibility. And then, after he said goodbye and relocked the door, he started up the stairs and then fell and broke his neck?"

Butler was dismissive. "He didn't break his neck by falling."

"But that's what the medical examiner found, and the police. Are we right?"

"Yes, we are."

"Will Caleb Ironwood agree?"

Butler said, "It won't change the facts."

Rabbit picked up the phone and took it over to the counter and put it beside the toaster. He said, "Someone already in the house wouldn't have had to use the back door."

Butler said, "A family member?"

"Anyone already in the house."

"But then it would've been smart to unlock the back door so it would look like the killer came in that way."

"Sometimes the smart move doesn't happen."

8

Through the efforts of General Ironwood's colleagues in intelligence, Butler was given an identification card created for the purpose of visiting the Bureau of Ships. It said that he worked for BUSANDA, the Bureau of Supplies and Accounts. If asked what he did there, he could say that he edited revisions of the Armed Services Procurement Regulations (ASPR). If asked why he was at Ships, he would need to be creative, but he could certainly suggest that he was monitoring the expenditure of public funds. Basically, the ID card permitted him to have lunch in the Ships cafeteria, and he became a familiar face there. In conversations with the staff, he soon learned when to approve of cost-cutting measures (seldom) and when not to (often). Having worked for the government before, he was already familiar with the various retirement benefits. There was plenty to talk about.

In the cafeteria line, a pleasant woman, perhaps in her mid-forties, tried to be helpful. "The chicken tetrazzini is better than the spaghetti Bolognese." He thought that it was a close question.

The woman was plump, with very white skin and rosy cheeks. He didn't think the cheeks were created by rouge.

They might come from the bloom of good health, or perhaps hypertension. Her name was Helene, but he didn't quite catch her last name.

When they had paid for their selections, he asked, "May I join you for lunch?"

She looked pleased and said, "Why certainly."

At first, they talked about the weather. Then they moved on to popular music. She liked the Beatles. Why not? But Butler was not prepared to discuss the subject in depth. He told her he was new to BuShips and wanted to learn about the character of the place, office politics, how to get along there, how to avoid minefields. She said she liked her work and the people were nice, mostly.

He said, "They told me that a man in my office, a man named Waverly, died recently. Did you know him?"

"Not really. Are you his replacement?"

"No, I don't do submarines. But I'm curious about him. He was young, wasn't he? Is there radiation exposure in this building? The last place I worked had a cancer cluster."

"Don't worry about that. He had an accident."

"A car crash?"

"No, an accident at home. He drilled through the sheetrock into an electric line, or something like that."

"That's too bad. Was he a nice guy, a good colleague?"

"I didn't really know him." She finished her coffee. "The truth, I think, is that he wasn't outgoing. Nobody I know was friendly with him."

Butler said, "Maybe he was standoffish."

"Yes, maybe so." They picked up their trays and took their dishes to the counter. She said, "He was married to a general's daughter. He seemed to have money. I think people felt that he had an attitude of superiority."

"That's seldom appealing."

She said, "Yes, it takes compassion to tolerate the rich."

Butler honored her with a rare smile. They agreed to meet for lunch again.

That afternoon another person in the office questioned Butler about his job. "If you aren't in submarines, what sort of work do you do—to the extent that it isn't classified?" Butler had seen Helene talking to that man.

"Right now I'm handling congressional relations."

"What sort of thing?"

"Mostly constituent complaints. You know, someone in the congressman's district has a problem with the Navy, so the constituent contacts his congressman and asks the politician to intervene. Actually, it's usually not just ordinary voters, it's companies that have contracts with the Navy, suppliers of goods or services. So then we have to look into it and prepare a report or write a letter for SecNav. A lot of it involves collecting information, knowing where to look, knowing who has the answer."

"Is that the sort of work you've always done?"

"No. The thing that was my biggest success was designing the Pentaburger stand in the center of the Pentagon courtyard. I'm the guy who created the five-sided hamburger. I even designed the machine that stamps them out." Butler knew it was a claim that would be difficult to check.

"You were trained as a designer?"

"I was a history major."

*

As he walked to his car, Butler saw walking toward him a man he knew as Hugo Bettendorff, but the man had used other names. Butler was aware that Bettendorff had done covert work for various government agencies—only of the US government, Butler thought. Bumping into him was not a random event. It never was.

The man said, "Hello, Butler. What brings you here?"

"Hello, Hugo, I'm working at the Bureau of Ships now."

"So I'm told." Hugo Bettendorff always wanted it to be clear that he was one step ahead. "I understand that you've been asking questions about John Waverly."

Butler did not deny it. "As always, you're well-informed."

"Are you working for Angleton?"

James Jesus Angleton was the chief of counterintelligence at the CIA, the Agency's chief spy-catcher.

"No, I'm not."

"Who are you working for?"

"I don't think I can tell you that. You understand. I'm a confidential agent."

"Yes, I understand. And you know damn well that you can't afford to not tell me."

The two men looked at each other in a staring contest. Bettendorff was taller. He won.

Butler said, "John Waverly was General Ironwood's son-in-law. He died in a very peculiar fall. His neck was broken, just so. Ironwood wants to find out more about it. I'm helping him."

"Angleton is interested in John Waverly."

"Why?"

"Why's he interested in anybody? You figure it out. And, because you are poking at it, asking questions about Waverly, now Angleton is interested in you."

"My only interest is General Ironwood's interest."

"And what does Rabbit Maranville have to do with it?"

"He's a friend of General Ironwood."

"Well, now you know that your questions about Waverly have made Jim Angleton aware of you. You should keep that in mind."

As Bettendorff was walking away, he turned back to Butler and said, "You might want to look at Waverly's gambling. He wasn't good at picking horses."

*

Since Angleton was interested in Butler, Butler became interested in Angleton. One spook could haunt another. But Angleton was a dangerous adversary—he was smart, he drank enough to make him unpredictable, and he was pathologically suspicious.

Butler reported to Rabbit on his inquiries at the Bureau of Ships and they scheduled another meeting in Saranac Lake. Rabbit liked to look at the person he was talking to, and Ironwood could join them there.

It was safer to meet at a public place because Rabbit's camp was often watched by Angleton's men and Rabbit couldn't sweep the house for bugs every day. That was too much work. Tables in the back room at the Full Moon were usually empty if you picked the right time of day.

Ironwood was a few minutes late and apologized to Rabbit and Butler as he arrived. "I got lost." As soon as he sat down, he said to Butler, "Tell me about Angleton." Rabbit had told Ironwood about Angleton's interest in John's death.

Without interpretive comment, Butler gave an account of his encounter with Bettendorff.

The general said, "You didn't talk to Angleton, only to one of his boys?"

Butler said, "That's right. Angleton wouldn't dirty his hands with me, but Bettendorff wasn't making it up. He was acting on instructions."

"Why's Angleton so concerned about the death of my son-in-law, a minor civil servant? What's the CIA's interest in this?"

"When I asked Bettendorff that question, he strongly suggested that it was Angleton's job, a counter-intel interest. He said, 'You figure it out.' It was clear to me he meant that Angleton thought Waverly was a security risk, involved in the loss of secrets."

Rabbit said, "But why's Angleton upset about our inquiry into it? If we discover new information about the circumstances of Waverly's death, that could be helpful. We might find clues about whether the Soviets killed him."

Ironwood said, "Maybe Angleton doesn't want our investigation because his people were involved in the death"

Rabbit said, "To be clear about it, are you suggesting that our people killed him?"

"That's not beyond the realm of possibility. But I'm simply trying to figure out why they're so concerned about our questions that they, in effect, threaten us, tell us to stay out of it. Why would they do that?"

Rabbit rubbed the bowl of his pipe on his nose. It made the pipe shiny. "When we suspect someone of being a security risk, we don't just execute him without due process of law."

Butler said, "That might depend on how much they know about what the man had done, and how urgent they felt the problem was. Sometimes there isn't time for the niceties, and maybe it would depend on who would be embarrassed by putting the man on trial."

Rabbit and Ironwood both received this in silence.

Then Rabbit said, "If you've seen that, I hope you won't tell me about it." He turned to Ironwood. "Did you have reason to believe that John was a security risk?"

Ironwood paused and took a deep breath. "I didn't like John. I didn't want my daughter to marry him, but I certainly didn't think any such thing."

Rabbit said, "What didn't you like about him?"

"I thought he didn't treat Mary as well as he should have, and he was humorless."

Rabbit finished his coffee. "Standard stuff. Standard complaints about sons-in-law. Petty stuff." Rabbit turned to Butler. "I think we need to find out more about what's bothering Angleton. Do you know anybody you could talk to about that?"

Butler said, "I think so. One of the agents I worked with at the Agency is now working for Angleton. I think he trusts me. He'll certainly be more friendly than Bettendorff."

9

Rabbit had two ways to heat the camp, a cast iron stove in the kitchen and a large stone fireplace in the living room. Both burned wood. The back wall of the fireplace formed one wall of the dining room, and the chimney extended up through two bedrooms on the second floor and heated the whole upstairs. The fireplace was nine feet wide, and the heavy andirons could hold logs more than a yard long. Rabbit had a copper wash boiler on the hearth that was usually filled with shorter split birch, but the stock was depleted. He went out to the woodshed and brought in another armload. Carrying the wood, he stumbled on the porch steps and was lucky not to fall. He had found that his balance was not as good now. But he was still moving.

Although it wasn't very cold in the house yet, Rabbit liked to have a fire beside him while he read. He laid a fire but did not light it. The birch was well-dried and would burn hot. An especially hot fire might ignite creosote, but he kept the chimney clean.

The phone rang. It was Butler and he wasted no time getting down to business Social graces didn't appeal to him. "There's a big investigation going on in counter-intel. They see that the Soviets had someone inside, maybe still have, probably at the Navy, and one of the people under suspicion is the late John Waverly, which brings it very close to General Ironwood, so the investigation I'm doing is clearly of interest. Somebody I talked to at BuShips told them about us. Angleton's boys don't like it if we're looking at the same things they are. We might show them up." Rabbit moved the phone to his other ear—the better one. Butler continued. "They say we're getting in their way, and they think we're looking over their shoulders, and then they wonder who we're protecting. The fact that we're working with Ironwood is a big negative. His involvement looks to them like he's trying to cover his tracks."

Rabbit said, "I'm confident that Caleb Ironwood would never give our secrets to our enemies. But if John Waverly was sending things to a Soviet network—if he was—that suggests several possibilities. One is that the Soviets thought Waverly was going to get caught and, if that happened, he'd negotiate a deal and expose the network. So they got rid of him. Or maybe they didn't like the material he'd been giving them, thought he'd sent them in the wrong direction, had created a screen. Or maybe one of our over-enthusiastic patriots killed him in order to plug the leak."

"I'm only one man. Which one of your theories do you want me to pursue?"

"What's your judgment? Which one seems most likely to you?"

"It's hard for me to investigate the Soviets. They could be anywhere in our government or at a private defense contractor or in a think tank. I don't know where they are, or who they are. I can't cover all your possibilities."

"But you think we shouldn't ask Ironwood for more help, help in getting us more manpower?"

"Ironwood's involvement carries real risk." There was static on the phone. Butler and Rabbit both wondered whether their conversation was being recorded. Butler continued, "I want to explore Angleton's motives. Why's he so worried about having us look into the death of Ironwood's son-in-law? It makes sense for the general to be interested in it, but why does Angleton want to stop us?" Butler thought that it wouldn't hurt at all to have Angleton hear their suspicion.

Rabbit said, "If Waverly was a Soviet asset and the Soviets have a cleanup crew here, getting rid of loose ends, that's certainly a matter for Angleton's interest. We want to know about that."

Butler said, "Trying to find Waverly's killer seems like a very indirect way to hunt for the KGB. And Waverly had a personal life. He was a gambler—I don't know whether the general knew about that. Maybe it was one of the things he didn't like about Waverly, but Ironwood didn't tell us about it. Bettendorff told me. And Waverly came into some money recently—he bought a house on Chesapeake Bay. Maybe he won a big pot—maybe one of his horses came in. Or, maybe he also lost a big pot of money, maybe an even bigger pot. Maybe he owed money to people who were unhappy about not being paid, people who know how to break necks. What does Angleton know about that? Has he looked into it? Or maybe one of Angleton's boys who knows how to break necks did the job. How rough does Angleton play? Do you know?"

"No, of course I don't really know."

"I'd like to talk to General Ironwood. I want to find out whether he knew about the gambling. I'd also like to find out whether he ever crossed Angleton. It seems like Angleton has it in for him, maybe."

"There's nothing preventing you from talking to Ironwood. Go right ahead."

"Roger, wilco."

Rabbit said, "You've been watching too many war movies."

*

General Ironwood and his wife had returned to D.C. and Butler arranged to meet with him there. The Ironwoods were living in a small apartment building on 19th Street, NW, not far from the Hilton. The general told Butler that he could meet at eight a.m. and Butler readily accepted. The next morning, Mrs. Ironwood met him at the door and offered him bacon and eggs. He declined, with thanks. Then she disappeared.

General Ironwood was freshly shaved, and his white hair had been brushed. He was wearing a blue and white striped oxford cloth shirt with a button-down collar (probably from Brooks Brothers, Butler thought), a light grey cardigan sweater made of soft wool, khaki trousers (not Army issue), and tan leather slippers. Nonetheless, he looked ready to review the troops. Very fit. He was the racquetball champion in his age bracket at the Pentagon Officers Athletic Club.

The two men sat in the living room. Ironwood said, "Why do you suppose Bettendorff gave you the tip about John Waverly's gambling?" Rabbit had briefed Ironwood on the latest report from Butler.

"Bettendorff wanted something from me."

"Did he want you to give him information?"

"No, he wanted me to keep quiet about some information."

"Ah, I see. You know something."

"Yes. I know many things, sir." Butler stood. Ironwood remained seated. "But one more thing I'd like to know. Were you aware that Waverly bought a home at Scientists' Cliffs on Chesapeake Bay?"

Ironwood turned in his chair to face Butler. "I thought they were renting a house there, renting from Professor Atwood of the University of Delaware."

"The real estate tax records show that John Waverly bought the property from Professor Atwood about a year ago."

"That's news to me."

Butler pulled from his pocket a small notebook and a pen. He said, "Where did the money come from?"

"I don't know."

Butler said, "Of course Angleton suspects that the money maybe didn't come from gambling winnings…He thinks it came from the Soviets." Ironwood didn't move. Butler continued, "How could we investigate that?"

"Beats me. I suppose you know how to investigate."

"All I can do is ask the right questions and listen closely to the answers."

"You're the investigator. And you tell me Angleton is working on it. His office has a hundred agents — more than a hundred."

"Yes. We're unlikely to do better, and the Soviets know how to make money look like gambling winnings if they think they need to do that.... Aqueduct paper isn't hard to produce ... But bookies seldom give invoices."

Ironwood said, "If you find a list of numbers, it's usually a book code. Especially if they're in sets of three — the first is the page number, the second is the line, the third is the word. Then all you need is to identify the book."

Butler just looked at him, disdainfully. He wasn't sure whether Ironwood was being insulting or was kidding. After a pause, Butler said, "You and I must have gone to the same school."

Ironwood smiled. Then he said, "There's something we should look at. I think Angleton may be the key to this, or at least one key. He's a dodgy character. He drinks too much, and his motives and alliances are questionable. He's a relentless spy catcher, which is fine, but he does odd things that are hard to explain."

"It sounds to me like you don't have a high opinion of him."

Ironwood snorted with laughter. "Angleton was a student at Yale at the same time I was. We didn't like each other."

"Why not?"

"Essentially social class, I think. He was a lot fancier than I was."

"Fancy? How?"

"He was the editor of *Furioso*, a literary magazine, and they published poetry by Ezra Pound, E. E. Cummings, and William Carlos Williams. Angleton corresponded with those poets."

"So what?"

"So he thought he was a big deal. He considers himself a poet. He's an arrogant bastard. Where did he get that British accent? Went to a British prep school, I think."

"Tell me more."

"We're cut from different cloth. I'm from the backwoods of West Virginia, and he grew up in luxury in Milan, Italy. His father was a cavalry officer who served with General Pershing and then became the chief of the American Chamber of Commerce in Italy. I was a public school boy."

"His family was rich."

"At least compared to mine they were . . . . He's a plotter, not a field man. During the war, he worked for OSS while I was parachuting into Poland behind enemy lines."

"I get it. You'd like to clip his wings and he'd like to clip yours."

"Yeah. That's about it, I suppose. Do you know about Mary Pinchot Meyer? The murder on the Georgetown towpath?"

"No, when was that?"

"In the fall of 1964. It was in all of the newspapers."

"I was in Guatemala then. Working. Tell me about it."

"It's an unsolved case. At first, it looked like a purse snatching gone bad, but then more facts emerged that didn't fit."

"Who was killed?"

"Do you know who Cord Meyer is?"

"Sure. He's one of the top men at the Agency."

"The woman who was killed was his ex-wife. They were married for thirteen years, but divorced in 1958. Even more important, perhaps, Mary Meyer was Jack Kennedy's lover at the time of his death. That wasn't well-known, but there were people who knew it. She was murdered not quite a year after Kennedy was assassinated. The report of the Warren Commission had just come out and she was very critical of their 'lone gunman' theory, a theory that is full of holes. So Mary Meyer was getting attention, especially from the Georgetown set. Her ex-husband was in charge of covert operations at the CIA. Her sister was married to Ben Bradlee, of the *Washington Post*. She was *very* well-connected, in a good position to know things and she was trouble. Put it together. What does that all add up to?"

Butler said, "How was she killed?"

"She was shot. Walking along the C and O towpath, in the open air, in daylight. She was an artist, worked in a studio behind her house in Georgetown, went for a walk when she finished painting for the day. Neighbors heard shots. There were a couple of witnesses some distance away."

"It doesn't sound like a well-planned operation."

"No, but they got away with it. It worked."

Butler was skeptical. "It sounds more like a crime of opportunity. Spur of the moment."

"What kind of opportunity? There was no purse to snatch. She wasn't carrying one. Sexual assault? In the open air, in the middle of the afternoon, with public access? Pretty unlikely. There was no evidence of sexual assault."

Butler sat down. "What does Angleton have to do with it? And how's it connected to the death of John Waverly?"

"What you're hearing from Bettendorf is that Waverly was a Soviet spy. Let's suppose, for the sake of argument, that that was true."

Butler pulled out his notebook.

Ironwood said, "Since Mary Meyer rejected the Warren Commission's conclusion that Lee Harvey Oswald shot Kennedy, conspiracy theorists immediately said that someone, probably at CIA, had been eager to shut her up. Oswald had Russian connections. He spent time in Russia. If Oswald and John Waverly were in the same Soviet network, had the same handlers, Angleton would certainly be interested in that."

Ironwood paused. Butler said, "What else?"

Ironwood continued. "There are several possibilities. The anti-Castro Cubans who invaded at the Bay of Pigs expected air cover. They were recruited by the CIA, and the invasion was planned at the CIA and financed with CIA money. It was probably a Cord Meyer operation—at the least, he was involved. It failed because Jack Kennedy refused to provide airplanes at the beachhead. Also, Castro may have been warned that the invasion was coming, so he sent in his planes and the dissident Cubans were bombed and machine-gunned on the open beach, slaughtered. Planners at the CIA were furious at Kennedy's refusal to use planes. Castro was furious at Kennedy for the invasion attempt, the attempt to kill him. The Soviet Union was furious for the same reason—which may have been the motivation for Oswald. In any event, there were plenty of people who might have wanted to assassinate Kennedy."

"Are you suggesting that the CIA was involved in a conspiracy to kill the president?"

"I'm not suggesting anything. I'm simply asking questions and saying that we should be open to exploring possibilities, even distasteful ones, even possibilities that seem improbable. The CIA is a very large, very complex place. it has people there, people in high positions, who have objectives we can't see. It's opaque — by design. Cord Meyer was head of the United World Federalists. What in the hell is he doing at the CIA running covert operations? What in the hell is that about?" He paused. "I didn't work for the CIA. I was simply an Army officer. The Army is straightforward, a place where you know who is giving the orders. I don't know how the CIA works. You did some work for them. Maybe you know. Rabbit Maranville is an old, long-time CIA man. No doubt he has some close friendships there. I don't know how he feels about Cord Meyer."

Butler wrote in his notebook and said, "I could move around asking some questions."

Ironwood said, "Watch for Angleton's involvement. When you look into it, I think you'll see his fingerprints all over this. Why? Why is Angleton so concerned about John's death? The obvious possibility is that the reason he's pushing us away from the investigation is that he's afraid we'll discover that CIA, probably one of his agents, put John at the bottom of those stairs."

*

After meeting with Butler, Ironwood called Rabbit. He

said, "I wish I understood Butler better. He's an enigma. I wish I knew what makes him tick."

"I told you at the beginning, Caleb, that his greatest asset as an agent is that he tends to disappear. He's inconspicuous. He's taciturn. If he were memorable, he'd lose his advantage."

'He makes me uncomfortable."

"He's not a hail fellow well-met, that's for sure. He'll never be your buddy. But he does the job."

Ironwood paused. "Okay."

10

At Coreys, the sun was bright, and the ponds were smooth. A flotilla of aluminum canoes was crossing the water, probably a Scout troop or a group organized by one of the outfitters and heading toward the Stony Creek. Rabbit was working in the kitchen washing accumulated dishes when he heard a car pull into the front yard. It drove across the grass, which annoyed him. He went out to see who it was.

J. J. Angleton was just getting out of the car.

Angleton said, "It's a nice day."

Rabbit said, "Yes. It's a surprise to see you."

"Why are you still inside on such a nice day?"

"Not that I'm not pleased to see you, Jim, but why are you coming to visit if you thought I wouldn't be here on such a nice day? It's a long way from D.C."

"I'm looking for General Ironwood."

"I assume he's at his camp on Raquette Lake."

Angleton said, "His place is only accessible by water."

"So you came here instead."

"Yes. I did. "

"Why'd you think Ironwood would be here?"

"He often is, isn't he?"

"Lately he has been. Let's go inside and have a cup of coffee." They walked into the living room.

Angleton said, "No coffee. This isn't a social call. You or your agents have been asking questions about the death of John Waverly."

"I don't have agents anymore, Jim. I'm retired. Have a seat."

They sat.

"But you have people who help you. Have there been inquiries?"

"Yes, there have. John Waverly, as you well know, was Caleb Ironwood's son-in-law. Caleb and I both regard the circumstances of Waverly's death as suspicious, so we've been looking into it. Caleb is understandably interested in how it happened."

"And why it happened?"

Rabbit said, "Sure, I suppose so."

"What have you found out?"

"Not much. We don't have police powers, of course, so there's a limit to what we can do."

Angleton said, "Maybe Waverly had been into something that he shouldn't have and it got him killed."

"Maybe. We considered marital infidelity. Husbands can be angry."

"I'm not interested in angry husbands…I'm told that General Ironwood was at a conference at Sea Island, Georgia, when his son-in-law died."

Rabbit said, "People saw him there. I wasn't there, so all I know is what I've been told. Why don't you ask General Ironwood?"

"I already have. And I'll ask again. I'll keep asking."

"That sounds like you, Jim. Why are you interested in

Waverly's death? What does it have to do with counterintelligence?"

"Have you ever heard of Samuel Aldrich?"

"Sure. He handled two of our Soviet assets in New York City under my jurisdiction. Aldrich did some sloppy work. But Waverly was never involved in intelligence. He was at the Bureau of Ships, working with submarine data. He wouldn't have had any business with Aldrich."

"Not our business, at least."

"Maybe theirs?"

"That would be what I would be interested in."

"What does General Ironwood have to do with this?"

"I'm going to read you in on some of it because I need your help. You know the rules as well as I do."

"Sure. I'm still bound."

Angleton said, "One of our agents in Moscow reports that Pentagon documents have gone there. Always a major concern. " Without being invited to do so, Angleton stood and opened the door onto the screened porch. He looked at the mountains. "The particular combination of seeds in a burlap bag will often tell us where those seeds came from. The sorting of seeds is meticulous work, but it's a little easier with documents. Some of the things now in Moscow probably came from Aldrich, but other documents include submarine design specs. And there are also force estimates and contingency plans that almost certainly came from someone close to Ironwood."

"Surely you don't suspect Caleb Ironwood of giving classified information to the Soviets, or to any foreign power."

"I just follow the facts, Rabbit. What was Ironwood's relationship with his son-in-law?"

"Tepid, I think, not especially close. It's a normal family. Ironwood's daughter has a young son and she's now pregnant."

"John Waverly was the father of both children?"

"So far as I know. Caleb had a grandfatherly relationship, I think. Family dinners and that sort of thing."

Angleton picked up a fly swatter and examined it as if it were unfamiliar. "I'm very sure that Waverly did great harm to the nation, Rabbit. I don't know yet whether he was working with Aldrich or whether he had his own Soviet handler, but in either event it looks like some of the material came from Ironwood—the force estimates and contingency plans."

"As you well know, Jim, our hard-working public servants often don't have enough time during the day to complete all the tasks we give them. They work extra hours after dinner, sometimes well into the night. They know they aren't supposed to take classified material home, but when they leave the office they sometimes just put the things they're working on into their briefcases and then spread the files out on their desks at home. It's a security violation, of course, but I might even have done it. No doubt you would not have. But I don't like to sleep at the office. I like a change of clothes. I don't know how often Waverly was at Ironwood's, but I think it's possible that he could have had access to Caleb's home office. Perhaps the daughter, Mary, and her husband may even have had a key to the Ironwood apartment. Again, you could ask Caleb."

"Again, I already have. I'm going to interview him more. I think John Waverly's death is connected to Soviet espionage, one way or another. But I'll warn you. Be careful about what you get involved in."

"I worked at the Agency for a long time, Jim. I know what a minefield it is. I'll watch both my front and my back, and I wish you well."

11

The Maranvilles and the Ironwoods did not travel together, but both couples went home to the District of Columbia for a fall visit. The colors in the Adirondacks were beautiful in late September and early October, but after the leaves had fallen from the maples, birches, and aspens Washington was more hospitable. It was then cool enough to be in D.C.

Rabbit and Penny lived in the Kalorama Triangle neighborhood, near the high Taft Bridge over the Rock Creek gorge. They had a large apartment in a limestone building built in the 1920s, a co-op with one apartment per floor. Guests were received downstairs and shown to a sitting room by an elderly man in a white linen jacket. He was called George. The Maranvilles may not have known whether George was his first or his last name — perhaps they did, but they didn't need to. Tax records of the District listed him as "George Washington." Butler was shown to the elevator when the Maranvilles indicated that they were ready to receive.

The elevator, run by an operator twenty-four hours per day, of course, opened to their apartment, not onto a hallway. The anteroom, long and narrow, with a refectory table and two ladder-back chairs, served both the public spaces at the front of the apartment and the bedrooms at the rear.

Rabbit greeted Butler at the elevator. He said, "Let's talk in the living room. It overlooks a small park." Rabbit offered coffee. He always offered coffee and the offer was always declined.

The comfortable armchair in which Butler sat was near a small painting, an Edward Hopper. He studied the painting. Rabbit found this lack of eye contact disconcerting but tolerated it.

Butler said, "I interviewed Cord Meyer. He was at Langley when his ex-wife, Mary, was killed. Other people at Langley confirm that. The Meyers were divorced but he was, of course, immediately informed about her death and he cooperated in the police investigation. He thinks she was probably the victim of a sexual assault, when she fought back and was shot. I also talked to a police detective with the name of Crooke. I think if I were Officer Crooke I'd get the name changed. He told me about the gunshots. There were two, one to her chest and one to her temple. The medical examiner found that both shots were fired at close range—there were powder burns on her clothing and on her skin."

Rabbit said, "It doesn't sound like a purse snatching."

"Right." Butler looked at his notebook. "The detective said, 'A pistol whip across the forehead would have got him the purse.' But no purse was found at the scene and no wallet, no ID, so initially the police thought it was a robbery, but then later her purse was found at her studio. Apparently, she didn't carry it with her when she went for walks …. She also had a diary. It confirmed that she was sleeping with Jack Kennedy and had been for some time.

Ben Bradlee, the editor of the *Washington Post* who is publishing the Watergate investigation stories, is the husband
of Mary Meyer's younger sister, Tony. They searched for
the diary in Mary's house and her studio. I interviewed
him, not her. She was too distraught. Bradlee wasn't eager to talk to me, but since Watergate he's made so many
speeches about the public's right to know that he couldn't
really refuse. The most interesting thing I learned from him
was that he and Tony found Angleton already in Mary's
house looking for the diary. Angleton said the door was
unlocked, but he's known at the Agency as 'the locksmith.'
He didn't find the diary, but Tony gave it to him after she
found it."

"So why was Mary Meyer killed?"

"That's the big question. The placement of the shots
could be interpreted as an execution. And some people
have interpreted them that way. So, by that theory, the killing was done to silence her, but silence her about what?
Surely not just because she was criticizing the lone gunman theory of the Warren Commission. What could she
have known? Maybe something about the CIA?"

Rabbit said, "If it was an Agency operation, it was incompetent."

"Not so incompetent that they got caught. Whoever
did it got away with it."

"True. But it doesn't sound like an Agency operation.
They wouldn't do it that way. It's too public, too open, too
noisy, too much publicity. Too gory."

Butler said, "There's one more intriguing fact. Shortly
after Mary's death, before her identity became known — re-

member that she wasn't carrying any ID—Bradlee got a call at his office telling him that a woman who fit the description of his sister-in-law had been murdered on the towpath. There'd been a report on the radio about an unnamed victim. The call to Bradlee came from Langley. The timing of the call is crucial and somewhat unclear. But CIA was sure on top of it, quickly."

" That doesn't make sense. There's something wrong with the story. If people at the Agency planned a hit on the president's mistress, why would they call Bradlee to tip him off? They know that the *Post* can identify where calls come from. I'm tempted to say that it simply didn't happen! But that's not an analysis, it's just a reaction. There can always be a rogue actor within a big institution like the CIA. There are many, many agents there, and they can go nuts just like people anywhere else, maybe more so. But what are the facts? That telephone call just makes no sense…So what's the alternative? Was the killing just a random act of violence?"

Butler said, "The placement of the shots suggests an intentional killing."

Rabbit said, "A suspect was arrested and then acquitted. Did he do it?"

"There was no real evidence that he did. A very weak case—he simply happened to be in the neighborhood."

"What about eyewitnesses? What can they tell us?"

"Essentially nothing, apparently. I haven't interviewed either of them, but I've read the police reports and the trial testimony. Their shaky testimony is the principal reason that the suspect was acquitted. One witness was on the other side of the canal, a long way from the towpath. The other, a lieutenant in the Marines, didn't come forward until the next day and he didn't have a clear view of the shooting either. Apart from the race of the shooter, the descriptions that the witnesses gave when they were first interviewed didn't match the defendant. About all that fit was that he was 'a black man'."

"Could we learn anything more by talking to them?"

"I don't think so. The police and the trial attorneys did a good job with them."

Rabbit said, "That leaves me with questions. Did Mary Meyer know the same people that John Waverly did? Did they maybe have the same handler?"

"You think she was a Soviet spy?"

"It's only a question. But the mistress of the President of the United States would be a prize asset. Or did she really know something about JFK's assassination? …What do we know about Waverly's love life?"

Butler said, "Nothing, really. I didn't find any evidence of extramarital activity."

"Did you look for it?"

"The problem is that you have to know where to look. Without a thread to start pulling on, there's nothing to unravel."

Rabbit said, "Mary Meyer was killed eight years before John Waverly. That's a long time in the spy business or, for that matter, in the infidelity business. It's unlikely that Waverly's love life would provide any connection to Mary Meyer's networks. Treason is a pretty demanding job. I think it probably exhausted Waverly's supply of intrigue.

Stealthy meetings with Soviet couriers and handlers, the tending of dead drops, probably didn't leave much time for secret trysts with lovers. Still, it would be interesting to know whether the medical examiner found any STDs. STDs have been known to make wives angry."

Butler said, "I doubt that's what the examiner was looking for."

"Right."

"I'll see if I can find a gossipy neighbor."

*

Three days later, Butler came to see Rabbit again. He said, "I tried looking into Waverly's love life, without being too obvious about it, and I found nothing. He appears to have been admirably dull. He was no Jack Kennedy. And if we go around asking more questions about Waverly's sex life, we'll stir up a hornets' nest. I think that would be for no good purpose. My instinct is that it's a dead end."

"Okay, where do we look next?"

Butler took his notebook from his pocket. "General Ironwood has been blowing smoke about Mary Meyer. I think he wants to divert us from where we should be looking."

"Where's that"?

"At him." Butler turned some of the pages in his notebook. "General Ironwood was at Sea Island, Georgia, at the time. Maybe we should look at that. I'd like to go to Sea Island. Weather is good there this time of year."

"Do you play golf?

"No, I swim. But I can work as a caddy, or a waiter. And I collect."

"What do you collect?"

"Mostly sea shells, but sometimes information."

*

Rabbit met with Caleb Ironwood at Martin's Tavern in Georgetown. He felt he needed to tell Caleb that Butler would go to Sea Island.

"Butler is interested in that conference you attended."

"Why?"

"I'm not sure. He seems to think that someone there may have been involved in the Soviet spy ring and perhaps in John's death. People who were there had access to material that went to Moscow.""

Ironwood was skeptical. "The conference was still going on when John died. The people who were at Sea Island couldn't have done it."

Rabbit said, "Kim Philby was brilliant at making it look like he was in a particular place when he was actually somewhere else. Once he was in Bulgaria but created evidence that he was in London the whole time—his milk was taken in at his bachelor flat, and so on. He didn't have to use the electricity or the gas at his flat, he just had to make the meters say that he'd used it. Or perhaps he was really in London when he was thought to be in Bulgaria. One or the other. Doing that is mostly a matter of making the audience watch a rabbit being pulled out of a hat while the magician hides the key to the handcuffs. Philby was also very good at pretending to be drunk. I think Butler's occasional intoxication may be mostly an act."

"Butler isn't as bright as Philby."

"No. And we aren't either." Rabbit smiled.

General Ironwood didn't like that, but he didn't press it. He said, "You and I were in the intelligence business. We collected facts and then we had to figure out what they meant, the why of it, why people were doing what we were able to see. So what in the hell was Angleton up to here? Angleton is the key to it. He's a loose cannon. Breaking into houses, picking locks, for Christ's sake, Why? Should we ignore that?"

"I don't see the connection, Caleb."

"That's because you haven't tried to. You haven't thought about it."

"Butler's investigating it."

After they finished their crabcakes, Rabbit said, "Why didn't you see immediately that John's death wasn't caused by a fall?"

"That wasn't as clear to me then as it is now, but in our family conversations during the first day or two after John's death I suggested the possibility that someone might have killed him. Mary had a fit about that and accused me of adding to her pain. Ellen told me to shut up. So I did."

Rabbit said, "The importance of an issue depends upon the time. Some issues become smaller; others become bigger. The real question is, why would a professional assassin be visiting the Waverly house in the middle of the night? Who would want to do that?"

12

Butler flew to a small airport on St. Simons Island and then took a hotel shuttle to Sea Island, nearby. He paid cash to both the airline and the shuttle. He could have flown to a larger airport at either Savannah or Jacksonville and then rented a car to drive to the resort, which is about sixty miles from each of those cities, but he intended to stay at least several days, perhaps a week or two, and he knew it would be difficult to park a car at the resort that long unless he was a paying guest. He also didn't want a rental car company to make a record that he was there, even though he didn't plan to use his own name. He had several driver's licenses and credit cards to choose from.

He quickly got a job at the resort as part-time help, filling in where needed. He worked as a greeter, meeting arriving guests and helping with their luggage; as a caddy at the golf course; as a waiter during busy periods in the dining room and at private parties; and as a custodian of life preservers and beach umbrellas at the waterfront. The combination of tasks was useful because it brought him into contact with many of the other employees. His lack of personality was also helpful because the regulars did not regard him as a threat to either their jobs or their romances. He was, apparently, someone to talk to but not a player.

The supervisor of the chambermaids was a woman named Edith, known as Eddy. She was friendly, and she greeted him warmly every time she saw him. He estimated that Eddy was somewhere over fifty, but he wasn't sure how far over. Her hair was a peculiar copper color, a color that almost certainly didn't come from nature. She had wide hips, a noticeable belly, substantial, solid thighs, and a raucous laugh. He liked her, and he joined her for lunch. Or, more accurately, she came to his table. He asked her about her work.

On the second day of this, Eddy said, "I have to watch out for the maids. Some of them look for opportunities to walk in on a couple while they're going at it. That might happen by accident once, but if it happens twice, the maid is gone. We can't have it. It isn't good for business. If the sheets get soiled, that's a part of the deal. The customers pay money for that." She smiled broadly. "This is no job for voyeurs. I won't have it."

She continued smiling broadly.

He said, "That makes sense."

She said, "And they won't walk in on you and me either, Larry."

He was using the name Larry Wiggins. He had an old set of cards and licenses in that name.

He said, "You know, Eddy, I'm not going to be staying here. I'm a guy who moves on. I float."

"That's okay."

"So let's don't have any misunderstanding."

"For God's sake, look at me. I don't get that many offers. You should do what I do — take your opportunities."

He said, "Shouldn't we kiss first? I usually kiss first."

"We could do that. I think maybe there's more to you than you let on."

Most of the employees were housed in a building that resembled a barracks. They had shared rooms, but Eddy was long-term, a supervisor, and well-paid. She had a room of her own in the hotel. It was small, but it was private.

Butler's wife was more attractive and more languorous, but Eddy was energetic and enthusiastic. He was grateful. So was she.

*

When handling the dirty towels and bed linens coming into the laundry, Butler wore rubber gloves. Asked why he was wearing gloves, he said, "Who knows what kinds of germs these wealthy white people have?" The laundry workers, black and white, all laughed. One said, "You're just as white as they are, Larry, but maybe not so flush."

One morning in the dining room after breakfast hours, as Butler was clearing away dishes and serving platters, he struck up a conversation with Alice. She was an attractive, fortyish waitress who lived in the town.

After discussion of the job and where they were from, Butler said, "Does the resort sometimes have big conferences here, meetings with thirty or forty participants?"

"Oh yes, sure. We had a big one in early August. Famous people were here."

"What was the conference about?"

"It was all very secret. We couldn't go in the meeting

room while it was going on. The men had to come out to get their coffee. All the papers were locked up every day in the hotel's safe. But sometimes we heard things they said to each other after a session was over, or in the morning before they got going. We all tried to figure out what they were talking about. It was almost a game. Eventually we decided that they were trying to make the Vietnam War popular."

"Popular? Wars aren't popular"

"Sure they are. World War Two was popular."

Butler said, "Yeah, it was popular in families that didn't have someone get killed." He picked up two more platters. "How long did the conference go on?"

"Three days. But there was time for golf. They only talked about four hours a day, in two sessions, morning and afternoon, and not everyone went to every session. At these kinds of things, each part usually has a special topic. But even the schedule of the topics was all secret, all locked up."

"So, how were they going to make the Vietnam War popular?"

Alice said, "Who knows? But we heard some things."

"For example? What did you hear?"

"Well, after one of the meetings, Mr. Haldeman said –"

Butler interrupted, "Haldeman, as in the White House?"

"Yes, I think that's right. Haldeman said to another man, 'I don't think advertising can sell a war,' and the other man replied, 'Why not? It sells everything else,' and then Haldeman said, 'Winning would be popular.' I think the other man was an Army general. I heard him called general, but he wasn't in uniform. I think Haldeman was telling him to win, to do his job right."

"But Haldeman was there?"

"Yeah, and also Joseph Alsop, the newspaper columnist." Alice smiled. "I heard some of the men say 'bee, bee, dee and oh' several times. At first I thought it was the code name for a secret weapon, maybe a poison gas. But then I found out that it was just the initials of an advertising agency."

"What sort of advertising did they have planned, or did they have in mind?"

"We don't know. We didn't hear that part ….But some of it was funny. I heard one of them shout, loud, 'Cleaner than clean!' Someone answered him, 'It's been used.'"

*

Butler worked for two days at the golf course, part of the time as a caddy and part of the time cleaning equipment. A log book in the golf office listed names of guests who had reserved times, and the book was preserved because it recorded the presence on the course of movie stars, U.S senators, and even a president. The book was proudly displayed, and Butler was happy to look at it. He paid close attention to August 6th and 7th. John Waverly died in the night between those two days. The book showed that General Ironwood was scheduled to play on the morning of August 6th, at the same time as Judge Wilson Griffin. Their titles were used in the book, presumably so that caddies would address them properly.

When his work at the golf course ended, Butler went to Eddy's room. He asked her whether she knew who Judge Griffin was.

"Sure," she said, "He lives here, some of the time. He's from Atlanta but he has a second home on land owned by the resort, near the golf course."

"What can you tell me about him?"

"He's not the most popular guest."

"A lousy tipper?"

"Yeah, but worse than that. He's a pill. Lords it over everyone. Has a scowl on his face all the time. He looks like he's sentencing someone to death, or at least to a very long prison term."

"Who can tell me more about him?"

"You might try Lefty Lewis. He's a good little guy."

"Little?" Butler was small. He said, "Smaller than me?"

"Yes, Larry, smaller than you. But he's not a boy. He's probably thirty. He works as a caddy and sometimes as a bartender."

"Where can I find him?"

"He lives in the staff apartments." She took off her bra. "Why are you asking these questions? Who are you working for?"

"I'm just naturally curious. I'm not working."

"Yeah, okay." She sat on the edge of the bed.

*

The weather had turned cool on the Georgia coast. It was time for that to happen, he supposed. Guests were no longer swimming in the ocean but Butler was nonetheless still sometimes assigned to beach duty. There were always sunbathers. The resort had a heated pool, of course, but some guests preferred the beach, where they could look at the ocean. The sunbathers were almost exclusively middle-aged women who passed time recumbent on loungers, aging their skin while their husbands played golf.

Butler liked water but he didn't like sand. Sand stuck to your skin, got inside your bathing suit, and was generally uncomfortable. He didn't mind the salt in the water, but he preferred water that was confined within concrete walls, held captive. He found the unruly nature of the ocean unsettling. There were also a lot of creatures in it, things that might be good to eat, or might not, but in either case he wasn't happy to go swimming with them. At low tide you could smell them.

He had arranged for Lefty Lewis to meet him at the beach at five, the hour when the ladies went to any of several bars that served cocktails with fruit in them.

Lewis was, indeed, smaller than Butler, perhaps five feet even. He was also slim. He could have been a featherweight boxer. His movements were quick and precise. He had straight black hair, long in the current style, and it broke over the collar of his jacket. The management would be telling him to get it cut. His eyes were large and brown, but he was not a handsome man.

Lewis said, "Eddy tells me that the two of you are getting along good."

Butler didn't comment.

"She also tells me that you're looking for information on Judge Wilson Griffin."

Butler said, "Do you want a drink? The icebox has beer or Coke."

"I'd take a beer."

"Let me see what kind we've got." The drinks were in a metal box with ice. "Looks like it's Bud today."

He handed a bottle and the opener to Lewis and took a beer for himself. "I'll join you."

When Lewis took the bottle and opener, Butler observed that he was left-handed and wondered whether the nickname referred only to that.

Lewis said, "Judge Griffin is a federal judge, a powerful man. He's very well-protected. And I don't think you can bribe him."

"I'm not interested in bribing him. I'm just looking for information. Nothing scandalous."

"Are you a lawyer? Do you have a case in his court?"

"No, I'm not a lawyer and I'm not working on any case that Judge Griffin is handling. I just want to confirm some facts. Do you know the judge?"

Spread around on the beach were a number of inflated balls, probably a dozen of them, large and small, that people, large and small, could play with at the beach. One of Butler's jobs was to pick up the balls and put them in the beachhouse overnight. He started doing that, and Lewis walked along with him.

Lewis said, "Yeah, sure, I know the judge. Sometimes I caddy for him and sometimes I bartend at his house."

"Tell me about him. Do you like him?"

"Like him? He's not the kind of guy you like. You maybe respect him, or fear him, or even ignore him, I can imagine all of those. But *like* him, nah."

"Okay, just tell me what he looks like."

"There's something about his long neck, with all the loose skin, makes me think of a turkey."

"A turkey?"

"A turkey contemplating Thanksgiving." Lefty picked up two beachballs and said, "I'll help you, Larry." He tossed one of the balls in the air and caught it. "When his neck gets severed for Thanksgiving, then who's going to write his judgments?"

Butler said, "Those turkeys have clerks."

Lefty didn't even smile, but he said, "Judge Griffin looks lower class — his facial structure, his shoulders."

"There's no such thing as a lower class body structure."

"Sure there is. Humphrey Bogart, for example. The Maltese Falcon, the African Queen."

"Proves my point," said Butler. "Humphrey Bogart came from a wealthy family."

"No, can't be."

"Where do you think he got the name Humphrey?" They took a load of beachballs to the office. "So, what else can you tell me about him?"

Lefty said, "One of the jobs of the bartender is to change the tape when the music stops. I can tell you that Griffin doesn't like Miles Davis or Sarah Vaughn. Too modern."

"Maybe also too black?"

"I don't know. Maybe."

Butler put three more beachballs into the office and shut the door. "You said you've caddied for Griffin. Do you remember whether you did that on a morning in early August?"

"I don't remember, but I might have a record of it."

"The log book at the golf course tells me that Griffin partnered with General Caleb Ironwood on August sixth."

"Because I do so many different gigs, I keep a schedule in a date book." He removed a small book from his pocket. "The book that I'm holding in my hand." He turned the pages. "You said August sixth?"

"That's right."

"I didn't caddy for him that day, but I worked a party at his house that evening."

"Do you know whether General Ironwood was at that party?"

"I don't know. There were about thirty people there, and I don't know Ironwood."

"Just tell me about the party at Griffin's house."

"There isn't much to tell. It was all people from the conference. Buttoned-up. The men were over-the-hill tough guys with too much money and the women were the female version of that. Some of them in frilly dresses."

"I'm interested in General Ironwood."

"What does he look like?"

"He looks like a general, an old one. In good shape."

"I think I know who Ironwood is. Tall, with white hair, in his sixties, very erect posture, head up, wears glasses with those light gray plastic frames. Anonymous glasses. Those are military-issue. I saw a lot of them when I was working at the Naval Air Station."

"The man sounds like Ironwood."

"I saw him at the conference, at their coffee breaks. I was tending the coffee pot."

"Was he at Griffin's party?"

"I don't remember him there. But he could've been. You might want to ask Eddy. She worked the party in order to make extra money. When the resort caters parties at houses located on the grounds, employees have opportunities to work overtime and make good money. Eddy probably assigned that perk to herself. She might know whether Ironwood was there."

"I'll ask her."

Lefty said, "Here's the way those parties work. When there's an open bar, the resort charges the customer a flat rate per person. So the customer, in this case Judge Griffin, gives the resort a count and the amount billed is based on the number of people there. One of the jobs of the bartender is to count the number of guests to make sure that there aren't more people there than should be. Since I was bartending that night, I kept a count, which I gave to the management. I don't have that written down in the datebook, but I may have a record of it at home, or Eddy may have that."

"Did you get to see the guest list? And would you still have it?"

"No, I was only given the count and I never saw the guest list. Eddy may be able to get it if it still exists."

"I'll have to talk to her."

"I gather you shouldn't have trouble doing that."

"Yep. Should I ask Judge Griffin about it?"

"He probably wouldn't talk to you. If you ask him about Ironwood, he's going to wonder why it's any of your business. Just the way I wonder why it's your business." Lefty finished his beer. "Griffin isn't a sweetheart. One evening in the bar, not during the conference but more recently, I overheard him tell one of the guests that all of the people in jail deserve to be there. It wasn't hard to overhear. He bellows. He said only guilty people are put in jail. He said that if the trial courts make mistakes, the appeals court corrects them. He looked thoughtful and serious when he said it."

Butler chuckled, which was as close as he ever came to a laugh.

Lefty said, "He wasn't kidding. He really believes that, or says he does."

"That's good to know. What bullshit!"

"I don't know who you work for, Larry, but I hope you're going to stick it to some the bastards who want to run the world"

"The bad news, Lefty, is that they don't just want to."

*

That night, Butler asked Eddy. "Lefty tells me that you worked a party at Judge Griffin's house on the evening of August sixth."

"Yes, I remember it. We provided the food — small meatballs on toothpicks, and cheeseballs rolled in ground-up pecans, also on toothpicks. There was no fondue so I didn't have to set up Sterno fires, but there were lots of toothpicks. I helped in the kitchen and carried trays around to the guests."

"Was General Ironwood there?"

"I'm not sure."

"Do you know what he looks like?"

"Oh yes. I remember him. Handsome man. And I know which room in the hotel was his."

"Your maids change the bed linens. Could I find out whether Ironwood's bed was slept in the night of Griffin's party?"

"We don't keep records of which beds are slept in. If the guest paid for the room, that bed is theirs for the night. We don't care where they sleep, and we don't ask questions about it."

"No, of course not. Sorry."…"But you don't remember whether Ironwood was at the party at Judge Griffin's."

"No. He might've been there. I'm just not sure."

"Would you know whether he was on the guest list—whether he was in the count for the number of guests?"

"I don't have the guest list, but I have the resort's file on the party, the billing information—because we provided the food, the serving staff, and the bar. The file's in the second drawer on the left in my desk."

"Let's take a look at it."

"You aren't going to get me in trouble are you?"

"Nothing could get you in trouble, Eddy. You're golden. And the management will never hear about this."

The file showed that Griffin contracted for a party with thirty people, twenty-eight guests plus Judge and Mrs. Griffin. It also showed, however, that the Griffins were charged for only twenty-eight people because two of the invited guests never arrived.

Butler asked, "Is that unusual?"

"No, happens all the time. Plans change."

"But there isn't a record of who didn't show?"

"No, there isn't."

*

The next morning Butler had a message in his mailbox telling him to report to the business office. When he arrived there, he was handed a "Notice of Termination" and severance pay, which amounted to his pay for the remainder of the week. He was told that he was being fired because the management had received reports that he was asking questions about the guests. The secretary added, "You're gone. And they want you off the property by dinnertime. Pack your bag."

Butler talked to Eddy. She said, "It was Alice. I'm sorry, it's my fault. I gave her a kitchen job she didn't like and she got back at me by taking it out on you. She knew about our relationship. That's the way this place works. Alice'll pay for it."

Butler said, "Don't be too hard on Alice. She's just a blabbermouth. It's time for me to be going anyway. I told you I was a rolling stone." He gave her a hug. "Take it easy, Eddy, you're a good person."

She said, "I'll miss you, Larry." But there were no tears.

13

At the top of the hill overlooking the Stony Creek Ponds, Rabbit was sitting on the new deck, enjoying sunshine. He was wearing warm clothes. Someone with an icebreaker had created a long runway for a loon that made the mistake of staying too long. Rabbit was not at all sure that the loon would be able to take off, but he hoped it would. He liked having loons on the pond, and they tended to return to familiar places.

The telephone rang. It was James J. Angleton, with a complaint. "Butler has been asking questions about Mary Pinchot Meyer. Why?"

"Caleb Ironwood thought it might have some connection to the death of his son-in-law."

"How? How can they be connected? Mary died in 1964. Eight years ago. And they say some of my theories are crazy!"

"I think what interests Ironwood is your connection to the case."

"Oh, for Christ's sake. Mary Meyer was a family friend. We went through all that eight years ago. There's nothing in it…Unless…Unless Caleb Ironwood knows something I don't. He certainly knew more about John Waverly than I did. But where's the connection to Mary Meyer? Did

Waverly have friends in Georgetown? Possibly a woman? Women have odd ties. My wife was a friend of Mary's. I'll ask Cicely. She has good ideas. She's a poet. Maybe a poet can tell us something about it. I studied poetry, you know. I believe poets have things to tell us, a deeper understanding. But, unfortunately, the explanation is probably more prosaic than that."

Rabbit suspected that Angleton had been drinking. "We won't get in your way, Jim."

"My interest in Waverly's death is to find the network. I think the Soviets probably killed him to close that path. If we'd been onto him in time, and had squeezed him, he would've given us his handler. That could've led us to the network. Finding his killer might do the same thing."

*

Hugo Bettendorff dropped by the Ironwood residence unannounced. Ellen was home. He said, "I apologize for bothering you, Mrs. Ironwood. I'm Hugo Bettendorff from Mr. Angleton's office. I have just a few questions."

She invited him in, rather grudgingly.

He said, "Did you know Mary Pinchot Meyer?"

"The woman who was killed on the Georgetown towpath? Caleb mentioned that he suggested someone look into that.…Mary and I overlapped at Brearley; I believe."

"Yes, and also at Vassar. Did you know her?"

"Not really. Not in school. But I'm sure I must have met her. Brearley and Vassar both have get-togethers for alums from time to time … She was an artist, I believe."

"Yes, she was. Associated with Kenneth Noland of the Washington Colorist school."

"Oh. I'm afraid I don't know much about art."

"Ah, that's too bad. But perhaps you might have shared an interest with her in the ACLU or the NAACP, or the World Federalists."

Mrs. Ironwood looked at the ceiling. "Army officers' wives are thin on the ground in those organizations."

"There are exceptions. Cord Meyer had been a Marine officer, and he was a leader of the World Federalists while he was married to her." Bettendorff frowned. "Perhaps an Army officer doing intelligence work would find it useful to have some contacts in those organizations."

"I wouldn't know. My interests run more to gardening and literature."

"At Vassar you were the president of the Students for Norman Thomas, the socialist candidate for president."

Ellen Ironwood stiffened in her chair. "Thomas seemed to be a man of integrity with good values. Better than the candidates of the two major parties.""

"Mary Pinchot was a member of your executive committee."

"Was she?"

"And you were active in the United World Federalists when Cord Meyer was the head of that organization."

"I don't believe Mary was married to him then."

"For someone who didn't know her, you're well informed about her bio."

Mrs. Ironwood remained silent.

Bettendorf said, "I'm not buying it."

"Mr. Bettendorff, what you are buying or not buying is of very little interest to me." She looked at him squarely. "Now, I need to get on with my needlework. I don't have time for bullshit."

Bettendorff stood. He loomed over her. "I assure you, Mrs. Ironwood, that we care very much about the death of your friend, Mary Meyer, and also the death of your son-in-law."

He left without further words from either of them.

*

The nine a.m. coffee crowd at the Full Moon was assembled in full force. Several tables held lively and boisterous conversationalists, but Rabbit was at a small table of his own, protected with a newspaper in front of his face.

He went to the counter for coffee and the waitress said, "Would you like a doughnut with your coffee, Sheriff Maranville?"

He said, without smiling, "No, thank you, and I'm not a sheriff."

"Well, you're retired now, but you were a police official. Right?"

"I'm retired, that's right. And the other part is close, but not a sheriff."

"Okay. Well, you're always welcome here."

"Thank you."

He assumed that the transmission of news from Joe Cioni's grocery store in Tupper Lake to the Full Moon in Saranac Lake had some static on the line. He went back to his newspaper.

A few minutes later, Caleb Ironwood appeared on the other side of the newspaper. He said, "I tracked you down."

"I'm not hard to find. I'm a creature of habit." He nodded toward the empty chair. "Please join me."

"Is it okay to talk here?"

"Well, that depends on what you want to say, I suppose, but it's so noisy in here that it would be hard for anyone to follow our conversation. We may even have difficulty doing it."

Caleb sat. "Well. McGovern carried only one state. Not even his home state."

"Yes, the American people had a choice between burglary and World War Two heroism, and they resoundingly chose burglary. They are a practical people, not given to romantic gestures."

"The closer I get to electoral politics," Caleb said, "the more skeptical I become about it."

"I don't think skeptical is a strong enough word. I think disgusted would be closer to the mark."

"But Nixon is smart."

"Yes. Needy and smart. Not an attractive combination."

Caleb went to the counter for coffee. When he returned, he said, "Ellen was visited by Hugo Bettendorff at our apartment. He went out of his way to let her know that they had investigated her fully. They were eager to tell her that they knew about her juvenile explorations of socialism. Why would they want to do that?"

"Angleton is suspicious by nature and he loves to intimidate."

"He wants us to back off. He's uncomfortable with us digging on it. Why?"

Rabbit said, "The death of Mary Meyer made the Agency look bad. She had too many connections to CIA—through Cord, through the Angletons, both wife and husband, and through Jack Kennedy. That attracted unwanted attention, and the Agency thrives on secrecy. It has a culture of secrecy, and Angleton is protecting that. It's one of the things, maybe even the primary thing, that makes the Agency feared. And fear is essential to its effectiveness. Angleton understands that. The associations of JFK and maybe of Mary Meyer brought out the worst suspicions of the American people."

Caleb said, "Maybe some of them correct?"

Rabbit paused, and then said in a lower voice, "There's always that possibility"

14

Rabbit feared that his telephones were tapped, both in Washington and at Coreys. Conversations in public places were safer. If he returned to D.C., he could meet with Butler in a park, a train station, or a hotel lobby, but he didn't want to go to D.C. again. He liked the approach of winter in the Adirondacks. The first snow was always a joy. So Butler was paid for another trip north.

Rabbit said to him, "We've met at the Full Moon a couple of times. If we go back there again, my former employers will wire the place. Let's go to the Bide-a-Wee instead. It's a tavern located east of Saranac on the road to Lake Placid and it has a colorful history. I'll explain."

"When do you want me there?"

"Where will you be staying?"

"I'll be at the Hot Sara, with a view of the mountains."

Hot Sara was an affectionate name for the Hotel Saranac.

"How about tomorrow at the Wee at eighteen hundred hours? We could have a hamburger."

"I'll be there."

*

Butler saw Rabbit's small Ford on the gravel lot of the roadhouse, parked at the end of a row of pickup trucks. Inside, the bar was crowded with customers who were laughing loudly, but the big room next to it was dimly lit and quiet. At first, he did not find Rabbit, who was seated at a table by a window on a side wall. It was almost dark out, but there was enough light from the window to produce a silhouette, and Rabbit waved an arm.

To get to Rabbit's table, Butler had to walk past a life size cardboard figure of a yeoman warder of the Tower of London, a Beefeater. The decor of the Bide-a-Wee is a collection of artifacts representing British culture and tradition, broadly and whimsically defined. It celebrates all of the nationalities of the United Kingdom. In addition to the Beefeater, there is an Irish harp made of plastic and decorated with shamrocks, a plaster cast of a statue of Gelert, the noble Welsh dog who was mistakenly and tragically killed after he had saved a child from being eaten by a wolf, and a framed collection of swatches of Scottish tartans. The bartender is a man named Beatty Burke who attempts any accent native to the British Isles. If you ask him whether he speaks Welsh or Gaelic or Cornish, he will reply, "I don't speak it, but I understand a bit of it." And then you are supposed to respond, "Aye, just like my dog." And then everyone laughs and has a drink.

Rabbit pointed Butler toward a chair away from the window and said, "Hastings would never have sat at this table. He always wanted a solid wall behind him, with a clear view of the door, and preferably a solid, heavy table in front of him."

"Who's Hastings?"

"Good question. God knows what his real name is. He's a Brit, maybe ex-Army, maybe ex-Special Operations, maybe both. He describes himself as a professional assassin. Someone in our government, definitely not me, hired him to help with a problem at Camp Drum. To make a long story short, do you see that big table against the back wall?"

Butler nodded.

"Hastings was sitting there a couple of years ago with one of my agents and the agent's wife. A KGB team, three men, walked in that front door you just came through. Shooting immediately followed. The three KGB men were killed, and Hastings was seriously wounded. One of the KGB men was Hastings's son."

"Did Hastings kill his own son?"

"No, that kill was credited to my agent. Actually, through highly imaginative work in the Agency's press office, all three of the kills were credited to my agent because five years earlier we reported that Hastings died. Since the agent's wife was unarmed and Hastings was dead, it followed as night follows the day that the agent must have killed all three." Rabbit pointed to the large table along the back wall. "If you go look, you'll see several bullet holes in the table and the wall, carefully preserved. The framed collection of Scottish tartans has a neat round hole in the glass, near the center. Hastings was sitting with his head just below those tartans. There's a copper plaque on the wall that gives a short version of the story…. Now, do you have anything to report from Sea Island?"

"Yes, but nothing as wild as that."

The waitress came over and they ordered two hamburgers and two pints of Guinness.

After the waitress had gone, Butler said, "First I should tell you that I was fired by the resort because they heard that I was asking questions about guests. I think I was clumsy and pushed too hard. But I got the information there was to get. I'm sorry if it makes it more difficult for you to deal with General Ironwood. If the resort contacts him and tells him that an investigator was asking questions about him, that might cause trouble for you. But the resort doesn't know my real name."

Rabbit said, "Ironwood won't have any trouble figuring it out. He knows that you were going to Sea Island. I told him. I just didn't tell him that you were going to be asking about him."

"He'll be angry."

"Only if he knows about it." Rabbit took his pipe out and then put it away again. "I don't think the resort is likely to contact him. Why would they? It would suggest that he might've been hurt or damaged by his time at the resort. Why would they want to tell him that? They won't want to be the bearers of bad news."

"I let them think that they were punishing me by sending me away. It's always good to let people feel that they've been successful."

"Good point." Rabbit thought that maybe Butler was more subtle than he had previously appreciated.

"Okay, I focused on August sixth, the day before the night when John Waverly died. General Ironwood played golf that morning. The resort has a record that he made a reservation to play at nine-thirty with a judge named Wilson Griffin, a federal judge. There were also two other players in a foursome."

Rabbit said, "It would be interesting to know what Caleb's score was that morning. It might indicate whether he was tense. But I don't suppose the resort records the scores."

"No, probably not. They also don't have a record of what Ironwood did that afternoon. Presumably, he went to one of the sessions of the conference, but I couldn't find anyone who actually remembered seeing him there. That may not be too significant because almost all of the conference participants went home after the program ended, so I mostly talked to staff and staff weren't in the meeting room."

The waitress brought the two pints of Guinness. Conversation at the table stopped.

Then Butler continued. "Ironwood's golf partner, Judge Griffin, owns a house in a sort of high-end neighborhood associated with the resort. Wealthy Georgians have weekend or vacation homes there, especially people who like to play golf, and Griffin had a private party on the evening of August sixth at his house for participants in the conference. The resort catered the party. There are some records about that. This is crucial because, if Ironwood was at that party, there's no realistic way, no way at all without a private jet, that he could have got back to Arlington before John Waverly died. It takes about nine to ten hours to drive from Arlington, Virginia, to Sea Island—more when the traffic is bad."

Rabbit said, "Did you question Judge Griffin?"

"No, I didn't. I knew that would be awkward and could be dangerous. If I asked him whether Ironwood was at the party, he'd wonder why I was concerned about that. If I told him that I worked for Ironwood, why wouldn't I just ask Ironwood? Griffin could then easily call the general to ask why I was interested in when he was at the conference ... I don't think we want Griffin poking into the question of whether Ironwood was at Sea Island when Waverly died. So I decided it was better to stay away from it. And I don't think we want to tell Griffin what my role was."

"You used good judgment. It's better to keep Judge Griffin out of it. I don't know him, but he's an unpredictable element."

"So I talked to the bartender at the party and one of the waitresses. The waitress knew what Ironwood looked like and the bartender thought he knew. Neither one of them remembers him being there, but they both said it was possible that he could have been."

"How many people at the party?"

"About thirty."

The hamburgers arrived at that point and there was another brief pause in the conversation. "It would be hard to be sure about it in a crowd that big. That's quite a few."

Butler said, "There's another fact. The resort counts the number of guests, for the billing, but they don't take names. There were two fewer guests than had been planned for. Two people didn't show. I don't know who they were."

"Two people missing could be one couple that didn't show."

"Yes, it could. But most of the men didn't bring their

wives along. Wives wouldn't be paid for on the expense account."

"So we don't know that Caleb was there, and we also don't know that he wasn't there."

"That's about it."

Rabbit said, "How would Caleb have arranged to get from Sea Island to Arlington and then back again, at the right times, without being conspicuous?"

"That's the really tricky part."

The waitress came over and asked whether they liked their hamburgers. Both men were polite.

Then Butler continued, "There are a couple of small airports nearby that he could have used. One is at Brunswick, Georgia, a small city on the mainland just across from the islands. Delta has flights to Brunswick. It's about twelve miles from the resort. And McKinnon Field on St. Simons Island is even closer. It was a Naval Air Station during World War Two, but it became a civilian airport in the late forties. Military aircraft still sometimes use the field. Some of the Pentagon people at the conference came that way. Maybe also ranking civilian officials."

Rabbit said, "Those were probably Special Air Mission flights. I've flown SAM. When they have seats available, they'll let unscheduled passengers ride along, provided that the passengers have the rank. A general would be accommodated, if possible."

"And that's a real possibility. I went over to McKinnon Field and asked questions, and I'll get to that, but first I checked with Delta at Brunswick, and they didn't have a Caleb Ironwood on any flight in the month of August. Of course, he could've used another name if he had the ID. But Delta had only one outgoing flight that might have worked."

Butler handed Rabbit a pamphlet. "Here's Delta's schedule. You can read it while I go to the men's room."

Rabbit said, "An efficient use of time."

When Butler returned, Rabbit said, "Caleb surely had alternative ID when he was running intelligence operations, but I'm not sure whether he still has it."

"The Pentagon keeps records on that. There's a Benjamin Franklin Haycraft who is General ironwood. But he didn't use that ID in Georgia. I checked. So I went to St. Simons Island, to McKinnon Field. There's a master sergeant there who loads the SAM flights, supervises the passengers and checks credentials. I don't think that's his only duty, but I don't know what else he does. I talked to him."

"Would he recognize Ironwood? Would he know him if he saw him?"

"Hold your horses! Eat your hamburger. You're getting ahead of my story."

"Sorry." Rabbit addressed the hamburger.

"The sergeant wasn't cooperative, or didn't want to be cooperative, but I got something out of him. First he told me that he wasn't going to talk about any of it without a direct order from top brass. Maybe from top Pentagon brass—someone who outranks Ironwood. He said he knows that covert stuff goes on that can't be talked about and shouldn't be talked about."

"What did you say to that?"

"I said, okay, that's right. I told him that all I wanted to know was who got on an airplane—something that happened in the daytime with other people watching."

"Or not watching."

"Right. Then I described Ironwood, but I only referred to him as 'General Ironwood.' Here's his response; I wrote it down." Butler looked at his notebook. "The sergeant said, 'I don't argue with three-star generals. When a lieutenant general asks you to do something, you do it.' I hadn't described Ironwood as a lieutenant general. I'm not sure whether the sergeant's use of his rank was deliberate or whether it was just careless."

Rabbit said, "I'm betting he did it on purpose."

"Yeah. Me too. I think he knew who Ironwood was, recognized him. But he sure wasn't going to tell me whether Ironwood was on any particular flights."

"But it's a possibility. Where does that leave us? Which flights did he take?"

Butler said, "I'm betting on the Delta flights using an alias and payment in cash. On the military flights there would have been greater risk that someone would recognize him, especially because there were military and White House people at the conference who could use SAM."

"That sounds right. But if he flew on Delta, what was the sergeant trying to tell you by talking about a lieutenant general?"

"Maybe the general he was talking about was some other lieutenant general. Or maybe Ironwood talked to the sergeant but then decided not to take a SAM flight because it was too risky, or it had the wrong schedule."

Rabbit said, "Or maybe the sergeant was not really trying to tell you anything. He was just being uncooperative. We don't know. But Caleb would have had options."

Butler said, "I also checked the movement of cars. General Ironwood had a car at Sea Island, but I was unable to determine whether it was a rented car or a car he brought from home. He could have rented a car using an alias and then paid in cash. But he had a car. I talked to the guy at the resort who parks cars and supervises parking. He said that Ironwood was assigned parking. The car jockey doesn't really know whether Ironwood's car went in and out, but he said that the cars of the conference guests were all parked in one section and that they mostly just stayed there throughout the conference."

"It isn't very certain."

"No, it isn't. And there's also a shuttle that runs to the Brunswick airport, and to McKinnon Field on request. The shuttle is free for guests. They just tip the driver."

"What about transportation at the D.C. end of the trip?"

"Paying cash to taxis works."

They finished their hamburgers and their Guinness. The waitress was on the ball. She removed their plates and asked, "Cheesecake and coffee or more Guinness?"

They each ordered another Guinness.

While the stout was drawn, Rabbit said, "Let's do an inventory. What do we have? There are a number of pieces. First, I think Caleb was not at Judge Griffin's party. He might have been, but I think Eddy or Lefty Lewis would have spotted him. He's pretty impressive. I think it's a lot more likely that he was one of the two missing guests. Then there's the travel. Driving is highly unlikely. There are too many miles, and it takes too long. Even if he left Sea Island at noon on the sixth, it would be stretching it and cutting it close to drive to Arlington, commit the murder, and then drive back to Sea Island and get there in time for the closing sessions of the conference on the seventh."

Butler said, "That didn't happen."

"So he would have had to fly. He had options." Rabbit had the Delta schedule in front of him. "There was an outgoing flight from Brunswick on Delta in the afternoon of the sixth and a return flight early on the seventh. He could have used whatever name was on a card he had in his pocket and paid cash. Or there was the military flight option. He might have talked or intimidated his way onto a flight from McKinnon. Maybe, just maybe, the sergeant let the rank slip out because he didn't like being intimidated or conned. Payback works that way. But that's just speculation. And we don't know whether Caleb slept at the resort on the night of the sixth. He might have or he might not."

Butler said, "There isn't enough to convict."

"No, there isn't. But I say we bluff. I'm going to tell Caleb you discovered that he wasn't at Sea Island on the night of August sixth. We'll see how he reacts."

"He's your friend."

"Yes, probably a dangerous, guilty friend." Rabbit toyed with his glass of stout. "I think he's lied to me. If he was at Sea Island on the night of the sixth, he'll produce witnesses."

"Maybe he was with a woman."

"If I read Caleb right, he's more likely to be a murderer

than an adulterer. Pick your sin." He stood. "Let's go look at the copper plaque and examine the bullet holes. We can talk as we walk." They spoke quietly and stopped talking when they passed the only occupied table. "If he was with a woman, I think he'll tell me. He'd rather confess to that. And I think he'll calculate that I'd keep my mouth shut about adultery but maybe not about murder."

"You're a tough man, Rabbit."

"I've been told that before. I don't really enjoy the tough-guy role. I don't seek out these things, I hope. I hope I don't, but sometimes I trip over them and I have to deal with them."

Then Rabbit said, "Or maybe I'm drawn to trouble."

They both read the plaque on the wall, silently. It said,

The bullet holes seen here came from shots fired by three men who invaded the building heavily armed and wearing bullet-proof vests. They were later found to be employed by a foreign government. All three men were killed by Captain Joe Boudreau of the U.S. Air Force, acting in defense of the patrons of this establishment.

Butler said, "Boudreau must be one hell of a marksman."

"As you know, there's a longer story lying behind that. With 'lying' being the operative word."

15

The Maranvilles and the Ironwoods did not coordinate their travel schedules, but the Ironwoods returned to the Adirondacks only two days after Rabbit and Penny. Caleb was at Raquette Lake, but Rabbit knew that he needed to have a difficult conversation with him, and he needed to do it soon.

It was easier for them to meet at Rabbits camp because there was ice on Raquette Lake. And Rabbit preferred to have the meeting on his home ground, not Caleb's.

As usual, Caleb was right on time. He was dressed in his best Class A civilian suit. He didn't need the uniform.

Rabbit said, "You look like you're going to church."

"Perhaps I am."

"Jim Angleton came here.

"Here?"

Rabbit pointed to an upholstered chair in the living room. "A car pulled up into the front yard and I went out to meet it. It was Angleton. He said he was looking for you." Rabbit paused and looked at Caleb. "So they've been watching you. And now me. Us."

"Why?"

"Yes, why? I think Angleton suspects that we're conspiring."

"What sort of conspiracy?"

"What do you think it might be?"

"God knows. Angleton sees conspiracies everywhere. He's a dangerous man."

Rabbit said, "Yes, a little paranoid, which may be a desirable trait in his line of work, but he certainly isn't stupid. And he's dogged."

"You and I know there's nothing in it."

"Do we? He's interested in John Waverly, and John's death."

Caleb stirred in his chair. "What interest, what kind of interest?"

"Angleton's usual interest. His work." Rabbit took a pipe from a pocket of his jacket. He said, "Angleton seems to think that John was sending secrets to an established Soviet network. In Angleton's mind, at least, it has something to do with a CIA employee suspected of selling secrets."

Rabbit watched Caleb, looking for a reaction of anger, surprise, shock. But he didn't see any change. Nothing. Caleb simply got up from his chair, barely hesitated, and went out the back door of Rabbit's house and down the hill to the water. Rabbit didn't know what to make of it.

Caleb was gone for half an hour. When he returned, his suit was rumpled. He said, "It's my worst nightmare come true."

"You knew."

"Yes. First, I suspected, then later I knew. I saw the money, or what it bought. John was in it for the money, for Christ's sake." Caleb sat slowly in the living room's closest chair, his head in his hands. Rabbit saw that he had been crying. "It was tormenting me. I was distraught. I thought I needed to fix it."

"How bad was it?"

"There were lives at stake. The messages he sold to the Soviets blew the cover of two of our agents in Moscow and got them killed. The submarine plans he sent could result in ships being sunk, hundreds of lives lost. If I'd waited, more lives might have been lost—they likely would have been. Weigh the balance."

"Angleton was already on it and would have pursued it."

"How long would it have taken him to get the job done, while more of our people died and my son-in-law lined his pockets? My goddamn treacherous son-in-law." Caleb had his hands in his pockets. He leaned forward from the waist. "If John hadn't fallen and broken his neck, Angleton would have continued investigating and John would have sold more secrets before Angleton got enough evidence to arrest him. Then there would have been a public trial, my daughter would have been disgraced, and the stress would have been bad for her pregnancy, her blood pressure. I prevented greater harm to many people and perhaps the nation."

"Was there a fight?"

"No, there was no fight." Ironwood looked at his hands, palms up. "I simply did what had to be done."

"He was a lot younger than you, Caleb. How did you manage it?"

"I was trained. He was not. And I surprised him."

Rabbit spread a hand across his forehead and used the thumb to massage one temple and his long fingers to massage the other. "We found that you weren't at the Sea island conference that night. You left there and came back to D.C."

Caleb said, "If you just keep quiet, Rabbit, John's death will remain accidental. There's no reason for the medical examiner's verdict to be reopened."

"I'm not the only person who knows, Caleb. Butler knows."

Butler was a freelance investigator who had worked for both Rabbit and Caleb.

"If you keep quiet, he'll follow your lead."

Rabbit cleared his throat, then looked down. "Why? Why should he?"

"Because he respects you. If you ask him to stay quiet, he'd respect your authority."

"Don't count on it. My authority? I'm a retired has-been. And you don't have your command now."

"I could offer him money. Not a lot, but an amount worth having."

"You don't want to do that. That's another crime. And it's harder to defend than the death. The broken neck could've been an accident. Hush money can't be. It never looks accidental."

"We've already paid him to investigate. This could just be another payment."

Rabbit pulled out his tobacco pouch. "Angleton is digging into this. He'll keep after it. That's the way he works. He knows about Butler. And Butler won't risk obstruction of justice or perjury for your benefit. He's looking forward to a comfortable old age. He isn't going to take the fall for you, Caleb. He was offended, angry really, that you lied to him, tried to con him about being at Sea Island the whole time."

Caleb stood. "You're angry too, Rabbit. That's why you want me punished."

"Angry? No, I don't think so."

"Disappointed then?"

"Perhaps.... Why did you agree to join me in the investigation, to cooperate?"

"I thought it was pretty obvious that the death wasn't accidental."

"It's occurred to me that you agreed to the investigation so you could stay close to it, see what was going on, maybe even impede it if you saw an opportunity."

"Yes, I did think about that." Caleb took a step toward Rabbit. "If I'm such a bad person, why aren't you afraid of me?"

Rabbit didn't stand. "What makes you think I'm not?"

"I can see that you're not. I know how to read people. Why aren't you afraid of me? I could break your neck as easily as I broke John's."

Rabbit fumbled with his tobacco pouch and spilled a small amount while loading his pipe. "I guess I must think you wouldn't do that." He brushed the tobacco off his trousers. "And I don't think you're really that good at reading people."

"Why wouldn't I do it? If I'm so evil...."

"If you really want to finish me off, there's a pistol in the top drawer of that small marble-topped chest by the front door."

Caleb walked over to the chest. He opened the drawer, removed the pistol cautiously, held it in his hand, and examined it. "It's loaded. There are bullets."

"Of course."

"Why? What for?"

"Protection."

"It wouldn't stop a bear." Caleb looked at the pistol again. "It's unsafe to store a loaded gun in an unlocked drawer."

"Yes, it is. But, if you need protection in a hurry, you won't have time to unlock the drawer or load the gun. And it hasn't been there long. I only put it there this morning, while you were gone."

"Well, a loaded pistol. That's a surprise. Did you think you'd be able to get to it if you needed it today?"

"I hoped so"

"I'll bet I could break your neck before you could get the drawer open. You had too many years behind a desk."

"Let's don't test it. Then, too, it would be extremely difficult for you to get away with it. There aren't many people around here for you to blame it on." Rabbit stood, "I don't think you're evil, but you're human and you have human failings. You're capable of doing self-serving things. Humans do that. It's one of the traits that permits us to survive."

"Then why do I deserve to be locked up? Why do I need to be punished? "

"It isn't mostly you who needs it, Caleb, it's the world. The world needs to see that private executions are punished. We need more order than that. Order is important.

The work you and I did for many years was intended to maintain order."

"For Christ's sake, Rabbit. That's crackly-dry-abstract. This is my goddamn life we're talking about!" Caleb turned his back on Rabbit and slammed his fist against a wall faced with varnished pine. The impact knocked snowshoes hung on the wall onto the floor. " Stop being a bureaucrat. Where's your humanity?"

Rabbit said, "If you want to discuss this, I don't know how else to talk about it. I suppose we could just howl at each other, like wolves."

"I don't think I'm a wolf."

"No, of course you're not." Rabbit looked out the window, toward the mountains. "Why'd you do it? Some people might call it a moral failing, moral blindness. I call it a survival instinct."

"My survival or yours?" Caleb picked up the snowshoes and put them on a table. "Given your career, you can't be thinking some nonsense about the sanctity of life."

Rabbit faced him, "I made decisions that took lives. I even made decisions that particular persons needed to die. I'm not much worried about mortal sin. I've never been a believer and I'm not expecting an afterlife. Regardless of what I do, I'm not going to be rewarded with immortality. That doesn't happen. So sin doesn't come into it. Duty does. Killing and lying in the service of the nation are one thing. When they're done to save your own ass, they're something else." He continued looking at Caleb, evenly. Rabbit didn't move. "But we need an orderly process for meting out punishment."

Caleb smiled. A slight, rueful smile. "Goddamn law-yers. It's all about procedure." He turned, stepped toward the front door, but then stopped. He said, "You can't prove it."

"No, probably not. But there's enough to persuade the police that they should see you as a prime suspect, the principal suspect. And, once they start really looking, with Angleton helping them, they might find other things that implicate you. Other lies. They'll get closer, build a case." Rabbit paused. "Or you might get a pass—in recognition of your service to the nation. But they'd know you did it, and word would get around, inevitably. It always does. The invitations for the social events of the diplomatic corps would dry up."

"Why are you doing this?"

"That's a good question. I've thought about it. I think the simple answer is that it's the right thing to do. We can't just let you decide to kill someone because he's a bad guy. There are a great many bad people in the world. Should we be free to start eliminating them, one by one? There are people who believe that you and I are both very bad guys. You were a general in our military. Since many peo-ple think the Vietnam War was illegal and immoral, they think you are a war criminal. I worked for CIA. Enough said. When people start making their own decisions about justice, watch out! That's why we can't let you get away with this, Caleb. Without a legal process, no one is safe."

"Jesus! What a speech."

"It's an old one, Caleb. It was all figured out by our dis-tant ancestors, a very long time ago."

Caleb was standing by the front door. " You're obviously eager to regard yourself as a good man. You want to do
your duty. But duty to whom, or to what? To the Agency?
John's death isn't a matter of concern to CIA. The nation's
security was improved by John's death. The KGB, I'm sure,
found it discouraging. And you aren't a law enforcement
officer. You never were. The Agency has no police powers.
What are you playing at? What duty?"

"When it comes right down to it, Caleb, you're a military commander. You think like a military commander. But
you don't really believe in the chain of command. As you
said a few minutes ago, you don't respect process, you don't
see the value of it. What you want is control. For your own
reasons, for the sake of your family, you wanted to determine the outcome. You weren't willing to leave the decision
to others, so you executed John without due process."

"It was a battlefield decision, not something to be decided in an office at the Pentagon or at Langley."

He opened the door. "What about the human values,
Rabbit? Humanity, loyalty, compassion, friendship, decency?"

"Decency? Since when is breaking someone's neck, rendering him lifeless, a decent act?"

"Retribution against a traitor is decent. It should happen. And regard for the welfare of your friends is decent.
Friendship is valuable. Maybe there's even a duty to your
friends."

Rabbit said, "I think you're not required to tolerate a
friend's conduct that you wouldn't tolerate in someone else.
And perhaps you shouldn't. But I think you'll do the hon-

orable thing, Caleb, and it's certainly better to do it sooner rather than later."

"And what is the honorable thing, in your view?"

"Confess. Give the authorities the facts, the full, true story, and let them decide how to proceed."

"That's asking a lot."

"Yes, it is. But you've lived honorably for too many years to ruin it now."

"Cut the Ivy League crap, Rabbit."

"Strange as it may seem, some of that crap is actually worth taking seriously, worthy of respect. But I don't need to argue that case. You know I'm right."

"You're a sanctimonious sonofabitch."

"How much did Mary know about his crimes?"

"I didn't ask and she didn't tell me. Sometimes a mystery is better."

"What about your wife, Ellen? How much did she know?"

Caleb froze. Then he spoke, very quietly and very slowly. "Rabbit, for God's sake. Ellen and Mary don't deserve your wrath. They had nothing to do with this! For God's sake, leave them alone. There isn't much I wouldn't do to prevent harm to them. What do you want from me? What can I give you?"

"Take responsibility."

Caleb turned toward the door but then stopped. "Alright. I'll do it, if that'll satisfy your sense of the rightness of things, some abstract idea of justice. But how will that help? How will ruining me help?"

"So long as you keep talking, Caleb, I think you'll reach the right conclusion."

Caleb walked out the door and closed it behind him, gently.

There was now a slight mist, another reluctant rain. Rabbit had already brought the flag inside. He flew the American flag every day except when it rained. The flag was never left out in a rain.

16

Penny was still in D.C. He called her that evening. He said, "What's on in D.C.?"

"I went to the National Gallery and said hello to your favorite Modigliani nude."

"Ah yes, how I miss her!"

"You scoundrel."

"I met with Caleb this afternoon. In effect, I made accusations and he argued with me. Needless to say, the conversation was tense, but it wasn't as bad as I'd feared it might be. He was angry, and fearful. He left the house for a time and I saw when he returned that he'd cried. It wasn't good, but it wasn't violent."

"I'm going to come up to see you."

"I'd welcome that."

*

The telephone rang the next day in the early afternoon. It was Ellen Ironwood. She said, "Rabbit, I'm worried about Caleb. He's gone off in the car and I don't know where he is. Is he at your house?"

"No, Ellen, he isn't here, and I haven't heard from him since I saw him yesterday."

"He told me that he had a very difficult conversation with you. He was upset."

"I was upset too."

"I haven't seen him like this before. Will the two of you be able to reconcile, to work it out? I certainly hope so."

"I hope so too. I have great regard for Caleb, in many ways."

"Has he done something wrong, or have you?"

"I think he made a serious mistake, one that could get him into trouble."

Ellen paused for a moment and then said, "Excuse me please, I'm going to sit down....What did the two of you talk about?"

"John's death."

"I was afraid of that. What did he tell you?"

"Not much. Mostly, I told him."

"How much do you know?"

"How much do *you* know? First I should tell you that there's always a chance that my phone may be tapped. It often is. Maybe more than often."

Ellen said, "We should get together. I don't know when Caleb will be coming home. Are you available today?"

"Do you have a car?"

"Yes.'

Rabbit said, "Do you know the Adirondack Hotel in Long Lake? It's about half way between your place and mine, and it has a good kitchen."

"I know the place. I could meet you there in about two hours."

"That would work. Two hours from now."

*

The Adirondack Hotel is a large, white, frame building, the original part of which was built in the 1850s. It has twenty guest rooms just across the road from a sandy beach on Long Lake. Airplanes with pontoons are anchored at the shore, and tourists hire them for sightseeing. If your meal is timed right, you get to see one land.

Rabbit and Ellen ordered fish stew, a house specialty. Ellen said, "At this point, Rabbit, I think we need to trust each other."

Rabbit said, "That's often a good thing to do, but it's always dangerous."

Ellen frowned but started to speak. "I've now talked to Caleb, so he knows I'm talking to you."

"You have his consent?"

"Not exactly, but I don't need his consent to talk to you." Ellen rearranged her silverware. "We've had a rough time in our family for the past three months. I'm not sure whether the time Caleb's been spending with you contributed to the tensions or whether you provided a refuge, a relief for him."

"What's been the trouble?"

"At first, he thought John had too much money—bought a new car and a fancy camera. And then, later, there was a vacation house on the Chesapeake Bay at Scientists' Cliffs. Caleb asked John where the money came from. They argued. Essentially, John told Caleb that it was none of his damn business. Initially, I was inclined to defend John. I told Caleb to let John and Mary live their own lives, solve their own problems. I thought Caleb was being a busybody, interfering."

"What about Mary? What did she say?"

"Mary was being quiet, but I could see she was upset."

"Did you question her?"

"Yes, but only a little. She was clearly having trouble with John, and I didn't want to pry."

"But you changed your mind."

"Yes, I did." Ellen wiped her mouth with the linen napkin. She lowered her voice, almost to a whisper. "Angleton came to see Caleb."

"Never a welcome visit. What was the subject?"

"Documents from Caleb's office were found in Moscow. They were estimates of force for foreign countries, what Caleb calls 'punching power.'"

Rabbit said, "The information in those documents exposes our sources. Often you can pretty well tell where the information must have come from. So that blows our covert agents in those countries. It's the sort of thing that gets people killed. Angleton was right to be worried."

"Angleton was on the warpath. He was sure that the things came from Caleb's office and everyone in the office was under suspicion, including Caleb himself."

"But Caleb's retired. Would he have had access to the documents?"

"The papers go back to the time when he was still there."

"How would John have got hold of them? He worked at Ships."

"John could have seen the papers on Caleb's desk. Caleb always continued working after he came home."

"And he brought classified material home with him, as he shouldn't have?"

Ellen said, "As he shouldn't have, but everyone who is busy does it."

"Right. Soviet agents count on it. Just as our agents in Moscow count on their officials taking stuff home…I did it too, and Angleton damn well knows it."

"Of course, but he likes to pretend that he doesn't."

Rabbit said, "Caleb was very upset about it, so he consulted you."

"Yes, he did. We have a good relationship, and I think he values my judgment, and my support. And of course it affected our relationship with Mary and John…What are you going to do, Rabbit?"

"To tell you the truth, Ellen, I don't know. But I'll need to make a decision soon. I regard Caleb as a friend; I like him. But this is murder. There's not much legal defense for what he did. Necessity wouldn't work—not the way it's defined in the law. They'd say he should've let the legal process play out. So I can't just say, 'Oh, well.'…I have to give it thought, and that'll take some time. This is a grave matter for Caleb, of course, but it's a serious matter for me, too. I'm a lawyer, after all".

Ellen said, "You're worried about being disbarred."

"Not really. I'm retired. My career is definitely over, no matter what, and I'm near the end of my life."

"But you don't want the disgrace. Caleb doesn't either."

"I don't think it's the same. I didn't kill anyone."

"I love him, Rabbit."

"I understand that."

"I don't love you."

"I understand that too."

"You're jealous of him because he's a stronger person than you are."

"Oh, for Christ's sake, Ellen" He stood. "I'll get the check. I think we're done talking."

17

When Penny arrived at Coreys in the early evening, her greeting to Rabbit was, "The house looks clean! A few pine needles, but that's no problem a broom wouldn't solve."

"Thank you for the compliment."

Penny said, "You're thin, Charles, and you have dark circles under your eyes."

"I'm perfectly fine, Penelope, I'm in the prime of life, ready to wrestle a bear."

Her use of his baptismal name was a good-natured rebuke, and he replied in kind. It was an old game.

She said, "You're tired. I'll fatten you up. But you're out of bread. I'll make some. It smells like balsam here, which isn't bad, but I'll make it smell like bread baking."

He said, "Even better."

Penny was wearing a red maxi coat made of a dense, tightly woven wool, tailored gray slacks, well-pressed, and a white cotton flannel blouse with a paisley scarf. She removed the coat and the scarf and put on an apron. She was tall and slim and had pure white hair. She would not have been out of place at the National Gallery, but the coat would have been too warm there.

The flour was in a sturdy paper bag on the counter. Last year the flour had been in a canister because there were mice, but this year the mice eradication program appeared to have been successful, so far. She took out a large bowl and put in water, dry yeast, salt, and a small amount of honey. After the yeast had begun to bubble, she scooped a generous amount of flour into the bowl and beat the mixture with a wooden paddle. She said, "How was Caleb?"

"He's old, Penny. Like me, he's serving a life sentence of social isolation. His hearing and eyesight are both failing, but he's still strong and energetic and his reflexes are good. His balance isn't what it was. He's had falls. That's how it starts. I call it dying by inches. He's a bit depressed. What more do we need to do to him? Does he need to have humiliation added to his afflictions?"

"That depends upon what sins he's committed. Stop whining. You're lucky to be alive and still devising arguments, even if they aren't as good as they used to be." She spread more dry flour on the counter. "The problem is, you identify with Caleb. He's you."

"Yes, I suppose he is. In many ways. I hope not completely."

"And that's why you're sympathetic to him."

"I'd say 'understanding' rather than 'sympathetic.'"

"Whatever." She scraped the mixture from the bowl onto the flour spread on the counter and started working the flour into the mixture, using her hands. It was physical and messy. She said, "I think your righteousness is becoming less enthusiastic. That's a good thing. I'm glad to see it. Righteousness too often leads to zeal, and zeal is suspect—it smacks of excess, ill-considered action, a lack of proper restraint. Zealots aren't my favorite people."

He stood next to her and watched her kneading the flour.

Penny said, "You're bearing up under this very well."

"Am I?"

"Yes. You haven't been emotional about it, Rabbit."

"You know me. I don't do emotion. I think that's why you married me. You wanted peace and quiet."

"That was an important part of it. But I assumed you were always thinking about something—you had something on your mind. But I've seen you angry."

"Seldom."

"Yes, seldom. I know the Agency valued your calm."

"Probably. The phrase is 'cool under fire.' The steady hand. At the Agency, if you got upset about every piece of bad news, every crisis, you'd be dysfunctional."

But she hadn't finished dealing with zealots. "Zeal corrupts people's ideas about what defines honor and duty, about what honor and duty require in the particular circumstances." The dough was still sticky, so she sprinkled another handful of flour on the counter and went back to kneading the dough. "Can you still talk to Caleb?"

Rabbit said, "I think so. He tried to reassure me. He said he wouldn't harm me—except he implied pretty strongly that he'd do something serious if I caused legal trouble for Ellen or Mary. He's a puzzle. He's a cool customer, but passions within him run deep. He was capable of killing John in a very calculated way, and without any obvious upset to himself. I don't really know what to make of him."

Penny said, " I suppose that the loss of your friendship with Caleb is one of the less serious consequences."

"Yeah, well, I don't think it's possible to accuse a friend of murder, and not only accuse him but investigate him and establish that he probably is a murderer, and still have the friendship remain intact. The damage to the friendship is small potatoes, relatively, but it's a real loss."

"You're not allowing room for forgiveness, especially over time. You're still being the CIA man." She picked up the dough and slammed it hard on the counter in order to improve the texture of the bread.

Rabbit said, "Forgiveness over time is less likely when there's less time. Caleb and I aren't going to just forget this, of course, neither one of us will."

"No, of course not, but you can adapt, revise. "

"You think we should kiss and make up?"

"Not exactly." She slammed the dough on the counter again.

Rabbit stepped back. He said, "I'd hoped to do something positive. My career was mostly negative. The work had to be done, I think, but I didn't build, I excavated. I was mostly concerned with subversion, sometimes promoting it and sometimes preventing it. In my old age, I want to avoid making mistakes. It's too late for me to be able to correct them now. It's too late. So I'm sympathetic to error, misjudgment. We make mistakes. But Caleb made a very serious one."

Penny said, "Humanity requires sentiment and an awareness of frailty. Rationality can be carried too far. We destroy too much."

"My life has been devoted to making difficult judgments. Maybe it's time for me to stop making them. Maybe I shouldn't trust my judgment now. It's too late."

"I think I know what you mean. But I wouldn't put it that way." She stopped kneading the bread and turned toward him. "Can you withdraw from this, now that you've opened it up? Can you just walk away from it? Angleton is investigating."

"It was found to be an accidental death. That verdict stands until someone goes into court and persuades a judge to set it aside and order a new investigation. I don't see anyone asking for that. At this point, the law's satisfied that there's been no wrong. And the family is satisfied. They don't want the ruling to be changed, not only for Caleb's benefit but for Ellen's and Mary's. And the police aren't interested."

"It was a murder."

"Yes, in theory it probably was, as the law defines it. But the law, in the operational sense, has ruled it an accidental death. New evidence could change that."

Penny said, "And you have new evidence .... If Caleb didn't kill John, why would he come back from Sea Island on August sixth, just for one night?"

"I've thought about that. If Caleb came home, maybe he came because he hoped to prevent Ellen and Mary from killing John. But he failed to prevent it."

"You have what Caleb told you."

"I know what he said. Maybe he was lying to protect them."

Penny picked up the dough and put it into an old maple bowl that was always used as the place for dough to rise. She covered it with a clean dishtowel and set the bowl on the kitchen table, near the stove where there was warmth that would help the rising. She said, "Don't you have a duty to disclose crimes?"

"There's a difference, both morally and legally, between

the duty to report a crime that's planned but hasn't happened yet and the reporting of a crime that's already done, complete. The reason for the first is to prevent the crime, prevent the harm. If the crime is theft, then the property or money might be returned, maybe, but in the case of murder the harm won't be undone. If the crime is murder, reporting it after the fact is only good for punishment. "

"It seems pretty important to punish murder."

"True. That's what I said to Caleb. Nonetheless, there's a difference. But there's another problem. Someone else knows about all this. He's an investigator we hired, named Butler. I'd be taking some risk if I failed to disclose this."

"How much risk?"

"I don't know. Clearly, I'll need to talk to Butler."

Penny said, "What would happen to Caleb if you reported your findings to the authorities?"

"Well, there'd be further investigation. I think it's pretty clear that he'd become a principal suspect in John's murder."

"Would he be convicted?"

"First of all, if he was charged, there'd be the question of whether he'd plead guilty or not guilty. I don't have enough experience with criminal law to know what would make sense or how he'd be advised. Maybe the facts would be hard to prove, less certain, or the expert testimony about the broken neck would be more equivocal. His lawyer would certainly offer the jury an alternative explanation of how John died. My own view initially was that the Soviets had probably killed John to shut him up."

"Would Caleb get any consideration, get a break, because of his distinguished military service?"

"That would be more likely to enter in at the sentencing, but the prosecutor would have some discretion."

"Who would the prosecutor be?"

"Well, it would be a Virginia case, in the state courts."

"How awful! The family would be destroyed."

"Yes, no doubt. But the defense would make the argument, of course, that John deserved to be killed. There'd be some sympathy for the family, I think."

She said, "There'd be mud slung all round."

"Yes, and the government wouldn't like that. The Army wouldn't like it, or DoD, or CIA, the FBI, all of them. None of them would look good. That may be one of the reasons why it's been quiet so far."

Penny said, "If Ellen and Mary knew about John's crimes, they must've been very upset—and very angry. It will be interesting to see whether Mary carries John's new child to term. Assuming that it's John's child." She took off her apron. "We'd all be better off if greed, vice, and treason were consistently punished, and decency and virtue were rewarded. What would be wrong with giving the decent person a break? The law should adopt a decency defense."

"The problem is that that's too squishy. The law needs to be reasonably certain. Decency is in the eye of the condemnor."

Penny said, "I think a jury could recognize authentic decency."

*

And then they had nearly the same conversation about six more times.

18

Rabbit's meeting with Butler needed to be face-to-face. Telephones would be less secure, and Butler might have to be persuaded that keeping quiet was the right thing to do. He took pride in his work. He'd need to be handled carefully. Deference and accommodation might be helpful. Rather than ask Butler to make a trip north, therefore, Rabbit traveled to Washington. The Ironwoods were now in the Adirondacks, which was another good reason for the meeting to be in D.C., more removed. Rabbit and Penny's apartment in D.C. was probably not monitored now, at least not as a routine matter, but he arranged for it to be swept as a precaution.

After an exchange of pleasantries, and after Butler had received a sizeable check, Rabbit said, "My friend, we've concluded the matter of John Waverly."

"What are you going to do?"

"Ah, yes. What am I going to do? Or, as Lenin put it, 'What is to be done?' Well, I don't know about you, but I plan to read a book. Or perhaps I'll return to the Adirondacks and go snowshoeing along the Raquette River."

"What about General Ironwood?"

"He's retired. I assume he'll continue to do what retired people do. Maybe build birdhouses. Maybe he'll read a book too. Or maybe even write one."

"You know what I mean."

"Yes, you're right, of course I do. Please forgive me. With regard to the death of John Waverly, the legal system has reached a conclusion. I don't propose to challenge it, or upset it, or get in the way. I'll let the people who are not retired do their work."

"You're going to remain silent?"

"I am."

"Do you think I should too?"

"Yes, I do. You, however, will of course make your own decision about that. But I've decided to stay silent."

Butler examined his shoelaces. "Ironwood told you he did it. Don't we have a duty to disclose that, to blow the whistle?"

"What do we know to a certainty? We think, we believe, that Ironwood did it, but we don't know that."

"He confessed to you."

"Yeah, you're right, it was pretty clear. And he had plenty of time to think about it while he was walking down by the water. Caleb is very smart. But what if he was taking the blame in order to protect someone else? What if Caleb didn't really do it, but his wife or his daughter, John's wife, did? That seems to me a real possibility."

Butler said, "Waverly was only forty years old and he weighed two ten. Even with the two women working together, would they have been able to subdue him, break his neck, twist it to sever his spinal cord, and then move the body to make the death look like a fall? That seems pretty damn unlikely. And how likely is it that they'd work together on it? Even if they're very tough ladies, and angry enough and reckless enough to do it, how likely is it that both of them would have the guts to plan it and carry it out? This killing was planned! It wasn't done on impulse."

"Maybe the women could have done it if he was drugged."

"The pathologist tested his blood for alcohol and opiates. Found a very small amount of alcohol, no drugs."

"But there's other compounds or chemicals that can incapacitate someone. Insulin, for example. Since those other drugs weren't tested for, we don't know whether they were used. We simply don't know. Or maybe the women did it with help from someone stronger, who might have been Caleb or possibly a hired man. I think the women knew what Waverly had done, and they were furious at him for ruining the family. Watch to see whether Mary has an abortion."

Then Rabbit took off his glasses, pinched the bridge of his nose, and rubbed his eyes. He said, "Would you like a beer?"

"No."

Rabbit would have liked one, but he did without it. "False confessions are an odd phenomenon. The police are well aware of it."

"You're going to just let him get away with it."

Rabbit said, "Are you sure you don't want a beer? I'm going to have one." Butler just shook his head. When Rabbit returned with beer in a glass, he continued. "In my opinion, the United States is better off without John Waverly. Russia is not better off but the United States is. His treason cost us lives. If Caleb Ironwood got rid of him, that was a public service done at some risk and cost to himself. You and I aren't getting in the way of any additional investigation. The authorities are free to do their work. I'm not proposing to give Ironwood a medal, but maybe he deserves one."

Butler was not persuaded. "If we have to defend ourselves, will that be an adequate defense?"

"So long as we're not withholding documents that have been subpoenaed, and are not concealing real evidence, we won't be prosecuted. We're not burying anything in the backyard. The police have more compelling things to do. It's one of the laws of physics—bodies at rest tend to remain at rest." Rabbit took out his pipe. "Besides, I'd get Edward Bennett Williams to defend us. He's an old friend. We'd skate before the ink was dry." He took tobacco from the pouch and tamped it into the bowl. "Why would the Waverly investigation get going again? If anyone thought that the Soviets had killed John in order to shut him up, CIA and the FBI would be all over it. But you and I don't think the Soviets did it and, so far as we know, nobody else thinks that either. The legal process is done with it. There's a medical examiner's verdict." Rabbit lit his pipe but continued talking. "I saw a lot a treachery in my time at the Agency, treachery both outside and inside, but Waverly is one of the worst. The sonofabitch was only in it for the money. Unlike the Cambridge spies—Burgess, Maclean, Philby, and Blunt—communism didn't enter into Waverly's motivation. He was a capitalist to the end. He wanted the vacation house at Scientists Cliffs."

Butler said, "Have you told Ironwood about your decision?"

"No."

"But you met with him and told him that he could've left the Sea Island conference?"

"Yes."

"How did it go?"

"There were some angry words, but nothing worse."

"Could you still change your mind about what you're going to do or not do?"

"I could if I wanted to, I suppose, but I don't think I will."

"Let me know if you decide to go public."

"Of course. I certainly will."

"Okay, you're the boss."

"No, I'm not. I'm not anybody's boss now. I'm just an old man, retired, enjoying quiet days in the Adirondacks. I look for projects to occupy my time."

19

Two days later, Rabbit had gone back to the Adirondacks, but Penny stayed in D.C. to attend a meeting of the board of directors of Interfaith Action.

Rabbit was eating butterbean soup with Caleb at the Adirondack house. The dining table was old and unpainted, with obvious repairs, but it was covered by an embroidered white linen tablecloth.

Caleb said, "This soup is substantial."

Rabbit said, "At the very least." He put his spoon down beside the bowl on his plate. "I said to you a while back that the reason you should face justice wasn't that you deserved it but that the world needed it. It's now clear to me that the world isn't listening. It's been told that John's death was accidental, and the world has gone on about its business. It isn't paying attention. So I suppose we can just let you get away with it." Rabbit looked at Caleb. "But maybe you should promise me that you'll never do it again."

Caleb said, "Can't do that."

"Why not?"

"You might misbehave."

"Please don't treat this as a joke, Caleb. That might cause me to change my mind."

"What do you plan to do now?"

"Exactly nothing."

"I didn't mean to make light of it." Caleb finished his bowl of soup. "Why did you load a pistol and put it in that drawer? Did you really think I was going to harm you?"

"I was reasonably certain that you killed John. So I thought you were capable of violence."

Caleb said, "John was a criminal, despicable, venal, a traitor. You, so far as I know, are none of those things. I like to think that I'm a rational man. He was a great danger to our country and to my family." He paused. "I'd never harm you to protect myself. I'd only act to protect the nation and the people I love and treasure."

Rabbit said, "Don't relax too much. Butler could talk. He takes pride in his work and he solved this. But he doesn't cultivate the media and he's immune to flattery. He doesn't like people and he doesn't like to talk."

"The news media would love the story."

"But influential people would want to keep it quiet. The government doesn't look good in its handling of the matter — the loss of important secrets to Moscow, the wrong verdict from the medical examiner, a very serious crime by a three-star general, the failure of the Agency and the FBI to plug the leak. They'd all do their best to lock it up."

"Do you still want me to confess?"

"Well, you don't need to rush into it."

Caleb loosened his tie. Snow was falling steadily. There was no wind, so the snow was distributed evenly over Caleb's car, about six inches deep.

Caleb stood and put on his overcoat. "I'd better get going before the snow gets worse. The boat trip from the store's dock to my dock is no longer possible. There's too much ice. Ellen and I are renting a cabin in the village. I hope she doesn't get stuck on her return from Old Forge."

Rabbit said, "Give Ellen and Mary my fond best wishes, please."

Caleb said, "I'll do it," and he went out the door.

It took him five minutes to brush and scrape the snow off his car.

*

Rabbit called Penny. "I talked to Caleb. He won't have many good days left. I hope he'll be free to spend them on his porch overlooking Raquette Lake, or tending his lawn filled with daisies and New York asters. The snow will melt in a few months. The flowers will grow again like weeds. I suppose they are weeds. You mow them off and they come right back. Then they bloom and look like a garden. Caleb deserves that. He's earned it.

"He parachuted into Poland behind enemy lines in the big war. When he was in the Pentagon, he worked hard and took risks. In dealing with his son-in-law, he took another risk. Apart from the threat of prosecution, he probably put his name on the list of Soviet execution targets, targets for reprisal. Caleb violated an unwritten rule, an understanding among field agents, although maybe he'd be granted an exception because the agent was his son-in-law.

"It's all byzantine and too much for a desk man. But the Soviets will probably leave him alone. They got what they wanted from Waverly, and we got what we wanted from Caleb. He's used up, but he can live free like this for another few years, perhaps. And he should. Then it's the Old Soldiers' Home, the Veterans Administration hospital, or the cyanide pill he's been saving since 1942. But not the Virginia criminal court."

"Does he really have a cyanide pill?"

"No. I just made that up. I've no reason to believe that he does. But once upon a time they were standard issue in the intelligence business." He cleared his throat. "It occurs to me that an expiration date on a bottle of cyanide pills would have a nice double meaning."

20

Rabbit didn't sleep well. There was an almost full moon, so bright that light was coming through the windows and casting shadows of the cereal boxes on the kitchen table. The sky was cloudless, and the moon appeared to be closer. Moonlight reflected from snow at four a.m. was bright enough to read by. And he did—but only the backs of the cereal boxes. He hoped that the bright moon would be followed by a sunny day.

In the afternoon, Rabbit got a call from the Agency's man who handled liaison with Army Intelligence. "Have you heard about Caleb Ironwood?"

Rabbit hesitated. "No, what?"

"He died in a car crash late yesterday."

After a silence that seemed long, Rabbit said, "It's awful." He paused again, and then said, "Details."

"General Ironwood was driving. No passenger. The car hit a bridge abutment on the main road near Forestport, south of Old Forge. At a high rate of speed. There was some snow on the road, but it wasn't icy. Sand had been spread."

"He hadn't been drinking." It was not a question.

"That's right. No evidence of that."

"Were there skid marks, evidence of braking?"

"No."

Rabbit did not respond. The caller said, "Because he was in intelligence work, Angleton will be interested in this."

"No doubt. But I don't think he'll find anything he doesn't already know."

"Surely General Ironwood hadn't sold anything."

"No. Certainly not."

"Still. There'll be concern."

Rabbit said, "There's always concern. I'll talk to Angleton."

*

An Army officer in full dress uniform, a captain, informed Ellen Ironwood of Caleb's death—very formally, very properly, but with compassion. It was always done in person, not by telephone. The officer had some difficulty locating her. The Army had been informed that the Ironwoods were at Raquette Lake, north of Old Forge, more than an hour's drive from the place where Caleb died, but the Raquette Lake locals told the captain that the Ironwood place was not occupied because the lake was frozen. Nonetheless, the captain, a resourceful officer, found her at the rented house and delivered the message, an unpleasant duty. He offered help in transporting the body and arranging the funeral. He said that, if the family wished it, the general would be buried with military honors. He also told Mrs. Ironwood that Rabbit had been informed about the general's death.

She telephoned Rabbit.

Rabbit said, "I'm very sorry, Ellen. If there's anything I can do."

"I went into his office. On the desk was a tablet, with this written in a firm hand, 'Tell Rabbit that I'. That was all. What was he going to tell you, Rabbit?"

"I don't know."

"Why did he stop writing? Did he say anything to you?"

"He said a great many things, Ellen. I don't know what to make of it."

She was calm. "His death looks like suicide. Do you think this was intended to be a suicide note? Then maybe he stopped writing because he thought better of it."

"The note doesn't really tell us anything."

"Unless there's something we don't know that will bring us comfort, Mary and I would prefer peace and quiet. John fell, as the medical examiner found. Perhaps that's what Caleb was writing to you about."

"Yes. Caleb and I talked about it yesterday. I thought he was feeling better. I certainly hoped so. I don't think I said anything to make it worse."

"I'm sure you didn't, but why did you do the investigation, Rabbit?"

He paused. "I'm not sure.'"

"You ought to have a better answer than that. Caleb is dead....Do you feel guilty?"

Rabbit was silent.

"You should."

"I told him I wasn't going to report anything."

"The damage was already done."

That was the end of the call.

*

Angleton called. "What do you think we should do, Rabbit?"

"Let's just let the medical examiner's verdict stand. We don't need to disgrace the unborn child."

"You have relevant facts."

"Look, Jim, John Waverly's death is not my responsibility. It never was, and it certainly isn't now. I'm retired. And Waverly's death isn't your responsibility either. Your job, an important one, is to stop the losses of our secrets. When Waverly was alive, he was an important target of your investigations. He needed to be stopped. But his death cut off that channel to the Soviets. Your only concern at this point is to identify his Soviet contacts here and put them out of business. Waverly is dead, gone, past tense."

"Sometimes the manner in which a man met his death tells me where I ought to be looking."

"You have plenty of reasons to look for the KGB, whether or not they killed John Waverly."

Angleton said, "Yes, I suppose there's nothing more to be accomplished by investigating either one of the deaths. We know what happened to both of them. In this country, persons charged with crimes have the right to confront their accusers. Waverly can't be tried in absentia or post mortem. And Caleb also."

"That's surely one of the reasons Caleb wanted him dead, and himself."

"My concern is to roll up the network."

*

The call from Penny was the third. She had seen the standard obits in the *Post* and the *Star*. There had been no speculation about suicide. Rabbit had already told her that Ironwood knew there would be no report to authorities.

Rabbit said to Penny, "If Caleb hadn't trusted me, he'd be alive today. John's death wouldn't have been investigated if I hadn't pushed it."

"That isn't true. You told me that Angleton was already investigating."

"He was only interested in the spy network. He didn't care about John's death unless it told him something about the spies. He was letting the medical examiner's finding stand."

Penny hummed a few bars of a song. Rabbit thought it might be Louis Armstrong's "Someday," but he wasn't sure because it's a difficult song to hum. Then she said, "Why did Caleb agree to join you in looking into it?"

"He couldn't say no. It was pretty clear that John was, in fact, the victim of a murder, and it would have been very suspicious if Caleb hadn't been interested in that. And there were other possible killers—most notably a Soviet hit squad doing damage control, and there was always the possibility of angry, jealous husbands. I think that, at the beginning, Caleb felt pretty safe. If Butler hadn't asked about the Sea Island travel, we wouldn't have found that Caleb could've done it. And being involved in the investigation permitted Caleb to keep an eye on me and influence the direction of the questions. He probably thought he could control me."

"Then he didn't know you very well."

"Hope, dear. Hope misled him."

"I should go make a condolence visit to Ellen Ironwood."

"You could do that but let me give you some background. Ellen called me soon after she was informed of Caleb's death. She'd found a cryptic note, apparently incomplete. It said only, 'Tell Rabbit that I'. Then it stopped. It could have been the beginning of a suicide note. We don't know why he stopped writing — maybe he was interrupted, or maybe he changed his mind. Ellen, of course, wondered what Caleb was going to tell me."

Penny said, "It said 'tell Rabbit that I'? There are a lot of possibilities."

"Yes. Maybe it was going to say, 'I am sorry,' or 'I forgive him,' or 'I hate his guts'. More likely, I suppose, he may have wanted to say something self-serving."

"It doesn't really matter which it was. He was a troubled man. He did what he did. And that was a pretty definitive end to it.... I feel sorry for Ellen."

Rabbit said, "Be careful. I strongly suspect that Ellen knew about John's crimes, and maybe she even knew that Caleb intended to kill him. She arranged for Mary and Max to be at her house, not at John's, at the time. In my showdown with Caleb, I asked him point-blank about how much Ellen and Mary knew, and he became very upset, very angry. I think it probably tells us that Ellen, at least, knew quite a bit. Too much, really.... Caleb probably calculated that when he sacrificed himself I would feel guilt or remorse and then back off and leave Ellen and Mary alone. If he thought that, he was right."

Penny said, "He made his own decisions, Rabbit. You didn't make the decisions for him. He made bad choices." Penny's voice became louder and brighter. "I'm going to come up to the Adirondacks for a week or two."

"I'd like that, but it's starting to get very cold here."

"We have wool blankets and warm clothes and the electric heaters."

"And we could have a fire in the fireplace. It doesn't heat the house very much, but it's nice to look at."

"And we could snuggle."

"Be careful. This phone may be tapped. Angleton has been here."

*

Rabbit put down the telephone, picked up the snowshoes that were on the table, and hung them back on the wall where they had been before Caleb knocked them down. Perhaps he would even find interest in using them this winter.

The rain had stopped, and the sky had cleared, but the weather was still unsettled. The pond was mirror smooth. An unbroken border of dark green lined the far shore. Above the water and its border the mountains were now visible, the nearer ones a lighter shade of green and the farther ones silver blue. Rabbit thought that photographs never captured it. Some paintings came closer but not many.

The landscape was disconcerting. Trees and mountains across the lake were repeated in the water, but upside down.

AUTHOR'S NOTE

Rabbit Maranville had supporting roles in three of my earlier books, almost walk-on parts. I decided that it was now time for him to have his own story. The character is loosely based on Squirrel Ashcraft (Edwin Maurice Ashcraft III) who was the director of domestic operations at the CIA in the 1950s and 1960s. The basic outline of Ashcraft's biography is very similar to that of Maranville—a Chicago lawyer who had gone to Princeton and then Northwestern Law School, practiced law in the family firm established by his grandfather in the 19th century, served in Navy intelligence in WWII and was spotted there by Wild Bill Donovan, who recruited him for service in the new CIA, first in Chicago and then in Washington.

Squirrel Ashcraft played jazz piano and held jam sessions at his home in Evanston with Marian and Jimmy McPartland, Eddie Condon, and musicians from the Bob Crosby band, including Bob Haggart. There are reports that, when he was at Princeton, Ashcraft sat in with Bix Beiderbecke.

The material about Mary Pinchot Meyer's death and the investigation following it owes much to Ben Bradlee's memoir, *A Good Life*, and to *The Ghost* by Jefferson Morley, which is an excellent, comprehensive biography of James

Jesus Angleton. Other information about Angleton's life and career was drawn from Robin Winks, *Cloak & Gown*, a well-written history focusing on the CIA's recruitment of Angleton and other students and faculty at Yale.

I'm grateful for the help of a perceptive group of readers, including Chris Angus, William Conger, Charles McManus, Evan Meagher, Bob Nelson, Meg Randall, Irv Slate, Katherine Sodergren, Miriam Weizenbaum, and Harvey Wilcox. They made important suggestions that improved the work. David Collins, Carole Mabus, David Heckman, and Jay Hook contributed especially helpful criticism. I am also grateful to the late Don Burke Denby, Sr., for singing as he walked to the grocery store. As always, Anne Heinz was the first person I consulted for advice on plot details, character development, recipes, and matters of tone and taste. I owe a large debt to all of these helpful friends and allies.

J. H.
June 2024, Tupper Lake

Jack Heinz is the author of *Rebellion, Love, Betrayal* (2019), *Six Spies in Saranac* (2020), and *Engagement in Saranac* (2022). He and his wife, Anne, live in Evanston, Illinois, and Tupper Lake, New York.